William King, John Nichols

The original works of William King

William King, John Nichols

The original works of William King

ISBN/EAN: 9783743401754

Manufactured in Europe, USA, Canada, Australia, Japa

Cover: Foto ©Andreas Hilbeck / pixelio.de

Manufactured and distributed by brebook publishing software (www.brebook.com)

William King, John Nichols

The original works of William King

THE ORIGINAL WORKS

OF

WILLIAM KING, LL.D.

ADVOCATE OF DOCTORS COMMONS;
JUDGE OF THE HIGH COURT OF ADMIRALTY
AND KEEPER OF THE RECORDS IN IRELAND,
AND VICAR GENERAL TO THE LORD PRIMATE.

NOW FIRST COLLECTED INTO THREE VOLUMES:
WITH HISTORICAL NOTES, AND MEMOIRS OF THE AUTHOR.

VOLUME THE THIRD.

He, void of envy, guile, and luft of gain,
Pour'd forth his unpremeditated ftrain.

LONDON,

PRINTED FOR THE EDITOR; AND SOLD BY N. CONANT,
SUCCESSOR TO MR. WHISTON, IN FLEET-STREET.
MDCCLXXVI.

USEFUL MISCELLANIES:

PART THE FIRST.

CONTAINING,

I. A PREFACE of the Publisher of the Tragi-comedy of JOAN OF HEDINGTON.

II. The Tragi-comedy of JOAN OF HEDINGTON. In Imitation of SHAKESPEARE.

III. Some Account of HORACE'S Behaviour during his Stay at TRINITY COLLEGE, in CAMBRIDGE. With an ODE, to entreat his Departure thence; together with a Copy of his Medal, taken out of TRINITY-COLLEGE Buttery, by a Well-wisher to that SOCIETY.

[IV. An ANSWER to CLEMENS ALEXANDRINUS's Sermon upon *Quis Dives falvetur*,]

VOL. III.   B

THE PUBLISHER
TO
THE READER.

IT is many years fince, that this Tragi-comedy of Joan of
Hedington came to my hands, when the truth of the facts
were frefh in memory. However, it is hoped that time has fo
far buried fome of them in oblivion, that now it may feem a
fable; and that a murder like that of hanging-up of Joan,
would never be attempted to be committed, by a perfon of breeding, in fo polite a town as that of Hedington.

I have been credibly informed that, foon after its compofition,
the parts were given out to feveral ingenious perfons for action.
But that defign failed, becaufe fome decorations for the ftage
were wanting, and the mufick between the acts, which was to
have been very long, was not fully perfected. I have had in-
formation likewife that the Prologue was not written by the
Author, or rather Authors, of the Play, but by a perfon of good
elocution and graceful prefence, who was to have fpoken it; and
would, by his delivery, have equaled Rofcius, Alleyn [a], Burbage,
or Betterton.

The Prologues of the Ancients were introductory to the Play,
and feldom pretended to wit; but gave an account of the Author of it, and whether it were of his own compofure, or a tranflation; and infifted moft u,on entreaties for the good-nature,
attention, and filence of their audience:

[a] Edward Alleyn, founder of Dulwich College, born Sept. 1, 1566, was
in high reputation in 1592, as appears from an Epigram of Ben Jonfon.
Haywood calls him — "Proteus for fhape, and Rofcius for a tongue."
He was one of the original actors in Shakefpeare's plays, a principal per-
former in Jonfon's; mafter of the Fortune Playhoufe near Whitecrofs-
ftreet, and keeper of the king's wild beafts. He began to build the College
at Dulwich in 1614; which he finifhed, at the expence of ten thoufand
pounds, in 1617. He met with many difficulties in the eftablifhment of
his foundation, it being oppofed by lord Bacon; but obtained the royal
licenfe, June 19, 1621. He died Nov. 25, 1626; and was buried in his
own chapel.

Date

Date operam, et cum silentio animadvortite,
Ut pernoscatis, quid sibi Eunuchus velit [b];

 " Attend, and list in silence to our play,
 " That ye may know what 'tis the *Eunuch* means;"

is the conclusion of the Prologue to that celebrated Play of
Terence, which gained the repeated applause of Rome. And to
the same purpose, though in more words, is the conclusion of
the Prologue to Phormio: only in the latter he complains that
one of their Plays, which was Hecyra, was not suffered to be
acted, by reason of the disturbance and noise of the spectators:

Date operam, adeste æquo animo per silentium;
Ne simili utamur fortunâ, atque usi sumus,
Cùm per tumultum noster grex motus loco est [c],
Quem Actoris virtus nobis restituit locum,
Bonitasque vostra adjutans, atque æquanimitas.

 " Give ear; be favourable; and be silent !
 " Let us not meet the same ill fortune now,
 " That we before encounter'd, when our troop
 " Was by a tumult driven from their place;
 " To which the Actor's merit, seconded
 " By your good-will and candour, has restor'd us."

The Prologues of all the Plays of Terence seem to have been
written by the Actors; at least not to have exceeded their capacity. In that of Hecyra, the principal Actor, Lucius Ambivius
Turpio, upon his own account, entreats their silence, that he
might be encouraged to study new parts, and purchase fresh copies
for their diversion:

Meâ causâ causam hanc accipite, et silentium date,
Ut lubeat scribere aliis, mihique ut discere
Novas expediat, posthac pretio emptas meo.

[b] To these quotations from the Comic Poet we have annexed the
beautiful translation of his happiest imitator.

[c] Alluding to the disturbances on the first attempt to represent the
Hecyra, or " Stepmother."

  " — When first
 " It was presented, such a hurricane,
 " A tumult so uncommon interven'd,
 " It neither could be seen, nor understood:
 " So taken were the people, so engag'd,
 " By a rope dancer,"

         COLMAN.

         " Admi;

" Admit this plea for my fake, and be filent;
" That other Poets may not fear to write;
" That I too may hereafter find it meet
" To play new pieces bought at my expence [d]."

The Epilogues of the Ancients were of a more concife nature than their Prologues, and came up even to a Lacedæmonian brevity. Thaïs and Bacchis, or Myfis and Phrygia, the ladies or chamber-maids of thofe times, were not forced to change their cloaths, and after the Play come to regale the audience with an Epilogue, not becoming the modefty of their fex. Nor did Lucius Ambivius Turpio, or Lucius Attilius Præneftinus, prefume to huff and threaten their audience, and to throw lightning and thunder amongft them, as has been done in thefe latter ages, and been very judicioufly reflected on by Mr. Bayes in his " Rehearfal." The Epilogues of three Comedies of Terence, the Eunuchus, the Heautontimorumenos, and Phormio, proceed to no farther an extent than that of thefe four words, *Vos valete et plaudite*, " Ye, farewell; and clap your hands!" But that of Hecyra curtails this exuberance, and is content with two, *Vos plaudite*, " Clap your hands;" and thofe of Andria and Adelphi condefcend fo far as to have only one, viz. *Plaudite*, " Clap your " hands [e]."

The

[d] From the two prologues to the " Hecyra," and fome paffages in Horace, we may collect that riots, parties, &c. were as common in Rome as in England; and that a firft night was as terrible, and the town as formidable, to Cæcilius and Terence, as to the puny authors of our days. The high reputation of Ambivius Turpio (the Actor who fpoke this Prologue, and probably the Manager of the Company) as well as the efteem which Terence had for him, is evident; and we conceive no unfavourable idea of the Town-criticks of thofe times, who could liften to fuch a plea urged by the Actor, and fo candidly acquiefce in all that he faid in his own commendation. We have feen indeed, and it is to be hoped fhall fee again, an Acting Manager in our time, to whom modern Authors have as much reafon to be partial as Terence to Ambivius; but, though he has helped out many a lame Play with a lively Prologue, I believe he would hardly venture to make fuch an addrefs to the publick as this before us.   COLMAN.

[e] All the old Tragedies and Comedies acted at Rome concluded in this manner. *Donec* CANTOR, *Vos* PLAUDITE, *dicat*, fays Horace. Who the *Cantor* was, is matter of difpute. Monf. Dacier thinks it was the whole

The Prologues and Epilogues of our antient English Poets were probably of the like compofition, though fome of them were made by the Authors themfelves ; but moft ran upon the fame fubject. I fhall proceed no farther at prefent upon this point, becaufe I defign a compleat Differtation concerning all the Prologues and Epilogues that have come to my hands, to fhew the priftine fimplicity of them, and the licentioufnefs that has daily crept in upon them in fucceeding ages.

I have been affured that one of the Authors of this Tragicomedy ufed often to lay before him the Prologue of Ben Jonfon to his moft applauded Play, called, " The Fox [f] ;" which does not yield to any Comedy of any other nation whatfoever, for the juftnefs of thought, propriety of expreffion, and the true painting of the characters ; and may be faid to be the moft excellent, as to the variety of incidents, the feveral cataftrophe's, and the compleat working-up of the whole defign. The piece is what I have thought fitting to lay before the Reader ; it being remarkable for the number of the verfe, and the quaintnefs of the expreffion.

The PROLOGUE to " THE FOX" of BEN JONSON.

" Now, luck yet fend us ! and a little wit
 " Will ferve, to make our PLAY hit ;
" (According to the palates of the feafon)
 " Here is rhyme, not empty of reafon.
" This we were bid to credit, from our *Poet*,
 " Whofe true fcope, if you would know it,
" In all his *Poems* ftill hath been this meafure,
 " *To mix profit with your pleafure* ;

Chorus ; others fuppofe it to have been a fingle Actor ; fome the Prompter, and fome the Compofer. Before the word *Plaudite*, in all the old copies, is an Ω, which has alfo given rife to feveral learned conjectures. It is moft probable, according to the notion of Madam Dacier, that this Ω, being the laft letter of the Greek alphabet, was nothing more than the mark of the tranfcriber, to fignify the end, like the Latin word *Finis* in modern books ; or it might, as Cook fuppofes, ftand for 'Ωδὸς, *Cantor*, denoting that the following word *Plaudite* was fpoken by him.   COLMAN.

 [f] In which, *Burbage* figured as the principal Comedian.

                " And

" And not as fome (whofe throats, their envy failing)
　" Cry hoarfely, *All be writes is railing* :
" And, when his PLAYS come forth, think they can flout them,
　" With faying, *He was a year about them.*
" To thefe there needs no *lie*, but this his *creature*,
　" Which was two months fince no feature ;
" And, though he dares give them five lives to mend it,
　" 'Tis known, five weeks fully penn'd it :
" From his own hand, without a *co-adjutor*,
　" *Novice, journeyman*, or *tutor.*
" Yet, thus much I can give you, as a token
　" Of his PLAY's worth, No eggs are broken ;
" Nor quaking cuftards with fierce teeth affrighted,
　" Wherewith your rout are fo delighted ;
" Nor hales he in a *gull*, old ends reciting,
　" To ftop gaps in his loofe writing ;
" With fuch a deal of monftrous and forc'd *action*,
　" As might make Beth'lem a faction :
" Nor made he his PLAY from jefts ftol'n from each table,
　" But makes jefts to fit his *fable* ;
" And fo prefents quick *Comedy* refined,
　" As beft *Criticks* have defigned,
" The *laws* of Time, Place, Perfons, he obferveth,
　" From no needful *rule* he fwerveth.
" All gall and copperas from his ink he draineth ;
　" Only a little falt remaineth,
" Wherewith he'll rub your cheeks, till (red with laughter)
　" They fhall look frefh a week after."

In my opinion, the moft remarkable paffages in this Prologue may be applied to the Tragi-comedy of " Joan of Hedington." For, in the firft place, if a Poet takes care " to mix profit with " pleafure," and endeavours that his " rhime be not empty of " reafon," a " little wit" will make his Play " hit," and gain it a deferved fuccefs. In this performance, the main defign is to promote an univerfal good, by expofing vice, and fhewing the dangers it leads perfons into, either of lofs of limbs, or life itfelf; and when virtue is the chief aim, all good people will be *pleafed* to fee the contrary to it difregarded. And, fince the diction is eafy and proper, there is no occafion for points, puns, quibbles, old jefts, or forced expreffions ; fince our prefent age, like that of

Auguſtus, is more inclinable to reliſh the natural beauties of Terence, than the mean pretenſions to wit that were uſed by Plautus, and afterwards exploded by Horace. The Prologue goes on, that it was objected to the author of " The Fox," that " all he wrote was railing;" whereas indeed he " drained all gall " from his ink, and left only a little ſalt." So, if perſons will do irregular actions, it is not a lampoon to tell them of it, and reprove them with ſome ſmartneſs; and this is ſo far from reflection, that it ſhews the irregularities of a very few are diſcountenanced by a larger part, and ought at leaſt to ſhame thoſe decaying members into a compliance with better examples. When the Prologue ſays, " the Author was not above five weeks about his " Play;" ſomething might likewiſe be ſaid of this, that the working it up did not coſt ſo much time as the birth of an elephant, or the production of the famous Oration of Iſocrates. Laſtly, the Prologue takes notice,

" The *laws* of Time, Place, Perſons, he obſerveth,
" From no needful *rule* he ſwerveth."

And in this Poem it may be remarked, that, notwithſtanding the ſhortneſs of it, it ſtill keeps up to the *rule* of Horace :

Neve minor, neu ſit quinto productior Actu
Fabula, quæ poſci vult, et ſpectata reponi. Ars Poet. ver. 189.

Which is,

" The Play which you deſign ſhould often pleaſe,
" Muſt have Five Acts, and neither more nor leſs."

Mr. CREECH's Tranſlation.

Then as to the *time* of the action, I have ſeen none (except " The " Adventures of Five Hours ⁘," and ſome few Tragedies in imitation of the French) that can come near it; for the whole ſpace of time does not ſeem in probability to be of greater extent than that of Maſter Churchwarden's fetching up the cows, and his wife's milking them. The *place* for the performance of the action is comprehended in the ſmall vicinage of Hedington, in which ſtreet every body ſees every body, and every body knows every thing. There is no running from thence to Cowley, ſo to Hinkſey, and then back to Marſton, as we have parallel inſtances in moſt of Shakeſpeare's Tragedies. Then for the *manners* of the perſons, they are entirely carried on throughout: Mother Harris and Mother Franklin do not talk like Mr. Cole; neither do

⁘ A Tragi-comedy by Sir William Tuke; printed 1663, Folio.

a
Father

Father Clerkenwell or Mr. Atſon approach the ſpirit of Mr. Pindar; for, as Horace has it, ver. 236.

Nec ſic enitar Tragico differre colori,
Ut nihil interſit, Davúſne loquatur, et audax
Pythias, emunćto lucrata Simone talentum ;
An cuſtos famulúſque Dei Silenus alumni.

Which verſes are admirably improved by Mr. Creech [h], who indeed has been a ſecond Horace, if not a ſuperior genius to him, and had done greater wonders if he had received the lights which have been given ſince his deceaſe to that Author, and lately communicated to the Publick [i].

" They muſt not make all Perſons talk alike,
" The *city valet*, and the *country Dick*;
" The *chamber-maid* grown impudently bold,
" When ſhe has robb'd the *lecher* of his gold :
" The *downright farmer*, and the *dowdy ſot*,
" Or elſe the *briſk companion* o'er his pot."

Here are great notices of the ſignificancy of the Latin tongue, not to be found in any Commentator except Mr. Creech.

Davus is to ſignify a *city valet* and a *country Dick*.

[h] Mr. Thomas Creech was born at Blandford in Dorſet, in 1659, ſon of Thomas Creech, gent. educated at Sherborn ſchool, entered at Wadham College, Oxford, 1675; took the degree of A. B. 1680; M. A. 1689 ; and the ſame year was elected probationer fellow of All Souls. In 1701, he was preſented by his college to the living of Welling in Hertfordſhire. He was a good philoſopher, divine, and poet ; but, through ſome diſappointment either in love or in his expectations, laid violent hands on himſelf before he had taken poſſeſſion of his living. He publiſhed Lucretius in Engliſh, 1682, 8vo ; in Latin, 1695, 8vo; a Tranſlation of Horace, 1684, 8vo ; of Theocritus, with Rapin's Diſcourſe of Paſtorals, 1684, 8vo ; of Manilius, 1700. He tranſlated the Lives of Pelopidas in Corn. Nepos and Plutarch, and that of Solon in the latter ; with his Laconic Apophthegus, Eſſay on Socrates's Demon, and the two firſt Books of Sympoſius, the thirteenth Satire of Juvenal, and ſome Poems of Ovid and Virgil. He was alſo author of ſeveral verſes and tranſlations in the Miſcellany Poems.—On his father's monument in Blandford Church, this Poet is called " The learned, much-admired, and " much-envied Mr. Creech." See Hutchins, Hiſt. of Dorſet, vol. I. p. 83.

[i] Dr. Bentley's Horace was firſt publiſhed in 1711.

Simo

have not as yet any account of their Epitaphs, which I generally collect from all parishes once in ten years.

Joan of Hedington, whether by the bruises she might have received in the struggle she made for the last efforts of life (as will appear in the Play, when she was tied to the beam by Pindar), or by the concern she might have for the affront she had received after having lived so long in the neighbourhood, or being agitated by the Furies, ran distracted, and in that violent condition disclosed the secret transactions of her life; but undoubtedly what she then delivered was like a sick woman's dream, inconsistent with itself, incoherent in its parts, and a mixture of some grounds of truth, veiled with a cloud of fabulous inventions, raised from an irregular imagination: so that no great observation could be made from what she said. However, it gave occasion to a Poem, called "Joanna Furens;" which, being a rhapsody of Latin and "English, came but to few hands, and has since perished.

Having been already longer than I at first designed, I shall make my remarks upon the Play much shorter than I would have done otherwise.

Revenge and Friendship are two great bases upon which a Play may be built; and they apparently have the predominance in this Interlude. The provocation, the injury, the thirst after *revenge*, and the accomplishment of it, and that by the help of *friendship*, run through the whole contexture.

The Drama is opened by Mother Shephard and Mr. Churchwarden, two grave persons; as is that of the Adelphi in Terence:

Senes qui primi venient, hi partem aperient :
In agendo partem ostendent.

    "Part the old men, who first appear, will open ;
    "Part will in act be shewn."

Mitio and Demea, the two brothers, were in the first Scene to display their own characters, and to continue them throughout. So Mrs. Shephard, in the first Scene, declares her dislike to vice ; and, having been an exact observer of the whole transaction, concludes the Play with a very remarkable and useful piece of morality.

It has been objected to this Play, that the Scene between Mother Harris and Joan of Hedington has too much freedom of language, which they are pleased to term *scolding*. But to this it may be answered, that both of them preserve their character, for ill

words

words will follow ill deeds; and it may be further said, that, in the Tragedies of the Antients, both Greek and Latin, there are examples of greater intemperance in speech, scolding imprecations, and ill language; and that these persons speak more like Princesses than Medea or Hecuba. In Terence's Andria, the scolding scene between Myfis and Davus is the most artificial of all that Comedy, which, though not the wittiest, is esteemed one of the most nicely wrought pieces of that Author. The whole turn of the Play depends upon it; and Davus (ver. 801) commends himself for it, in these words:

> *Paulum intereffe cenfes, ex animo omnia,*
> *Ut fert natura, facias, an de induftriâ?*

> " Is there then
> " No difference, think you, whether all you say
> " Falls naturally from the heart, or comes
> " With cold premeditation [k]?"

Scolding must be scolding; and there are no other words it can be put into but those of Nature. Joan and Mother Harris had their nails to fight with: but it would have been ridiculous to have introduced them with their helmets and launces, like Joan of Arc or the Amazonian Hippolyta.

It has likewise been objected, that, Joan of Hedington's calling not being commendable in its own nature, the Author ought not to have made her justify herself so far as to say, " she had been " honeft in her calling." But for this there is an example in the Adelphi of Terence; where Sannio, though he confeffes,

> *Leno fum, fateor, pernicies communis adolefcentium,*
> *Perjurus, peflis.*

> " Well, I am a Pimp [l],
> " The common bane of youth, a perjurer :
> " A public nuifance,".

has

---

[k] The words of Davus to Myfis in this speech have the air of an oblique praife of this scene from the Poet himself, shewing with what art it is introduced, and how naturally it is fuftained. COLMAN.

[l] This seems (says Mr. Colman) to be a tranflation from Diphilus, from whom this part of the fable was taken.

> " No calling is more baneful and pernicious,
> " Than that of a Procurer." WESTERHOVIUS.

The Procurer was a common character in the Comedy of the Antients; but,

if

have not as yet any account of their Epitaphs, which I generally collect from all parishes once in ten years.

Joan of Hedington, whether by the bruises she might have received in the struggle she made for the last efforts of life (as will appear in the Play, when she was tied to the beam by Pindar), or by the concern she might have for the affront she had received after having lived so long in the neighbourhood, or being agitated by the Furies, ran distracted, and in that violent condition disclosed the secret transactions of her life; but undoubtedly what she then delivered was like a sick woman's dream, inconsistent with itself, incoherent in its parts, and a mixture of some grounds of truth, veiled with a cloud of fabulous inventions, raised from an irregular imagination: so that no great observation could be made from what she said. However, it gave occasion to a Poem, called " Joanna Furens;" which, being a rhapsody of Latin and " English, came but to few hands, and has since perished.

Having been already longer than I at first designed, I shall make my remarks upon the Play much shorter than I would have done otherwise.

Revenge and Friendship are two great bases upon which a Play may be built; and they apparently have the predominance in this Interlude. The provocation, the injury, the thirst after *revenge*, and the accomplishment of it, and that by the help of *friendship*, run through the whole contexture.

The Drama is opened by Mother Shephard and Mr. Churchwarden, two grave persons; as is that of the Adelphi in Terence:

Senes qui primi venient, hi partem aperient :
In agendo partem ostendent.

" Part the old men, who first appear, will open ;
" Part will in act be shewn."

Mitio and Demea, the two brothers, were in the first Scene to display their own characters, and to continue them throughout. So Mrs. Shephard, in the first Scene, declares her dislike to vice ; and, having been an exact observer of the whole transaction, concludes the Play with a very remarkable and useful piece of morality.

It has been objected to this Play, that the Scene between Mother Harris and Joan of Hedington has too much freedom of language, which they are pleased to term *scolding*. But to this it may be answered, that both of them preserve their characters, for ill

words

words will follow ill deeds; and it may be further said, that, in the Tragedies of the Antients, both Greek and Latin, there are examples of greater intemperance in speech, scolding imprecations, and ill language; and that these persons speak more like Princesses than Medea or Hecuba. In Terence's Andria, the scolding scene between Mysis and Davus is the most artificial of all that Comedy, which, though not the wittiest, is esteemed one of the most nicely wrought pieces of that Author. The whole turn of the Play depends upon it; and Davus (ver. 801) commends himself for it, in these words:

> *Paulum interesse censes, ex animo omnia,*
> *Ut fert natura, facias, an de industriâ?*
>
>   " Is there then
> " No difference, think you, whether all you say
> " Falls naturally from the heart, or comes
> " With cold premeditation [k] ?"

Scolding must be scolding; and there are no other words it can be put into but those of Nature. Joan and Mother Harris had their nails to fight with: but it would have been ridiculous to have introduced them with their helmets and launces, like Joan of Arc or the Amazonian Hippolyta.

It has likewise been objected, that, Joan of Hedington's calling not being commendable in its own nature, the Author ought not to have made her justify herself so far as to say, " she had been " honest in her calling." But for this there is an example in the Adelphi of Terence; where Sannio, though he confesses,

> *Leno sum, fateor, pernicies communis adolescentium,*
> *Perjurus, pestis.*
>
>   " Well, I am a Pimp [l],
> " The common bane of youth, a perjurer;
> " A public nuisance,".

                   has

[k] The words of Davus to Mysis in this speech have the air of an oblique praise of this scene from the Poet himself, shewing with what art it is introduced, and how naturally it is sustained. COLMAN.

[l] This seems (says Mr. Colman) to be a translation from Diphilus, from whom this part of the fable was taken.

   " No calling is more baneful and pernicious,
   " Than that of a Procurer." WESTERHOVIUS.
The Procurer was a common character in the Comedy of the Antients; but,
                    if

has said juft before,

> *Lene fum.* AESCH. *Scio.* SA. *At ita ut ufquam fide fuit quif-*
> *quam optuma.*
>
> " I'm a Procurer [m]. AESCH. True. SA. And in my way
> " Of as good faith as any man alive."

It has been further faid, that the foliloquy of Joan of Hedington in the fecond Scene of the firft Act, and her expreffions in the fecond Scene of the third Act, are too lofty for her character. But this criticifm will wholly vanifh, when thefe lines of Horace's Art of Poetry [n] are thoroughly confidered; and it will be allowed that Comedy upon occafion may admit of elevated expreffions.

> *Verfibus exponi Tragicis res Comica non vult:*
> *Indignatur enim privatis ac propè focco*
> *Dignis carminibus narrari cœna Thyeftæ,*
> *Singula quæque locum teneant fortita decenter.*
> *Interdum tamen & vocem Comœdia tollit,*
> *Iratufque Chremes tumido delitigat ore.*

Which is thus tranflated by Mr. Creech, with his ufual improvement and brightnefs:

> " A *Comic* Story hates a *Tragic* ftyle,
> " *Bombaft* fpoils *humour*, and *diftorts* a *fmile*,

---

if we may pronounce from their remains, we may venture to fay that the character was never fo finely painted in any part of their works as in the following lines of Shakefpeare:

> " Fie, firrah, a bawd, a wicked bawd!
> " The evil that thou caufeft to be done,
> " That is thy means to live. Doft thou but think,
> " What 'tis to cram a maw, or cloath a back,
> " From fuch a filthy vice? Say to thyfelf,
> " From their abominable and beaftly touches,
> " I drink, I eat, array myfelf, and live!
> " Canft thou believe thy living is a life,
> " So ftinkingly depending! Go, mend, mend!"
>
> *Meafure for Meafure.*

[m] He fays this to Æfchines, to intimidate him, alluding to the privileges allowed to the Romans at Athens, on account of the profit accruing to the republick from their traffick in flaves. It was forbidden to abufe them, on pain of difinheritance. COLMAN.

[n] Ver. 89.

" And

“ And *tragical Thyestes'* barbarous feast .
“ Scorns *mean* and *common words*, and hates a jest :
“ Let every subject have what fits it best.
“ Yet *Comedy* may be allow'd to rise,
“ And rattle in a passion or surprize."

I hope it will give no offence, that Mr. Cole, Act II. Scene 1. amongst the terrible things which he supposes to be at Shotover, declares that he should not be frighted if *camels* were there; whereas a camel is an innocent harmless creature. But it must be considered, that the notion that he had raised to himself of a camel was impressed upon his imagination from the fight he had had of them in old tapestry hangings, and might therefore think they had a physical terribility equal to their bulk. But I must refrain; and omit the defence of particular expressions, various readings, &c. and beg the Reader's kind acceptance of these endeavours, as being, &c.

A. D. 1712.

THE TRAGI-COMEDY

OF

JOAN OF HEDINGTON.

SCENE, *HEDINGTON.*

In Imitation of SHAKESPEARE.

THE PROLOGUE.

GALLANTS, we here prefent you with a Play,
The product of a country holiday.
'Tis ufual now with Prologues to be witty.
But we are not; good faith, the more the pity!
Our Play won't make you laugh, nor make you cry,
For 'tis a perfect Tragi-comedy.
We have no hopes for this our homely treat,
But that, for being fhort, you'll think it fweet.

ACT I. SCENE I.

SCENE, *The High Street in* HEDINGTON.

Enter Mother SHEPHARD *and the* CHURCHWARDEN,

Mother SHEPHARD.

INDEED, Mr. Churchwarden, as I was faying before, this
fame Joan of Hedington is a naughty woman,

CHURCHW. I cannot help it, Neighbour.

M. SHEP. She does not keep a civil houfe, and is a difgrace to
the town; for Gentlemen dare not come to my houfe to drink,
for fear they fhould be thought to go to Joan's.

CHURCHW. Have you good ale, Mother?

M. SHEP. Yes, that I have, marry.

CHURCH. Why then, people will come, for all Joan, I warrant you. But I muft go fetch up the cows. Ha! here are
Gentlemen a coming.

M. SHEP.

M. SHEP. He! a pox on them! They are going to Franalin's. However, I have got some good North-country customers still; and here are two of them coming.

SCENE II.

Enter Father CLERKENWELL *and Mr.* ATSON.

M. SHEP. You are very welcome, Masters: I am glad to see you.

F. CLERK. Have you got good ripe ale, Mother?

M. SHEP. Yes, indeed, Sir: but I have but a little.

ATS. How much?

M. SHEP. A dozen and a half.

F. CLERK. What is that between us two? But come, let us go in. Wash the two-quart mug, for I am a-dry; two of them may quench my thirst a little for the present. Stay, give us a quarter of tobacco.   [*Exeunt.*

❖ ❖ ❖ ❖

ACT II.   SCENE I.

SCENE, *The High Street.*

Enter JOAN OF HEDINGTON *and* Mother HARRIS.

JOAN. MARRY come up, you are so proud with your black bag [o]!

HARRIS. Well, it was none of your money paid for it.

JOAN. But your daughter's did. You are so proud of that minxs, and think to spoil my custom!—But I would have you to know that I am sounder than e'er a Harris of you all.

HARRIS. You sounder! I would have you to know, I scorn to let such pitiful rogues come into my house as you have to do with.

JOAN. I would have you to know, I have as good customers come to my house as any woman in Hedington—no disgrace to you, Goody Harris.

M. HARRIS. Sure you might have had a Mistress under your girdle when you spoke to me, hussey.

[o] N. B. Joan wore a Hat, and Mother Harris a Hood.   KING.

JOAN. Huffey me no huffey, Mrs. Slopdawdry. I will pull your black bag for you. I am a better woman than yourself. I have been an old Parifhioner here, and gone to church, and all the town know I have been honeft in my calling ; and to be abufed by fuch a goffip as you, that are come to put off your pocky ware in our parifh !

M. HARRIS. No more pocky ware than yourfelf.

JOAN. You lye, you Whore. I'll tear your eyes out.

[*Fall a fighting,* JOAN *beats* Mother HARRIS *off the Stage, calling her* Whore *and* Bitch, *the other crying.*

SCENE II. *The High Street.*

JOAN OF HEDINGTON *fola.*

Let's view the mighty act which I have done:
The thing is worthy Joan of Hedington.
I, that have favour'd youngfters many a fcore,
Was ne'er affronted at this rate before
By fuch an upftart, tawdry, pocky whore ;
She from the Maggoty Pie away was fent,
Becaufe fhe had not trade to pay her rent.
At Hinkfey then they would not let her ftay,
Becaufe fhe kept a bawdy-houfe, they fay ;
But now, I think, I've given the whore her due.
Shall I be *buffied* by a bitch like you ?
No, I have beat her, and the drab is gone :
I will reign miftrefs of this place alone,
And be the topping dame of Hedington.

But I think I had beft go home, and drink a dram of brandy.
[*Exit* JOAN.

ACT III.   SCENE I.

SCENE, Mother HARRIS's *Houfe.*

Enter Mother HARRIS, FRANK HARRIS, *and Mr.* COLE.

FRANK. THIS is intolerable, that my mother fhould be abufed by fuch a drab as Joan of Hedington ! I will be revenged, whatever it coft me.   [*Mother* HARRIS *groans.*
COLE.

COLE. Alas, my dear, torment thyfelf no more:
And you, dear mother, ceafe to fob and groan.
For, let me never more be happy made
By the enjoyment of my lovely Frances,
If I don't fatisfy your dire revenge.

HARRIS. Ay, Mr. Cole, nothing could oblige me and my
daughter more, than if you would revenge me on that witch.

FRANK. Ay, do, my dear; ftudy how to revenge my mother
of that witch. You are a fcholar; cannot you conjure?

[COLE *walks about, mufing.*

COLE. I'll break her windows—windows fhe has none,
And then her lattice is not worth the breaking.
I'll go and drink her brandy, and not pay her;
But not to pay for't would be ungenteel,
And I can ne'er be guilty of a thing
That does not favour of a gentleman.
But ftay —
I have a friendfhip with a certain man,
Cunning and clofe, and trufty to his friend,
Pindar, my eyes delight, my other felf;
He promis'd me, that, difputations done,
He'd take a walk, and meet me at this place.
Oh, for his coming now, when moft I want him!
He'll find a fpeedy way to my revenge,
And gratify my mother and my miftrefs.
Two heads are always wifer far than one,
And, when to mine his counfels fhall be join'd,
We'll plague this faucy Joan, with force united.

I believe, Mrs. Frances, it would do your mother good, to drink
fome of this warm flip.

M. HARRIS. I cannot drink flip, if it was flip of gold, till I
am revenged.

FRANK. Dear Mr. Cole, help my mother but in this one
bufinefs; and I will love you better than ever I did Mr.
Warburton.

COLE. Blefling attend you for this laft expreffion!
O what a vaft reward is this you promife!
Thy love, for which I many a time would die,
Is to be gain'd now upon eafy terms.
Were Joan on t'other fide of Shotover,

And

And all the way ftuck full of bears and lions ;
Were fnakes and camels there, and living toads,
I'd fetch her, though fix giants ftood to guard her.
This I could do alone, with fingle ftrength.
But, when I fhall have Pindar's force and counfel,
I'd dare — indeed what would I not dare then ?

    HARRIS. I think you muft carry me to the bed, to lie down
a little.

    FRANK. Pray, mother, ftay a little : here is Crendon the
bagpiper.

    M. HARRIS. Mufic encreafes melancholy thoughts :
But brings no eafe to minds opprefs'd with grief.

[They carry her off.

S C E N E II.   JOAN's Houfe.

Enter Father CLERKENWELL and ATSON.

    F. CLERK. Here, who is within here ? Give me a quartern
of brandy.

    ATS. And me another. Joan, we muft go up the ftone ftairs.

    JOAN. Hold, two words to a bargain. You owe me a groat
for laft time.

    F. CLERK. Joan, where's your helper ?

    JOAN. She is gone a hay-making.

    F. CLERK. Well then, I will go to Mother Harris.

    JOAN. Rather than that, I will do any thing,
Wipe off old fcores, and let you run on new.
I freely do forgive the groat you owe me.
But mention not, oh, fpeak not any more
That odious, filthy, pocky name of Harris ;
For, when I hear it once, my curdled blood
Chills at my heart, and trembles in my veins.
Be'nt fo unkind, dear Clerky, to go thither ;
I vow you make me weep with your unkindnefs.

    F. CLERK. I be'nt unkind, Joany ; I vow, you make me cry
too. I wo'nt go, Joany, I wo'nt.

    ATS. No, he fhan't go. Come, let us all three go up ftairs,
and be friends ; and bid your hufband burn us a pint of brandy.

[Exeunt.
A C T

ACT IV. SCENE I.

SCENE, *A Field adjacent to* Mother HARRIS's *House.*

Enter Mr. PINDAR *and Mr.* COLE.

PIND. I TELL you, friend, from henceforth be at eafe.
The lovely Frances foon fhall be your own,
And Mother Harris have her wifh'd revenge.

COLE. Thou beft of friends, let me embrace thee clofe;
Let's both away, and perfect thy defign.

PIND. Hold, you muft ftay behind; I'll act alone,
To fhew how much Pindar will do for Cole.
You, in my abfence, comfort up your mother,
Put fugar in her ale, 'twill eafe her grief;
And you and gentle Frances fearch the hen-rooft,
That, when I bring home news of your revenge,
With a large difh you lovers may be ready
In eggs and bacon to proclaim my welcome.
But, hold, I want a rope.

COLE. Here's one lies ready.

PIND. 'Tis well.   Good-bye.   [*Exeunt.*

COLE. Now, ye propitious ftars, be guides to Pindar!
For never man fo freely undertook
To ferve his friend in fuch a dangerous moment!

SCENE II.   Mother HARRIS's *Parlour.*

Enter FRANK HARRIS *leading* Mother HARRIS, *and Mr.* COLE.

M. HARRIS. Lord! Mr. Cole, that fugared ale was very good.
I did not care if we had the other flaggon.

Enter Mrs. FRANKLIN,

Mrs. FRANKL. I am forry to fee you fo ill, Mrs. Harris;
that fame Joan's a fawcy huffey, fhe beat me one day too

COLE. Ah, Mrs. Franklin, this is kindly done, to come to
comfort us in our diftrefs.

M. FRANKL. I am willing to do any neighbourly kindnefs.
Lord! forfooth, you are black and blue: you muft put on fome
wet brown paper.

COLE. [*Afide to* FRANK HARRIS.] This Mrs. Franklin is
a very good woman; fhe underftands chirurgery, I fee. Will
you pleafe to walk in, and drink, Mrs. Franklin?   [*Exeunt.*

C 3

ACT V.   SCENE I.

SCENE, JOAN'S *House.*

JOAN OF HEDDINGTON *sola.*

I AM glad they are gone; they were two swinging fellows.

Enter Mr. PINDAR.

PIND. How do you do, Joan?

JOAN. Pretty well, Sir; though, I must beg your pardon, I do not remember your name.

PIND. I believe not. I was never here before. But Mr. Hopman, of Cripfy, recommended me to you for a gill of brandy, and a firk or two up the *stone stairs,* little Joan — up the *stone stairs,* little Joan.

JOAN. Will you pleafe, Sir, to have your brandy before you go up, or burnt againft you come down?

PIND. Againft I come down, little Joan.

SCENE II.   JOAN'S *Chamber.*

Mr. PINDAR *folus.*

I'll do it; and yet methinks my heart relents.
Why fhould I murder her that never hurt me?
Not me, indeed: but fure my friend is me,
And, fince this Joan has dar'd to be fo bold
To injure Cole, fhe muft have injur'd Pindar.
Hence then compaffion and all tender thoughts;
For Mother Harris foon fhall be reveng'd,
And by this hand of mine.

Enter JOAN.

My dear, come fit down upon the bed, little Joany.

> [*As fhe is going to fit down, he toffes the noofe of the rope over her head.*

JOAN. What is this for?

PIND. No hurt, little Joany! no hurt!

> [*He pulls the noofe, and ties her up to the beam.*

'Tis done, and now I'll inftantly to Cole,
And bring him joyful news of his revenge.

> [*Exit.*

SCENE

SCENE III.   Mother SHEPHARD's *House*.

Mother SHEPHARD *and the* CHURCHWARDEN.

CHURCHW. Lord, mother, have you heard the news?

M. SHEPH. No, not I; what news?

CHURCHW. Why, there is such a clutter about Joan's door, you would admire at it; poor Joan has been almost hanged. A Scholar came and tied her up to a beam in her chamber; and, if her husband had not come and cut her down, she had been hanged by this time.

M. SHEPH. Well, I always said she would come to a bad end; it is but what she deserves, for being such a whore.

CHURCHW. Well, I am glad the poor woman is not hanged, for all that.

M. SHEPH. Women, whose honour should be still their guide,
When once they give it up, and go aside,
Into a numerous maze of mischiefs run,
As may be seen by Joan of Hedington!

E P I L O G U E.

OUR Play is done; and, if it chance to please,
  We shall be mighty glad, and much at ease;
But, if it should not please you, Sirs! what then?
Why our young Poet ne'er will write again;
For he's as proud and surly as old BEN!

SOME

Some Account of HORACE's Behaviour during his Stay at TRINITY COLLEGE in CAMBRIDGE. With an ODE to entreat his Departure thence. Together with a Copy of his Medal, taken out of TRINITY COLLEGE Buttery, by a Well-wisher to that SOCIETY.

HAVING had some intimacy with Horace, and likewise an acquaintance with several of the Fellows of Trinity College, I have been so curious as to collect some particulars concerning his stay and behaviour at that place; where he lay indeed, and eat and drank at the Master's lodge; but his apartment was magnificently fitted up, and his entertainment profusely provided for, at the cost of the Fellows and Scholars. He declared often, that his mind had presaged to him that he should come into Great Britain, from the very time he wrote the Thirty-fifth Ode of his First Book, to Fortune, where he implores her to preserve Cæsar in his journey and voyage to Britain:

> *O Diva, gratum quæ regis Antium,*
> *Præsens vel imo tollere de gradu*
> > *Mortale corpus, vel superbos*
> > > *Vertere funeribus triumphos,* &c.

> " Great Goddess, Antium's guardian power,
> " Whose force is strong and quick to raise
> " The lowest to the highest place;
> " Or, with a wondrous fall,
> > " To bring the haughty lower,
> " And turn proud triumphs to a funeral, &c."   CREECH.

> *Serves iturum Cæsarem in ultimos*
> *Orbis Britannos, et juvenum recens*
> > *Examen, Eoïs timendum*
> > > *Partibus, Oceanóque rubro.*

> " Preserve great Cæsar! Cæsar leads
> " To distant Britain. Guide his fate, ⚹
> " And keep the glory of our state,
> > " The youth that must infest
> > " With arms the haughty Medes,
> " And scatter fears and slavery through the East."
> > > > > CREECH.
> > > > > > And

And he actually prophesied concerning his coming into Britain in the Fourth Ode of his Third Book; where he declares he would undertake that voyage, by the help of the Muses, though he was naturally afraid of the sea, and a great coward according to his own character:

> *Utcunque mecum vos eritis: libens*
> *Infanientem navita Bosporum*
>   *Tentabo, et arentes arenas*
>   *Litteris Assyrii viator.*
> *Visam Britannos hospitibus feros,*
> *Et lætum equino sanguine Concanum.*
>   *Visam pharetratos Gelonos,*
>   *Et Scythicum inviolatus amnem.*

> " Whilst you my feeble ship shall guide,
> " I'll singly stem the proudest tide:
> " I'll travel through the farthest East,
> " Where never mortal foot hath prest;
> " Britain's inhospitable flood,
> " And Thracians pleas'd with horses blood,
> " On Scythian sands I'll boldly tread,
> " And stoutly see the quiver'd Mede."

CREECH.

But in short, it seems, Horace would go any where for good entertainment; and, as their ill fate would have it, came to Trinity College, to exercise their hospitality; which he has done to some purpose, as will appear hereafter. Whilst he was at Rome, he familiarly told Albius Tibullus, in the Fourth Epistle of his First Book,

> *Me pinguem, et nitidum bene curatá cute vises,*
> *Quem ridere voles, Epicuri de grege porcum.*

> " Then come and see me now grown plump and fine,
> " When you would laugh at one of Epicurus' swine."

CREECH.

He is much improved since that time, and is become *totus teres atque rotundus*, as round as a bowl, or the hoop of a tierce of claret; so that, when the Fellows saw this black unwieldy outlandish *pig* come into their " kitchen-garden (which the College " Cooks used to have for pot-herbs, sallads, &c. but has since " been forcibly disposed of [by the Master], by taking the key " and giving it to one of the Fellows, expressly against the con-
" sent

" fent of the Seniors ᴾ;" they might apprehend, in the very worſt ſenſe of the proverb, that " a *bog* was got into their peaſe;" for he ravaged them like an Iriſh *cocberer*, who never departs as long as he can find a ſingle potatoe.

When he firſt came, he cried out againſt merchants, for importing wine, and drinking out of plate; and gave in his bill of fare very ſparingly. Some chicory, mallows to looſen his body, and now and then a few olives, were all that he deſired; and would often repeat theſe verſes of the Thirty-firſt Ode of his Firſt Book :

> — *dives et aureis*
> *Mercator exficcet culullis*
>   *Vina Syrâ reparata merce,*
> *Diis carus ipſis; quippe ter et quater*
> *Anno reviſens æquor Atlanticum*
>   *Impune : me paſcunt olivæ,*
>   *Me cichorea, levéſque malvæ.*

> " — The merchant now, come ſafe to land,
> " In golden goblets quaffs the wine,
>   " His Syrian wares and voyage gain'd.
> " He chiefeſt darling of the Gods;
>   " For twice a year he plows the main,
> " He rides the proud Atlantic floods,
>   " And yet makes ſafe returns again.
> " Me *chicory* and *olives* feed,
>   " Me looſening *mallows* nobly feaſt;
> " They give what Nature's wants can need,
>   " And kindly fill the eaſy gueſt."   CREECH.

But ſoon afterwards he ſhews himſelf not to be ſo eaſy a gueſt; and declares himſelf for " banquets," *Nos convivia;* for rummaging, careleſſneſs, and debauchery:

> *Nos convivia, nos prælia virginum*
> *Sečtis in juvenes unguibus acrium*
> *Cantamus, vacui, ſive quod urimur,*
>   *Non præter ſolitum leves.*   Od. I. vi.

ᴾ See Remarks upon a Letter, by Mr. Miller, Fellow of Trinity College, p. 69. KING.

" I ſing

"   I fing foft boys and virgins wars,
"   How foon they fmile, how angry foon :
"   With clofe-par'd nails and tender tooth,
"   They all invade the ruffling youth ;
"   Thus urge my frolick on,
"   And bid farewell, a long farewell, to cares."
Then there was nothing to be heard of from him, but

"   Hang forrow, caft away care ;
"   The College is bound to find us :
"   For you and I and all muft die,
"   And leave the world behind us !"

Or elfe, as Mr. Creech has paraphrafed upon the Ninth Ode of
the Firft Book, in the true ftrain of a Ballad,

"   All cares and fears are fond and vain,
"   Fly vexing thoughts of dark *to-morrow* :
"   What chance *fcores* up, count perfect gain ;
"   And banifh bufinefs, banifh forrow."

And then Horace would repeat twenty Songs to the fame pur-
pofe, which appear in his Works, and are tranflated by his admired Friend Mr. Creech ; for, during his ftay in College, he
gained fome fmattering in the Englifh ; and, being informed that
Mr. Creech, who had tranflated his Works, was the fame perfon
who had tranflated Lucretius, he had a great veneration for him,
for having, as far as in him lay, propagated the Epicurean principles : for Horace had always a bent to that Philofophy rather
than any other, notwithftanding his pretended recantation, which
he publifhed in the Thirty-fourth Ode of his Firft Book,

Parcus Deorum cultor, et infrequens,
Infanientis dum fapientiæ
    Confultus erro : nunc retrorfum
       Vela dare, atque iterare curfus
Cogor relictos.———

"   I, that but feldom did adore,
"   I that no God but Pleafure knew,
"   Whilft mad Philofophy did blind,
"   And Epicurus fool'd my mind,
"   Muft keep that impious courfe no more,
"   But turn my fails and fteer anew."

He pretended to have been converted by a clap of thunder, or
perhaps took the advice of a grave perfon, whofe maxim it is,
                                                    " that

" that a man fhould have the face of religion, for it would do
" him fervice in the world." But I never heard that Horace,
whilft in College, "kept Chapel ?" himfelf; but that he has
hindered other perfons from minding Divinity, which fhould
have been their proper ftudy, rather than to find out *que's*, and
atque's, and *vel's*, and *nec's*, and *neque's*, at the expence of a
thoufand pounds a year and upwards, defigned for much better
ufes than to correct an old Latin Song-book, not to fay worfe of
it, notwithftanding all the graces and beauties of its language.

During his ftay, he took every opportunity to recommend drinking and pleafure.   Was it Spring-time, that was moft proper :

Solvitur acris Hyems grata vice Veris, et Favoni ;
 Trahúntque ficcas machinæ carinas :
At neque jam ftabulis gaudet pecus, aut arator igni,
 Nec prata canis albicant pruinis.   Od. I. iv.

And therefore, as Mr. Creech fays, he advifes his Friend to live
merrily :

" Sharp Winter melts, Favonius fpreads his wing,
 " A pleafing change, and bears the Spring :
" Dry fhips drawn down from ftocks now plow the main,
 " And fpread their greedy fails again :
" Nor ftalls the ox, nor fires the clown, delight ;
 " And fields have loft their hoary white."

For, according to this Author, the Spring makes him thirfty ;
and he attributes his defire of liquor more to the feafon, than his
own inclination :

Jam Veris comites, quæ mare temperant,
Impellunt animæ lintea Thraciæ :
Jam nec prata rigent, nec fluvii ftrepunt
 Hybernâ nive turgidi, &c.

Adduxere fitim tempora, Virgili :
Sed preffum Calibus ducere Liberum
Si geftis, juvenum nobilium cliens
 Nardo vina merebere.   Od. IV. xii.

" The foft companions of the Spring,
 " The gentle Thracian Gales,
" Spread o'er the Earth their flowery wing,
 " And fwell the greedy merchant's fails :

q Remarks upon a Letter, &c. p. 141.   r Ibid.

              " The

" The ſtreams, not ſwoln with melted ſnow,
  " In fair mæanders play ;
" To quiet ſeas they ſmoothly flow,
  " And gently eat their eaſy way, &c.

" The Seaſon, Virgil, brings us thirſt ;
  " And, if you mirth deſign
" With noble youths, bring ointment firſt,
  " And I'll provide thee racy wine."   CREECH.

But Winter was the ſeaſon he moſt delighted in, which was the time for jollity, not only for profuſeneſs in drink, but in firing,

    — vetuſtis extruat lignis focum.   Epod. ii.

Then the fire was to be built high with dry and blazing logs ; and then he uſed to ſtir up his friends to mirth, with his Thirteenth Epode :

    Horrida tempeſtas cælum contraxit ; et imbres
    Nivéſque deducunt Jovem, &c.

The latter part of which has been ſince tranſlated into that common but chearful ſong,

    " Old Chiron thus preach'd to his pupil Achilles ;"

which concludes to this purpoſe,

    " But, all the while you lie before the town,
    " Drink, and drive care away ; drink, and be merry :
    " You'll ne'er go the ſooner to the Stygian Ferry.

And, amidſt his plenteous cups, he would ſtill be commanding to lay on more fire. " Who is there ?" Bring " coals, billets, turf, " ſedge, charcoal [1], any thing ; but do not let us ſtarve." And then he would break out into theſe words of the Ninth Ode of his Firſt Book,

    Vides, ut altâ ſtet nive candidum
    Soraƈte, nec jam ſuſtineant onus
      Sylvæ laborantes : gelíque
        Frigora conſtiterint acuto ?

    Diſſolve frigus, ligna ſuper foco
    Largè reponens : atque benigniùs
      Depreme quadrimum Sabinâ,
        Oh Thaliarche, merum diotâ.

---

[1] Remarks upon a Letter, &c. p. 168,

    " See how the hills are white with snow,
       " The seas are rough, the woods are tost,
    " The trees beneath their burthen bow,
       " And purling streams are bound in frost.
    " Dissolve the cold with noble wine,
       " Dear friend, and make a rouzing fire;
    " 'Gainst cold without, and care within,
       " Let both with equal force conspire."   CREECH.

One of Horace's qualities was, that he never wanted to go home, but would keep up his company till fun-rising, as he tells us in the Twenty-first Ode of his Third Book :

    Vivæque producent lucernæ,
      Dum rediens fugat astra Phœbus.

The Reader must pardon the want of a Translation to these verses, because Mr. Creech tells us in his Preface, " That some " principles he had made him *cautious* of some Odes, and that " he had passed by three more upon a different account." I cannot tell upon what account; but this Ode happened to be so unfortunate as to be one of them.

Although he pretended to be no newsmonger or politician, nor to concern himself how the war was managed, or who paid taxes, so he enjoyed his ease and pleasure ;

    Quid bellicosus Cantaber, & Scythes, &c.   Od. II. xi.
    " What fierce Cantabrians, what the Scythians dare,
    " Make, friend, no object of thy care, &c."

yet he was a religious observer of all public rejoicings for any victory; he never failed to be the most zealous assistant at a gawdy[t] or a bonfire. At such times, he used to be the ring-leader of his companions ; and this was generally the beginning and burthen of his Song :

    Nunc est bibendum, nunc pede libero
    Pulsanda tellus: nunc Saliaribus
      Ornare pulvinar Deorum
        Tempus erat dapibus, sodales.   Od. I. xxxvii.
    " Now, now, 'tis time to dance and play,
    " And drink, and frolick all the day;

    [t] A feast, a festival, a day of plenty; a word still used in the universities.   JOHNSON.

        'Tis

    " 'Tis time, my friends, to banish care;
    " And coftly feafts
    " With thankful hearts prepare
    " In hallow'd fhrines, and make the Gods your guefts."

It feems, he was more peculiarly accuftomed to obferve the Firft of March, for many years together.

Martiis cælebs quid agam Kalendis,
Quid velint flores, et acerra thuris
Plena, miraris, &c.   Od. III. viii.

    " What I, a Batchelor, intend,
    " My learned Lord, and noble friend,
    " In *Mars his Calends,* you admire ;
    " What mean *thofe flowers that crown my head,*
    " The coals on green turf altars laid,
    " Where in fmall cenfers *thankful fweets* expire."

                            CREECH.

And then he was fo modeft as to afk Mæcenas to lay afide thoughts of public bufinefs :

Negligens, ne quà populus laboret :
Parce privatus nimiùm cavere.

    " Negleft the various turns of ftate,
    " The fports of chance, or nods of fate :"   Ibid.

and to defire him to drink a hundred cups to his health, and fit up till day-light ; which was but a moderate requeft for fo great a man to do for fuch a friend.

Sume, Mæcenas, cyathos amici
Sofpitis centum, et vigiles lucernas
Perfer in lucem.

    " Let watching tapers chafe the night,
    " And rifing morn reftore the light."   Ibid.

Horace was refolved to keep up the good cuftom in England, though it was after fomething a different way from what he ufed to do at Rome. A friend of his, coming into his chamber on the *Calends of March,* which is more generally known by the Title of " St. David's-day," found him very complaifant to the feafon. Inftead of his veffel of *old wine,* he was very plentifully provided with a *cragg* of *Welfh ale* ; inftead of the " flowers that " ufed to crown his head," he had got a prodigioufly over-grown

     5   leek

leek in his hat; and the "thankful fweets" were much more fatisfactorily fupplied with the odour of a dozen of warm crufts and a whole cheefe toafting before the fire.

He was of a flattering temper; and there was no trufting to him, or any perfon that belonged to him. He that promifes over-much is fure to perform nothing. At one time no perfon was fo great with him as Mæcenas, as we fee by the Seventeenth Ode of his Second Book, where he takes an horrible oath, that he will affuredly " die the fame day with Mæcenas;" and that nothing fhould part them, not even the " breath of the fire- " fpitting Chimæra," nor the forces of " the hundred-handed " Gyas:" but there was nothing of all this (as well as fome other things) to be depended on.

As he grew daily more unweildy, fo he fell into the Dutch faction; and was extremely pleafed with a Book I had then by me, but is fince loft, which was an Edition of his Odes and Epodes, in a fair character, with a tranflation on the other fide into Dutch profe. It might be very elegant for aught I know, being not much converfant in that language; all that I can remember of it is,

O nata mecum confule Manlio.   Od. III. xxi.

𝔚𝔥𝔞𝔫 𝔐𝔦𝔧𝔫 𝔥𝔢𝔢𝔯 𝔐𝔞𝔫𝔩𝔦𝔲𝔰 𝔅𝔬𝔲𝔯𝔤𝔬𝔲𝔯𝔪𝔞𝔢𝔰𝔱𝔢𝔯 𝔴𝔞𝔢𝔰.

I fancy it might not be improper for Horace to take a journey to Amfterdam, to fee what improvements he can make of him- felf in Holland. In the mean time, there was a prodigious and unufual confumption of bread, ale, and firing, in the lodge; fo that the fellows made a public complaint. They thought they were not obliged to pay for Horace's maintenance, whilft he was recruiting himfelf with fome few emendations of his work. They alledged, " That if any Benefactor, Farmer, or out- " lying Officer of the College, be invited to the table of the " Mafter, Major Fellows, or Scholars, the College is to bear the " charge; but, if the Mafter, or any Member of the College, " invite any elfe, he muft pay the College the value of the dinner " or fupper [*]."

The entertainment of fuch a gueft as Horace ran the College to great expence, and the Mafter to great extravagance in his demands from the Fellows.

[*] Remarks upon a Letter, &c. p. 164.

Mr.

Mr. Miller, in his " Remarks on the Letter," fays, " I will " infert but one account of what the Mafter has taken, befides " his ftatutable allowances, and that in the compafs of one year, " though he was abfent about half the time ᵂ.

From the SENIOR BURSAR.	l.	s.	d.		l.	s.	d.
Coals,	63	12	0	Small Beer,	45	0	0
Commencement-money,	6	13	4	Bread,	59	7	0
Weftminfter Election,	5	0	0	Flour,	9	0	0
Chamber Rent,	24	0	0	Bran,	1	10	4
From the JUNIOR BURSAR.				Dove-houfe,	5	0	0
Extraordinaries,	47	10	8	From the STEWARD.			
Mafter's Gardener,	2	0	0	Linen, about	12	0	0
Billets,	17	2	0	Audit Exceedings,	4	0	0
Turf and Sedge,	14	9	9	Brawn,	3	10	0
Charcoal,	15	0	0	Chandler,	10	0	0
From the PANDOXATOR.				Extra Commons,	41	12	0
Ale,	62	16	0	Servants Commons, more than Statute,	22	4	0

ᵂ Dr. Bentley, who was appointed mafter of Trinity College, by king William, in 1700, to reftore difcipline and learning in that College, endeavoured it to an eminent degree, proceeding up to the bottom f em very directly, and examining every candidate for fcholarfhips and fellowfhips thoroughly, and feemed as nearly as poffible to have given every one the place he really deferved; but at an election for fellowfhips, about 1703 or 1704, he ventured *for once only,* as he faid, " to recede from " that excellent rule, *Detur Digniffimo,* " in favour of Mr. Stubbs, nephew to the vice-mafter. Thus, fays Mr. Whifton, " he broke in upon his " integrity, and I think he never after returned to it." He carried matters with fo high a hand in the government of this college, that, in 1709, a complaint was brought againft him, before Dr. John Moore, bifhop of Ely, as vifitor, by feveral of the fellows, who, in order to have him removed from the mafterfhip, charged him with embezzling the public money, and other mifdemeanours. In anfwer to this, he prefented a defence to the Bifhop, which was publifhed in 1710, under the title of " The prefent State of Trinity College," 8vo.; and thus began a lafting quarrel, which, having the nature of a *bellum inteftinum,* was carried on, like other civil wars, with the moft virulent animofity on each fide, till, after above twenty years continuance, it ended at laft in the Doctor's favour. There is a large account of this difpute, and a lift of the feveral books written about it, in the " Biographia Britannica."

"On the whole, this one year, besides his statute-table, al-
"lowances, and dividend, he took 454 *l.* 6 *s.* 1 *d.* ; for one far-
"thing of which there is no colour of statute.

"And there are six or seven of those Items, which, for any
"thing I can find, are original encroachments of his own ; and the
"rest he has enlarged to the degree of amazement. How much
"bread, &c. he had in reference to the whole College, and as
"much as two other Colleges in the University ; and how much
"in comparison to former Masters ; is reserved to the evidence
"on the articles. One single article, that of his fire, which
"amounts to 110 *l.* 3 *s.* 9 *d.* is so much, that scarce any Noble-
"man in England, I believe no Archbishop, spent the like in
"the time. This fuel must be sold, or otherwise embezzled ; for,
"if he had kept a continual fire in every chimney of his lodge
"all that time, it could not have consumed so much."

The same Author goes on to shew, p. 170, how much the
Master exceeded the account of Mountague, in the following particulars, for several years :

Senior Bursar's Books.	l.	s.	d.
Anno			
1707 For Coals for the Lodge,	77	14	8
1708 — — —	63	6	8
1709 — — —	76	10	0
Pigeon-meat,	3	1	2
Billets for the Lodge,	9	0	0
Turf and Sedge,	15	7	0
Billets for both Assizes,	1	10	0
Pigeon-meat,	5	3	5
Pandoxator's Office,			
1708 Flour, 22 Bushels,	9	0	0
Bread,	59	6	0

Junior Bursar's Books.	l.	s.	d.
Anno			
1708 Billets for the Lodge,	17	2	0
Turf and Sedge,	14	9	9
Billets for both Assizes,	3	0	0
Small Beer, 100 Barrels,	45	0	0
Ale, 314 Craggs,	62	6	0
1709 Flour, 13 Bushels, 1 Peck,			
Bread,	33	6	0
Small Beer, 101 Barrels,	45	9	0
Ale, 38 Craggs,	17	12	0

It may seem very extraordinary that one single person should
in a year expend 284 *l.* 6 *s.* 1 *d.* in bread, beer, and firing ; but,
I think, I have abundantly justified the Master, in shewing that he
had a *Guest* who was able to consume that and much more. But
then it was for the credit of the Society, that they once entertained a person of that eminence ; and it will redound to their
immortal honour, not only in Great Britain, but throughout all
Europe. However, the young *lads*, as they will be gibing and
scoffing at their betters, would often accost Horace with these

line

lines of his own, at the end of the Second Epistle of his Second Book; telling him, that gaiety was more proper for their youth than his age; and therefore desired him to rusticate himself, and retreat to his own sty :

Lusisti satis, edisti satis, atque bibisti :
Tempus abire tibi est, ne potum largius æquo
Rideat, et pulset lasciva decentius ætas [x].

These verses not being translated by Mr. Creech, whose translation may likewise be deficient in other particulars; I shall present the Reader with a Paraphrase of these lines, and a Medal of Horace, in his present bulk and proportion.

Advice to HORACE, to take his Leave of TRINITY COLLEGE [y], in CAMBRIDGE.

HORACE, you now have long enough
  At Cambridge play'd the fool :
Take back your criticizing stuff
  To Epicurus' School.

But, in excuse of this, you'll say,
  You're so unwieldy grown,
That, if amongst that herd you lay,
  You scarcely should be known.

How many butter'd crusts you've tost,
  Into your weem so big,
That you're more like (at College cost)
  A *porpoise* than a *pig*.

[x] These lines have, with the most beautiful imagery, been applied to himself by one of the politest Criticks of the present age, in the close of an admirable "Dissertation on the Idea of Universal Poetry."

[y] " Where BENTLEY late tumultuous wont to sport
  " In troubled waters, but now sleeps in *port* :
  " The mighty Scholiast, whose unwearied pains
  " Made HORACE dull, and humbled MILTON's strains."

See Dunciad, Book iv. ver. 201, &c. The great SCRIBLERUS explains the second line " retired into harbour;" but the learned SCIPIO MAFFEI understands it (and we cannot but subscribe to his opinion) of a certain *wine*, of which this Professor invited him to drink abundantly.

                                        But

But you from head to foot are *brawny,*
   And so from side to side :
You measure (were a circle drawn)
   No longer than you're wide.

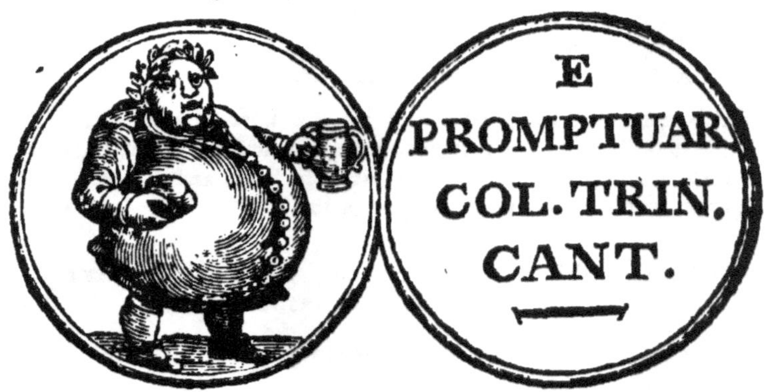

Then bless me, Sir, how many craggs
   You've drunk of potent ale !
No wonder if the belly swaggs,
   That's rival to a *whale.*
E'en let the Fellows take the rest,
   They've had a jolly tasler :
But no great likelihood to feast,
   'Twixt Horace and the Master.

I shall give a further account of the proceedings of Horace;
which perhaps may discover some points of learning that have
hitherto lain secret. In the mean time, I entreat the Reader to
accept of these,

From, &c.

AN ANSWER[a]

TO

CLEMENS ALEXANDRINUS'S SERMON,

UPON

Quis Dives falvetur? " What Rich Man can be faved?"
Proving it eafy for a Camel to go through the Eye of a Needle.
Delivered at the Devil's Arfe of Peak[b].

WHEN we come to be " laid up in the fepulchres of our
" fathers, the laft ftage of our throne of mortality," the
                                                    fituation

[a] Afcribed to Dr. King, on the authority of " Mifcellaneous Poems,
" Tranflations, and Imitations, by feveral Hands," publifhed by Lintot,
in 2 vols. 12mo. 1720; the firft volume, by Pope, the Duke of Buckingham, Gay, Betterton, and Dryden; the fecond, by King, Smith, Dibben,
Fenton, Yalden, Rowe, Southcott, Broome, Ward, and Daniel. The
collection, though commonly afcribed to Mr. Pope, was entirely formed
by Lintot.

[b] This little piece evidently alludes to, and was occafioned by, the
famous Sermon preached by Dr. White Kennet, afterward Bifhop of
Peterborough, on the death of William the firft Duke of Devonfhire,
and publifhed under the title of " A Sermon preached at the Funeral of
" the Right Noble William Duke of Devonfhire, in the Church of All-
" Hallows in Derby, on Friday, Sept. 5, 1707; with fome Memoirs of
" the Family of Cavendifh," 8vo. 1708. It gave great offence at the time
of its publication; and was very feverely animadverted upon by the
well-known John Dunton, in a pamphlet entitled, " The Hazard of a
" Death-bed Repentance, fairly argued, from the late Remorfe of William
" late Duke of Devonfhire, with ferious Reflections, &c. &c. The whole
" refolving that nice Queftion, *How far a Death-bed Repentance is poffible
" be fincere?* And is publifhed by way of Anfwer to Dr. Kennet's Ser-
" mon, &c." 8vo, 1708. This Sermon occafioned Mr. Pope to take
notice of Dr. Kennet in the following very fevere lines:
          " When fervile Chaplains cry, that birth and place
          " Indue a Peer with honour, truth, and grace;
          " Look in that breaft, moft dirty Dean! be fair:
          " Say, can you find out one fuch lodger there?"
                    Imitations of Horace, Book II. Ep. ii. ver. 220.
Dr. Kennet was born Aug. 10, 1660; in June, 1678, was entered of
Edmund Hall, Oxford; B. D. in May, 1683; M. A. in 1685; D. D. in
D 3   1699;

situation seems to be somewhat horrid [c]: but, upon review, " the
" Elysian vallies open with greater amazement, and the rocky
" *monumental* hills *of marble*, that hang over in a more aweful
" guard of it, seem to be Art insulting Nature." It is not " parts,
" corrupted in the finest head, on the surface of which straws
" and feathers may swim, while weightier matters lie at the bot-
" tom [d];" it is not " knowledge, defined by some to be a bubble in
" the water, a meteor in the air, or a tumor and spectacle;" it is not
" being of a society for promoting stock sand work-houses, for erec-
" ting parochial libraries [e];" or writing " Parochial Antiquities [f],"
that can preserve us from having " *gravel* in our mouths [g]." Upon
this deplorable occasion, although my writings have sunk into
contempt and disuse, yet I shall once again attempt " a seri-
" ous and rational discourse," under these two " paradoxes,"
which " my love of singularity makes me fond to maintain." I
shall shew, first, how a good rich man may be never the worse for
living oddly. Secondly, I shall explain the use of my *plank* [h] and
door, in all cases of desperate extremities.

As to the first point. A good rich man " may allow himself
" to climb up any hill within his reach; to fatigue himself within-
" doors; to acquire heat, and expell moisture; to take a com-
" fortable breakfast, and then walk round his lodgings; to have a
" dinner provided for him about twelve o'clock; to have a candle
" with ten or twelve tobacco-pipes before him; then to shut the
" door, and fall a smoaking and writing, and thinking how to
" digest what he had fed upon; to be jealous of being burnt for
" a heretick, and afraid of the Bishop of Sarum [i]; to run beyond

1699; in 1701, archdeacon of Huntingdon. By the management of
Bp. Burnet, he preached the abovementioned sermon in 1707; and, by
the succeeding duke's recommendation, obtained the deanry of Peterborough; of which see he was consecrated bishop, Nov. 9, 1718. He
died Dec. 19, 1728.
 [c] See Dr. Kennet's Sermon, p. 1.   [d] P. 26.   [e] P. 31.
 [f] Published by Dr. Kennet, in 4to, 1695.   [g] Sermon, p. 32.   [h] P. 34.
 [i] Dr. Seth Ward, who at one period of his life had spoken of Mr.
Hobbs's Writings in very favourable terms, but afterward wrote against
them. In 1661 he was made dean, and next year bishop, of Exeter; in
1667 was translated to Salisbury; and in 1671 made chancellor of the
Garter, being the first Protestant Bishop that ever was so. He died Jan. 6,
1688-9, aged 71, after having had for many years the misfortune to
outlive his senses.

" sea

" fea in a fright, and be driven back by the fame : not to endure
" contradiction, or an empty houfe ; in his ficknefs, to ride upon
" a feather-bed in a coach; to hate any thoughts or difcourfe of
" death ; to make himfelf a warm coat the winter before he dies;
" and if then he falls into a pit, to catch hold of one of the Devil's
" *cloven feet* [k] ;" or of my *plank*, which, under the next head, I
fhall prove worth both of them.

Far be it from me to deny, that *gloves, fcarves, funeral fermons,*
and *memoirs,* &c. are proper to be ufed at the *obfequies* of the
dead, " who too often affect fecrecy and filence," as their exe-
cuters do " a parcimonious narrownefs of mind [l]." But thefe are
things of an inferior confideration to my *plank* and *wicket.* Some
philofophers " have been glad to creep out of the world at any
" hole [m] ;" but I have a new " *door* of hope for them," provided
" they be men of parts and figure, and will give me *crape*
enough to " confecrate their memory" with my *decorums.* I have
before infinuated, that a good rich witty man may do any thing
but be damned. But I fee fome people pricking up their ears
there. You, Goodman Two-fhoes, and you, Gammer Two-fhoes,
and you, Tom Trap, and you, Dick Froft, and you, Goody
Gurton, that have lain in ftraw ever fince your bed was taken
away for plunder in the civil wars ; let me tell you, you are
" poor ftupid wretches ;" your " duller flame will be more eafily
" extinguifhed ; you meaner finful *fcrubs* are generally given
" over to a reprobate mind ;" your barley-bread and peafe-pudding
make you *heavy* and *ftupid* ; and, " if you do not take care,
" you will die as ftupidly as you lived." Therefore look to it,
and begin to repent as foon as you can ; the fooner the better for
you who are poor people. But Heaven forbid that I fhould
preach this doctrine to you, Mr. Alderman OCCASI; or to you, Mr.
ON-ALL the Recorder ; to you, the worfhipful Mr. Juftice CON-
FORM ; or to you, my honoured patronefs, Lady MITY ! You
are gentlefolks all ; you are perfons of greateft wit, and wealth,
and ability, in this rich and ingenious corporation ; whom I am
glad to fee at church now and then, as your leifure will permit
you. I befeech you not to furmife that I mean the leaft part of
this to your Honours. All that I mean is this : " Ordinary abilities
" may be altogether funk by a long vicious courfe of life [n]." But

---

[k] All thefe circumftances are related by Dr. Kennet of the celebrated
Mr. Hobbs. Sermon, &c. p. 107.

[l] P. 3.   [m] A faying of Mr. Hobbs, p. 116.   [n] P. 35.

                                    it

it is an undoubted *maxim*, " That perfons of diftinguifhed fenfe
" and judgement, by their nobler and brighter parts, have an ad-
" vantage of underftanding the worth of their fouls before they
" refign them." Therefore, Gentlefolks, I have referved for you
an expedient, called " A death-bed repentance." After you
" have made *fhipwreck* of a good confcience," I have a *plank*
for you, upon which "one or two" (I believe I can make room
for you *four* gentry) " may efcape °." But, do you hear, you
" meaner finful wretches," that do not fit upon *cufhions*, and are not
afleep, and have no vote in the veftry ; it will be little comfort
for you, in this *ftorm*, to " expect the like deliverance." Confider
what has been faid ; and you will not haftily repent—of what you
have heard.

° Sermon, p. 34.

THE

THE ART OF COOKERY;

IN IMITATION OF

HORACE'S ART OF POETRY.

WITH SOME

LETTERS to Dr. LISTER and Others

Occasioned principally by the Title of a Book publifhed by the Doctor, being the Works of APICIUS COELIUS, " concerning the Soups and Sauces of the Ancients [a]."

With an Extract of the greateft Curiofities contained in that Book.

By the Author of THE JOURNEY TO LONDON.

Humbly infcribed to the Honourable BEEF STEAK CLUB.

[a] " Apicius Cælius, de Opfoniis, five Condimentis, five Arte Co- " quinaria, Libri Decem. *Amftelod.* 1709," 8vo.

THE PUBLISHER

TO

THE READER.

IT is now-a-days the hard fate of fuch as pretend to be Authors, that they are not permitted to be mafters of their own works; for, if fuch papers (however imperfect) as may be called a *copy* of them, either by a fervant or any other means, come to the hands of a Bookfeller, he never confiders whether it be for the perfon's reputation to come into the world, whether it is agreeable to his fentiments, whether to his ftyle or correctnefs, or whether he has for fome time looked over it; nor doth he care what name or character he puts to it, fo he imagines he may get by it.

It was the fate of the following Poem to be fo ufed, and printed with as much imperfection and as many miftakes as a Bookfeller that has common fenfe could imagine fhould pafs upon the town, efpecially in an age fo polite and critical as the prefent.

Thefe following Letters and Poem were at the prefs fome time before the other paper pretending to the fame title was crept out: and they had elfe, as the Learned fay, groaned under the prefs till fuch time as the fheets had one by one been perufed and corrected, not only by the Author, but his Friends; whofe judgement, as he is fenfible he wants, fo is he proud to own that they fometimes condefcend to afford him.

For many faults, that at firft feem fmall, yet create unpardonable errors. The number of the verfe turns upon the harfhnefs of a fyllable; and the laying a ftrefs upon improper words will make the moft correct piece ridiculous. Falfe concord, tenfes, and grammar, nonfenfe, impropriety, and confufion, may go down with fome perfons; but it fhould not be in the power of a Bookfeller to lampoon an Author, and tell him, " You did write all " this: I have got it; and you fhall ftand to the fcandal, and I " will have the benefit." Yet this is the prefent cafe, notwithftanding there are above threefcore faults of this nature; verfes tranfpofed, fome added, others altered, or rather that fhould have been altered, and near forty omitted. The Author does not value himfelf upon the whole; but, if he fhews his efteem for Horace, and can by any means provoke perfons to read fo ufeful a treatife; if he fhews his averfion to the introduction of luxury, which may tend to the corruption of manners, and declares his love to the old Britifh hofpitality, charity, and valour, when the arms of the family, the old pikes, mufkets, and halberts, hung up in the hall over the long table, and the marrow-bones lay on the floor, and " Chevy Chace" and " The old Courtier of the Queen's" were placed over the carved mantle-piece, and the beef and brown bread were carried every day to the poor; he defires little farther, than that the Reader would for the future give all fuch Bookfellers as are before fpoken of no manner of encourage-ment.

LETTERS

L E T T E R S

T O

Dr. LISTER and OTHERS.

L E T T E R I.
To Mr. ———

DEAR SIR,

THE happiness of hearing now and then from you extremely
delights me; for, I must confess, most of my other Friends
are so much taken up with politicks or speculations, that either
their hopes or fears give them little leisure to peruse such parts
of Learning as lay remote, and are fit only for the closets of the
Curious. How blest are you at London, where you have new
Books of all sorts! whilst we at a greater distance, being destitute
of such improvements, must content ourselves with the old store,
and thumb the Classicks as if we were never to get higher than
our Tully or our Virgil.

You tantalize me only, when you tell me of the Edition of a
Book by the ingenious Dr. Lister, which you say is a Treatise
De Condimentis & Opsoniis Veterum, " Of the Sauces and Soups
" of the Ancients," as I take it. Give me leave to use an expression, which, though vulgar, yet upon this occasion is just and
proper : You have made my mouth water, but have not sent me
wherewithal to satisfy my appetite.

I have raised a thousand notions to myself, only from the title.
Where could such a treasure lay hid? what Manuscripts have
been collated? under what Emperor was it written? Might it not
have been in the reign of Heliogabalus, who, though vicious
and in some things fantastical, yet was not incurious in the grand
affair of *eating?*

Consider, dear Sir, in what uncertainties we must remain at
present. You know my neighbour Mr. Greatrix is a learned
Antiquary.

Antiquary.   I shewed him your Letter ; which threw him into such a dubiousness, and indeed perplexity of mind, that the next day he durst not put any *catchup* in his *fish-sauce*, nor have his beloved *pepper*, *oil*, and *lemon*, with his *partridge*, left, before he had seen Dr. Lister's Book, he might transgress in using something not common to the Ancients.

Dispatch it, therefore, to us with all speed ; for I expect wonders from it.   Let me tell you ; I hope, in the first place, it will, in some measure remove the barbarity of our present education : for what hopes can there be of any progress in Learning, whilst our Gentlemen suffer their sons, at Westminster, Eaton, and Winchester, to eat nothing but *salt* with their *mutton*, and *vinegar* with their *roast beef*, upon holidays ? what extensiveness can there be in their souls ; especially when, upon their going thence to the University, their knowledge in *culinary matters* is seldom enlarged, and their diet continues very much the same ; and as to *sauces*, they are in profound ignorance ?

It were to be wished, therefore, that every family had a French tutor ; for, besides his being Groom, Gardener, Butler, and Valet, you would see that he is endued with a greater accomplishment ; for, according to an ancient Author, *Quot Galli, totidem Coqui,* " As many Frenchmen as you have, so many Cooks you may de- " pend upon ;" which is very useful, where there is a numerous issue.   And I doubt not but, with such tutors, and good house-keepers to provide *cake* and *sweet-meats*, together with the tender care of an indulgent mother, to see that the children eat and drink every thing that they call for ; I doubt not, I say, but we may have a warlike and frugal Gentry, a temperate and austere Clergy ; and such Persons of Quality, in all stations, as may best undergo the *fatigues* of our *fleet* and *armies*.

Pardon me, Sir, if I break off abruptly ; for I am going to Monsieur D'Avaux, a person famous for easing the tooth-ach by *revulsion*. He has promised to shew me how to strike a lancet into the jugular of a *carp*, so as the blood may issue thence with the greatest effusion, and then will instantly perform the operation of stewing it in its own blood, in the presence of myself and several more Virtuosi. But, let him use what *claret* he will in the performance, I will secure enough to drink your health and the rest of your friends.					I remain, Sir, &c.

L E T T E R

LETTER II.
To Mr. ————

SIR,

I SHALL make bold to claim your promise, in your laſt obliging Letter, to obtain the happineſs of my correſpondence with Dr. Liſter; and to that end have ſent you the encloſed, to be communicated to him, if you think convenient.

LETTER III.
To Dr. LISTER, preſent.

SIR,

I AM a plain man, and therefore never uſe compliments; but I muſt tell you, that I have a great ambition to hold a correſpondence with you, eſpecially that I may beg you to communicate your remarks from the Ancients, concerning *dentiſcalps*, vulgarly called *tooth-picks*. I take the uſe of them to have been of great antiquity, and the original to come from the inſtinct of Nature, which is the beſt miſtreſs upon all occaſions. The Egyptians were a people excellent for their Philoſphical and Mathematical obſervations: they ſearched into all the ſprings of action; and, though I muſt condemn their ſuperſtition, I cannot but applaud their invention. This people had a vaſt diſtrict that worſhiped the *crocodile*, which is an animal, whoſe jaws, being very oblong, give him the opportunity of having a great many teeth; and, his habitation and buſineſs lying moſt in the water, he, like our modern Dutch *whitſters* [b] in Southwark, had a very good ſtomach, and was extremely voracious. It is certain that he had the water of Nile always ready, and conſequently the opportunity of waſhing his mouth after meals; yet he had farther occaſion for other inſtruments to cleanſe his teeth, which are ſerrate, or like a ſaw. To this end, Nature has provided an animal called the *ichneumon*, which performs this office, and is ſo maintained by the product of its own labour. The Egyptians, ſeeing ſuch an uſeful ſagacity in the *crocodile*, which they ſo much reverenced, ſoon began to imitate it, great examples eaſily drawing the multitude; ſo that it became their conſtant cuſtom

———————

[b] Whoſe tenter-grounds are now almoſt all built upon.

to pick their teeth, and wash their mouths, after eating. I cannot find in Marsham's " Dynasties [c]," nor in the " Fragments of
" Manethon [d]," what year of the moon (for I hold the Egyptian
years to have been *lunar*, that is, but of a month's continuance)
so venerable an usage first began : for it is the fault of great
Philologers, to omit such things as are most material. Whether
Sesostris, in his large conquests, might extend the use of them,
is as uncertain ; for the glorious actions of those ages lay very
much in the dark. It is very probable that the public use of
them came in about the same time that the Egyptians made use
of *juries.* I find, in the Preface to the " Third Part of Modern
" Reports," that " the Chaldees had a great esteem for the

[c] Sir John Marsham was born Aug. 23, 1602; educated at Westminster, and sent from thence to St. John's College, Oxford. He studied
the law at the Middle Temple, and was appointed one of the six clerks in
Chancery in 1638 ; was deprived of that place by the parliamentarians,
but restored to it by King Charles II, who knighted him in 1660, and
made him a baronet three years after. The title of the learned Historian's
work here alluded to is " Canon Chronicus Ægyptiacus, Ebraicus,
" Græcus, &c." and is at once a proof of his great erudition, profound
judgement, and indefatigable industry. The first edition of it was printed
at London, in folio, 1672 ; it was re-printed at Leipsic, in 4to, 1676 ;
and again at Franeker, in 4to, 1696 ; and very soon rendered the author's name famous throughout Europe. It is well known that the
Egyptians, like the Chinese, pretended to incredible antiquity ; and had,
in the list of their Dynasties, extended their chronology to 36,525 years.
These Dynasties had long been rejected as fabulous : but Sir John Marsham
has reduced them to Scripture chronology, by proving them to be not
successive, but *collateral.* Some things which he has advanced have been
contradicted, if not confuted, by men of learning. But it is no wonder
that one traveling in the darkness of antiquity, as he did, should sometimes
miss his way. Le Clerc says, " summo studio antiquitates Ægyptias col-
" legit." Dr. Wotton says, " he was the first who made the Egyptian
" antiquities intelligible." And the learned Dr. Shuckford tells us,
" no tolerable scheme can be formed of the Egyptian history, that is
" not, in the main, agreeing with his." He died May 25, 1685.

[d] High priest of Heliopolis in the time of Ptolomæus Philadelphus, at
whose request he wrote his history, comprizing a period of 53,535 years,
pretending to take his accounts from the sacred inscriptions on the pillars
of Hermes Trismegistus. His Dynasties were transcribed by Eusebius,
in his Chronica. See Bp. Stillingfleet's Origines Sacræ, book i. c. 2.

" number

" number TWELVE, becaufe there were fo many figns of the
" Zodiack; from them this number came to the Egyptians,
" and fo to Greece, where Mars himfelf was tried for a murder,
" and was acquitted." Now it does not appear upon record,
nor any *ftone* that I have feen, whether the jury clubbed, or
whether Mars treated them, at dinner, though it is moft likely
that he did; for he was but a quarrelfome fort of perfon, and
probably, though acquitted, might be as guilty as Count Koningfmark [e]. Now the cuftom of *juries* dining at an eating-houfe,
and having glaffes of water brought them with *tooth-picks* tinged
with vermilion fwimming at the top, being ftill continued, why
may we not imagine, that the *tooth-picks* were as ancient as the
dinner, the *dinner* as the *juries*, and the *juries* at leaft as the *grand-
children* of Mitzraim? Homer makes his heroes feed fo grofsly,
that they feem to have had more occafion for *fkewers* than *goofe-*

[e] Charles John lord Koningfmark, &c. a native of Drefden, and a necef-
fitous adventurer, was tried and acquitted from being an acceffary to the
murder of Thomas Thynne, efq. Feb. 21, 1681-2.—Mr. Thynne was
married to the lady Elizabeth Percy, countefs of Ogle, fole daughter and
heirefs to Jofceline earl of Northumberland, but was murdered in his
coach, Feb. 12, 1681-2, before confummation, by three affaffins, fuppofed
to be fuborned by count Koningfmark, who had made fome advances to
the lady Ogle. That lady was betrothed in his infancy to Henry Cavendifh
earl of Ogle, only fon to Henry duke of Newcaftle, who, dying Nov. 1,
1680, before he was of an age to cohabit with her, left her a virgin
widow. Mr. Thynne, who married her when fhe was fcarcely fifteen, was
prevailed on by her mother to travel another year before he bedded her;
in which interval fhe became acquainted with Koningfmark; who, having
no hopes of obtaining her whilft her hufband lived, is fuppofed to have
contrived his death. The lady, however, detefted this bafe and inhuman
conduct, and foon after married the great duke of Somerfet. The ftory
of the murder, which is well known by the reprefentation of it on an
entablature of Mr. Thynne's monument in Weftminfter Abbey, may be
feen in Rerefby's " Memoirs," p. 135.—The three affaffins (Uratz,
Borofky, and Stern) were hanged in Pall Mall, March 10, 1681-2.—
Koningfmark is faid to have been killed in a quarrel in Hungary, in
1686, in the 31ft year of his age; but we are, with more probability,
informed, that when king George II. made fome alterations in his palace
at Hanover, the count's body was found under the floor. His fifter (miftrefs to Auguftus II, king of Poland) was mother of the famous marfhal
Saxe. Granger, vol. IV. p. 237.

VOL. III.　　　　　　　　E　　　　　　　　*quills.*

quills. He is very tedious in defcribing a Smith's forge and an anvil; whereas he might have been more polite, in fetting out the *tooth-pick-cafe* or painted *fnuff-box* of Achilles, if that age had not been fo barbarous as to want them. And here I cannot but confider, that Athens, in the time of Pericles, when it flourifhed moft in fumptuous buildings, and Rome in its height of empire from Auguftus down to Adrian, had nothing that equalled the Royal or New Exchange, or Pope's-head-Alley, for curiofities and *toy-fhops*; neither had their Senate any thing to alleviate their debates concerning the affairs of the univerfe like *raffling* fometimes at Colonel Parfons's [f]. Although the Egyptians often extended their conquefts into Africa and Ethiopia, and though the Cafre Blacks have very fine teeth; yet I cannot find that they made ufe of any fuch inftrument; nor does Ludolphus [g], though very exact as to the Abyffinian empire, give any account of a matter fo important; for which he is to blame, as I fhall fhew in my Treatife of " Forks and " Napkins," of which I fhall fend you an Effay with all expedition. I fhall in that Treatife fully illuftrate or confute this paffage of Dr Heylin [h], in the Third Book of his " Cofmography," where he fays of the Chinefe, " That they eat their meat with "two fticks of ivory, ebony, or the like; not touching it with " their hands at all, and therefore no great foulers of linen. " The ufe of filver forks with us, by fome of our fpruce gal- " lants taken up of late, came from hence into Italy, and from " thence into England." I cannot agree with this learned Doctor in many of thefe particulars. For, firft, the ufe of thefe *fticks* is not fo much *to fave linen,* as out of pure neceffity; which arifes from the length of their nails, which perfons of great quality in thofe countries wear at a prodigious length, to prevent all poffibility of working, or being ferviceable to themfelves or others; and therefore, if they would, they could not eafily feed themfelves with thofe claws; and I have very good authority, that in the Eaft, and efpecially in Japah, the Princes have their meat put into their mouths by their attendants.. Befides, thefe fticks are of no ufe but for *their* fort of meat, which, being *pilau,* is all boiled to rags. But what would thofe fticks fignify to carve a *turkey-cock,* or a *chine of beef?* Therefore our *forks* are

[f] The White's, Almack's, or Arthur's, of thofe days.

[g] See the fecond volume of this collection, p. 91.

[h] See fome account of Dr. Heylin, in our Author's " Adverfaria."

of quite different shape: the steel ones are bidental, and the silver
generally resembling tridents; which makes me think them to
be as ancient as the Saturnian race, where the former is appro-
priated to Pluto, and the latter to Neptune. It is certain that
Pedro Della Valle, that famous Italian Traveller, carried his
knife and *fork* into The East Indies; and he gives a large account
how, at the court of an Indian Prince, he was admired for his
neatness in that particular, and his care in wiping *that* and his
knife, before he returned them to their respective repositories.
I could wish Dr. Wotton, in the next edition of his " Modern
" Learning," would shew us how much we are improved, since
Dr. Heylin's time, and tell us the original of *ivory knives*, with
which young heirs are suffered to mangle their own *pudding*;
as likewise of *silver* and *gold knives*, brought in with the desert
for carving of *jellies* and *orange-butter*; and the indispensable necessity of a *silver-knife* at the side-board, to mingle *sallads* with,
as is with great learning made out in a Treatise called Acetaria,
concerning " Dressing of Sallads." A noble Work! But I
transgress —

And yet, pardon me, good Doctor, I had almost forgot a thing
that I would not have done for the world, it is so remarkable. I
think I may be positive, from this verse of Juvenal[l], where he
speaks of the Egyptians,

Porrum et cepe nefas violare, et frangere morsu,

that it was " sacrilege to chop a leek, or bite an onion." Nay,
I believe that it amounts to a demonstration, that Pharaoh Necho
could have no true *lenten porridge*, nor any *carrier's sauce* to his
mutton; the true receipt of making which sauce I have from an
ancient MS. remaining at the Bull Inn in Bishopsgate-street,
which runs thus:

" Take seven spoonfuls of spring water; slice two onions of
" moderate size into a large saucer, and put in as much salt as
" you can hold at thrice betwixt your fore-finger and thumb, if
" large, and serve it up." *Prolatum est.*

HOBSON, Carrier to the University of Cambridge.
The effigies of that worthy person remains still at that Inn[k];
and I dare say, that not only Hobson, but old Birch, and many

others

<hr>

[l] Sat. XV. 9.

[k] Hobson, by the help of common sense, and a constant attention to a
few frugal maxims, raised a much greater fortune than a thousand men of

                              genius

others of that mufical and delightful profeffion, would rather
have been labourers at the Pyramids with that *regale*, than to
have reigned at Memphis, and have been debarred of it. I break
off abruptly. Believe me an admirer of your worth, and a fol-
lower of your methods towards the increafe of Learning, and
more efpecially your, &c.

✳✳✳✳✳

LETTER IV.
To Mr. ———

SIR,

I AM now very ferioufly employed in a Work that, I hope,
may be ufeful to the Publick, which is a Poem of the " Art
" of Cookery," in imitation of Horace's " Art of Poetry," infcribed to Dr. Lifter, as hoping it may be in time read as a preli-
minary to his Works. But I have not vanity enough to think it
will live fo long. I have in the mean time fent you an imitation
of Horace's invitation of Torquatus to fupper, which is the Fifth
Epiftle of his Firft Book [l]. Perhaps you will find fo many faults
in this, that you may fave me the trouble of my other propofal;
but, however, take it as it is :

> If Bellvill can his generous foul confine
> To a fmall room, few diſhes, and fome wine,
> I fhall expect my happinefs at nine.
> Two bottles of fmooth Palm, or Anjou white,
> Shall give a welcome, and prepare delight,

genius and learning educated in that Univerfity ever acquired, or were
even capable of acquiring. He was, to ufe the citizen's phrafe, A MUCH
BETTER MAN than Milton, who has written two quibbling epitaphs
upon him. But, if that great Poet had never lived, Hobfon's name would
have been always remembered; as he took an effectual method of perpe-
tuating his memory, by erecting a handfome ftone conduit at Cambridge,
fupplying it by an aqueduct, and fettling feven lays of pafture-ground towards the maintenance of the fame for ever. He died, in the time of the
plague, 1630, in the 86th year of his age. See more of him in the
Spectator, Nº 509. His will is in Peck's Collections. Granger, vol. II.
p. 400.

    [l] This Epiftle has been imitated by Dr. Swift, in " Toland's Invitation
" to Difmal, to dine with the Calves Head Club," vol. XVI. p. 357.

Then for the Bourdeaux you may freely afk,
But the Champaigne is to each man his flafk.
I tell you with what force I keep the field;
And if you can exceed it, fpeak, I'll yield.
The fnow-white damafk enfigns are difplay'd,
And glittering falvers on the fide-board laid.
Thus we'll difperfe all bufy thoughts and cares,
The General's counfels, and the Statefman's fears :
Nor fhall fleep reign in that precedent night,
Whofe joyful hours lead on the glorious light,
Sacred to Britifh worth in Blenheim's fight.
The bleffings of good-fortune feem refus'd,
Unlefs fometimes with generous freedom us'd.
'Tis madnefs, not frugality, prepares
A vaft excefs of wealth for fquandering heirs.
Muft I of neither wine nor mirth partake,
Left the cenforious world fhould call me Rake?
Who, unacquainted with the generous wine,
E'er fpoke bold truths, or fram'd a great defign?
That makes us fancy every face has charms ;
That gives us courage, and then finds us arms :
Sees care difburthen'd, and each tongue employ'd,
The poor grown rich, and every wifh enjoy'd.
   This I'll perform, and promife you fhall fee
A cleanlinefs from affectation free :
No noife, no hurry, when the meat's fet on,
Or when the difh is chang'd, the fervants gone :
For all things ready, nothing more to fetch,
Whate'er you want is in the Mafter's reach.
Then for the company, I'll fee it chofe,
Their emblematic fignal is the Rofe.
If you of Freeman's raillery approve,
Of Cotton's laugh, and Winner's tales of love,
And Bellair's charming voice may be allow'd,
What can you hope for better from a crowd ?
But I fhall not prefcribe.   Confult your eafe,
Write back your men, and number as you pleafe :
Try your back-ftairs, and let the lobby wait ;
A ftratagem in war is no deceit.
           I am, Sir, yours, &c.
               E 3   LETTER

L E T T E R V.

To Mr. ————

I HERE fend you what I promifed, a " Difcourfe of Cookery," after the method which Horace has taken in his " Art of " Poetry," which I have all along kept in my view; for Horace certainly is an Author to be imitated in the delivery of *precepts*, for any art or *fcience*. He is indeed fevere upon OUR fort of learning in fome of his *Satires*; but even there he inftructs, as in the Fourth Satire of the Second Book, ver. 13.

> *Longa quibus facies ovis erit, illa memento,*
> *Ut fucci melioris, et ut magis alba rotundis,*
> *Ponere : namque marem cohibent callofa vitellum.*

> " Choofe eggs oblong; remember they'll be found
> " Of fweeter tafte, and whiter than the round :
> " The firmnefs of that fhell includes the male."

I am much of his opinion, and could only wifh that the world was thoroughly informed of two other truths concerning *eggs*. One is, how incomparably better *roafted eggs* are than boiled; the other, never to eat any butter with *eggs* in the *fhell*. You cannot imagine how much more you will have of their flavour, and how much eafier they will fit upon your ftomach. The worthy perfon who recommended it to me made many profelytes; and I have the vanity to think that I have not been altogether unfuccefsful.

I have in this Poem ufed a plain, eafy, familiar ftyle, as moft fit for precept; neither have I been too exact an Imitator of Horace, as he himfelf directs. I have not confulted any of his Tranflators; neither Mr. Oldham [m], whofe copioufnefs runs into Paraphrafe; nor Ben Jonfon, who is admirable for his clofe following

[m] John Oldham, born Aug. 9, 1653, was a bachelor of Edmund Hall, Oxford; A. B. in 1674, and foon after ufher to the free fchool at Croydon. In this fituation, fome of his poetry having been handed about, he was honoured with a vifit by the earls of Rochefter and Dorfet, Sir Charles Sedley, and other perfons of diftinction. In 1678, he was tutor to the fon of Judge Thurland, and in 1681 to a fon of Sir William Hickes. By the advice of Sir William and the affiftance of Dr. Lower, he applied for about a year to the ftudy of phyfic; but, poetry being predominant, he haftened to London, and became a perfect votary to the bottle, yet without

lowing of the original; nor yet the Lord Rofcommon [n], fo excellent for the beauty of his language, and his penetration into the very defign and foul of that Author.   I confidered that I went upon a new undertaking; and though I do not value myfelf upon it fo much as Lucretius did, yet I dare fay it is more innocent and inoffenfive.

Sometimes, when Horace's rules come too thick and fententious, I have fo far taken liberty as to pafs over fome of them; for I confider the nature and temper of Cooks, who are not of the moft patient difpofition, as their under-fervants too often experience.   I wifh I might prevail with them to moderate their paffions, which will be the greater conqueft, feeing a continual heat is added to their native fire.

Amidft the variety of difeffions that Horace gives us in his "Art of Poetry," which is one of the moft accurate pieces that he or any other Author has written, there is a fecret connexion in reality; though he doth not exprefs it too plainly; and therefore this Imitation of it has many breaks in it.   If fuch as fhall condefcend to read this Poem would at the fame time confult Horace's original Latin, or fome of the aforementioned Tranflators, they would find at leaft this benefit, that they would re-

out finking into the debauchery of his contemporary wits.   He was patronized by the earl of Kingfton, who would have made him his chaplain if he would have qualified himfelf.   He lived with the earl, however, till his death, which was occafioned by the fmall-pox, Dec. 9, 1683.   He was particularly efteemed by Mr. Dryden; who has done him great juftice in "Verfes to his Memory."   His works have been frequently printed in one volume, 8vo; in 1722 in 2 vols. 12mo. with the Author's Life; and very lately, under the infpection of Capt. Thompfon, in 3 vols. 12mo.

[n] Wentworth Dillon, earl of Rofcommon, was born in Ireland; and educated in Yorkfhire, under the tuition of Dr. Hall, afterward bifhop of Norwich.   When the troubles began in England, he was fent to finifh his ftudies in Normandy, under the learned Bochart.   At the Reftoration, he was appointed captain of the band of gentlemen penfioners.   Refigning this poft, he went to Ireland, and was made captain of the guards by the duke of Ormond.   But the pleafures of the Englifh court being powerful motives for his return, he was made mafter of the horfe to the duchefs of York. He now began to be diftinguifhed as a poet; and projected with Mr. Dryden the fixing of a ftandard to our language; a project which religious commotions foon defeated.   He died Jan. 17, 1684.   His poems, which are good, but not numerous, are printed in the "Works of the Minor "Poets."

E 4

collect

collect those excellent instructions which he delivers to us in such elegant language.

I could wish the Master and Wardens of the Cooks Company would order this Poem to be read with due consideration; for it is not lightly to be run over, seeing it contains many useful instructions for human life. It is true, that some of these rules may seem more principally to respect the Steward, Clerk of the Kitchen, Caterer, or perhaps the Butler. But the Cook being the principal person, without whom all the rest will be little regarded, they are directed to him; and the Work being designed for the universal good, it will accomplish some part of its intent, if those sort of people will improve by it.

It may happen, in this as in all works of Art, that there may be some terms not obvious to common Readers; but they are not many. The Reader may not have a just idea of a *swoled mutton*, which is a sheep roasted in its wool, to save the labour of fleaing. *Bacon* and *filbert tarts* are something unusual; but, since *sprout tarts* and *pistachio tarts* are much the same thing, and to be seen in Dr. Salmon's " Family Dictionary," those persons who have a desire for them may easily find the way to make them. As for *grout*, it is an old Danish dish; and it is claimed as an honour to the ancient Family of Leigh, to carry a dish of it up to the coronation. A *dwarf pye* was prepared for King James the First, when Jefferey his dwarf rose out of one armed with a sword and buckler °; and is so recorded in history, that there are few but know it. Though *marinated fish, hippocraes,* and *ambigues,* are known to all that deal in Cookery; yet *terrenes* are not so usual, being a silver vessel filled with the most costly dainties after the manner of an *oglio*. A *surprize* is likewise a dish not so very common; which, promising little from its first appearance, when open abounds with all sorts of variety; which I cannot better resemble than to the Fifth Act of one of our modern Comedies. Lest *Monteth, Vinegar, Taliessin,* and *Bossu,* should be taken for dishes of rarities; it may be known, that Monteth was a gentleman with a scalloped coat, that Vinegar keeps the ring at Lincoln's Inn Fields, Taliessin was one of the most ancient Bards amongst the Britons P, and Bossu one of the

most

° See the note on ver. 255. of " The Art of Cookery."

P Taliessin, chief of the Bards, flourished in the sixth century. His works are still preserved, and his memory held in high veneration among

his

moſt certain inſtructors in criticiſm that this latter age has produced 9.

I hope it will not be taken ill by the Wits, that I call my Cooks by the title of ingenious; for I cannot imagine why Cooks may not be as well read as any other perſons. I am ſure their *apprentices*, of late years, have had very great opportunities of improvement; and men of the firſt pretences to literature have been very liberal, and ſent in their contributions very largely. They have been very ſerviceable both to *ſpit* and *oven*; and for theſe twelve months paſt, whilſt Dr. Wotton with his " Modern " Learning" was defending *pye-cruſt* from ſcorching, his dear Friend Dr. Bentley, with his " Phalaris," has been ſinging of *capons*. Not that this was occaſioned by any ſuperfluity or te-diouſneſs of their writings, or mutual commendations; but it was found out by ſome worthy patriots, to make the *labours* of the *two Doctors*, as far as poſſible, to become uſeful to the publick.

Indeed Cookery has an influence upon mens actions even in the higheſt ſtations of human life. The great Philoſopher Pytha-goras, in his " Golden Verſes," ſhews himſelf to be extremely nice in eating, when he makes it one of his chief principles of morality to abſtain from *beans*. The nobleſt foundations of honour, juſtice, and integrity, were found to lye hid in *turnips*; as appears in that great Dictator, Cincinnatus, who went from the plough to the command of the Roman army; and, having brought home victory, retired to his cottage: for, when the Samnite ambaſſadors came thither to him, with a large bribe, and found him dreſſing *turnips* for his repaſt, they immediately returned with this ſentence, " That it was impoſſible to prevail " upon him that could be contented with ſuch a *ſupper*." In ſhort, there are no honorary appellations but what may be made uſe of to Cooks; for I find throughout the whole race of Char-lemaigne, that the Great Cook of the Palace was one of the prime miniſters of ſtate, and conductor of armies: ſo true is that maxim of Paulus Æmilius, after his glorious expedition into Greece, when he was to entertain the Roman People, " that

his countrymen. Both Merlin and Talieſſin had propheſied, that the Welſh ſhould regain their ſovereignty over this iſland; which ſeemed to be accompliſhed in the houſe of Tudor. GRAY.

9 See the note on ver. 585.

" there was equal skill required to bring an army into the field,
" and to set forth a magnificent entertainment [r]; since the one
" was as far as possible to annoy your enemy, and the other to
" pleasure your friend." In short, as for all persons that have
not a due regard for the learned, industrious, moral, upright, and
warlike profession of Cookery, may they live as the ancient
inhabitants of Puerte Ventura, one of the Canary Islands, where,
they being so barbarous as to make the most *contemptible* person
to be their *butcher*, they had likewise their *meat* served up *raw*,
because they had no fire to dress it; and I take this to be a
condition bad enough of all conscience!

As this small Essay finds acceptance, I shall be encouraged to
pursue a great design I have in hand, of publishing a Bibliotheca
Culinaria, or the " Cook's Complete Library," which shall begin
with a Translation, or at least an Epitome, of Athenæus, who
treats of all things belonging to a Grecian Feast. He shall be
published, with all his *comments*, *useful glosses*, and *indexes*, of
a vast copiousness, with cuts of the *basting-ladles*, *dripping-pans*,
and *drudging-boxes*, &c. lately dug up at Rome, out of an old
subterranean skullery. I design to have all Authors in all languages upon that subject; therefore pray consult what Oriental
Manuscripts you have. I remember Erpenius, in his Notes
upon Locman's [s] Fables (whom I take to be the same person
with Æsop) gives us an admirable receipt for making the *sour
milk*, that is, the *bonny clabber*, of the Arabians. I should be
glad to know how Mahomet used to have his *shoulder of mutton*
dressed. I have heard he was a great lover of that joint, and
that a maid of an Inn poisoned him with one, saying, " If he is

---

[r] This maxim seems to have been adopted by the gallant contriver of
the modern festival of " The Oaks."

[s] By birth an Abyssinian of Ethiopia or Nubia, and sold among the
Israelites as a black slave in the reigns of king David and Solomon. He
is by many supposed to be the same with the Æsop of the Greeks. And
indeed we find in the apologues of Locman in Arabic many particulars
that are seen in Æsop's fables; so that it is not easy to determine whether the Greek or the Arabian are the originals. That species of instruction, however, is more agreeable to the genius of the Oriental than of the
Western nations; and Planudes, in his fabulous Life of Æsop, borrowed
many of his materials from traditions he found in the East concerning
Locman, concluding them to have been the same person.—See the Preface
to " The Art of Love."

" a Pro-

" a Prophet, he will discover it; if he is an impostor, no matter
" what becomes of him." I shall have occasion for the assistance
of all my Friends in this great work. I some posts ago desired
a Friend to enquire what Manuscripts Sol. Harding, a famous
Cook, may have left behind him at Oxford. He says, he finds
among his Executors several admirable *bills of fare* for *Aristotle*
suppers, and entertainments of country strangers, with certain
prices, according to their several seasons. He says, some pages
have large black crosses drawn over them; but for the greater
part the Books are fair and legible.

Sir, I would beg you to search Cooks Hall, what Manuscripts
they may have in their Archives. See what in Guildhall: what
account of *custard* in the Sword-bearer's Office: how many tun
He, a Common Cryer, or a Common Hunt, may eat in their life-
time. But I transgress the bounds of a Letter, and have strayed
from my subject, which should have been, to beg you to read the
following lines, when you are inclined to be most favourable to
your Friend; for else they will never be able to endure your just
censure. I rely upon your good-nature, and I am

Your most obliged, &c.

L E T T E R VI.
To Mr. ———

DEAR SIR,

I HAVE reflected upon the discourse I had with you the other
day, and, upon serious consideration, find that the true understanding of the whole " Art of Cookery" will be useful to all
persons that pretend to the *belles lettres,* and especially to Poets.

I do not find it proceeds from any enmity of the Cooks, but
it is rather the fault of their Masters, that Poets are not so well
acquainted with good eating; as otherwise they might be, if
oftener invited. However, even in Mr. D'Urfey's ' presence,
this I would be bound to say, " That a good dinner is brother
" to a good poem :" only it is something more substantial; and,
between two and three a clock, more agreeable.

' See, in vol. II, " Useful Transactions," Part ii. No 3.

I have

'I have known a supper make the most diverting part of a Comedy. Mr. Betterton [u], in " The Libertine [w]," has set very gravely with the leg of a chicken: but I have seen Jacomo very merry, and eat very heartily of pease and buttered eggs under the table. The Host, in " The Villain [x]," who carries tables, stools, furniture, and provisions, all about him, gives great content to the spectators, when from the crown of his hat he produces his cold capon; so Armarillis (or rather Parthenope, as I take it) in " The Rehearsal," with her wine in her spear, and her pye in her helmet; and the Cook that slobbers his beard with sack posset, in " The Man's the Master [y];" have, in my opinion, made the most diverting part of the action. These embellishments we have received from our imitation of the ancient Poets. Horace, in his Satires, makes Mæcenas very merry with the recollection of the unusual entertainments and dishes given him by Nasidienus; and with his raillery upon garlick in his Third Epode. The Supper of Petronius, with all its machines and contrivances, gives us the most lively description of Nero's luxury. Juvenal spends a whole Satire about the price and dressing of a single fish, with the judgement of the Roman Senate concerning it. Thus, whether serious or jocose, good eating is made the subject and ingredient of poetical entertainments.

I think all Poets agree that Episodes are to be interwoven in their Poems with the greatest nicety of art; and so it is the same thing at a good table: and yet I have seen a very good Episode (give me leave to call it so) made by sending out the leg of a goose, or the gizzard of a turkey, to be broiled: though I know that Criticks with a good stomach have been offended that the unity of action should be so far broken. And yet, as in our Plays, so at our common tables, many Episodes are allowed, as slicing of cucumbers, dressing of sallads, seasoning the inside of a surloin of beef, breaking lobsters claws, stewing wild ducks, toasting of cheese, legs of larks, and several others.

[u] Thomas Betterton, with justice esteemed the Roscius of his age, was born in 1635, came upon the stage in 1656, and continued on it with great reputation more than 50 years. He died Apr. 28, 1710. Sir Richard Steele, who attended the ceremony of his funeral, published a paper in " The Tatler" to his memory, vol. III. No 167.

[w] A Tragedy by Thomas Shadwell, acted 1676.

[x] A Tragedy by Thomas Porter, acted 1663.

[y] A Comedy by Sir William Davenant, acted 1669.

A Poet,

A Poet, who, by proper expreſſions and pleaſing images, is to lead us into the knowledge of neceſſary truth, may delude his audience extremely, and indeed barbarouſly, unleſs he has ſome knowledge of this " Art of Cookery," and the progreſs of it. Would it not ſound ridiculous to hear Alexander the Great command his *cannon* to be mounted, and to throw red hot bullets out of his *mortar-pieces?* or to have Statira talk of *tapeſtry hangings,* which, all the Learned know, were many years after her death firſt hung up in the Hall of King Attalus? Should Sir John Falſtaff complain of having dirtied his *ſilk ſtockings,* or Anne of Boleyn call for her *coach;* would an audience endure it, when all the world knows that Queen Elizabeth was the firſt that had her *coach,* or wore *ſilk ſtockings.* Neither can a Poet put *hops* in an Engliſhman's drink before *hereſy* came in: nor can he ſerve him with a diſh of *carp* before that time: he might as well give King James the Firſt a diſh of *aſparagus* upon his firſt coming to London, which were not brought into England till many years after; or make Owen Tudor preſent Queen Catharine with a *ſugar-loaf,* whereas he might as eaſily have given her a *diamond* as large; ſeeing the *iceing* of *cakes* at Wood-ſtreet Corner, and the *refining* of *ſugar,* was but an invention of two hundred years ſtanding; and before that time our Anceſtors ſweetened and garniſhed all with *honey;* of which there are ſome remains, in *Windſor bowls,* *baron bracks,* and large *ſimnels,* ſent for preſents from Lichfield.

But now, on the contrary, it would ſhew his reading, if the Poet put a *hen turkey* upon a table in a Tragedy; and therefore I would adviſe it in Hamlet, inſtead of their painted trifles; and I believe it would give more ſatisfaction to the Actors. For Diodorus Siculus reports, how the ſiſters of Meleager, or Diomedes, mourning for their brother, were turned into *hen-turkeys;* from whence proceeds their ſtatelineſs of gate, reſervedneſs in converſation, and melancholy in the tone of their voice, and all their actions. But this would be the moſt improper meat in the world for a Comedy; for melancholy and diſtreſs require a different ſort of diet, as well as language: and I have heard of a fair lady, that was pleaſed to ſay, " that, if ſhe were upon a " ſtrange road, and driven to great neceſſity, ſhe believed ſhe " might for once be able to ſup upon a *ſack poſſet* and a *fat* " *capon.*"

I am

I am sure Poets, as well as Cooks, are for having all words
nicely chosen and properly adapted; and therefore, I believe,
they would shew the same regret that I do, to hear persons of
some rank and quality say, "Pray cut up that goose. Help me
"to some of that chicken, hen, or capon, or half that plover;"
not considering how indiscreetly they talk, before *men of art*,
whose proper terms are, "*Break that Goose*;"—"*sruss that*
"*Chicken*;"—"*spoil that Hen*;"—*sauce that Capon*;"—"*mince*
"*that Plover*."—If they are so much out in common things,
how much more will they be with *bitterns, herons, cranes*, and
peacocks? But it is vain for us to complain of the faults and
errors of the world, unless we lend our helping-hand to retrieve
them.

To conclude, our greatest Author of Dramatic Poetry, Mr.
Dryden [z], has made use of the mysteries of this Art, in the Prologues to two of his Plays, one a Tragedy, the other a Comedy;
in which he has shewn his greatest art, and proved most successful.
I had not seen the Play for some years, before I hit upon almost
the same words that he has in the following Prologue to "All
"for Love."

   "Fops may have leave to level all they can,
   "As Pigmies would be glad to top a man.
   "Half-wits are fleas, so little and so light,
   "We scarce could know they live, but that they bite.
   "But, as the rich, when tir'd with daily feasts,
   "For change become their next poor tenant's guests:
   "*Drink hearty draughts of Ale from plain brown bowls,*
   "*And snatch the homely Rasher from the coals:*

[z] John Dryden was born at Aldwincle, in Northamptonshire, Aug. 9,
1631; was educated at Westminster, under Dr. Busby; and from
thence elected, 1650, to Trinity College, Cambridge. In 1668, he was
appointed historiographer and poet laureat; which places he lost at the
Revolution, 1688: but his generous patron the earl of Dorset, out of his
private estate, made up to him the loss of his pension. He married the
lady Elizabeth Howard, daughter to the earl of Berkshire; and died May 1,
1701. A list of his works (too numerous for the compass of a note) may
be seen in the "Biographia Britannica." In one of the three prints prefixed to his "Virgil," 8vo, Mr. Dryden is represented in a long and large
wig. It was from his wearing such a wig that Swift compares him to a
lady in a lobster, vol. I. p. 292.

"So

" So you, retiring from much better cheer,
" For once may venture to do penance here;
" And, since that plenteous Autumn now is past,
" Whose Grapes and Peaches have indulg'd your taste,
" Take in good part from our poor Poet's board,
" Such shrivel'd Fruit as Winter can afford."

How *sops* and *fleas* should come together, I cannot easily account for; but I doubt not but his *ale, rasher, grapes, peaches,* and *shriveled apples,* might " Pit, Box, and Gallery," it well enough. His Prologue to " Sir Martin Mar-all" is such an exquisite Poem, taken from the same Art, that I could wish it translated into Latin, to be prefixed to Dr. Lister's Work. The whole is as follows :

<h2 style="text-align:center">PROLOGUE.</h2>

" Fools, which each man meets in his dish each day,
" Are yet the great regalia's of a Play :
" In which to Poets you but just appear,
" To prize that highest which cost them so dear,
" Fops in the town more easily will pass,
" One story makes a statutable ass :
" But such in Plays must be much thicker sown,
" Like yolks of eggs, a dozen beat to one.
" Observing Poets all their walks invade,
" As men watch woodcocks gliding through a glade,
" And when they have enough for Comedy,
" They 'stow their several bodies in a pye,
" The Poet's but the Cook to fashion it,
" For, Gallants, you yourselves have found the wit.
" To bid you welcome, would your bounty wrong.
" None welcome those who bring their *cheer* * along."

The image (which is the great perfection of a Poet) is so extremely lively, and well painted, that methinks I see the whole Audience with a dish of buttered eggs in one hand, and a woodcock pye in the other. I hope I may be excused, after so great an example; for I declare I have no design but to encourage Learning, and am very far from any designs against it. And therefore I hope the worthy gentleman who said that the " Journey to

* Some Criticks read it *Chair.* KING.

" London"

" London [b]" ought to be burnt by the common hangman, as a
Book, that, if received, would difcourage ingenuity, would be
pleafed not to make his bonfire at the upper end of Ludgate-
ftreet, for. fear of endangering the Bookfellers fhops and the
Cathedral.

I have abundance more to fay upon thefe fubjects; but I am
afraid my firft courfe is fo tedious, that you will excufe me both
the fecond courfe and the defert, and call for pipes and a candle.
But confider, the Papers come from an old Friend; and fpare
them out of compaffion to,

      SIR, &c.

✳✳✳✳✳

L E T T E R VII.

To Mr. ———

SIR,

I AM no great lover of writing more than I am forced to, and
therefore have not troubled you with my Letters to congratulate your good fortune in London, or to bemoan our unhappinefs
in the lofs of you here. The occafion of this is, to defire your
affiftance in a matter that I am fallen into by the advice of fome
Friends; but, unlefs they help me, it will be impoffible for me
to get out of it. I have had the misfortune to — write; but,
what is worfe, I have never confidered whether any one would
read. Nay, I have been fo very bad as to defign to print; but
then a wicked thought came acrofs me with " Who will buy?"
For, if I tell you the title, you will be of my mind, that the very
name will deftroy it: " The Art of Cookery, in Imitation of
" Horace's Art of Poetry; with fome familiar Letters to Dr.
" Lifter and others, occafioned principally by the title of a Book
" publifhed by the Doctor, concerning the Soups and Sauces of
" the Ancients." To this a Beau will cry, " Phough! what
" have I to do with Kitchen-ftuff?" To which I anfwer, " Buy
" it, and then give it to your Servants." For I hope to live to fee
the day when every miftrefs of a family, and every Steward, fhall
call up their children and fervants with, " Come Mifs Betty,
" how much have you got of your *Art of Cookery?*" " Where did
" you leave off, Mifs Ifabel?"—" Mifs Kitty, are you no farther

[b] Printed in vol. I. p. 187.

                                                             " than

" than *King Henry and the Miller* ?"—Yes, Madam ; I am come to
" — His name shall be enroll'd
" In Eftcourt's [c] Book, whose gridiron's fram'd of gold.
" Pray, Mother, is that our Mafter Eftcourt ?"—" Well, child,
" if you mind this, you shall not be put to your *Affembly's Ca-*
" *techifm* next Saturday." What a glorious fight it will be, and
how becoming a great family, to fee the Butler out-learning the
Steward, and the painful Scullery-maid exerting her memory far
beyond the mumping Houfe-keeper ! I am told that, if a Book is
any thing ufeful, the Printers have a way of pirating on one another,
and printing other perfons copies, which is very barbarous. And
then shall I be forced to come out with " The True Art of
" Cookery is only to be had at Mr. Pindar's, a Patten-maker's,
" under St. Dunftan's Church, with the Author's Seal at the Title-
" page, being Three Saucepans, in a Bend proper, on a Cook's
" Apron, Argent. Beware of Counterfeits." And be forced to
put out Advertifements, with " Strops for Razors, and the beft
" Spectacles, are to be had only at the Archimedes, &c."

I defign propofals, which I muft get delivered to the Cooks
Company, for the making an order that every apprentice shall
have the " Art of Cookery" when he is bound, which he shall
fay by heart before he is made free ; and then he shall have Dr.
Lifter's Book of " Soups and Sauces" delivered to him for his
future practice. But you know better what I am to do than I.
For the kindnefs you may shew me, I shall always endeavour to
make what returns lay in my power. I am yours, &c.

L E T T E R   VIII.

To Mr. ——

DEAR SIR,

I CANNOT but recommend to your perufal a late exquifite
Comedy, called " The Lawyer's Fortune ; or, Love in a
" Hollow Tree [d];" which piece has its peculiar emblifhments,

and

[c] See note on ver. 519.
[d]   " — Left a chafm fhould intervene,
    " When Death had finifh'd Blackmore's reign,

and is a Poem carefully framed according to the niceſt rules of the " Art of Cookery :" for the Play opens with a ſcene of good Houſewifry, where Favourite the Houſe-keeper makes this complaint to the Lady Bonona.

" FAV. The laſt mutton killed was lean, Madam. Should not " ſome fat ſheep be bought in ?

" BON. What ſay you, Let-acre, to it?

" LET. This is the worſt time of the year for ſheep. The " freſh graſs makes them fall away, and they begin to taſte of " the wool; they muſt be ſpared a while, and Favourite muſt " caſt to ſpend ſome ſalt meat and fiſh. I hope we ſhall have " ſome fat calves ſhortly."

What can be more agreeable than this to the " Art of Cookery," where our Author ſays,

" But, though my edge be not too nicely ſet,
" Yet I another's appetite may whet;
" May teach him when to buy, when ſeaſon paſt,
" What's ſtale, what's choice, what's plentiful, what *waſte*,
" And lead him through the various maze of taſte."

In the Second Act, Valentine, Mrs. Bonona's ſon, the conſummate character of the Play, having in the Firſt Act loſt his Hawk, and conſequently his way, *benighted and loſt, and ſeeing a light in a diſtant houſe, comes to the thrifty widow Furioſa's,*

" The *leaden crown* devolv'd to thee
" Great Poet of the hollow-tree!"   SWIFT, Rhapſody on Poetry.

Sir William Grimſton, bart. (created viſcount Grimſton and baron of Dunboyne in the kingdom of Ireland, June 3, 1719), when a boy, wrote a Play, to be acted by his ſchool-fellows, intituled, " The Lawyer's For-" tune; or, Love in a Hollow Tree;" printed in 4to, 1705; a performance of ſo little merit, that his Lordſhip at a more advanced period of life endeavoured by every means in his power to ſuppreſs it; and this he might poſſibly have accompliſhed, had he not been engaged in a diſpute with the ducheſs of Marlborough, about the Borough of St. Albans. To render him ridiculous in the eyes of his conſtituents, her Grace cauſed an impreſſion of this Play to be printed, with an Elephant in the Title-page dancing on a Rope. This edition his Lordſhip purchaſed; but her Grace, being determined to accompliſh her deſign, ſent a copy to be reprinted in Holland, and afterward diſtributed the whole impreſſion among the Electors of St. Albans; for which place he was choſen repreſentative, in 1713, 1714, and 1727. He died Oct. 15, 1756.

(which

(which is exactly according to the rule, " A Prince, who in a
" Foreft rides aftray !") *where he finds the old gentlewoman card-
ing, the fair Florida her daughter working on a parchment, whilft
the maid is spinning.* Peg reaches a chair; fack is called for; *and
in the mean time the good old gentlewoman complains fo of rogues;
that fhe can fcarce keep a goofe or a turkey in fafety for them.
Then Florida enters, with a little white bottle about a pint, and
an old-fafhioned glafs, fills and gives her mother; fhe drinks to
Valentine, he to Florida, fhe to him again, he to Furiofa, who fets it
down on the table. After a fmall time, the old Lady cries,* " Well,
" it is my bed-time; but my daughter will fhew you the way to
" yours : for I know you would willingly be in it." This was
extremely kind ! Now, upon her retirement (fee the great judgement of the Poet !) fhe being an old gentlewoman that went to
bed, he fuits the following regale according to the age of the
perfon. Had boys been put to bed, it had been proper to have
" laid the *goofe* to the fire," but here it is otherwife : for, after
fome intermediate difcourfe, he is invited to a repaft; when he
modeftly excufes himfelf with, " Truly, Madam, I have no
" ftomach to any meat, but to comply with you. You have, Ma-
" dam, entertained me with all that is defirable already." *The
Lady tells him,* " cold Supper is better than none ;" *fo he fits at
the table, offers to eat, but cannot.* I am fure, Horace could not
have prepared himfelf more exactly ; for (according to the rule,
" A Widow has cold Pye"), though Valentine, being love-fick,
could not eat, yet it was his fault, and not the Poet's. But, when
Valentine is to return the civility, and to invite Madam Furiofa,
and Madam Florida, with other good company, to his mother the
hofpitable Lady Bonona's (who, by the bye, had called for two
bottles of wine for Latitat her Attorney), then affluence and
dainties are to appear (according to this Verfe " Mangoes,
" Potargo, Champignons, Caveare"); and Mrs. Favourite the
Houfe-keeper makes thefe moft important enquiries.

" FAV. Miftrefs, fhall I put any Mufhrooms, Mangoes, or
" Bamboons, into the Sallad ?

" BON. Yes, I pr'ythee, the beft thou haft.

" FAV. Shall I ufe Ketchop or Anchovies in the Gravy ?

" BON. What you will."

But, however magnificent the Dinner might be, yet Mrs. Bonona,
·as the manner of fome perfons is, makes her excufe for it, with,

F 2

" Well,

" Well, Gentlemen, can ye spare a little time to take a short
" dinner? I promise you, it shall not be long." It is very probable, though the Author does not make any of the guests give a
relation of it, that Valentine, being a great sportsman, might
furnish the table with game and wild-fowl. There was at least
one Pheasant in the House, which Valentine told his mother of the
morning before. " Madam, I had a good flight of a Pheasant-
" cock, that, after my Hawk seized, made head as if he would
" have fought; but my Hawk plumed him presently." Now it is
not reasonable to suppose that, Vally lying abroad that night, the
old gentlewoman under that concern would have any stomach to
it for her own supper. However, to see the fate of things, there
is nothing permanent; for one Mrs. Candia making (though
innocently) a present of an Hawk to Valentine, Florida his mistress grows jealous, and resolves to leave him, and run away with
an old sort of fellow, one Major Sly. Valentine, to appease
her, sends a message to her by a boy, who tells her, " His master,
" to shew the trouble he took by her misapprehension, had sent
" her some visible tokens, the Hawk torn to pieces with his own
" hands;" *and then pulls out of the basket the wings and legs of a
fowl.* So we see the poor bird *demolished,* and all hopes of wild-
fowl destroyed for the future: and happy were it if misfortunes
would stop here. But, the cruel Beauty refusing to be appeased,
Valentine takes a sudden resolution, which he communicates to
Let-acre the Steward, to *brush off,* and *quit his habitation.* However it was, whether Let-acre did not think his young Master
real, and Valentine having threatened the House-keeper to kick
her immediately before for being too fond of him, and his boy
being raw and unexperienced in traveling, it seems they made
but slender provision for their expedition; for there is but one
Scene interposed, before we find distressed Valentine in the most
miserable condition that the joint Arts of Poetry and Cookery
are able to represent him. There is a Scene of the greatest horror, and most moving to compassion, of any thing that I have
seen amongst the Moderns; " Talks of no pyramids of Fowl,
" or bisks of Fish," is nothing to it; for here we see an innocent
person, unless punished for his Mother's and House-keeper's extravagance, as was said before, in their Mushrooms, Mangoes,
Bamboons, Ketchup, and Anchovies, reduced to the extremity of
eating his *cheese without bread,* and having no other drink but
water.

water. *For he and his boy, with two saddles on his back and
wallet, came into a walk of confused trees, where an owl hollows,
a bear and leopard walk across the desart at a distance, and yet
they venture in;* where Valentine accosts his boy with these lines,
which would draw tears from any thing that is not marble:

" Hang up thy wallet on that tree
" And creep thou in this hollow place with me,
" Let's here repose our wearied limbs till they more
          " wearied be]

" BOY. There is nothing left in the wallet but one piece of
" cheese.   What shall we do for bread?
" VAL. When we have slept, we will seek out
" Some roots that shall supply that doubt.
" BOY. But no drink, Master?
" VAL. Under that rock a spring I see,
" Which shall refresh my thirst and thee."

So the Act closes; and it is dismal for the Audience to consider how Valentine and the poor boy, who, it seems, had a coming stomach, should continue there all the time the musick was
playing, and longer.   But, to ease them of their pain, by an invention which the Poets call *catastrophe*, Valentine, though with
a *long beard*, and very *weak* with fasting, is reconciled to Florida,
who, embracing him, says, " I doubt I have offended him too
" much; but I will attend him home, cherish him with cordials,
" make him broths," (poor good-natured creature! I wish she
had Dr. Lister's Book to help her!) " anoint his limbs, and be
" a nurse, a tender nurse, to him."   Nor do blessings come alone;
for the good Mother, having *refreshed him with warm baths,
and kept him tenderly in the house,* orders Favourite, with repeated injunctions, " to get the best entertainment she ever yet
" provided, to consider what she has and what she wants, and to
" get all ready in few hours."   And so this most regular work is
concluded with a dance and a wedding-dinner.   I cannot believe
there was any thing ever more of a piece than the Comedy.   Some
persons may admire your meagre Tragedies; but give me a Play
where there is a prospect of good meat or good wine stirring in
every Act of it.

Though I am confident the Author had written this Play
and printed it long before the " Art of Cookery" was thought

of, and I had never read it till the other Poem was very nearly perfected; yet it is admirable to fee how a true rule will be adapted
to a good work, or a good work to a true rule. I fhould be
heartily glad, for the fake of the publick, if our Poets, for the
future, would make ufe of fo good an example. I doubt not
but, whenever you or I write Comedy, we fhall obferve it.

I have juft now met with a furprizing happinefs; a Friend that
has feen two of Dr. Lifter's Works, one " De Buccinis Fluviatilibus
" et Marinis Exercitatio," an Exercitation of Sea and River
Shell-fifh; in which, he fays, fome of the chiefeft rarities are the
pizzle and *fpermatic veffels* of a Snail, delineated by a microfcope,
the *omentum* or *caul* of its throat, its *Fallopian tube*, and its *fub-*
crocean teflicle; which are things Hippocrates, Galen, Celfus,
Fernelius [e], and Harvey [f], were never mafters of. The other
curiofity is the admirable piece of Cœlius Apicius, " De Opfoniis,
" five Condimentis, five Arte Coquinaria, Libri decem," being
Ten Books of Soups and Sauces, and the Art of Cookery, as it is
excellently printed for the Doctor, who in this fo important affair
is not fufficiently communicative. My Friend fays, he has a
promife of leave to read it. What Remarks he makes I fhall
not be envious of, but impart to him I love as well as his

Moft humble fervant, &c.

[e] Born in Picardy about the end of the fifteenth century. He made
a remarkable progrefs in his ftudies at Paris. Before he applied himfelf entirely to phyfic, he taught philofophy in the College of St. Bar-
bara; which he was forced to quit on the great increafe of his practice.
He was much efteemed by Henry II, when Dauphin; who could not
prevail on him to accept the place of firft phyfician till fome years after he
came to the throne. Fernelius got a vaft eftate by his bufinefs; and was
the author of many valuable works, which, with his Life by William
Plantius his difciple, have been frequently re-printed.

[f] Dr. William Harvey, born April 2, 1578, and immortalized by his
difcovery of the circulation of the blood. He had the happinefs, in his
life-time, to find the clamours of ignorance, envy, and prejudice, againft
his doctrine, totally filenced, and to fee it univerfally eftablifhed. It has,
by length of time, been more and more confirmed; and every man now
fees and knows it from his own experience. Dr. Harvey died June 3, 1657.
His works, with an admirable portrait of the Author, were publifhed, in
one volume, 4to, by the College of Phyficians, in 1766, with an elegance
which reflects the higheft honour on that refpectable body.

T H E

THE

ART OF COOKERY,

IN IMITATION OF

HORACE'S ART OF POETRY.

TO DR. LISTER g.

INGENIOUS LISTER, were a picture drawn
  With Cynthia's face, but with a neck like Brawn;
With wings of Turkey, and with feet of Calf,
Though drawn by Kneller h, it would make you laugh!
Such is, good Sir the figure of a Feast,   5
By some rich Farmer's wife and sister dreft;
Which, were it not for plenty and for steam,
Might be resembled to a sick man's dream,
Where all ideas huddling run so fast,
That Syllabubs come first, and Soups the last.   10
Not but that Cooks and Poets still were free,
To use their power in nice variety;
Hence Mackarel seem delightful to the eyes,
Though drefs'd with incoherent Gooseberries.
Crabs, Salmon, Lobsters, are with Fennel spread,   15
Who never touch'd that herb till they were dead;
Yet no man lards salt Pork with Orange-peel,
Or garnishes his Lamb with Spitchcock'd Eel.
  A Cook perhaps has mighty things profefs'd,
Then sent up but two dishes nicely drefs'd,   20
What signify Scotcht-collops to a Feast?

g See an account of Dr. Lister, vol. I. p. 189.

h Sir Godfrey Kneller was at the head of his profeffion, from the reign
of Charles II, to that of George I; and had the honour to draw the
portraits of ten crowned heads, befides feveral electors and princes, and
most of the nobility of England,

Or you can make whip'd Cream ; pray what relief
Will that be to a Sailor who wants Beef ;
Who, lately ship-wreck'd, never can have eafe,
Till re-eftablifh'd in his Pork and Peafe ?
When once begun, let induftry ne'er ceafe
Till it has render'd all things of one piece :
At your Defert bright Pewter comes too late,
When your firft courfe was all ferv'd up in Plate.
 Moft knowing Sir ! the greateft part of Cooks
Searching for truth, are cozen'd by its looks.
One would have all things little ; hence has tried
Turkey Poults frefh'd, from th' Egg in Batter fried ;
Others, to fhew the largenefs of their foul,
Prepare you Muttons fwol'd, and Oxen whole.
To vary the fame things, fome think is art.
By larding of Hogs-feet and Bacon-tart,
The tafte is now to that perfection brought,
That care, when wanting fkill, creates the fault.
 In Covent-Garden did a Taylor dwell,
Who might deferve a place in his own Hell :
Give him a fingle coat to make, he'd do't ;
A veft, or breeches fingly ; but the brute
Could ne'er contrive all three to make a fuit :
Rather than frame a Supper like fuch cloaths,
I'd have fine eyes and teeth without my nofe.
 You that from pliant Pafte would fabricks raife,
Expecting thence to gain immortal praife ;
Your knuckles try and let your finews know
Their power to knead, and give the form to dough ;
Chufe your materials right, your feafoning fix,
And with your Fruit refplendent Sugar mix :
From thence of courfe the figure will arife,
And elegance adorn the furface of your Pies.
 Beauty from order fprings : the judging eye
Will tell you if one fingle plate's awry.
The Cook muft ftill regard the prefent time,
T'omit what's juft in feafon is a crime.
Your infant Peafe t' Afparagus prefer,
Which to the Supper you may beft defer.

Be cautious how you change old bills of fare,
Such alterations should at least be rare;
Yet credit to the Artist will accrue,
Who in known things still makes th' appearance new.
Fresh dainties are by Britain's traffick known,   65
And now by constant use familiar grown;
What Lord of old would bid his Cook prepare,
Mangoes, Potargo, Champignons, Caveare?
Or would our thrum-capp'd Anceftors find fault
For want of Sugar-tongs, or Spoons for Salt?   70
New things produce new words, and thus Monteth
Has by one veffel fav'd his name from death.
The Seafons change us all.   By Autumn's froft,
The fhady leaves of trees and fruit are loft.
But then the Spring breaks forth with frefh fupplies,   75
And from the teeming Earth new buds arife.
So Stubble Geefe at Michaelmas are feen
Upon the fpit; next May produces Green.
The fate of things lies always in the dark,
What Cavalier would know St. James's Park¹?
For Locket's ftands where gardens once did fpring,
And Wild-ducks quack where Grafshoppers did fing;
A Princely Palace on that fpace does rife,
Where Sedley's ᵏ noble Mufe found Mulberries.

Since

ⁱ In the time of king Henry VIII, the Park was a wild wet field;
but that prince, on building St. James's palace, inclofed it, laid it out in
walks, and, collecting the waters together, gave to the new-inclofed ground
and new-raifed building the name of St. James.   It was much enlarged by
Charles II; who added to it feveral fields, planted it with rows of lime-
trees, laid out the Mall, formed the canal, with a decoy, and other ponds
for water fowl.   The " Lime-trees or *Tilia*," whofe bloffoms are incomparably fragrant, were probably planted in confequence of a fuggeftion of
Mr. Evelyn, in his " Fumifugium," publifhed in 1661.   (See p. 48. of
an edition re-printed by B. White in 1772.)   The improvements lately
made feem in fome meafure to have brought it into the ftate it was in
before the Reftoration; at leaft, the Wild-ducks have in their turn given
way to the Grafsboppers.

ᵏ Sir Charles Sedley was born at Aylesford, in Kent, about 1639.   At
17 years of age, he was a fellow commoner of Wadham College, Oxford;
and returned to his own country without taking any degree.   At the Re-

ftoration,

Since Places alter thus, what conftant thought
Of filling various difhes can be taught ?
For he pretends too much, or is a fool,
Who'd fix thofe things where Fafhion is the rule.   85

    King Hardicnute, midft Danes and Saxons ftout,
Carouz'd in nut-brown Ale, and din'd on Grout :   90
Which difh its priftine honour ftill retains,
And, when each Prince is crown'd, in fplendour reigns.

    By Northern cuftom, duty was exprefs'd
To friends departed, by their Funeral Feaft.
Though I've confulted Holinfhed [l] and Stow [m],
I find it very difficult to know

Who

floration, he came to London; commenced wit, courtier, poet, and gallant; and was fo much efteemed as to be a kind of oracle among the poets. Whilft the reputation of his wit increafed, he became poor and debauched, his eftate was impaired, and his morals much corrupted. In 1663, being fined five hundred pounds for a riot in Bow-ftreet, he became more ferious, and applied to politicks.—His daughter Catharine, having been miftrefs to James II. before he afcended the throne, was created countefs of Dor-chefter, Jan. 2, 1685. Sir Charles, who looked upon this title as a fplendid indignity purchafed at the expence of his daughter's honour, was extremely active in bringing about the Revolution; from a principle of gratitude, as he faid himfelf: " for, fince his majefty has made my " daughter a countefs, it is fit I fhould do all I can to make his daughter " a queen." He died Aug. 20, 1701. His works, which bear great marks of genius, were printed in 2 vols. 8vo. 1719. Amongft them is a comedy called " The Mulberry Garden," acted at the Theatre Royal 1668. That garden is alfo mentioned in feveral other comedies of the laft century.

[l] Raphael Holinfhed, who lived in the fixteenth century, publifhed his " Chronicles" in 2 vols. folio, 1577; and again in 3 vols. 1587. In the fecond edition, feveral fheets were caftrated, in compliance to queen Elizabeth and her miniftry; but thofe caftrations have been printed fepa-rately.

[m] John Stow was born about 1525, and died April 5, 1605. He greatly affifted Holinfhed in the laft edition of his " Chronicles ;" and publifhed his " Survey of London," in 1598, 4to. (fince frequently re-printed; the fifth edition, in 1720, in 2 vols. folio, by Mr. Strype, with additions, and the Author's Life). In 1600, he publifhed his " Flores " Hiftoriarum;" reprinted with additions about five years afterward; but, even in its improved ftate, it was a mere abridgement of a hiftory of this

nation,

Who, to refresh th'attendants to a grave,
Burnt-claret first or Naples-biscuit gave.

    Trotter from Quince and Apples first did frame
A Pye which still retains his proper name :   100
Though common grown, yet, with white Sugar strow'd,
And butter'd right, its goodness is allow'd.

    As Wealth flow'd in, and Plenty sprang from Peace,
Good-humour reign'd, and Pleasures found encrease.
'Twas usual then the banquet to prolong,   105
By Musick's charm, and some delightful song :
Where every youth in pleasing accents strove
To tell the stratagems and cares of Love.
How some succefsful were, how others crost :
Then to the sparkling glafs would give his toast,   110
Whose bloom did most in his opinion shine,
To relish both the Musick and the Wine.

    Why am I styl'd a Cook, if I'm so loth
To marinate my Fish, or season Broth,
Or send up what I roast with pleasing froth ;   115 }
If I my Master's *gusto* won't discern,
But, through my bashful folly, scorn to learn ?

    When among friends good-humour takes its birth,
'Tis not a tedious Feast prolongs the mirth ;
But 'tis not reason therefore you should spare,   120 }
When, as their future Burgefs, you prepare,
For a fat Corporation and their Mayor.
All things should find their room in proper place ;
And what adorns this treat, would that disgrace.

nation, which he had been above forty years collecting.—" Stow and
" Holingshed (said an able Writer in 1727), the jest and contempt of their
" learned and witty contemporaries, for long stories of *shews* and *sheriffs*,
" are become the serious amusement of our present Virtuosi.   Any unin-
" formed, senselefs heap of rubbish, under the name of a History of a
" Town, Society, College, or Province, have long since taken from us the
" very idea of a genuine compofition.   Every Monkish Tale, and Lye,
" and Miracle, and Ballad, are refcued from their duft and worms, to
" proclaim the poverty of our Forefathers ; whose nakednefs, it seems,
" their pious Posterity take great pleafure to pry into : for of all those
" Writings given us by the *Learned Oxford Antiquary* [HEARNE], there
" is not one that is not a disgrace to Letters ; moft of them are so to
" Common Senfe, and some even to Human Nature." *Critical Enquiry,*
&c. p. 63.

Some times the vulgar will of mirth partake,   125
And have exceſſive doings at their wake :
Even Taylors at their yearly Feaſts look great,
And all their Cucumbers are turned to Meat.
A Prince, who in a Foreſt rides aſtray,
And weary to ſome cottage finds the way,   130
Talks of no pyramids of Fowl or biſks of Fiſh,
But hungry ſups his Cream ſerv'd up in earthen diſh :
Quenches his thirſt with Ale in nut-brown bowls,
And takes the haſty Raſher from the coals :
Pleas'd as King Henry with the Miller free,   135
Who thought himſelf as good a man as he.
    Unleſs ſome ſweetneſs at the bottom lye,
Who cares for all the crinkling of the Pye ?
    If you would have me merry with your cheer,
Be ſo yourſelf, or ſo at leaſt appear.   140
    The things we eat by various juice controul
The narrowneſs or largeneſs of our ſoul.
Onions will make even Heirs or Widows weep;
The tender Lettuce brings on ſofter ſleep ;
Eat Beef or Pye-cruſt if you'd ſerious be :   145
Your Shell-fiſh raiſes Venus from the Sea;
For Nature, that inclines to ill or good,
Still nouriſhes our paſſions by our food.
    Happy the man that has each fortune tried,
To whom ſhe much has given, and much denied :   150
With abſtinence all delicates he ſees,
And can regale himſelf with Toaſt and Cheeſe !
    Your Betters will deſpiſe you, if they ſee
Things that are far ſurpaſſing your degree ;
Therefore beyond your ſubſtance never treat;   155
'Tis plenty, in ſmall fortune, to be neat.
'Tis certain that a Steward can't afford
An entertainment equal with his Lord.
Old age is frugal; gay youth will abound
With heat, and ſee the flowing cup go round.   160
A Widow has cold Pye ; Nurſe gives you Cake ;
From generous Merchants Ham or Sturgeon take.
The Farmer has brown Bread as freſh as day,
And Butter fragrant as the dew of May.

Cornwall

Cornwall Squab-pye, and Devon White-pot brings, 165
And Leicefter Beans and Bacon, food of Kings!
   At Chriftmas-time, be careful of your fame,
See the old Tenants table be the fame;
Then, if you would fend up the Brawner's head,
Sweet Rofemary and Bays around it fpread: 170
His foaming tufks let fome large Pippin grace,
Or midft thofe thundering fpears an Orange place;
Sauce like himfelf, offenfive to its foes,
The roguifh Muftard, dangerous to the nofe.
Sack and the well-fpic'd Hippocras the Wine, 175
Waffail the bowl with ancient ribbands fine,
Porridge with Plumbs, and Turkeys with the Chine.
If you perhaps would try fome difh unknown,
Which more peculiarly you'd make your own, 180
Like ancient failors ftill regard the coaft,
By venturing out too far you may be loft.
By roafting that which your Forefathers boil'd,
And boiling what they roafted, much is fpoil'd.
That Cook to Britifh palates is complete, 185
Whofe favoury hand gives turns to common meat.
   Though Cooks are often men of pregnant wit,
Through nicenefs of their fubject, few have writ.
In what an awkward found that Ballad ran,
Which with this bluftering paragraph began: 190

   There was a Prince of Lubberland,
A Potentate of high command,
Ten thoufand Bakers did attend him,
Ten thoufand Brewers did befriend him:
Thefe brought him Rifing-cruffs, and thofe 195
Brought him Small Beer, before he rofe.

   The Author raifes mountains feeming full,
But all the *cry* produces little *wool*:
So, if you fue a Beggar for a houfe,
And have a verdict, what d'ye gain? A Loufe! 200
Homer, more modeft, if we fearch his Books,
Will fhew us that his Heroes all were Cooks:
How lov'd Patroclus with Achilles joins,
To quarter out the Oxe, and fpit the loins.

Ob

Oh could that Poet live! could he rehearfe   205
Thy Journey, LISTER, in immortal verfe!
   MUSE, SING THE MAN THAT DID TO PARIS GO,
THAT HE MIGHT TASTE THEIR SOUPS, AND MUSHROOMS
     KNOW!
  Oh, how would Homer praife their dancing Dogs,
Their ftinking Cheefe, and Fricafee of Frogs!   210
He'd raife no fables, fing no flagrant lye,
Of Boys with Cuftard choak'd at Newberry;
But their whole courfes you'd entirely fee,
How all their parts from firft to laft agree.
   If you all forts of perfons would engage,   215
Suit well your Eatables to every age.
   The favourite Child, that juft begins to prattle,
And throws away his Silver Bells and Rattle,
Is very humourfome, and makes great clutter,
Till he has Windows on his Bread and Butter: 220
He for repeated Supper-meat will cry,
But won't tell Mammy what he'd have, or why.
   The fmooth-fac'd Youth, that has new Guardians chofe,
From Play-houfe fteps to Supper at the Rofe,
Where he a main or two at random throws: 225
Squandering of wealth, impatient of advice,
His eating muft be little, coftly, nice.
   Maturer Age, to this delight grown ftrange,
Each night frequents his club behind the Change,
Expecting there frugality and health,   230
And honour rifing from a Sheriff's wealth:
Unlefs he fome Infurance-dinner lacks,
'Tis very rarely he frequents Pontack's.
But then old age, by ftill intruding years,
Torments the feeble heart with anxious fears: 235
Morofe, perverfe in humour, diffident,
The more he ftill abounds, the lefs content,
His Larder and his Kitchen too obferves,
And now, left he fhould want hereafter, ftarves:
Thinks fcorn of all the prefent age can give,   240
And none thefe threefcore years knew how to live.
But now the Cook muft pafs through all degrees,
And by his art difcordant tempers pleafe,
And minifter to Health and to Difeafe.

Far from the Parlour have your Kitchen plac'd,   245
Dainties may in their working be difgrac'd.
In private draw your Poultry, clean your Tripe,
And from your Eels their flimy fubftance wipe.
Let cruel offices be done by night,
For they who like the thing abhor the fight.   250

Next, let difcretion moderate your coft,
And, when you treat, three courfes be the moft.
Let never frefh machines your Paftry try,
Unlefs Grandees or Magiftrates are by :
Then you may put a Dwarf into a Pye [n].   255
Or, if you'd fright an Alderman and Mayor,
Within a Pafty lodge a living Hare [o];
Then midft their graveft Furs fhall mirth arife,
And all the Guild purfue with joyful cries.

Crowd not your table : let your number be   260
Not more than feven, and never lefs than three.

'Tis the Defert that graces all the Feaft,
For an ill end difparages the reft :
A thoufand things well done, and one forgot,
Defaces obligation by that blot.   265
Make your tranfparent Sweet-meats truly nice,
With Indian Sugar and Arabian Spice :
And let your various Creams incircled be
With fwelling Fruit juft ravifh'd from the tree.
Let Plates and Difhes be from China brought,   270
With lively paint and earth tranfparent wrought.

[n] In the reign of Charles I, Jeffery Hudfon was ferved up to table, in
a cold pie, at Burleigh on the Hill, the feat of the duke of Buckingham ;
and, as foon as he made his appearance, prefented by the duchefs to the
queen, who retained him in her fervice. He was then feven or eight
years of age, and but eighteen inches in height ; and grew no taller till
after thirty, when he fhot up to three feet nine inches. The king's
gigantic porter once drew him out of his pocket, in a mafque at court, to
the furprize of all the fpectators. Soon after the breaking out of the civil
war, he was made a captain in the royal army ; attended the queen, in
1644, into France, where he fought a duel with Mr. Crofts, with piftols,
on horfeback, and killed his antagonift the firft fire. After the Reftoration, he was imprifoned in the Gatehoufe, on fufpicion of being concerned in the Popifh plot, and died in confinement in his fixty third year.
Granger, vol. II. p. 405.

[o] A joke which has been frequently put in practice.   The

The Feaſt now done, diſcourſes are renew'd,
And witty arguments with mirth purſu'd:
The cheerful Maſter midſt his jovial friends,
His glaſs " to their beſt wiſhes" recommends:
The Grace-cup follows to his Sovereign's health,
And to his Country, " Plenty, peace, and wealth."
Performing then the piety of *grace,*
Each man that pleaſes re-aſſumes his place:
While at his gate, from ſuch abundant ſtore,
He ſhowers his god-like bleſſings on the poor.
   In days of old, our Fathers went to war,
Expecting ſturdy blows and hardy fare:
Their Beef they often in their murrions ſtew'd,
And in their Baſket-hilts their Beverage brew'd.
Some Officer perhaps might give conſent,
To a large cover'd Pipkin in his tent,
Where every thing that every Soldier got,
Fowl, Bacon, Cabbage, Mutton, and what not,
Was all thrown into bank, and went to pot.
But, when our conqueſts were extenſive grown,
And through the world our Britiſh worth was known,
Wealth on Commanders then flow'd in apace,
Their Champaign ſparkled equal with their Lace:
Quails, Beccofico's, Ortolans, were ſent
To grace the levee of a General's tent.
In their gilt Plate all delicates were ſeen.
And what was Earth before became a rich Terrene.
   When the young Players get to Iſlington,
They fondly think that all the world's their own:
Prentices, Pariſh-clerks, and Hectors meet;
He that is drunk, or bullied, pays the Treat.
Their talk is looſe; and o'er the bouncing Ale,
At Conſtables and Juſtices they rail:
Not thinking Cuſtard ſuch a ſerious thing,
That Common Council Men 'twill thither bring;
Where many a man, at variance with his wife,
With ſoftening Mead and Cheeſe-cake ends the ſtrife.
Even Squires come there, and, with their mean diſcourſe,
Render the Kitchen, which they ſit in, worſe.
Midwives demure, and Chamber-maids moſt gay,
Foremen that pick the box and come to play.

Here find their entertainment at the height,
In Cream and Codlings reveling with delight.
What thefe approve the great men will diflike :   315
But here's the art, if you the palate ftrike,
By management of common things, fo well,
That what was thought the meaneft fhall excel ;
While others ftrive in vain, all perfons own
Such difhes could be drefs'd by you alone.   320
   When ftraiten'd in your time, and fervants few,
You'll rightly then compofe an *ambigue*:
Where firft and fecond Courfe, and your Defert
All in one fingle table have their part.
From fuch a vaft confufion 'tis delight,   325
To find the jarring elements unite,
And raife a ftructure grateful to the fight.
   Be not too far by old example led,
With caution now we in their footfteps tread :
The French our relifh help, and well fupply   330
The want of things too grofs by decency.
Our Fathers moft admir'd their Sauces fweet,
And often afk'd for Sugar with their Meat ;
They butter'd Currants on fat Veal beftow'd,
And Rumps of Beef with Virgin-honey ftrew'd.   335
Infipid Tafte, old Friend, to them who Paris know,
Where Rocombole, Shallot, and the rank Garlick, grow.
   Tom Bold did firft begin the ftrolling mart,
And drove about his Turnips in a cart :
Sometimes his Wife the Citizens would pleafe,   340
And from the fame machine fell Pecks of Peafe.
Then Pippins did in Wheel-barrows abound,
And Oranges in Whimfey-boards went round,
Befs Hoy firft found it troublefome to bawl,
And therefore plac'd her Cherries on a ftall ;   345
Her Currants there and Goofeberries were fpread,
With the enticing gold of Ginger-bread :
But Flounders, Sprats, and Cucumbers, were cried,
And every found and every voice was tried.
At laft the Law this hideous din fupprefs'd,   350
And order'd that the Sunday fhould have reft ;
And that no Nymph her noify food fhould fell,
Except it were new Milk or Mackarel.

There is no dish but what our Cooks have made,
And merited a charter by their trade.   355
Not French Kickshaws, or Oglio's brought from Spain,
Alone have found improvement from their brain;
But Pudding, Brawn, and White-pots, own'd to be
Th'effects of native ingenuity.
    Our British Fleet, which now commands the main,   360
Might glorious wreaths of victory obtain,
Would they take time; would they with leisure work,
With care would salt their Beef, and cure their Pork;
Would boil their liquor well whenc'er they brew,
THEIR CONQUEST HALF IS TO THE VICTUALER DUE.   365
    Because that thrift and abstinence are good,
As many things if rightly understood;
Old Crofs condemns all persons to be Fops,
That can't regale themselves with Mutton-chops.
He often for stuft Beef to Bedlam runs,   370
And the clean Rummer, as the Pest-house, shuns,
Sometimes Poor Jack and Onions are his dish,
And then he faints those Fryars who stink of Fish.
As for myself, I take him to abstain,
Who has good meat, with decency, though plain: 375
But, though my edge be not too nicely set,
Yet I another's appetite may whet;
May teach him when to buy, when season's past,
What's stale, what choice, what plentiful, what waste,
And lead him through the various maze of taste.   380
    The fundamental principle of all,
Is what ingenious Cooks THE RELISH call:
For, when the market sends in loads of food,
They all are tasteless till that makes them good.
Besides, 'tis no ignoble piece of care,   385
To know for whom it is you would prepare:
You'd please a Friend, or reconcile a Brother,
A testy Father or a haughty Mother:
Would mollify a Judge, would cram a Squire,
Or else some smiles from Court you may desire;   390
Or would, perhaps, some hasty Supper give,
To shew the splendid state in which you live.
Pursuant to that interest you propose,
Must all your Wines and all your Meat be chose.

Let men and manners every diſh adapt,   395
Who'd force his Pepper where his gueſts are *clapt?*
A cauldron of fat Beef and ſtoop of Ale
On the huzzaing mob ſhall more prevail,
Than if you give them with the niceſt art
Ragoûts of Peacocks-brains, or Filbert-tart.   400
    The French by Soups and *Haut-goûts* glory raiſe,
And their deſires all terminate in praiſe.
The thrifty maxim of the wary Dutch
Is, to ſave all the money they can touch :
" Hans," cries the Father, " ſee a Pin lies there,   405
" A Pin a day will fetch a Groat a year.
" To your Five Farthings join Three Farthings more;
" And they, if added, make your Halfpence Four !"
Thus may your ſtock by management encreaſe,
Your wars ſhall gain you more than Britain's peace.   410
Where love of wealth and ruſty coin prevail,
What hopes of Sugar'd Cakes or Butter'd Ale ?
    Cooks garniſh out ſome tables, ſome they fill,
Or in a prudent mixture ſhew their ſkill :
Clog not your conſtant meals; for diſhes few   415
Encreaſe the appetite, when choice and new.
Even they who will Extragavance profeſs,
Have ſtill an inward hatred for Exceſs.
Meat, forc'd too much, untouch'd at table lies,
Few care for carving trifles in diſguiſe,   420
Or that fantaſtie diſh ſome call *ſurprize.*
When pleaſures to the eye and palate meet,
That Cook has render'd his great work complete :
His glory far, like SIR-LOIN's KNIGHTHOOD, flies;
Immortal made, as KIT-CAT by his Pies.   425
    Good-nature muſt ſome failings overlook,
Not wilfulneſs, but errors of the Cook.
A ſtring won't always give the ſound deſign'd
By the Muſician's touch and heavenly mind :
Nor will an arrow from the Parthian bow   430
Still to the deſtin'd point direƈtly go.
Perhaps no Salt is thrown about the diſh,
Or no fried Parſley ſcatter'd on the Fiſh;

G 2

Shall

Shall I in paffion from my dinner fly,
And hopes of pardon to my Cook deny,   435
For things which careleffnefs might overfee,
And all mankind commit as well as he ?
I with compaffion once may overlook
A Skewer fent to table by my Cook :
But think not therefore tamely I'll permit   440
That he fhould daily the fame fault commit,
For fear the Rafcal fend me up the Spit !

   Poor Roger Fowler had a generous mind,
Nor would fubmit to have his hand confin'd,
But aim'd at all ; yet never could excel   445
In any thing but ftuffing of his Veal :
But, when that difh was in perfection feen,
And that alone, would it not move your fpleen ?
'Tis true, in a long work, foft flumbers creep,
And gently fink the Artift into fleep.   450
Even Lamb himfelf, at the moft folemn feaft,
Might have fome chargers not exactly dreft.

   Tables fhould be like pictures to the fight,
Some difhes caft in fhade, fome fpread in light,
Some at a diftance brighten, fome near hand,   455
Where eafe may all their *delicace* command :
Some fhould be mov'd when broken ; others laft
Through the whole treat, incentive to the tafte.

   Locket, by many labours feeble grown,
Up from the Kitchen call'd his eldeft Son :   460
" Though wife thyfelf," fays he, " though taught by me,
" Yet fix this fentence in thy memory :
" There are fome certain things that don't excel,
" And yet we fay are *tolerably well* :
" There's many worthy men a Lawyer prize,   465
" Whom they diftinguifh as of *middle* fize,
" For pleading well at Bar, or turning Books,
" But this is not, my Son, the fate of Cooks,
" From whofe myfterious art true pleafure fprings
" To *ftall* of Garter, and to *throne* of Kings.   470
" A fimple fcene, a difobliging fong,
" Which no way to the main defign belong.

                                                          " Or

" Or were they abfent never would be mifs'd,
" Have made a well-wrought Comedy be hifs'd :
" So in a Feaft no intermediate fault   475
" Will be allow'd ; but, if not beft, 'tis naught."
    He that of feeble nerves and joints complains
From Nine-pins, Coits, and from Trap-ball, abftains ;
Cudgels avoids, and fhuns the Wreftling-place,
Left Vinegar refound his loud difgrace.   480
But every one to Cookery pretends,
Nor Maid or Miftrefs e'er confult their friends.
But, Sir, if you would roaft a Pig, be free :
Why not with Brawn, with Locket, or with me ?
We'll fee when 'tis enough, when both eyes out,   485
Or if it wants the nice concluding bout.
But, if it lies too long, the crackling's pall'd,
Not by the Drudging-box to be recall'd.
    Our Cambrian Fathers, fparing in their Food,
Firft broil'd their hunted Goats on bars of wood.   490
Sharp Hunger was their feafoning, or they took
Such Salt as iffued from the native rock.
Their Sallading was never far to feek,
The poignant Water-grafs, or favoury Leek ;
Until the Britifh Bards adorn'd this Ifle,   495
And taught them how to roaft, and how to boil :
Then Talieffin rofe, and fweetly ftrung
His Britifh Harp, inftructing whilft he fung :
Taught them that honefty they ftill poffefs,
Their truth, their open heart, their modeft drefs,   500
Duty to kindred, conftancy to friends,
And inward worth, which always recommends ;
Contempt of wealth and pleafure, to appear
To all mankind with hofpitable cheer.
In after-ages, Arthur taught his Knights   505
At his Round Table to record their fights,
Cities eraz'd, encampments forc'd in field,   ⎫
Monfters fubdued, and hideous tyrants quell'd,   ⎬
Infpir'd that Cambrian foul which ne'er can yield.⎭
Then Guy, the pride of Warwick, truly great,   510
To future Heroes due example fet,

G 3

By his capacious cauldron made appear,
From whence the spirits rise, and strength of war,
The present age, to Gallantry enclin'd,
Is pleas'd with vast improvements of the mind.   515
He that of honour, wit, and mirth, partakes,
May be a fit companion o'er Beef-steaks,
His name may be to future times enroll'd
In Estcour's Book P, whose Gridiron's fram'd of Gold.
Scorn not these lines, design'd to let you know   520
Profits that from a well-plac'd Table flow.
   'Tis a sage question, if the Art of Cooks
Is lodg'd by Nature, or attain'd by Books:
That man will never frame a noble treat,
Whose whole dependance lies on some Receit.   525
Then by pure Nature every thing is spoil'd,
She knows no more than stew'd, bak'd, roast, and boil'd.
When Art and Nature join, th' effect will be
Some nice *Ragout*, or charming *Fricasee*.
   The lad that would his genius so advance   530
That on the rope he might securely dance,
From tender years enures himself to pains,
To Summer's parching heat, and Winter rains,
And from the fire of Wine and Love abstains;
No Artist can his Hautboy's stops command,   535
Unless some skilful Master form his hand;
But Gentry take their Cooks though never tried,
It seems no more to them than up and ride.
Preferments granted thus shew him a fool
That dreads a parent's check, or rods at school.   540
   Ox-cheek when hot, and Wardens bak'd, some cry;
But 'tis with an intention men should buy.

P That is, " be admitted a member of The Beef Steak Club."—
Richard Estcourt, who was a Player and Dramatic Writer, is celebrated in
the Spectator, as possessed of a sprightly wit and an easy and natural
politeness.   His company was much coveted by the great, on account of
his qualifications as a boon companion.   When the famous Beef Steak
Club was first instituted, he had the office of Providore assigned him; and,
as a mark of distinction, used to wear a small gridiron of gold hung
about his neck with a green silk ribband.   He died in the year 1713.

Others

Others abound with such a plenteous store,
That, if you'll let them treat, they'll ask no more;
And 'tis the vast ambition of their soul,   545
To see their Port admir'd, and Table full.
But then, amidst that cringing fawning crowd,
Who talk so very much, and laugh so loud,
Who with such grace his Honour's actions praise,
How well he fences, dances, sings, and plays;   550
Tell him his Livery's rich, his Chariot's fine,
How choice his Meat, and delicate his Wine;
Surrounded thus, how should the Youth descry
The happiness of Friendship from a Lye?
Friends act with cautious temper when sincere,   555
But flattering Impudence is void of care:
So at an Irish Funeral appears
A train of Drabs with mercenary tears;
Who, wringing oft their hands with hideous moan,
Know not his name for whom they seem to groan;   560
While real Grief with silent steps proceeds,
And Love unfeign'd with inward passion bleeds.
Hard fate of Wealth! Were Lords as Butchers wise,
They from their meat would banish all the *Flies!*
The Persian Kings, with Wine and massy Bowl,   565
Search'd to the dark recesses of the soul:
That, so laid open, no one might pretend,
Unless a man of worth, to be their Friend.
But now the Guests their Patrons undermine;
And slander them, for giving them their Wine.
Great men have dearly thus companions bought:
Unless by these instructions they'll be taught,
They spread the net, and will themselves be caught.

   Were Horace, that great Master, now alive,
A Feast with wit and judgement he'd contrive.   575
As thus:—Supposing that you would rehearse
A labour'd Work, and every Dish a Verse:
He'd say, " Mend this, and t'other Line, and this."
If after trial it were still amiss,
He'd bid you give it a new turn of face,   580
Or set some Dish more curious in its place.

If you perfift, he would not ftrive to move
A paffion fo delightful as Self-love.
　　We fhould fubmit our Treats to Criticks' view,
And every prudent Cook fhould read Boffu q.   585
Judgement provides the Meat in feafon fit,
Which by the genius dreft, its fauce is Wit.
Good Beef for Men, Pudding for Youth and Age,
Come up to the decorum of the Stage.
The Critick ftrikes out all that is not juft,   590
And 'tis even fo the Butler chips his Cruft.
Poets and Paftry-cooks will be the fame,
Since both of them their images muft frame.
Chimæra's from the Poet's fancies flow :
The Cook contrives his fhapes in real Dough.   595
　　When Truth commands, there's no man can offend,
That with a modeft love corrects his Friend,
Though 'tis in toafting Bread, or buttering Peafe,
So the reproof has temper, kindnefs, eafe.
But why fhould we reprove when faults are fmall ?   600
Becaufe 'tis better to have none at all.
There's often weight in things that feem the leaft,
And our moft trifling follies raife the jeft.
　　'Tis by his cleanlinefs a Cook muft pleafe,
A Kitchen will admit of no difeafe.   605
The Fowler and the Huntfman both may run
Amidft that dirt which he muft nicely fhun.

q M. Le Rene Boffu, a native of Paris, began the courfe of his ftudies at
Navarre ; where he difcovered an early tafte for polite literature, and foon
made a furprizing progrefs in all the valuable parts of learning. His firft
great publication was, a " Parallel, or Comparifon betwixt the Principles
" of Ariftotle's Natural Philofophy and thofe of Defcartes. Paris, 1674."
And next year produced his celebrated treatife on E. ic Poetry, which,
Mr. Boileau fays, is one of the beft compofitions on the fubject that ever
appeared in the French language. It has gone through feveral editions.
To one printed at the Hague, in 1714, F. Le Courayer has prefixed a difcourfe on that treatife, and fome encomiums on it ; and has alfo given fome
memoirs of the author, who died March 14, 1680, aged 42 ; and left a
vaft number of Mf. volumes, which are kept in the abbey of St. John de
Chartres. —

Empedocles,

Empedocles, a Sage of old, would raife
A Name immortal by unufual ways;
At laft his fancies grew fo very odd,   610
He thought by *roafting* to be made a God.
Though fat, he leapt with his unwieldy ftuff
In Ætna's flames, fo to have Fire enough.
Were my Cook fat, and I a ftander-by,
I'd rather than himfelf his Fifh fhould fry.   615
   There are fome perfons fo exceffive rude,
That to your private Table they'll intrude.
In vain you fly, in vain pretend to faft;
Turn like a Fox, they'll catch you at the laft.
You muft, fince bars and doors are no defence,   620
Even quit your houfe as in a peftilence.
Be quick, nay very quick, or he'll approach,
And, as you're fcampering, ftop you in your Coach.
Then think of all your fins, and you will fee
How right your guilt and punifhment agree: 625
Perhaps no tender pity could prevail,
But you would throw fome debtor into gaol.
Now mark th' effect of his prevailing curfe,
You are detain'd by fomething that is worfe.
  Were it in my election, I fhould chufe,   630
To meet a ravenous Wolf or Bear got loofe:
He'll eat and talk, and talking ftill will eat,
No quarter from the Parafite you'll get;
But, like a Leech well fix'd, he'll fuck what's good,
And never part till fatisfied with Blood.   635

LETTER

LETTER IX.

To Mr. ————

DEAR SIR,

I MUST communicate my happiness to you, because you are so much my Friend as to rejoice at it. I some days ago met with an old Acquaintance, a curious perſon, of whom I enquired if he had ſeen the Book concerning Soups and Sauces. He told me he had; but that he had but a very ſlight view of it, the perſon who was maſter of it not being willing to part with ſo valuable a rarity out of his Cloſet. I deſired him to give me what account he could of it. He ſays, that it is a very handſome Octavo; for, ever ſince the days of Ogilby [r], good paper and good print and fine cuts make a Book become ingenious, and brighten up an Author ſtrangely; that there is a copious Index; and at the end a Catalogue of all the Doctor's Works, concerning Cockles, Engliſh Beetles, Snails, Spiders that get up into the air and throw us down Cobwebs, a Monſter vomited up by a Baker, and ſuch like; which, if carefully peruſed, would wonder-

[r] "Here ſwells the ſhelf with OGILBY THE GREAT." *Dunciad; i. 141.* John Ogilby, famous for the number as well as the embelliſhment of his publications, was born at Edinburgh about Nov. 17, 1600. He was by profeſſion a dancing-maſter; but, getting lame by an accident, applied himſelf to ſtudy. He tranſlated the works of Virgil, and publiſhed them, with his own picture prefixed, in 8vo, 1649-50. It was re-printed in 1659, on royal folio; and has his picture before it, as moſt of the books which he publiſhed have. At fifty-four years of age, he learned the Greek tongue, and ſet about his tranſlation of Homer, which was publiſhed in 1660. The ſame year he alſo printed a very fine Bible at Cambridge. In 1662, he was appointed maſter of the revels in Ireland. On his return to London, he continued his employment of tranſlating and printing poetry till the great fire in September 1666, which deſtroyed his whole property. He had afterward the good fortune to be appointed his majeſty's coſmographer and geographic printer; and printed ſeveral great works, tranſlated or collected principally by himſelf. His laſt and greateſt undertaking was an "Atlas," which he did not live to finiſh; dying Sept. 4, 1676. He was employed by Charles II. to take a ſurvey of the roads of the kingdom; and the poſts were regulated according to that ſurvey. See Granger.—Winſtanley, in his "Lives of Poets," ſpeaks of "Ogilby's large volumes, his tranſlations of Homer and Virgil *done to* "*the life,* and with *ſuch excellent ſculptures:* and (what added great grace "to his works) he printed them all on *ſpecial good paper,* and in a *very* "*good letter.*"

fully

fully improve us. There is, it seems, no Manuscript of it in England, nor any other country that can be heard of; so that this impression is from one of Humelbergius, who, as my Friend says, he does not believe contrived it himself, because the things are so very much out of the way, that it is not probable any Learned Man would set himself seriously to work to invent them. He tells me of this ingenious remark made by the Editor, " That, whatever Manuscripts there might have been, they must " have been extremely vicious and corrupt, as being written out " by the Cooks themselves, or some of their Friends or Servants, " who are not always the most accurate." And then, as my Friend observed, if the Cook had used it much, it might be sullied; the Cook perhaps not always licking his fingers when he had occasion for it. I should think it no improvident matter for the State to order a select Scrivener to transcribe Receipts, lest ignorant Women and House-keepers should impose upon future ages by ill-spelt and uncorrect Receipts for potting of Lobsters, or pickling of Turkeys. Cælius Apicius, it seems, passes for the Author of this Treatise; whose science, learning, and discipline, were extremely contemned, and almost abhorred, by Seneca and the Stoicks, as introducing luxury, and infecting the manners of the Romans; and so lay neglected till the inferior ages; but then were introduced, as being a help to Physick, to which a Learned Author, called Donatus, says, that " the Kitchen " is a Handmaid." I remember in our days, though we cannot in every respect come up to the Ancients, that by a very good Author an old gentleman is introduced as making use of three Doctors, Dr. Diet, Dr. Quiet, and Dr. Merriman. They are reported to be excellent Physicians; and, if kept at a constant pension, their fees will not be very costly.

It seems, as my Friend has learnt, there were two persons that bore the name of Apicius, one under the Republick, the other in the time of Tiberius, who is recorded by Pliny, " to have had a " great deal of wit and judgement in all affairs that related to " Eating," and consequently has his name affixed to many sorts of Aumulets and Pancakes. Nor were Emperors less contributors to so great an undertaking, as Vitellius, Commodus, Didius Julianus, and Varius Heliogabalus, whose Imperial names are prefixed to manifold receipts; the last of which Emperors had the peculiar glory of first making Sausages of

Shrimps

Shrimps, Crabs, Oyfters, Sprawns, and Lobfters. And thefe
Saufages being mentioned by the Author which the Editor pub-
lifhes, from that and many other arguments the Learned Doctor
irrefragably maintains, that the Book, as now printed, could not
be tranfcribed till after the time of Heliogabalus, who gloried in
the Titles of Apicius and Vitellius, more than Antoninus, who
had gained his reputation by a temperate, auftere, and folid
virtue. And, it feems, under his adminiftration, a perfon that
found out a new Soup might have as great a reward as Drake * or
Dampier * might expect for finding a new Continent. My
Friend fays, the Editor tell us of unheard-of dainties; how
" Æfopus had a fupper of the tongues of Birds that could
" fpeak;" and that " his Daughter regaled on Pearls," though
he does not tell us how fhe dreffed them; how " Hortenfius left
" ten thoufand Pipes of Wine in his Cellar, for his Heir's drink-
" ing;" how " Vedius Pollio fed his Fifh-ponds with Man's
" Flefh;" and how " Cæfar bought fix thoufand weight of
" Lampreys for his Triumphal Supper." He fays, the Editor
proves equally to a demonftration, by the proportions and quan-
tities fet down, and the naufeoufnefs of the ingredients, that
the Dinners of the Emperors were ordered by their Phyficians;
and that the *Recipe* was taken by the Cook as the Collegiate
Doctors would do their Bills to a modern Apothecary; and that
this cuftom was taken from the Egyptians; and that this method
continued till the Goths and Vandals overran the Weftern Em-

* Born in Devonfhire in 1545. Before he had the royal fanction for
his depredations, he was a famous freebuoter againft the Spaniards. He
was the firft Englifhman that encompaffed the globe; which he performed
in two years and about ten months, from 1577 to 1579. Magellan, whofe
fhips paffed the South Seas fome time before, died in his paffage. On the
4th of April, 1581, her majefty conferred on Drake the honour of knighthood. In 1587, by burning 100 veffels at Cadiz, he fufpended the threatened invafion for a year; and about the fame time, took a rich Eaft
India carrack near the Terceras, by which the Englifh gained fo great in-
fight into trade in that part of the world, that it occafioned the eftablifhment of the Eaft India Company. In 1588, he was appointed vice-
admiral under lord Effingham, and acquitted himfelf in that important
command with his ufual valour and conduct. He died Jan. 28, 1595-6.

* Captain William Dampier was born in Somerfetfhire in 1652. He
was employed in a voyage to the South Seas, with Woodes Rogers, at the
time Dr. King wrote this Letter; from whence he returned in September,
1711. His voyage round the world is well known, and has gone through
many editions.

pire;

pire; and that they, by ufe, exercife, and neceffity of abftinence,
introduced the eating of Cheefe and Venifon without thofe additional Sauces, which the Phyficians of old found out to reftore
the depraved appetites of fuch great men as had loft their
ftomachs by an excefs of luxury. Out of the ruins of Erafiftra-
tus's Book of *Endive*, Glaucus Lorrenfis of *Cow-heel*, Mithæcus
of *Hot-pots*, Dionyfius of *Sugar-fops*, Agis of *Pickled Broom-buds*,
Epinetus of *Sack-poffet*, Euthedemus of *Apple-dumplings*, Hege-
fippus of *Black-pudding*, Crito of *Sowced Mackarel*, Stephanus
of *Lemon-cream*, Archites of *Hogs-harflet*, Aceftius of *Quince-
marmalade*, Hickefius of *Potted Pigeons*, Diocles of *Sweet-breads*,
and Philiftion of *Oat-cakes*, and feveral other fuch Authors, the
great Humelbergius compofed his Annotations upon Apicius;
whofe Receipts, when part of Tully, Livy, and Tacitus, have
been neglected and loft, were preferved in the utmoft parts of
Tranfylvania, for the peculiar palate of the ingenious Editor.
Latinus Latinius finds fault with feveral difhes of Apicius, and
is pleafed to fay they are naufeous; but our Editor defends that
great perfon, by fhewing the difference of our cuftoms; how
Plutarch fays, " the Antients ufed no Pepper," whereas all or at
leaft five or fix hundred of Apicius's Delicates were feafoned
with it. For we may as well admire that fome Weft Indians
fhould abftain from Salt, as that we fhould be able to bear the
bitternefs of Hops in our common drink: and therefore we
fhould not be averfe to Rue, Cummin, Parfley-feed, Marfh-
mallows, or Nettles, with our common Meat; or to have Pepper, Honey, Salt, Vinegar, Raifins, Muftard and Oil, Rue,
Maftick, and Cardamums, ftrown promifcuoufly over our Dinner
when it comes to table. My Friend tells me of fome fhort
obfervations he made out of the Annotations, which he owes to
his memory; and therefore begs pardon if in fome things he
may miftake, becaufe it is not wilfully, as that Papirius Petus
was the great patron of Cuftard: " That the *Tetrapharmacon*,
" a difh much admired by the Emperors Adrian and Alexander
" Severus, was made of Pheafant, Peacock, a wild Sow's Hock
" and Udder, with a Bread Pudding over it; and that the name
" and reafon of fo odd a difh are to be fought for amongft the
" Phyficians."
   The Work is divided into Ten Books; of which the Firft treats
of Soups and Pickles, and amongft other things fhews that Sauce-

pans were tinned before the time of Pliny; that Gordian ufed [7]
a Glafs of Bitter in a Morning; that the Antients fcalded their
Wine; and that burnt Claret, as now practifed, with Spice and
Sugar, is pernicious; that the Adulteration of Wine was as
antient as Cato; that *Brawn* was a Roman Difh, which Apicius
commends as *wonderful*; its Sauce then was Muftard and Honey,
before the frequent ufe of Sugar: nor were Sowced Hogs-feet,
Cheeks, and Ears, unknown to thofe ages. It is very probable,
they were not fo fuperftitious as to have fo great a delicate only
at Chriftmas. It were worth a Differtation between two learned
perfons, fo it were managed with temper and candour, to know
whether the Britons taught it to the Romans, or whether Cæfar
introduced it into Britain: and it is ftrange he fhould take no
notice of it; whereas he has recorded that they did not eat Hare's
flefh; that the Antients ufed to *marinate* their Fifh, by frying
them in Oil, and the moment they were taken out pouring
boiling Vinegar upon them. The Learned Annotator obferves,
that the beft way of keeping the Liquor in Oyfters is, by laying the deep Shell downwards; and by this means Apicius con-
veyed Oyfters to Tiberius when in Parthia. A noble invention,
fince made ufe of at Colchefter with moft admirable fuccefs!
What eftates might Brawn or Locket have got in thofe days,
when Apicius, only for boiling Sprouts after a new fafhion,
defervedly came into the good graces of Drufus, who then commanded the Roman armies!

The Firft Book having treated of Sauces or ftanding Pickles
for Relifh, which are ufed in moft of the fucceeding Receipts;
the Second has a glorious fubject, of Saufages, both with fkins
and without, which contains matters no lefs remarkable than
the former. The Antients that were delicate in their eating
prepared their own Mufhrooms with an Amber or at leaft a Silver
Knife; where the Annotator fhews elegantly, againft Hardouinus,
that the whole Knife, and not only the Handle, was of Amber
or Silver, left the ruftinefs of an ordinary Knife might prove
infectious. This is a nicety which I hope we may in time arrive to; for the Britons, though not very forward in inventions,
yet are out-done by no nations in imitation or improvements.

The Third Book is of fuch Edibles as are produced in Gardens. The Romans ufed *Nitre*, to make their Herbs look green;
the Annotator fhews our Salt-petre at prefent to differ from the

ancient

ancient *Nitre.* Apicius had a way of mincing them first with Oil and Salt, and so boiling them; which Pliny commends. But the prefent Receipt is, To let the Water boil well; throw in Salt and a bit of Butter; and so not only Sprouts but Spinage will be green. There is a moft extraordinary obfervation of the Editor's, to which I cannot but agree; that it is a vulgar error, that Walnut-trees, like Ruffian Wives, thrive the better for being beaten; and that long poles and ftones are ufed by boys and others to get the fruit down, the Walnut-tree being fo very high they could not otherwise reach it, rather out of kindnefs to themfelves, than any regard to the Tree that bears it. As for Afparagus, there is an excellent remark, that, according to Pliny, they were the great care of the ancient Gardeners, and that at Ravenna three weighed a Pound; but that in England it was thought a rarity when a Hundred of them weighed thirty; that Cucumbers are apt to rife in the Stomach, unlefs pared, or boiled with Oil, Vinegar, and Honey: that the Egyptians would drink hard without any difturbance, becaufe it was a rule for them to have always boiled Cabbage for their firft difh at Supper: that the beft way to roaft Onions is in Colewort Leaves, for fear of burning them: that Beets are good for Smiths, becaufe they, working at the fire, are generally coftive: that Petronius has recorded a little old Woman, who fold the *Agrefte Olus* of the Ancients; which honour I take to be as much due to thofe who in our days cry Nettle-tops, Elder-buds, and Cliver, in fpring-time very wholefome.

The Fourth Book contains the univerfal Art of Cookery. As Matthæus Sylvaticus compofed the Pandecits of Phyfic, and Juftinian thofe of Law; fo Apicius has done the Pandecits of his Art. In this Book which bears that infcription. The Firft Chapter contains the admirable Receipt of a *Salacacaby* of Apicius. Bruife in a Mortar Parfley-feed, dried Peneryal, dried Mint, Ginger, green Coriander, Raifins ftoned, Honey, Vinegar, Oil, and Wine; put them into a *Cacabulum*; three Crufts of Pycen-tine Bread, the Flefh of a Pullet, Goat Stones, Veftine Cheefe, Pine Kernels, Cucumbers, dried Onions minced fmall; pour a Soup over it, garnifh it with Snow, and fend it up in the *Caca-bulum.* This *Cacabulum* being an unufual veffel, my Friend went to his Dictionary, where, finding an odd interpretation of it, he was eafily perfuaded, from the whimficalnefs of the com-pofition, and the fantafticalnefs of Snow for its garnifh, that

the

the propereſt veſſel for a Phyſician to preſcribe to ſend to table upon that occaſion might be a Bed-pan. There are ſome admirable Remarks in the Annotations to the Second Chapter, concerning the Dialogue of Aſellius Sabinus, who introduces a combat between Muſhrooms, *Chats* or *Beccofico's*, Oyſters, and Redwings, a Work that ought to be publiſhed: for the ſame Annotator obſerves, that this Iſland is not deſtitute of Redwings, though coming to us only in the hardeſt weather, and therefore ſeldom brought fat to our tables; that the *Chats* come to us in April and breed, and about Autumn return to Africk; that experience ſhews us they may be kept in cages, fed with Beef or Wether Mutton, Figs, Grapes, and minced Filberds, being dainties not unworthy the care of ſuch as would preſerve our Britiſh hoſpitality. There is a curious obſervation concerning the diverſity of Roman and Britiſh diſhes; the firſt delighting in Hodge-podge, Gallimaufreys, Forced Meats, Juſſels, and Salmagundies; the latter in Spear-ribs, Surloins, Chines and Barons; and thence our terms of Art, both as to Dreſſing and Carving, become very different; for they, lying upon a ſort of Couch, could not have carved thoſe diſhes which our Anceſtors when they ſat upon Forms uſed to do. But, ſince the uſe of Cuſhions and Elbow-chairs, and the Editions of good Books and Authors, it may be hoped in time we may come up to them. For indeed hitherto we have been ſomething to blame; and I believe few of us have ſeen a diſh of Capon-ſtones at table (Lamb-ſtones is acknowledged by the learned Annotator that we have): for the art of making Capons has long been buried in oblivion. Varro, the great Roman Antiquary, tells us how to do it by burning of their ſpurs; which, occaſioning their ſterility, makes them Capons in effect, though thoſe parts thereby became more large and tender.

The Fifth Book is of Peaſe-porridge; under which are included, Frumetary [u], Watergruel, Milk-porridge, Rice-milk, Flumary, Stir-about, and the like. The Latin or rather Greek name is *Auſprios*; but my Friend was pleaſed to entitle it *Pantagruel*, a Name uſed by Rabelais [w], an eminent Phyſician.

There

[u] On which, Dr. King has written a very ingenious Poem.

[w] Rabelais, born about 1483, was firſt a Franciſcan, and then a Benedictine; but quitted both for the habit of a ſecular prieſt. After rambling about ſome time, he fixed at Montpelier, where he took the degrees in phyſic,

There are some very remarkable things in it; as, The Emperor
Julianus had seldom any thing but Spoon-meat at Supper: that
the Herb Fenugreek, with Pickles, Oil, and Wine, was a Roman
Dainty; upon which the Annotator observes, that it is not used
in our Kitchens, for a certain ungrateful bitterness that it has;
and that it is plainly a Physical Diet, that will give a stool; and
that, mixed with Oats, it is the best Purge for Horses: an excellent invention for frugality, that nothing might be lost; for
what the Lord did not eat, he might send to his Stable!

The Sixth Book treats of Wild-fowl; how to dress Ostridges,
(the biggest, grossest, and most difficult of digestion, of any Bird),
Phœnicoptrices, Parrots, &c.

The Seventh Book treats of things *sumptuous* and *costly*, and
therefore chiefly concerning *Hog-meat*; in which the Romans
came to that excess, that the Laws forbad the usage of Hogs-
harslet, Sweet-breads, Cheeks, &c. at their public Suppers;
and Cato, when Censor, sought to restrain the extravagant use
of Brawn, by several of his Orations. So much regard was
had then to the Art of Cookery, that we see it took place in
the thoughts of the wisest men, and bore a part in their most
important councils. But, alas! the degeneracy of our present
age is such, that I believe few besides the Annotator know the
excellency of a Virgin Sow, especially of the *black* kind brought
from China; and how to make the most of her Liver, Lights,
Brains, and Pettitoes; and to vary her into those fifty dishes
which, Pliny says, were usually made of that delicious Creature.
Besides, Galen tells us more of its excellences: " That fellow
" that eats Bacon for two or three days before he is to box or
" wrestle, shall be much stronger than if he should eat the best
" Roast Beef or Bag Pudding in the Parish."

The Eighth Book treats of such Dainties as *four-footed* Beasts
afford us; as, 1. the *Wild Boar*, which they used to boil with all
its bristles on. 2. The *Deer*, dressed with Broth made with
Pepper, Wine, Honey, Oil, and stewed Damsons, &c. 3. The
Wild Sheep, of which there are " innumerable in the Mountains
" of Yorkshire and Westmorland, that will let nobody handle
" them;" but, if they are caught, they are to be sent up with

physic, and practised with great reputation. He published, in 1532, some
pieces of Hippocrates and Galen; and his " History of Gargantua and
" Pantagruel" in 1535. He died in 1653.

an " elegant Sauce, prescribed after a physical manner, in form
" of an Electuary, made of Pepper, Rue, Parsley-seed, Juniper,
" Thyme dried, Mint, Penryal, Honey, &c." with which any
Apothecary in that country can furnish you. 4. *Beef,* with
Onion Sauce, and commended by Celsus, but not much approved
by Hippocrates, because the Greeks scarce knew how to *make*
Oxen, and *Powdering-tubs* were in very few Families : for Phyficians have been very peculiar in their Diet in all ages ; otherwife Galen would scarce have found out that young Foxes were
in season in Autumn. 5. The *Sucking Pig* boiled in Paper.
6. The *Hare,* the chief of the Roman *dainties*; its Blood being
the sweetest of any Animal, its natural fear contributing to that
excellence. Though the Emperors and Nobility had Parks to
fatten them in ; yet in the time of Didianus Julianus, if any one
had sent him one, or a Pig, he would make it last him three
days ; whereas Alexander Severus had one every meal, which
must have been a great expence, and is very remarkable. But
the most exquisite Animal was reserved for the last Chapter ;
and that was the *Dormouse,* a harmless creature, whose innocence
might at least have defended it both from Cooks and Phyficians.
But Apicius found out an odd fort of fate for those poor creatures ; some to be boned, and others to be put whole, with odd
ingredients, into *Hogs-guts,* and so boiled for Saufages. In ancient times, people made it their business to fatten them : Aristotle
rightly observes, that sleep fattened them, and Martial from
thence too poetically tells us that sleep was their only nourish-
ment. But the Annotator has cleared that point ; he, good man,
has tenderly observed one of them for many years, and finds
that it does not sleep all the Winter, as falfely reported, but
wakes at meals, and after its repast then rolls itself up in a ball
to sleep. This Dormouse, according to the Author, did not
drink in three years time ; but whether other Dormice do so, I
cannot tell, because Bambonfelbergius's Treatise " of Fattening
" Dormice" is lost. Though very costly, they became a common
dish at great entertainments. Petronius delivers us an odd Receipt for dressing them, and serving them up with Poppies and
Honey ; which must be a very foporiferous dainty, and as good
as Owl-pye to such as want a nap after dinner. The fondness
of the Romans came to be so excessive towards them, that, as
Pliny says, " the Censorian Laws and Marcus Scaurus in his
                                        " Consulship,

"Confulfhip, got them prohibited from public entertainments,"
But Nero, Commodus, and Heliogabalus, would not deny the
liberty, and indeed property, of their fubjects in fo reafonable
an enjoyment; and therefore we find them long after brought
to table in the times of Ammianus Marcellinus, who tells us
likewife, that "*fcales* were brought to table in thofe ages, to
"weigh curious Fifhes, Birds and Dormice," to fee whether they
were at the ftandard of excellence and perfection, and fometimes,
I fuppofe, to vie with other pretenders to magnificence. The
Annotator takes hold of this occafion, to fhew "of how great
"ufe fcales would be at the tables of our Nobility," efpecially
upon the bringing up of a difh of Wild-foul: "For if twelve
"Larks (fays he) fhould weigh below twelve ounces, they would
"be very lean, and fcarce tolerable; if twelve and down-weight,
"they would be very well; but if thirteen, they would be fat
"to perfection." We fee upon how nice and exact a balance the
happinefs of Eating depends!

I could fcarce forbear fmiling, not to fay worfe, at fuch ex-
actnefs and fuch dainties; and told my Friend, that thofe fcales
would be of extraordinary ufe at Dunftable; and that, if the
Annotator had not prefcribed his Dormoufe, I fhould upon the
firft occafion be glad to vifit it, if I knew its vifiting-days and
hours, fo as not to difturb it.

My Friend faid, there remained but Two Books more, one of
Sea and the other of River Fifh, in the account of which he
would not be long, feeing his memory began to fail him almoft
as much as my patience.

"'Tis true, in a long work, foft flumbers creep,
"And gently fink the Artift into fleep [x];"
efpecially when treating of Dormice.

The Ninth Book is concerning Sea Fifh, where, amongft other
learned Annotations, is recorded that famous Voyage of Apicius,
who, having fpent many millions, and being retired into Cam-
pania, heard that there were Lobfters of a vaft and unufual big-
nefs in Africa, and thereupon impatiently got on fhipboard the
fame day; and, having fuffered much at fea, came at laft to the
coaft. But the fame of fo great a man's coming had landed
before him, and all the Fifhermen failed out to meet him, and
prefented him with their faireft Lobfters. He afked if they had
no larger. They anfwered, "Their fea produced nothing more

<hr>

[x] Art of Cookery, ver. 449.

H 2

"excellent

" excellent than what they had brought." This honeſt freedom
of theirs, with his diſappointment, ſo diſguſted him, that he took
pet, and had the Maſter return home again immediately: and ſo,
it ſeems, Africa loſt the breed of one monſter more than, it had
before y.   There are many Receipts in the Book, to dreſs Cramp-
fiſh, that numb the hands of thoſe that touch them z; the Cuttle-
fiſh, whoſe blood is like ink ; the Pourcontrel, or Many-feet ;
the Sea-urchin or Hedge-hog ;   with ſeveral others, whoſe Sauces
are agreeable to their natures.   But, to the comfort of us Moderns, the Ancients often eat their Oyſters, a alive, and ſpread hard
Eggs minced over their Sprats as we do now over our Salt-fiſh.
There is one thing very curious concerning Herrings : It ſeems,
the Ancients were very fantaſtical, in making one thing paſs for
another ; ſo, at Petronius's Supper, the Cook ſent up a fat Gooſe,
Fiſh, and Wild-fowl of all ſorts to appearance, but ſtill all were
made out of the ſeveral parts of one ſingle Porker.   The great
Nicomedes, King of Bithynia, had a very delightful deception
of this nature put upon him by his Cook ; the King was extremely affected with freſh Herrings (as indeed who is not ?) ;
but, being far up in Aſia from the ſea coaſt, his whole wealth
could not have purchaſed one ; but his Cook contrived ſome ſort
of meat, which, put into a frame, ſo reſembled a Herring, that it
was extremely ſatisfactory both to this Prince's eyes and *guſto.*
My Friend told me, that, to the honour of the City of London,
he had ſeen a thing of this nature there ; that is, a Herring, or
rather a Salmogundy, with the head and tail ſo neatly laid, that
it ſurprized him.   He ſays, many of the *ſpecies* may be found at
the Sugar Loaf in Bell Yard, as giving an excellent reliſh to
Burton Ale, and not coſting above ſix pence, an inconſiderable
price for ſo imperial a dainty.

- The Tenth Book, as my Friend tells me, is concerning *Fiſh
Sauces,* which conſiſt of variety of ingredients, amongſt which is

y Lord Lyttelton's Nineteenth " Dialogue of the Dead " (perhaps the
moſt humourous in that admirable collection) ſeems to have been entirely
founded on the hints ſuggeſted by Dr. King.

z The wonderful electric properties of the *Torpedo* have been lately in-
veſtigated with the greateſt accuracy by the indefatigable reſearches of John
Walſh, eſq. F. R. S.

a The hiſtory of the ordering and generation of *green* Colcheſter oyſters,
by Col. Tuke, is in Sprat's Hiſt. of the R. S. p. 307.

generally

generally a kind of Frumetary. But it is not to be forgotten by any perfon who would boil Fifh exactly, that they threw them alive into the water, which at prefent is faid to be a Dutch Receipt, but was derived from the Romans. It feems, Seneca the Philofopher (a man from whofe morofe temper little good in the Art of Cookery could be expected), in his Third Book of Natural Queftions, correcting the luxury of the times, fays, the Romans were come to that daintinefs, that they would not eat a Fifh unlefs upon the fame day it was taken, " that it might tafte of " the Sea," as they expreffed it ; and therefore had them brought by perfons who rode poft, and made a great outcry, whereupon all other people were obliged to give them the road. It was an ufual expreffion for a Roman to fay, " In other matters I may " confide in you ; but in a thing of this weight, it is not con- " fiftent with my gravity and prudence. I will truft nothing but " my own eyes. Bring the Fifh hither, let me fee him breathe " his laft." And, when the poor Fifh was brought to table fwimming and gafping, would cry out, " Nothing is more " more beautiful than a dying Mullet !" My Friend fays, the Annotator looks upon thefe " as jefts made by the Stoicks, and " fpoken abfurdly and beyond nature ;" though the Annotator at the fame time tells us, that it was a law at Athens, that the Fifhermen fhould not wafh their Fifh, but bring them as they came out of the fea. Happy were the Athenians in good Laws, and the Romans in great Examples ! But I believe our Britons need wifh their Friends no longer life, than till they fee London ferved with live Herrings and gafping Mackarel. It is true, we are not quite fo barbarous but that we throw our Crabs alive into fcalding water, and tie our Lobfters to the fpit to hear them fqueak when they are roafted ; our Eels ufe the fame periftaltic motion upon the gridiron, when their fkin is off and their guts are out, as they did before ; and our Gudgeons, taking opportunity of jumping after they are flowered, give occafion to the admirable remark of fome perfons folly, when, to avoid the danger of the frying-pan, they leap into the fire. My Friend faid, that the mention of Eels put him in mind of the concluding remark of the Annotator, " That they who amongft the Sybarites " would fifh for Eels, or fell them, fhould be free from all " taxes." I was glad to hear of the word *conclude* ; and told him nothing could be more acceptable to me than the mention of the

H 3

Sybarites

Sybarites, of whom I shortly intend a History, shewing how they deservedly banished Cocks for waking them in a morning, and Smiths for being useful; how one cried out because one of the Rose-leaves he lay on was rumpled; how they taught their Horses to dance; and so their enemies, coming against them with *guitars* and *harpsichords*, set them so upon their *Round O's* and *Minuets*, that the form of their battle was broken, and three hundred thousand of them slain, as Gouldman [b], Littleton, and several other good Authors, affirm. I told my Friend, I had much overstayed my hour; but if, at any time, he would find Dick Humelbergius, Caspar Barthius, and another Friend, with himself, I would invite him to dinner of a few but choice Dishes to cover the Table at once, which, except they would think of any thing better, should be a Salacacaby, a Dish of Fenugreek, a Wild Sheep's head and appurtenance with a suitable Electuary, a *ragoût* of Capons Stones, and some Dormouse Sausages.

If, as Friends do with one another at a Venison-pasty, you should send for a plate, you know you may command it; for what is mine is yours, as being entirely your, &c.

---

[b] Francis Gouldman (who was educated at Christ's College, Cambridge, was sometime rector of S. Okenham in Essex, and died 1689) published a Latin and English Dictionary, in three parts, 1664, 4to; which was several times re-printed, and in 1674 much enlarged by W. Robertson, as it was again in 1678 by Dr. Scattergood. All the editions were printed at Cambridge.—The design of Gouldman, according to Dr. Littleton, his successor in this sort of learning, was rather to make new additions, then to correct former mistakes, or to throw out the many barbarous words which had crept into the Dictionaries then extant; for this reason Dr. Littleton (of whom see vol. II. p. 82.) undertook to reform it.—A Dialogue between Gouldman and Hesychius is printed in vol. I. p. 155.

THE

ART OF LOVE:

IN IMITATION OF

OVID DE ARTE AMANDI.

WITH A PREFACE,

CONTAINING

THE LIFE OF OVID.

The virtuous difpofition of our Author is no where more remarkably diftinguifhed than in this piece; wherein both the fubject and the example fo naturally lead into fome lefs chafte images, fome loofer love which ftands in need of a remedy.

BIOG. BRIT.

H 4

LORD HERBERT[a],

Eldeſt Son of his Excellency the Earl of PEMBROKE and MONTGOMERY[b]; Baron HERBERT of Caerdiff, Ross of Kendal, PARR, FITZ-HUGH, MARMION, ST QUINTIN, and HERBERT of Shutland; Knight of the Garter, &c. &c.

MY LORD,

THE following lines are written on a ſubject that will naturally be protected by the goodneſs and temper of your Lordſhip: for, as the advantages of your mind and perſon muſt kindle the flames of Love in the coldeſt breaſt; ſo you are of an age moſt ſuſceptible of them in your own. You have acquired all thoſe accompliſhments at home, which

[a] Henry lord Herbert ſucceeded to his father's titles in 1732, and died in 1749.

[b] Thomas earl of Pembroke, on the acceſſion of William and Mary, was ſent ambaſſador extraordinary to Holland; on his return to England, was ſworn of the privy council; made colonel of a regiment of marines, and appointed firſt commiſſioner of the admiralty; lord privy ſeal in March 1691; firſt plenipotentiary at Ryſwick in 1697; lord preſident of the council, May 11, 1699; lord high admiral of England and Ireland, Jan. 18, 1701-2. The latter poſt he reſigned in May 1702, to make room for the prince of Denmark; and was offered on that occaſion a great penſion, which he generouſly refuſed. He was appointed lord lieutenant of Ireland, April 17, 1707; and on the prince's death, Oct. 28, 1708, again lord high admiral. Toward the end of the year 1709, finding that office too fatiguing, he obtained permiſſion to reſign it. He died in 1732. To the patronage of this noble lord Dr. King was indebted for his offices of Judge of the High Court of Admiralty and Keeper of the Records in Ireland.

others

others are forced to feek abroad; and have given the world affurance, by fuch beginnings, that you will foon be qualified to fill the higheft Offices of the Crown with the fame univerfal applaufe that has conftantly attended your illuftrious Father in the difcharge of them. For the good of your Pofterity, may you ever be happy in the choice of what you love! And though thefe rules will be of fmall ufe to you that can frame much better; yet let me beg leave that, by dedicating them to your fervice, I may have the honour of telling the world, that I am obliged to your Lordfhip; and that I am moft entirely

Your Lordfhip's

Moft faithful humble fervant,

WILLIAM KING.

PREFACE.

P R E F A C E.

IT is endeavoured, in the following Poems, to give the Reader
of both fexes fome ideas of the Art of Love; fuch a Love as
is innocent and virtuous, and whofe defires terminate in prefent
happinefs and that of pofterity. It would be in vain to think of
doing it without help from the Antients, amongft whom none
has touched that paffion more tenderly and juftly than OVID.
He knew that he bore the mafterfhip in that Art; and therefore,
in the Fourth Book De Triftibus, when he would give fome account of himfelf to future ages, he calls himfelf " Tenerorum
" Lufor Amorum," as if he gloried principally in the defcriptions
he had made of that paffion. He tells us, he was a native of
Sulmo, a city of the Peligni, about ninety miles to the North
Eaft of Rome: that it was called fo from Solymus, a companion
of Æneas, who was the founder of it about four hundred years
before the building of that City. This Solymus married a
daughter of Æneas, who brought four with him from Troy:
the firft he left married in Thrace, the fecond in Peloponnefus,
and the third in Epirus. Ovid, in the Second Book of his Elegies,
inviting his Miftrefs to Sulmo, defcribes it as one of the moft
charming places that could be, to divert the fummer's heat; refrefhed with ftreams of water, rich paftures, corn, grapes, olives,
and fhade in abundance. Hercules Ciofanus, a native of the place,
has given a large and accurate account of it, before his excellent
obfervations upon Ovid's Works, which deferved the commendations of Muretus, Manutius, and Meliffus, the greateft wits of
that time. Ovid was born on the day when the two Confuls
Hirtius and Panfa were flain at Mutina, fighting againft Mark
Antony, who had been declared an enemy to the people of Rome;
which was on the twenty-firft ᶜ of March, in the 710th year after
the building of that City. Lucius, his father, was a Roman
Knight of an antient family, which had preferved that dignity
from the original of the order. Ovid had a brother, exactly a
year older than himfelf, named Lucius. They were both fent
to Rome for their education under the beft mafters, where the

ᶜ According to others, the *nineteenth*.

eldeft

eldeſt improved much in the ſtudies of the Law, and was maſter
of a vigorous and manly eloquence: but our Publius ſays, there
ſeemed to himſelf ſomething that was ſacred and celeſtial in the
Muſes, which ſtole all his inclinations; and though he conſidered
his Father's advice [d], which told him of the unprofitableneſs of that
ſtudy, and laid before him the miſerable poverty of Homer, and
therefore endeavoured to turn his ſtyle to Proſe, yet Verſes would
be intermixed, and the words fall into numbers without or even
againſt his will: ſuch was his natural genius and eaſineſs, that he
could no more refrain them, than a large ſpring can hinder itſelf
from ſending forth a pleaſing river. At twenty years old his
brother died, for whom he complains as having loſt a companion
and a friend. By this means he became heir to a large patrimony
in the territories of Sulmo, and to a houſe in that city, where
there is now the Church of Sancta Maria de Tumba; as alſo to
another houſe in Rome, near the Capitol, where is at preſent the
Church of Sancta Maria della Conſolatione; as likewiſe to plea-
ſant orchards upon the hills between the Flaminian and Claudian
ways, in which he might recreate himſelf with his Muſes. In
theſe he uſed to employ many hours, watering them, as he tells
us, with his own hands, as being moſt extremely delighted with
all ſorts of Gardening and Huſbandry. Some of his firſt Maſters
were Plotius Grippus and Marcellus (by ſome ſtyled Aurelius),
Fuſcus the Rhetorician, under whom he declaimed to admiration,
and gained ſo much reputation, that Marcus Annæus Seneca
reckons him amongſt the principal of his time. Ovid ſays, he
pleaded the cauſes of ſeveral criminals with good ſucceſs, and
that he ſeveral times was arbitrator, and managed matters ſo im-
partially, that the very perſons againſt whom he decreed applauded his juſtice. He bore ſuch offices as his dignity required,
and gave ſentences in ſuch Judicatories as by law he was called
to; but did never aſpire to be a Senator, as having a body not
fitted for labour, nor a mind patient enough to ſuſtain the cares of
ambition. He was of mean ſtature, ſlender of body, ſpare of
diet, and, if not too amorous, every way temperate. He drank
no wine but what was much allayed with water; neat in apparel;
of a free, affable, and courtly behaviour. He took the reſolution
of ſpending his time with perſons moſt noted for worth and learn-

d " Sæpe pater dixit, Studium quid inutile tentas?
" Mæonides nullas ipſe reliquit opes." Triſt. l. iv.

ing:

ing : amongſt whom, Cornelius Gallus a moſt wealthy and noble
Roman, and Marcus Varro, were his Patrons; Julius Græcinus
an eminent Grammarian, and that famous Author Julius Hyginus
keeper of the Palatine Library, were his particular friends. He
was ſo great an admirer of Portius Latro and his Sayings, that he
made uſe of many of them in his Verſes. His chief delight was
in the converſation of the Poets of his time, and he never thought
himſelf bleſt but in their company ; either when he was learning
the nature of Birds and Serpents, and the virtue of Herbs, from
Macer ; or the charms of Love's fires from Propertius ; or Heroic
Actions of the Theban War, equal to that of Troy, from Pon-
ticus ; or the reproof of Vice and Folly from the Iambicks of
Baſſus ; or, laſtly, all variety of learning and numbers from the
Lyre of Horace, to whom his liſtening ear was the more attentive, becauſe he firſt brought the Lyric meaſures amongſt the
Romans, for which he had ſufficient cauſe to glory. As Ovid
paid due regard to the Poets that preceded him, ſo he lets us know
that he did not want fitting reſpect from thoſe that were younger
than himſelf. He complains, not without reaſon, that he had
only a ſight of Virgil ; and that death hindered the friendſhip that
had elſe been between him and Tibullus, to whom he gives the
ſecond place amongſt the Elegiac Poets, as being ſucceſſor to
Gallus : he makes Propertius the Third, and was himſelf the
youngeſt. He began to write very ſoon, and had a reputation
before the age that others generally appeared in the world. He
owns, he had a heart that eaſily took fire, and that Love was the
ſubject of his Verſes : but it was without reflexion or diſreputa-
tion to any one, though ſome people pretended to find out the
perſon who was concealed under the feigned name of Corinna.
He had written his Heroical Epiſtles before ſuch time as the
regard he bore to Marcus Varro made him accept of a command,
and ſerve under him in Aſia. In his return from thence, he made
a ſtay at Athens, where he attained to the utmoſt exactneſs in the
Greek tongue : from thence he went to Alexandria, and in both
theſe places undoubtedly furniſhed himſelf with thoſe vaſt mines
and huge ſtores of Grecian and Egyptian learning, and all that
Hiſtory, Poetry, and moſt occult Philoſophy, which appear in all
his Works, but eſpecially in his " Metamorphoſes." Macer the
Poet, before mentioned, was his companion in theſe travels.
Having ſeen moſt of the Aſiatic cities, they came into Sicily toge-

ther,

ther, and diverted themfelves there for almoft a year's fpace with the rarities of that country. He had three wives; the firft when he was not quite fixteen years old, from whom, as he fays, for fufficient reafons, he was divorced; and fo likewife from the fecond, not for any real blame in her, but for diflike, according to the licentioufnefs of the times: but he extols often the chaftity and beauty of the laft, whom he inftructed in Poetry, and entirely affected, fhe continuing inviolably conftant to him, during all his misfortunes; notwithftanding many importunate folicitations. By the laft he had a daughter, named Perilla, married to Cornelius Fidus, by whom fhe had two children. He continued long in favour at the Court of Auguftus, till, in the fiftieth year of his age, he fell under the Emperor's difpleafure. The reafon is unknown at this time, and of little ufe to conjecture; though he fays that at Rome every one was acquainted with it*. He feems fatisfied that he had buried his father, being ninety years old; and his mother likewife, being antient, foon after him; that fo their old age might not be grieved at his misfortunes. He ex-preffes all the duty to them that fo good-natured a fon could do poffibly; and, if he could, would make their fhades fenfible, that it was an *error*, and not a *crime*, for which he fuffered. He received commands to *retire* to Tomi, a city of Sarmatia bordering on the Euxine Sea: for Cæfar would not give it fo harfh a name as *banifhment*. He had a fhip of his own in the Bay of Corinth, on which he made his voyage to the Euxine; and then performed the reft of his journey on foot to a place the utmoft and

---

* He fays in feveral parts of his works, the caufes of his mifery were two: his having compofed books on the Art of Love, and his having *feen fomething*. He does not tell us what it was he faw; but gives us to underftand, that his books contributed lefs to his difgrace than that did; and on his complaining to Love, that, after labouring to enlarge *his* empire, he obtained nothing for his reward but banifhment, Love anfwers,

" Utque hoc, fic utinam defendere cætera poffes:
" Scis aliud, quod te læferit, effe magis."

De Ponto, l. iii. ep. 3.

And in his Second Book De Triftibus, l. ii. ver. 103, he compares himfelf to unfortunate Actæon, who had undefignedly feen Diana naked, and fuffered for it. Various attempts have been made to conjecture what he *faw*; but it ftill remains an uncertainty.

moft

most inhofpitable of any that a Roman had ever been confined to. He complains of the dangers and miseries of his paffage, and the injuftice of his companions and fervants: but, refolved that his fpirit fhould not fink under his misfortunes, he made ufe of his refolution to overcome them, and prevailed fo far as to conquer his temper, that had been too much given up to eafe; and began to pafs his days in fome content, by means of thofe verfes which he made for his own fatisfaction, without any hopes of their coming to the perufal of others. And in this adverfity of the Poet his character appears with the greateft luftre: here he fhews a courage undaunted, a fpirit not to be caft down, a conftancy of love to the partner of his bed, and a friendfhip inviolable to thofe perfons of honour that he had confided in, many of which were of Confular dignity. He often folicited his repeal by the mediation of Germanicus Cæfar and others, or that he might at leaft be removed to fome more temperate clime: but, he fays, his hopes forfook him upon the death of Auguftus. Yet in the fixth year of his confinement he ftill continued to folicit it, and to thefe ends his writings out of Pontus were defigned: in one of them to his wife, he undertakes to fhew her, that his expedition was more dangerous than that which Jafon made for the Golden Fleece; as likewife in another to Pedo Albinovanus, a famous Poet, that he had undergone more than Ulyffes in all his twenty years: ingenioufly thus contriving to bring either of thofe noble fubjects to be comprehended in one of his fhort Epiftles. Some of thefe Letters were to his relations, as Rufus Fundanus, his wife's uncle; Suillius, that had married his wife's daughter; to Salanus and Severus, eminent Poets; to his friends Rufinus, Gallio, Tuticanus, Atticus, with whom he had been moft intimate, and many others: as to Maximus Cotta, who firft fent him a moft elegant Oration, and then the images of Auguftus, Tiberius, and Livia, which were a fight in thofe parts that occafioned great veneration. He writes to Veftalis, then Governor of Pontus, fprung from Daunus and the Alpine Kings; as likewife to Cotys, the fon of Cotys King of Thrace, who was then warring upon the Getes, to enlarge his territories, that he might be protected from thofe incurfions; and this, amongft others, he prays from the topic of Poetry, to which that Prince, it feems, was much addicted. He writes likewife to Græcinus, one of his oldeft acquaintance, to congratulate him upon his being defigned

Conful;

Conful; as likewife to Sextus Pompeius, when he had the like
view of that dignity; and at the fame time acknowledges, that
his life, and the continuance of it, had been owing to his good
offices. Nor did he omit writing to Meffalinus, fon to a celebrated Orator of that name, and a great favourite in the Court of
Auguftus : but one that he moft relied on was Fabius Maximus,
a man of the greateft honour, that would not defert a friend for
the frowns of Fortune; efpecially one that, as Ovid had done,
had loved and regarded him from the very time of his birth,
and had been dependant upon that family, and efpecially his
father, who was a perfon famous for his eloquence as well as his
great dignity, and was the firft Patron of Ovid's Mufe, having
encouraged him to venture his compofitions to try their fuccefs in
publick. But he loft this good friend in the fifth year of his
confinement; and therefore his expectation of relief was more
entirely thrown upon the confidence he had in the generofity of
Brutus, to whom he wrote many pathetic Letters on that occafion.
In the midft of the Getic wars, his good-humour gained fo far
upon their barbarous nature, that they became converfable with
him; fo that he attained their language to perfection, and made
it fubmit to numbers fo far, that he wrote a Poem in it. In an
Epiftle to Carus, who was Tutor to the two Cæfars, he tells
him, " The fubject was the praifes of Auguftus : that he taught
" them, that though the body of Auguftus was mortal, yet his
" divine part was gone to the heavens : that his fucceffor Ti-
" berius was equal to the virtues of his father, though his mo-
" defty would have made him refufe the title of Emperor: that it
" was queftionable whether Livia, reputed as the Vefta of her
" time for her modefty, was more happy and glorious in a
" hufband or a fon: that no family could be better fupported
" than the Emperor's, by two fuch fons as Germanicus and
" Drufus." He recited all this and much more to the Barbarians,
who by warlike figns teftified their applaufe; they exempted him
from all public burthens; they even againft his will fet garlands
upon his head; and ufed him in all refpects as kindly as his own
countrymen would have done : therefore he did not folicit a re-
moval out of any diflike to the people of the place, but for the
inclemency of the climate. He muft certainly have been a perfon univerfally beloved; for he had that happinefs, that Envy
never pretended to criticife upon any of his writings; for, as he

paid

paid due veneration to antiquity and the learned men of the time, so he owns that his Readers, whilst he was living, gave him such a portion of fame, as he rightly judged would last him to all posterity. As his birth was reported to have happened with that of Tibullus, one the most polite, the other the most ingenious, of the Elegiac Poets; so Livy is said to have died the same day with him, being the first of January, that in both he might be most nobly and honourably accompanied. Some Authors think that he died at Tomos, in the fifth year of Tiberius. Some say he lived seven years, nine months, and eleven days; others eight years, and some months; others nine, and others ten years, under his misfortunes. All which may be the more uncertain, since we have none of his Works since the Fourth Book of his Letters from Pontus, which were written in the sixth year. As he was honoured when living, so his funerals were celebrated by the Getes with universal sorrow. He was, as says Eusebius, buried near the gates of the city, where a monument was erected for him hard by a lake which retains his name. His Sepulchre is reported by Abraham Ortelius [f], who cites Gaspar Bruschius for his Author, to have been found in the year 1508, with a magnificent coverture, on which was this Epitaph:

FATUM NECESSITATIS LEX.

Hic situs est Vates, quem divi Cæsaris ira
Augusti, patria cædere jussit humo.
Sæpe miser voluit patriis occumbere terris,
Sed frustra; hunc illi fata dedere locum.

As translated by Mr. Sandys:

FATE THE LAW OF NECESSITY.

" Here lies that living Poet, by the rage
  " Of great Augustus banished from Rome,
" Who in his country sought to inter his age,
  " But vainly: fate hath lodg'd him in this tomb."

[f] A celebrated geographer, born at Antwerp in April 1527. He traveled a great deal in England, Ireland, France, Italy, and Germany; and became possessed of many rarities, in antique statues, medals, and shells. He published " Theatrum Orbis Terræ," and a " Thesaurus Geographicus, &c." and died June 10, 1598.

Ifabella Queen of Hungary, about the year 1540, fhewed to Petrus Angelus Barcæus, when he was at Belgrade, a filver pen with this infcription, " Ovidii Nafonis Calamus;" denoting that it had belonged to Ovid. This had not long before been found amongft fome old ruins, and fhe efteemed it as a venerable piece of antiquity. The elegant Poet Cœlius Calcagninus, when he was in Sarmatia, wrote an Elegy, wherein he defcribes the manners of the Scythians, and fays, " that not only Tomifvar but " other places contend for the refidence of Ovid; and that the " pen remains, wherewith he ufed to relieve his tedious hours in " thofe regions;" where Cœlius teftifies all to be true that Ovid has recorded of them. And certainly never any two Poets had a Mufe more like than thefe, fo fitted to the Elegiac ftyle. Calcagninus has a rarity in his Works not eafily to be found elfewhere, a copy of verfes all Pentameters; which whether they are not too foft, may be a queftion; however, being fhort, fhall be tranfcribed, though not attempted in Englifh :

> *Defle, Amor, ad Tumulum; folve, Elegëia, comas;*
> *Myrrha, tuos crimes; pone, Hyacinthe, tuos.*
> *Quintia obit, fed non Quintia fola obit :*
> *Rifus obit, obit Gratia, Lufus obit :*
> *Quintia obit, fed cum Quintia et ipfe obii ;*
> *Nec mea nunc anima in pectore fed tumulo eft.*
> *Hei mihi non pofthac decipietur Amor,*
> *Cui mater crebro Quintia vifa fuit,*
> *Inque hujus pofuit nefcius arma finus,*
> *Arma, inquam, quæ me furripuere mihi.*
> *Heu! heu! trifte jugum quifquis Amoris habet,*
> *Et prius ac norit fe periiffe perit.*

Angelus Politianus [g], another incomparable imitator of Ovid, bewails the exile and death of that Poet in ftrains fo foft and moving, that I cannot tell whether any language but the Latin is capable of expreffing it. Crifpinus, the learned Editor of the Dauphin's Ovid, has efteemed it fo much, as to let it be twice printed in thofe volumes. Nor does Julius Scaliger upon the fame fubject want fuch ftrokes as were ufual to fo great a Mafter.

[g] Born at Tufcany in July 1454. He was a prieft and canon of Florence. His works have been much admired, and frequently re-printed. He died in 1494.

The

The verfes which Ovid defired his wife might be upon his tomb in large characters were thefe:

Hic ego qui jaceo tenerorum Lufor Amorum,
Ingenio perii Nafo Poeta meo.
At tibi qui tranfis non fit grave quifquis amafti
Dicere, Nafonis molliter offa cubent!

In which he continues his opinion, that his mafterfhip in the Art of Love would be his glory, notwithftanding he had fuffered by it; and defires every traveller that had been in love would wifh foft reft to his bones, which they muft do unlefs they would be ungrateful.

As to his Works [h], his "Elegies to Corinna" were the firft that were produced in publick, which were in Five Books, but afterward by him reduced to Three. The fubjects fprung wholly from his own thoughts and imagination, nor does he feem to have borrowed any hint from the Greeks, with whofe language at that time in all probability he was not converfant. Of thefe, according to Mr. Dryden, it may be faid, "That, if they be compared "with thofe of Tibullus and Propertius, it will be found that "they feldom defigned before they wrote. And though the "language of Tibullus be more polifhed, and the learning of "Propertius, efpecially in his Fourth Book, more fet off to "oftentation; yet their common practice was to look no further "than the next line; whence it will inevitably follow, that they "can drive to no certain point. But Ovid has always the goal "in his eye, which directs him in his race; fome beautiful de- "fign, which he firft eftablifhes, and then contrives the means "which will naturally conduct him to his end." His next Work, in probability, was his "Epiftles;" which he afferts as his own invention, and therefore juftly glories in them. The wit of them is fo copious, that almoft every two lines may feem an Epigram. Mr. Dryden obferves, that "they are generally granted "to be the moft perfect piece of Ovid; and that the ftyle of them "is tenderly paffionate and courtly, two properties well agree- "ing with the perfons who are Heroines and Lovers." His next was his "Art of Love," in Three Books: concerning which it is hoped at prefent, that though heretofore they fell under the difpleafure of Auguftus; yet that now they are fo managed, as

[h] The beft edition of them is by Burman, Leyden, 1714, 4 vols. 4to.

that

that they may venture within the verge of the court without any
forbiddance.   About the fame time came forth his Two Books
of the " Remedies of Love," and a fmall one of the " Improve-
" ment of the Face ;" and fome few fuch pieces as that upon the
" Nut-tree," and perhaps fome others.   I fuppofe thefe to have
been all done before his travels into Greece and Egypt, in which
he made collections out of multitudes of Authors (befides
Parthenius of Chios, who treated on a like fubject) to compile
his Fifteen Books of " Metamorphofes ;" than which all Authors
agree that nothing can be more ingenious, nothing more excellent, artificial, or graceful, than the contexture of Fable with
Fable, which, in fuch diverfity of matter, are fo cunningly
woven together, that all appear but one feries.   Yet, as he was
going into banifhment, out of vexation at his own Poetry, which
was affigned (though only colourably) to have been the caufe of
it, he was refolved to burn them.   But there were too many
copies got abroad ; and therefore he excufes the faults that may
be in them, as not having received his laft correction : and yet
they are fome of the moft beautiful things that we have received
from the antients.   As moft perfons that love Poetry fome time
or another venture upon the Stage; fo Ovid, fhewed what he
could perform that way in a Tragedy called Medea[i], which is
now loft, but was then received with great applaufe.   Cornelius
Tacitus thinks that neither Afinius nor Meffala, in any of their
compofitions, came up to the Medea of Ovid : and Quintilian
fays, that by that Tragedy the Poet fhews how much he was
able to do, when he would rather temper than indulge his wit.
After his difmiffion from court, he had occafion to make ufe of a
fatirical ftyle, which he always before had induftrioufly avoided ;
but it was upon high provocation, and yet he does it under the
concealed Name of Ibis.   He is fuppofed to have written it in
full paffion, either in his voyage, or as foon as he came to the
Euxine fhore, againft a perfon that took occafion from his mif-
fortunes to fcandalize and reproach him ; to make his wife un-
eafy ; to endeavour to reduce him to the utmoft poverty by de-
priving him of his eftate, which Auguftus had entirely left him ;
for which clemency, in many excellent Verfes, the Poet is not
ungrateful.   He profeffes to have imitated Callimachus, who falls

i " Medea," by Mr. Glover, the author of " Leonidas," is perhaps
the moft claffical tragedy in the Englifh language.

upon

upon Apollonius Rhodius in a Poem under the same title. There can nothing include more of the antient Fable and History than this small Work; especially of such as have come to any fatal mischances. To alleviate his misfortunes, he wrote his Five Books " De Tristibus," which are a sort of Epistles ; but to persons he thought, for some reasons, it would then be improper to name. As likewise his Four Books of " Letters from Pontus," addressed to persons of the highest quality, as beforementioned, from whom he expected at least some hopes of the relaxation of his punishment. In all these, the serenity of his mind, the justness of the thought, the clearness and propriety of the expression, the evenness of the numbers, the tender moving of compassion, intermixed with various topicks of persuasive eloquence, have made Bellori affirm, that Ovid has made his very grief delightful; and that, whether he was upon the banks of Tiber, or upon those of the Danube, yet he still seemed to be in the midst of Helicon [k], It was here that Ovid composed his Twelve Books of the Fasti; which is as much as to say, he put the Roman Almanack and Calendar into verse : a bold undertaking ; and yet, in the Six Books [l] that remain, there is not only the most exact description of the Roman Ceremonies, Customs, and Antiquities [m]; but, in so obscure, barren, and dry a subject, he has proceeded with all the perspicuity, copiousness, splendid ornaments, and beautiful descriptions, that can be imagined : insomuch that Heinsius thinks nothing can be more easy, plain, and natural, than the story of Lucrece, where the impatience of young Tarquin and his companions, and the speed of their horses in carrying them to Rome, does not come up to that quickness of thought

[k] Mr. Cowley remarks, that, by the style of Ovid's Epistles *ex Ponto* and his *de Tristibus*, very unlike that of his Metamorphoses, one may see the humble and dejected spirit in which he wrote. The cold of the country, and his own despair, had benumbed his faculties.

[l] Many of the Learned suppose that no more than Six Books were ever written. In the second book de Tristibus, ver. 548, Ovid says,

" Sex ego Fastorum scripsi, totidemque libellos,

" Cumque sua finem mense volumen habet."

It is matter of doubt whether he means *six*, or *twice six*.

[m] Selden calls Ovid " a great canon lawyer," merely from these books, as giving us the best account of the religion and festivals of the old Romans.

which

which Ovid fhews in his comprehenfive verfes. In this retirement, Ovid likewife began his "Halieutica," or Book of Fifhes;
for it is a queftion whether he ever finifhed it: but by that which
remains it appears to have been an excellent and moft ufeful
Hiftory of Nature; wherein he defcribed many forts that were in
that fea, with their wonderful qualities, whofe very names had
before been unknown to Pliny, that moft induftrious Naturalift
among the Romans. This fubject Oppian afterward purfued in
Greek verfe, and dedicated to the Emperor Antoninus. Ovid
tells us of another Work that he compofed in Pontus, which was
"The Triumph of Germanicus," which, in his Epiftles from
thence to Salanus and Rufinus, he recommends to their protection.
But this is loft, as were feveral others: amongft which may be
reckoned his Confolation to Livia upon the Death of Drufus,
from whence Seneca has made ufe of many things in his Confo-
lations; his Epigrams, mentioned by Prifcian and Martial; his
Book "De Phænomenis," fpoken of by Probus and Lactantius; his Book againft Poetafters, quoted by Quihtilian; a Collection of Prophecies, and Two Books of the War of Actium,
dedicated to Tiberius Cæfar, but not completed. At his departure from Rome, he threw many things into the fire; which he
believed afterwards might have given fatisfaction to the Reader,
if they had not met with fuch an irreprievable condemnation.
There are feveral other things attributed to him; as, the Panegyrick to Pifo, the Nightingale, the Flea, and a Poem about an
Old Woman, in Three Books, which, being very filly, is very
fcarce; but Crifpinus tells us, the foolifh Author would impofe
it upon the world as if it were as true as Gofpel. In all his
Works, Ovid's wit is acknwledged to be luxuriant, which his
riper age would have corrected in his "Metamorphofes:" but he
fhews how difficult it would have been to him by the Letters
which he continued to write in his exile with the utmoft exuberance of thought and expreffion. Scaliger and Mr. Dryden
differ upon the point, whether Ovid knew how to leave off when
he had well begun; but then Mr. Dryden defcribes him as "vary-
"ing the fame fenfe a hundred ways, and yet that the moft fevere
"cenfor cannot but be pleafed with the prodigality of his wit:
"that every thing which he does becomes him; and if fome-
"times he appears too gay, yet there is a fecret gracefulnefs of
"youth which accompanies his writings." In Ovid's ftyle is a

native

native fimplicity, which whoever goes about to mend, will find he corrupts it. He fays more by Nature than Art can come up to. What he does, feems to be produced without pain; but it would be in vain for the greateft labour to attempt it. Scaliger takes notice, that ufing the fame word or expreffion too often is a fault of fome Authors that pretend to be correct; but that the Princes of the Poets, Virgil and Ovid, are free from the fufpicion of it. The obfervation is juft; and yet Ovid fhews how great a Mafter he was of words, by his repeating them even to advantage, as in thofe moft fweet Verfes of Phillis to Demophoon:

Credidimus blandis, quorum tibi copia, verbis;
Credidimus generi, nominibufque tuis.
Credidimus lacrymis; an et hæ fimulare docentur?
Hæ quoque habent artes, quáque jubentur, eunt.
Diis quoque credidimus; quo jam tot pignora nobis?
Parte fatis potui qualibet inde capi.

Which, amongft the moft ingenious Verfions of the Epiftles, I find thus tranflated by Mr. Edward Pooley [a]:

" I foolifhly believ'd the oaths you fwore,
" The race you boafted, and the Gods you bore,
" Who could have thought fuch gentle words e'er hung
" Upon a treachrous and deluding tongue?
" I faw your tears, and I believ'd them all:
" Can they lye too, and are they taught to fall?
" What needed all that numerous perjury?
" One was enough to one that lov'd like me."

Some have thought he had too much compaffion for his own failings, and that he rather loved than would any ways correct them. Seneca tells us, that, being defired by his Friends to leave out of his Works only three Verfes, he complied, on condition that he might fave three. Both parties wrote, and put the lines into the Arbitrator's hands, which, being produced, proved to be the fame. Two of them are recorded by Pedo Albinovanus the Poet, and his great Friend, who was there prefent; which were thefe:

Semibovemque virum, femivirumque bovem.
Sed gelidum Boream, egelidumque Notum.

[a] In the " Tranflation by feveral Hands," publifhed by Tonfon.

Whereby

Whereby it appears that his admirable wit did not want an anfwerable judgement in fuppreffing the liberties of his Verfe, if he had not affected it: and he was ufed to fay, that a mole did not mifbecome a good face, but made it more lovely. However, Ovid has had the greateft character among the Learned in all ages: for, befides the many great names beforementioned, Velleius Paterculus, a curious judge, joins him with Tibullus, as the two perfons that had brought their Poems to perfection. By Martial and others he is placed with Virgil, as being both confummate in their way. The Fathers Lactantius, St. Jerom, and St Auftin, have not denied his "Metamorphofis" its juft commendation. Planudes [*] tranflated it into Greek, to reftore that Learning, part of which had been brought from thence back again to his own country, Stephens moft juftly efteems him the beft Painter amongft the Poets. Heinfius thought, that whoever would be drawn to the life muft fit to him. And Raphael Regius fays, that his commanders, their ftratagems, and their battles, are fo touched by his pencil, that whoever views them attentively will imagine himfelf fo engaged, as to take part in their conflicts. And then no Poet has more naturally defcribed the manners of the perfons he mentions, nor is more fententious, nor better expati-

---

[*] A monk of Conftantinople; who lived at the end of the third and the beginning of the fourth century, and fuffered fome perfecution on account of his zeal for the Latin church. "Th t idiot of a Monk" (fays Dr. Bentley, Diff. on Æfop, p. 147) "has given us a Book, which "he calls *The Life of Æfop*, that perhaps cannot be matched in any lan-"guage for ignorance and nonfenfe,—But of all his injuries to Æfop, that "which can leaft be forgiven him is the making fuch a monfter of him "for uglinefs; an abufe, that has found credit fo univerfally, that all "the modern Painters fince the time of Planudes have drawn him "in the worft fhapes and features that Fancy could invent.—I wifh I "could do that juftice to the memory of the Phrygian, to oblige the "Painters to change their pencil; for it is certain, he was no deformed "perfon, and it is probable he was very handfome." In this particular, the Fabulift has had the fate of our Englifh Richard III; who, whatever other epithets he deferved, had no right to that of CROOKBACKED. One of the arguments, however, by which Dr. Bentley has vindicated the beauty of Æfop, is "becaufe his fellow flave was fair beyond ex-"ception;" a topic, which (it has been pleafantly obferved) may be of great ufe to all public focieties, becaufe it makes all the members of them alike wife and pretty. See "A fhort Account of Dr. Bentley's Humanity, "&c." p. 94. And fee above, p. 68.

ales upon the common-places of morality; as temperance, friendship, love of his country, labour, valour, learning, honesty, contempt of wealth, decay of outward beauty, and hopes of a lasting
reputation raised by virtue. It may from this small remark be
seen what opinion the world had of this Author, and how acceptable he was to them, when the same Regius, who wrote the
first Comment on the " Metamorphosis," vented fifty thousand
of them in his life-time. His person was in so great favour in his
prosperity, that his picture was cut in precious stones, and worn
by them in their rings. He mentions one of them with a crown
of ivy on his head, which, in one of his melancholy Letters, he
says was no longer a fitting ornament for him; and he speaks of
another set in a ring of gold. Our ingenious countryman Mr.
Sandys P tells us, he had seen his figure in a cornelian of exquisite
workmanship, and an old medal of silver stamped with his image;
and those he has placed before his Translation of the Metamorphosis. Hercules Ciofani q gives it us as delineated from an
antient marble found at Sulmo, and given him by his Friend
Julius Agapetus. Ursinus has a head of him in his collections.
There are several others; one from an antient medal in the
Dutch edition; another in the Dauphin's: but the most excellent, and that seems to approach nearest to the character of the
original, is that represented by Peter Bellori, Library-keeper and
Antiquary to the Queen of Sweden, among his images of antient
Philosophers, Poets, and Orators, set out in the year 1685; the
esteem which his most learned Excellency Spanhemius has shewn,

P George Sandys, son of Edwin archbishop of York, born about 1578,
published " Ovid's Metamorphosis, englished, mythologized, and repre-
" sented in figures, Oxford, 1632," folio. Francis Cleyn was the in-
ventor of the figures, and Solomon Sabang the engraver. He had before
published part of this translation; and in the preface to this second edition
he tells us, that he has attempted to collect out of sundry authors the
philosophical sense of the fables of Ovid. Mr. Dryden pronounced him
the best versifier of the last age. He was also an excellent geographer
and critic; and published in 1615 his travels to Turkey, &c. He was of
the privy-chamber to Charles I; and died in March, 1643-4. From the
Ovid of Sandys, and the Homer of Ogilby, Mr. Pope first took his taste for
poetry.

q This learned Italian, who published his annotations in 1578, was
induced to undertake that task from the honour he received in being the
countryman of Ovid. He is commended by Scaliger, for having written
well, and for being an honest man.

for it in his Differtations [r] will make others regard it. The medal is of brafs, with Ovid's Head on one fide, and on the Reverfe the Head of Menander Parrhafius, who caufed this Monument to be made for pofterity. Nicolaus Heinfius, in his laft Edition of Ovid, prefixed this head to it, as he received it from that exquifite treafure of Medals collected by Felicia Rondanina, a moft noble and learned Roman Matron. And the generofity and good-nature of Sir Andrew Fountain, in communicating it out of his great ftock of learned curiofities, is gratefully to be acknowledged [s].

'There has been in this Preface fo much faid of Ovid, that there may be lefs room to fpeak of the following imitation. It is at leaft fuch a one as Mr. Dryden mentions, " to be an endea-" vour of a later Poet to write like one who has written before " him on the fame fubject; that is, not to tranflate his words, or " be confined to his fenfe, but only to fet him as a pattern, and " to write as he fuppofes that Author would have done, had " he lived in our age and in our country. But he dares not fay " that Sir John Denham [t], or Mr. Cowley, have carried this Liber-" tine way, as the latter calls it, fo far as this definition reaches." But, alas! the prefent Imitator has come up to it, if not perhaps exceeded it. Sir John Denham had Virgil, and Mr. Cowley [u] had Pindar to deal with, who both wrote upon lafting foundations: but, the prefent fubject being Love, it would be unreafonable to think of too great a confinement to be laid on it. And though the paffion and grounds of it will continue the fame through all ages; yet there will be many little modes, fafhions, and graces, ways of complaifance and addrefs, entertainments and diverfions, which time will vary. Since the world will expect new things, and perfons will write, and the Antients have fo great

[r] De præftantia & ufu numifmatum antiquorum, Romæ, 1664, 4to. This learned writer and able ftatefman, after having been employed in embaffies at moft of the courts in Europe, died at London, Oct. 28, 1710, aged 81.

[s] Dr. King alludes to a Frontifpiece prefixed to his firft edition.

[t] Sir John Denham was born at Dublin in 16·5; and died March 19, 1668. His " Poems and Tranflations" have been frequently printed in one volume. That which Mr. Dryden fpeaks of is called " The De-" ftruction of Troy, &c."

[u] See note on ver. 2046.

a fund

a fund of Learning; whom can the Moderns take better to copy than such originals? It is most likely they may not come up to them; but it is a thousand to one but their imitation is better than any clumsy invention of their own. Whoever undertakes this way of writing, has as much reason to understand the true scope, genius, and force of the expressions of his Author, as a literal Translator: and after all, he lies under this misfortune, that the faults are all his own; and if there is any thing that may seem pardonable, the Latin ᵂ at the bottom shews to whom he is engaged for it. An Imitator and his Author stand much upon the same terms as Ben does with his Father in the Comedy ˣ: "What thof he be my Father, I an't bound Prentice to 'en." There were many reasons why the Imitator transposed several Verses of Ovid, and has divided the whole into Fourteen Parts rather than keep it in Three Books. These may be too tedious to be recited; but, among the rest, some were, that matters of the same subject might lie more compact; that too large a heap of precepts together might appear too burthensome; and therefore (if small matters may allude to greater) as Virgil in his " Georgicks," so here most of the parts end with some remarkable Fable, which carries with it some Moral: yet, if any persons please to take the Six first Parts as the First Book, and divide the Eight last, they may make Three Books of them again. There have by chance some twenty lines crept into the Poem out of the " Remedy of Love," which (as inanimate things are generally the most wayward and provoking) since they would stay, have been suffered to stand there. But as for the Love here mentioned, it being all prudent, honourable, and virtuous, there is no need of any remedy to be prescribed for it, but the speedy obtaining of what it desires. Should the Imitator's style seem not to be sufficiently restrained, should he not have afforded pains for review or correction, let it be considered, that perhaps even in that he desired to imitate his Author, and would not peruse them; lest, as some of Ovid's Works were, so these might be committed to the flames. But he leaves that for the Reader to do, if he pleases, when he has bought them.

ᵂ In the first editions of the " Art of Cookery" and of the " Art of " Love," Dr. King printed the original under the respective pages of his translations.

ˣ Congreve's Love for Love.

THE

ART OF LOVE.

PART I.

WHOEVER knows not what it is TO LOVE,
  Let him but read thefe verfes, and improve.
Swift fhips are rul'd by art, and oars, and fails :
Skill guides our chariots, Wit o'er Love prevails.
Automedon with reins let loofe could fly,   5
Tiphys with Argo's fhip cut waves and fky.
In Love-affairs I'm charioteer of Truth,
And fureft pilot to incautious youth.
Love 's hot, unruly, eager to enjoy ;.
But then confider he is but a boy.   10
Chiron with pleafing harp Achilles tam'd,
And his rough manners with foft mufick fram'd :
Tho' he'd in council ftorm, in battle rage,
He bore a fecret reverence for age.
Chiron's command with ftrict obedience ties   15
The finewy arm by which brave Hector dies.
That was *his* tafk, but fiercer Love is mine :
They both are boys, and fprung from race divine.
The ftiff-neck'd bull does to the yoke fubmit,
And the moft fiery courfer champs the bitt :   20
So Love fhall yield. I own, I've been his flave,
But conquer'd where my enemy was brave ?
And now he darts his flames without a wound,
And all his whiftling arrows die in found.
Nor will I raife my fame by hidden art,   25
In what I teach found reafon fhall have part :
For Nature's paffion cannot be deftroy'd,
But moves in Virtue's path when well employ'd.

Yet

Yet ſtill 'twill be convenient to remove
The tyranny and plagues of vulgar love.   30
May infant chaſtity, grave matrons' pride,
A parent's wiſh, and bluſhes of a bride,
Protect this Work ; ſo guard it, that no rhyme
In ſyllable or thought may vent a crime!
The Soldier that Love's armour would defy   35
Will find his greateſt courage is to fly :
When Beauty's amorous glances parley beat,
The only conqueſt then is to retreat :
But, if the treacherous Fair pretend to yield,
'Tis preſent death unleſs you quit the field.   40
Whilſt youth and vanity would make you range,
Think on ſome beauty may prevent your change :
But ſuch by falling ſkies are never caught,
No happineſs is found but what is ſought.
The huntſman learns where does trip o'er the lawn,   45
And where the foaming boar ſecures his brawn.
The fowler's low-bell robs the lark of ſleep,
And they who hope for fiſh muſt ſearch the deep :
And he that fuel ſeeks for chaſte deſire
Muſt ſearch where Virtue may that flame inſpire.   50
To foreign parts there is no need to roam :
The bleſſing may be met with nearer home.
From India ſome, others from neighbouring France,
Bring tawny ſkins, and puppets that can dance.
The Seat of Britiſh Empire does contain   55
Beauties that o'er the conquer'd globe will reign.
As fruitful fields with plenty bleſs the ſight,
And as the milky way adorns the night :
So *that* does with thoſe graceful nymphs abound,
Whoſe dove-like ſoftneſs is with roſes crown'd.   60
There tendereſt blooms inviting ſoftneſs ſpread,
Whilſt by their ſmalleſt twine the captive's led.
There youth advanc'd in majeſty does ſhine,
Fit to be mother to a race divine.
No age in matrons, no decay appears ;   65
By prudence only there you gueſs at years.
   Sometimes you'll ſee theſe Beauties ſeek the ſhade
By lofty trees in royal gardens made ;

Or at St. James's, where a noble care
Makes all things pleasing like himself appear;   70
Or Kensington, sweet air and blest retreat
Of him, that owns a Sovereign, though most great *y*.

    Sometimes in wilder groves by chariots drawn
They view the noble stag and tripping fawn.
On Hyde-Park's circles if you chance to gaze,   75
The lights revolving strike you with amaze.

    To Bath and Tunbridge they sometimes retreat,
With waters to dispel the parching heat;
But youth with reason there may oft admire
That which may raise in him a nobler fire;   80
Till the kind Fair relieves what he endures,
Caus'd at that water which all others cures.

    Sometimes at marriage rites you may espy
Their charms protected by a mother's eye,
Where to blest musick they in dances move,   85
With innocence and grace commanding love.
But yearly when that solemn night returns,
When grateful incense on the altar burns,
For closing the most glorious day e'er seen,
That first gave light to happy Britain's Queen;   90
Then is the time for noble youth to try
To make his choice with a judicious eye.
Not truth of foreign realms, not fables told
Of Nymphs ador'd, and Goddesses of old,
Equal those beauties who that circle frame;   95
A subject fit for never-dying fame:
Whose gold, pearl, diamonds, all around them thrown,
Yet still can add no lustre to their own.

    But when their Queen does to the Senate go,
And they make up the grandeur of the show;   100

    y George Prince of Denmark, consort to the Queen, greatly admired
these fine gardens.—They were purchased by King William from Lord
Chancellor Finch; were enlarged by Queen Mary; and improved by
Queen Anne, who was so pleased with the place, that she frequently supped
during the summer in the Green-house, which is very beautiful. Queen
Caroline extended the gardens to their present size, three miles and a half
in compass.

                                         Then

Then guard your hearts, ye makers of our laws,
For fear the judge be forc'd to plead his caufe;
Left the fubmiffive part fhould fall to you,
And they who fuppliants help be forc'd to fue.
Then may their yielding hearts compaffion take,
And grant your wifhes for your country's fake.
Eafe to their beauties wounds may goodnefs give;
And fince you make all happy, let you live.
    Sometimes thefe Beauties on New-market plains,
Ruling their gentle pads with filken reins,   110
Behold the conflicts of the generous fteeds,
Sprung from true blood, and well-attefted breeds.
There youth may juftly with difcerning eye
Through riding Amazonian habit fpy
That which his fwifteft courfer cannot fly.   115
    It is no treacherous or bafe piece of art,
T'approve the fide with which the Fair takes part:
For equal paffion equal minds will ftrike,
Either in commendation or diflike.
For, when two fencers ready ftand to fight,   120
And we're fpectators of the bloody fight,
Our nimble paffion Love has foon defign'd
The man to whom we muft and will be kind.
We think the other is not fit to win:
This is our conqueror ere fight begin.   125
If danger dares approach him, how we ftart!
Our frighted blood runs trembling to our heart:
He takes the wounds, but we endure the fmart,
And Nature by fuch inftances does prove,
That we fear moft for that which moft we love.   130
Therefore, if chance fhould make her faddle flide,
Or any thing fhould flip, or be untied,
Oh, think it not a too officious care
With eagernefs to run and help the fair.
We offer fmall things to the powers above: 135
'Tis not our merit that obtains their love.
So when Eliza, whofe propitious days
Revolving Heaven does feem again to raife;
Whofe ruling genius fhew'd a mafter-ftroke
In every thing fhe did, and all fhe fpoke;   140

Was

Was stepping o'er a passage, which the rain
Had fill'd, and seem'd as stepping back again;
Young Raleigh scorn'd to see his Queen retreat,
And threw his velvet cloak beneath her feet.
The Queen approv'd the thought, and made him great z.   145
    Mark when the Queen her thanks divine would give
Midst acclamations, that she *long may live*;
To whom kind Heaven the blessing has bestow'd,
To let her arms succeed for Europe's good.
No tyranny throughout the triumph reigns,   150
Nor are the captives dragg'd with ponderous chains:
But all declares the British subjects' ease,
And that their war is for their neighbours' peace.
Then, whilst the pomp of Majesty proceeds
With stately steps, and eight well-chosen steeds,   155
From every palace beauties may be seen,
That will acknowledge none but Her for Queen.
Then, if kind chance a lovely Maid has thrown
Next to a Youth with graces like her own,
Much she would learn, and many questions ask: 160
The answers are the Lover's pleasing task.
" Is that the *man* who made the French to fly?
" What place is Blenheim? is the Danube nigh?
" Where was't that he with sword victorious stood,
" And made their trembling squadrons chuse the flood?   165
" What is the *gold* adorns this royal state?
" Is it not hammer'd all from Vigo's plate?
" Don't it require a most prodigious care
" To manage treasures in the height of war?
" Must he not be of calmest truth possest   170
" Presides o'er councils of the Royal breast?
" Sea-fights are surely dismal scenes of war!
" Pray, Sir, were ever you at Gibraltar?
" Has not the Emperor got some Envoy here?
" Won't Danish, Swedish, Prussian Lords appear?   175
" Who represents the Line of Hanover?

    z Sir Walter Raleigh is well known to have been indebted to this
little mark of gallantry for his rise at court. See above, p. 93.

" Don't

" Don't The States General affift them all?
" Should we not be in danger, if they fall?
" If Savoy's Duke and Prince Eugene could meet
" In this folemnity, 'twould be complete.   180
" Think you that Barcelona could have ftood
" Without the hazard of our nobleft blood?
" At Ramillies what enfigns did you get?
" Did many towns in Flanders then fubmit?
" Was it the Conqueror's bufinefs to deftroy,   185
" Or was he met by all of them with joy?
" Oh, could my wifh but fame eternal give,
" The laurels on thofe brows fhould ever live!"
   The Britifh worth in nothing need defpair,
When it has fuch affiftance from the Fair.   190
As Virtue merits, it expects regard;
And Valour flies, where Beauty's the reward.

✠✠✠✠

P A R T   II.

IN Love affairs the Theatre has part,
   That wife and moft inftructing fcene of art,
Where Vice is punifh'd with a juft reward,   195
And Virtue meets with fuitable regard;
Where mutual Love and Friendfhip find return,
But treacherous Infolence is hifs'd with fcorn,
And Love's unlawful wiles in torment burn.
This without blufhes whilft a virgin fees,
Upon fome brave fpectator Love may feize,
Who, till *fhe* fends it, never can have eafe.
       As things that were the beft at firft
       By their corruption grow the worft;
       The modern Stage takes liberties   205
       Unfeen by our forefathers eyes.
       As bees from hive, from mole-hill ants;
       So fwarm the females and gallants,
       All crowding to the Comedy,
       For to be feen, and not to fee.   210

But, though thefe females are to blame,
Yet ftill they have fome native fhame :
They all are filent till they're afk'd,
And ev'n their impudence is mafk'd :
For Nature would be modeft ftill,   216
And there's reluctancy in will.
    Sporting and Plays had harmlefs been,
And might by any one be feen,
Till Romulus began to fpoil them,
Who kept a Palace, call'd ASYLUM;   220
Where Baftards, Pimps, and Thieves, and Pandars,
Were lifted all to be commanders.
But then the rafcals were fo poor,
They could not change a Rogue for Whore;
And neighbouring Jades refolv'd to tarry,   225
Rather than with fuch Scrubs they'd marry.
But, for to cheat them, and be wiv'd,
They knavifhly a farce contriv'd.
No gilded pillars there were feen,
Nor was the cloth they trod on green.   230
No Ghofts came from the cellar crying,
Nor Angels from the garret flying.
The Houfe was made of fticks and bufhes,
And all the Floor was ftrew'd with rufhes :
The Seats were rais'd with turf and fods,   235
Whence Heroes might be view'd and Gods.
Paris and Helen was the Play,
And how both of them ran away.
Romulus bad his varlets go
Invite the Sabines to his fhow.   240
Unto this Opera no rate is ;
They all were free to come in *gratis* :
And they, as girls will feldom mifs
A merry meeting, came to this.
There was much wifhing, fighing, thinking,   245
Not without whifpering and winking.
Their pipes had then no fhaking touch :
Their fong and dance were like the Dutch :
The whole performance was by men,
Becaufe they had no Eunuchs then.   250

But, whilſt the muſick briſkly play'd,
Romulus at his cue diſplay'd
The ſign for each man to his maid.
" Huzza !" they cry; then ſeize : ſome tremble
In real faſt, though moſt diſſemble. 255
·Some are attempting an eſcape,
And others ſoftly cry, " A rape !"
Whilſt ſome bawl out, " That they had rather
" Than twenty pound loſe an old father."
Some look extremely pale, and others red,
Some wiſh they'd ne'er been born, or now were dead,
And others fairly wiſh themſelves a-bed.
Some rant, tear, run; whilſt ſome ſit ſtill,
To ſhew they're raviſh'd much againſt their will.
Thus Rome began; and now at laſt, 265
After ſo many ages paſt,
Their rapes and lewdneſs without ſhame;
Their vice and villany's the ſame.
Ill be their fate who would corrupt the Stage,
And ſpoil the true correſtor of the age ! 570

PART III.

NOW learn thoſe arts which teach you to obtain
Thoſe beauties which you ſee divinely reign.
Though they by Nature are tranſcendent bright,
And would be ſeen ev'n through the gloom of night;
Yet they their greateſt luſtre ſtill diſplay 275
In the meridian pitch of calmeſt day.
'Tis then we purple view, and coſtly gem,
And with more admiration gaze on them.
Faults ſeek the dark; they who by moon-light woo,
May find their Fair-one as inconſtant too. 280
When Modeſty ſupported is by Truth,
There is a boldneſs that becomes your youth.
In gentle ſounds diſcloſe a Lover's care,
'Tis better than your ſighing and deſpair,

K 2

Birds may abhor their groves, the flocks the plain,
The Hare grown bold may face the Dogs again,
When Beauty don't in Virtue's arms rejoice,
Since Harmony in Love is Nature's voice.
But harden'd Impudence fometimes will try
At things which Juftice cannot but deny.
Then, what that fays is Infolence and Pride,
Is Prudence with firm Honour for its guide.
   The Lady's counfels often are betray'd
By trufting fecrets to a fervile Maid,
The whole intrigues of whofe infidious brain
Are bafe, and only terminate in gain.
Let them take care of too diffufive mirth ;
Sufpicions thence, and thence attempts, take birth.
Had Ilium been with gravity employ'd,
By Sinon's craft it had not been deftroy'd.
A vulgar air, mean fongs, and free difcourfe,
With fly infinuations, may prove worfe
To tender Females than the Trojan Horfe.
      •   Take care how you from Virtue ftray ;
      For Scandal follows the fame way,
      And more than Truth it will devife.
      Old Poets did delight in lies,
      Which modern ones now call *furprize.*
      Some fay that Myrrha lov'd her Father,
      That Byblis lik'd her Brother rather.
      And in fuch tales old Greece did glory :
      Amongft the which, pray take this Story.
         Crete was an Ifle, whofe fruitful nations
      Swarm'd with an hundred corporations,
      And there upon Mount Ida ftood
      A venerable fpacious wood,
      Within whofe centre was a grove
      Immortaliz'd by birth of Jove :
      In vales below a Bull was fed,
      Whom all the Kine obey'd as head ;
Betwixt his horns a tuft of black did grow,
But all the reft of him was driven fnow.
      (Our tale to truth does not confine us.)
      At the fame time one Juftice Minos,

That liv'd hard by, was married lately;   325
And, that his bride might ſhew more ſtately,
When through her pedigree he run,
Found ſhe was daughter to the Sun.
Her name Paſiphaë was hight,
And, as her Father, ſhe was bright.   330
This Lady took up an odd fancy,
That with this Bull ſhe fain would dance ye.
She'd mow him graſs, and cut down boughs,
On which his ſtatelineſs might browſe.
Whilſt thus ſhe hedges breaks and climbs,   335
Sure Minos muſt have happy times!
She never car'd for going fine,
She'd rather trudge among the Kine
Then at her Toilet ſhe would ſay,
    " Methinks I look *bizarre* to-day.   340
" Sure my glaſs lies, I'm not ſo fair:
" Oh, were this face o'ergrown with hair!
" I never was for top-knots born;
" My favourites ſhould each be horn.
" But now I'm liker to a Sow
" Than, what I wiſh to be, a Cow.—
" What would I give that I could lough!
" My Bull-y cares for none of thoſe
" That are afraid to ſpoil their cloaths:
" Did he but love me, he'd not fail   350
" To take me with my draggle-tail."
    Then tears would fall, and then ſhe'd run,
As would the Devil upon Dun.
When ſhe ſome handſome Cow did ſpy,
She'd ſcan her form with jealous eye.   355
Say, " How ſhe friſks it o'er the plain,
" Runs on, and then turns back again!
" She ſeems a Bear reſolv'd to prance,
" Or a She-aſs that tries to dance.
" In vain ſhe thinks herſelf ſo fine: 360
" She can't pleaſe Bull-y; for he's mine.
" But 'tis revenge alone aſſwages
" My envy when the paſſion rages.

K 3

" Here,

" Here, Rafcal, quickly yoke that Cow,
" And fee the fhrivel'd carrion plough.   365
" But fecond counfel's beft: fhe dies :
" I'll make immediate facrifice,
" And with the victim feaft my eyes.
" 'Tis thus my Rivals I'll remove,
" Who interpofe 'twixt me and what I love.   370
" Io in Egypt 's worfhip'd now,
" Since Jove transform'd her to a Cow.
" 'Twas on a Bull Europa came
" To that bleft land which bears her name.
" Who knows what Fate's ordain'd for me
" The languifhing Pafiphaë,
" Had I a Bull as kind as fhe !"
When madnefs rages with unufual fire,
'Tis not in Nature's power to quench defire;
Then Vice transforms man's reafon into beaft,   380
And fo the monfter's made the Poet's jeft.

✸✸✸✸

P A R T   IV.

LET Youth avoid the noxious heat of Wine :
   Bacchus to Cupid bears an ill defign.
The grape, when fcatter'd on the wings of Love,
So clogs the down, the feathers cannot move.   385
The boy, who otherwife would fleeting ftray,
Reels, tumbles, lies, and is enforc'd to ftay.
Then courage rifes, when the fpirit's fir'd,
And rages to poffefs the thing defir'd :
Care vanifhes through the exalted blood,   390
And forrow paffes in the purple flood ;
Laughter proceeds ; nor can he want a foul,
Whofe thoughts in fancied heaps of plenty roll.
Uncommon freedom lets the lips impart
Plain fimple truth from a diffembling heart.   395
Then to fome wanton paffion he muft run,
Which his difcreeter hours would gladly fhun ;

Where

Where he the time in thoughtless ease may pass,
And write his *billet-doux* upon the glass ;
Whilst sinking eyes with languishment profess   400
Follies his tongue refuses to confess.
Then his good-nature will take t'other sup,
If she'll first kiss, that he may kiss the cup.
Then something nice and costly he could eat,
Supposing still that she will carve the meat.   405
But, if a Brother or a Husband's by,
Whom the ill-natur'd world may call a spy,
He thinks it not below him to pretend
The open-heartedness of a true friend ;
Gives him respect surpassing his degree :   410
The person that is meant by all is *she*.
'Tis thought the safest way to hide a passion,
And therefore call'd the friendship now in fashion.
By secret signs and enigmatic stealth
She is the toast belongs to every health :   415
And all the Lover's business is to keep
His thoughts from anger, and his eyes from sleep,
He'll laugh ye, dance ye, sing ye, vault, look gay,
And ruffle all the Ladies in his play.
But still the Gentleman's extremely fine,   420
There's nothing apish in him but the wine.
    Many a mortal has been hit
    By marrying in a drunken fit.
    To lay this matter plain before ye,
    Pray hearken whilst I tell my story.   425
    It happen'd about break of day
    Gnossis a girl had lost her way,
    And wander'd up and down the Strand,
    Whereabouts now York Buildings stand :
    And half awake she roar'd as bad   430
    As if she really had been mad ;
    Unlac'd her boddice, and her gown
    And petticoats hung dangling down :
    Her shoes were slipt, her ankles bare,
And all around her flew her yellow hair.   435
    Oh, cruel Theseus ! can you go ;
    And leave your little Gnossis so ?

                                                    You

You in your fcull' did promife carriage,
And gave me proofs of future marriage;
But then laft night away did creep,   440
And bafely left me faft afleep.
Then fhe is falling in a fit;
But don't grow uglier one bit.
The flood of tears rather fupplies
The native rheum about her eyes.   445
The bubbies then are beat again :
Women in paffion feel no pain.
What will become of me ? oh, what
Will come of me ? oh, tell me that !

     Bacco was Drawer at the Sun,   450
And had his belly like his tun :
For blubber lips and cheeks all bloated,
And frizzled pate, the youth was noted.
He, as his cuftom was, got drunk,
And then went ftroling for a punk.   455
Six links and lantherns, 'caufe 'twas dark yet,
He prefs'd from Covent-Garden Market :
Then his next captives were the Waits,
Who play'd left he fhould break their pates.
But, as along in ftate he paffes,   460
He met a fellow driving affes :
For there are feveral folks, whofe trade is
To milk them for confumptive ladies.
Nothing would ferve but get aftride,
And the old Bell-man too muft ride.   465
What with their houting fhouting yell,
The fcene had fomething in't of hell.
And who fhould all this rabble meet,
But Gnoffy drabbling in the ftreet ?
The fright deftroy'd her fpeech and colour,   470
And all remembrance of her fculler.
Her conduct thrice bad her be flying :
Her fears thrice hinder'd her from trying.
Like bullrufhes on fide of brook,
Or afpin leaves, her joints all fhook.   475

                                        Bacco

Bacco cry'd out, " I'm come, my dear,
" I'll foon difperfe all thoughts of fear:
" Nothing but joys fhall revel here."
Then, hugging her in brawny arm,
Protefted, " She fhould have no harm :   480
" But rather would affure her, he
" Rejoic'd in opportunity
" Of meeting fuch a one as fhe :
" And that, encircled all around
" With glafs and candles many a pound,   485
" She fhould with bells command the bar,
" And call her rooms Suh, Moon, and Star :
" That the good company were met,
" And fhould not want a wedding treat."
In fhort, they married, and both made ye,   490
He a free Landlord, fhe a kind Landlady.
    The Spartan Lords their Villains would invite
To an excefs of drink in childrens fight.
The parent thus their innocence would fave,
And to the load of Wine condemn the flave.   495

P A R T   V.

THE feafon muft be mark'd for nice addrefs :
    A grant ill-tim'd will make the favour lefs.
Not the wife Gardener more difcretion needs
To manage tender plants and hopeful feeds,
To know when rain, when warmth, muft guard his flowers, 500
Than Lovers do to watch their moft aufpicious hours.
As the judicious pilot views from far
The influences of each rifing ftar,
Where figns of future calms or ftorms appear,
When fitting to be bold, and when to fear ;   505
So Love's attendant by long art defcries
The rife of growing paffion from the eyes.
Love has its Feftival as well as Faft,
Nor does its Carnival for ever laft.

What

What was a vifit, now is to intrude;   5ro
What's civil now, to-morrow will be rude.
Small figns denote great things: the happy man
That can retrieve a Glove, or falling Fan,
With grateful joy the benefit receives,
Whilft with defponding care his Rival grieves,   515
    Whene'er it may feem proper you fhould write,
Let Ovid the prevailing words endite;
By Scrope [a], by Duke [b], by Mulgrave [c], then be taught,
And Dryden's [d] equal numbers tune your thought,
                                                                Submiffive

    [a] Sir Car Scrope, one of thofe writers in the reign of King Charles
the Second, that Mr. Pope calls
    " The Mob of Gentlemen who write with eafe."
He was created a Baronet, January 16, 1666. The greater part of his
writings confift of Tranflations from Ovid, Virgil, and Horace, with fome
Love Songs and Lampoons. They are to be found in the volumes of
Dryden's Mifcellanies. He died fome time in the year 1680.

    [b] A writer of the fame clafs, and with about the fame degree of merit,
as Sir Car Scrope. He appears to have been of Cambridge, and a
friend to Mr. Otway, who has addreffed a Poetical Epiftle to him. His
Works are alfo printed in Dryden's Mifcellanies. " Dr. Duke (fays Swift)
" died fuddenly two or three weeks ago: he was one of the Wits when we
" were children; but turned parfon, and left it, and never wrote further
" than a prologue or recommendatory copy of verfes. He had a fine li-
" ving given him by the bifhop of Winchefter about three months ago;
" he got his living fuddenly, and he got his dying fo too." Journal to
Stella, Feb. 14, 1710-11. It appears by Le Neve that Dr. Duke was a
prebendary of Gloucefter.

    [c] John Sheffield, earl of Mulgrave, born about 1650, fucceeded his
father in that title in 1658. He was a man of uncommon wit and fpirit,
and of no lefs gallantry and politenefs. He cultivated an early acquaintance with Dryden and other men of genius; to whom he was indebted
for a much greater fhare of his reputation than was derived from his perfonal merit. He diftinguifhed himfelf early as a naval commander; lived
in great familiarity with the duke of York; and ferved him with the fin-
cereft attachment after he afcended the throne. He was inftalled knight
of the Garter, May 29, 1674; made a gentleman of the bedchamber, colonel of the old Holland regiment, governor of Hull, and commander of
the forces fent againft Tangier; lord chamberlain of the houfehold, Oct.
20, 1685; created marquis of Normanby, May 10, 1694; on the acceffion of queen Anne, lord privy feal; duke of Buckingham and Normanby, March 23, 1702; lord fteward of the houfehold, Sept. 1710;
                                                                prefident

Submiffive voice and words do beft agree   520
To their hard fortune who muft fuppliants be.
It was by fpeech like this great Priam won
Achilles' foul, and fo obtain'd his fon.
    HOPE is an ufeful Goddefs in your cafe,
And will increafe your fpeed in Cupid's race.   525
Though in its promifes it fail fometimes;
Yet with frefh refolution ftill it climbs.
Though much is loft at play; yet HOPE at laft
Drives on, and meets with fome fuccefsful caft.
Why then make hafte; on paper ting'd with gold,   530
By quill of dove, thy love-fick tale unfold.
Move fprightly, knowing 'tis for life you pufh:
Your Letter will not, though yourfelf might blufh.
'Tis no ignoble maxim I would teach
The Britifh Youth—to ftudy rules of fpeech.   535
That governs cities, that enacts our laws,
Gives fecret ftrength to juftice in a caufe.
To that the crowd, the judge, the fenate, yield:
'Gainft that ev'n Beauty can't maintain the field.
Conceal your art, and let your words appear   540
Common, not vulgar; not too plain, tho' clear.
Shew not your eloquence at the firft fight;
But from your fhade rife by degrees of light.
Drefs thoughts as if Love's filence firft were broke,
And wounded heart with trembling paffion fpoke.   545

prefident of the council, June 12, 1711. He died Feb. 24, 1720-21.
His writings were fplendidly printed in 2 volumes, 4to in 1723; and again
(but much caftrated) in 2 vols. 8vo, 1729. His poetry, though commended
by Rofcommon, Dryden, Lanfdown, Prior, Garth, and Pope, has incurred
the cenfure of Warton and of Walpole. The duke's only fon (by his
third wife Catharine daughter to the countefs of Dorchefter) dying at
Rome, 1735, juft when he had entered his twentieth year, left the famly
eftate to be inherited by natural children, of which the duke had feveral.
    d See above, p. 62. This truly great poet,
      " Dryden, the great high prieft of all the Nine,"
after having lived in exigencies, had a magnificent funeral beftowed on
him by the contribution of feveral perfons of quality. His *Prefaces*, Dr.
Swift fays, vol. VII. p. 64. have been of great ufe to modern Criticks;
      " Though merely writ at firft for filling
      " To raife the volume's price a fhilling."

    Suppofe that your firft Letter is fent back ;
Yet fhe may yield upon the next attack.
If not; by art a Diamond rough in hue
Shall brighten up all-glorious to the view.
Soft water-drops the marble will deftroy,
And ten years fiege prove conqueror of Troy.
    Suppofe fh' has read, but then no anfwer gave :
It is fufficient fhe admits her flave.
Write on ; for time the freedom may obtain
Of having mutual love fent back again.
    Perhaps fhe writes, but 'tis to bid you ceafe,
And that your lines but difcompofe her peace.
This is a ftratagem of Cupid's war :
She'd, like a Parthian, wound you from afar,
And by this art your conftancy would try :
She's neareft much when feeming thus to fly.
Purfue the fair difdain through every place
That with her prefence fhe vouchfafes to grace.
If to the Play fhe goes, be there, and fee
How Love rewarded makes the Comedy.
Fly to the Park, if thither fhe'd retire ;
Perhaps fome gentle breeze may fan the fire.
But if to Court, then follow, where you'll find
Majeftic Truth with facred Hymen join'd.
    It is in vain fome ftudy to profefs
Their inclination by too nice a drefs,
As not content with manly cleanlinefs.
Mien, fhape, or manner, no addition needs :
There's fomething carelefs that all art exceeds.
Adonis from his lonely folitudes,
Rough Thefeus landing from the briny floods,
Hippolytus frefh hunting from the woods,
O'er Heroines of race divine prevail'd,
Where powder'd wig and fnuff-box might have fail'd.
    No youth that's wife will to his figure truft,
As if fo fine to be accofted firft.
Diftrefs muft afk, and gratefully receive :
'Tis Heaven and Beauty's honour, they can give.
There's fome have thought that looking pale and wan,
With a fubmiffion that is lefs than man,

Might gain their end; but funk in the attempt,
And found, that which they merited, contempt.
  Gain but admittance, half your ftory's told:
There's nothing then remains but to be bold.
Venus and Fortune will affift your claim, 590
And Cupid dart the breaft at which you aim.
No need of ftudied fpeech, or fkilful rules:
Love has an eloquence beyond the fchools;
Where fofteft words and accents will be found
All flowing in to form the charming found. 595
Of her you love bright images you'll raife:
When juft, they are not flattery, but praife.
What can be faid too much of what is good,
Since an immortal fame is Virtue's food?
  For nine years fpace Egypt had fruitlefs ftood, 600
Without the aid of Nile's prolific flood,
When Thrafius faid, " That blefling to regain,
" The Gods require a ftranger fhould be flain."
" Be thou the man," (the fierce Bufiris cries:)
" I'll make th'advifer his own facrifice;
" Nor can he blame the voice by which he dies."
    Perillus, firft and laft of's trade,
    For Phalaris a Bull had made:
    With fire beneath, and water hot,
    He put the brafier in the pot, 610
    And gave him, like an honeft fellow,
    Precedence in his Bull to bellow.
The Tyrants both did right: No law more juft
Than, " He that thinks of ill, fhould feel it firft."
Curft be their arts, unftudied be their trade, 615
Who female truth by falfehood would invade:
That can betray a friend or kinfman's names,
And by that covert hide unlawful flames:
Whofe eager paffion finds its fure relief,
When terminating in another's grief: 620
Carelefs hereafter what they promife now,
To the Æolian winds commit their vow;
Then cite th' example of the faithlefs Jove,
Who laughs, they fay, at perjury in Love.

They

They think they have a thoufand ways to pleafe,   625
Ten thoufand more to rob the mind of eafe.
For, as the earth in various birth abounds,
Their humour dances in fantaftic rounds;
Like Proteus, can be Lion, River, Bear,
A Tree, or any thing that's fram'd of air.   630
Thus they lay fnares, thus they fet off their bait
With all the fine allurements of deceit.
But they who through this courfe of mifchief run
Will find that fraud is various, Virtue ONE.

     Achilles, a gigantic boy,   635
   Was wanted at the fiege of Troy:
   His country's danger did require him,
   And all the generals did defire him:
   For Difcord, you muft know, had thrown
   An Apple where 'twas two to one   640
   But, if a ftir was made about it,
   Two of the three muft go without it:
   And fo it was; for Paris gave it
   To Venus, who refolv'd to have it.
   (The ftory here would be too long;   645
   But you may find it in the Song.)
   Venus, although not over-virtuous,
   Yet ftill defigning to be courteous,
   Refolved to procure the varlet
   A flaming and triumphant harlot;   650
   Firft ftol'n by one fhe would not ftay with,
   Then married to be run away with.
   Her Paris carried to his mother,
   And thence in Greece arofe that pother,
   Of which old Homer, Virgil, Dante,   655
   And Chaucer, make us fuch a cant.
   It was a juft and noble caufe,
   The breach of hofpitable laws:
   Though done to one, yet common grief
   Made all unite to feek relief.   660
   But, when they fought the country round,
   There's no Achilles could be found.
   His mother was afraid t' have loft him,
   And therefore thus fhe did accoft him:

                    " My

" My pretty dear, let me perſuade ye   665
" This once for to becõme a lady.
" This petticoat and mantua take,
" And wear this nighttrail for my ſake.
" I've made your knots all of the ſmalleſt,
" Becauſe you're ſomething of the talleſt.   670
" I'd have you never go unlac'd,
" For fear of ſpoiling of your waiſt.
" Now languiſh on me—ſcorn me now—
" Smile—frown—run—laugh—I ſee 'twill do.
" You'd perfect all you now begin,   675
" Only for poking out your chin."
     Him thus inſtructed ſoon ſhe ſends
To Lycomede, and there pretends
It was a daughter of a Friend's,
Who, grown full large by country feeding,   680
Was ſent to her to mend her breeding.
Herſelf had now no child, nor no man
To truſt but him, poor lonely woman !
That might reward him well hereafter,
If he would uſe her as his daughter.   685
In choice of names, as Iris, Chloe,
Pſyche and Phillis, ſhe took Zoe.
Th' old man receiv'd her, and expreſt
Much kindneſs for his topping gueſt :
Shew'd her his girls ; ſaid, " Whilſt ſhe'd ſtay,   690
" His Zoe ſhould be us'd as they."
At firſt there much reſerv'dneſs paſt ;
But, when acquaintance grew at laſt,
They'd jeſt, and every one would ſhew
Her works, which ſhe could never do.   695
One ſaid, her fingers were moſt fitting
For the moſt fiddling work of knitting.
Then one her wedding-bed would make,
And all muſt help her for love's ſake.
Zoe undreſt in night-gown tawdry   700
With clumſy fiſt muſt work embroidery ;
Whilſt others try her greaſy clunches
With ſtoning currants in whole bunches.

Q   But

But there was one, call'd Dedamy,
Miftrufted fomething by the by,   705
And, fighing, thus one night fhe faid,
" Why, Zoe, mayn't we go to bed ?"—
" Soon as you pleafe, good Miftrefs Ded."

   The fleeting months foon roll about;
Time came when murder all muft out.   710
Zoe, for fear of the old man,
Into the army quickly ran;
And fav'd the flitting of his nofe,
By timely changing of her cloaths.

   Thus, whilft we Glory's dictates fhun,   715
Into the fnares of Vice we run:
And he that fhould his country ferve,
And beauty by his worth deferve,
In female foftnefs wanton ftays,
And what he fhould adore betrays.   720

PART VI.

BUT now, O happy Youth, thy prize is found,
  And all thy wifhes with fuccefs are crown'd.
Not Io Pœans, when Apollo's prais'd;
Not trophies to victorious Grecians rais'd;
Not acclamations of exalted Rome,   725
To welcome Peace with her Auguftus home;
Can more delight a brave and generous mind,
Than it muft you to fee a Beauty kind:
The bays to me with gratitude you'll give,
Like Hefiod and like Homer make me live.   730
Thus Pelops on triumphant chariot brought
Hippodamy with his life's danger bought.
Thus profperous Jafon, rich with golden fleece,
On Argos' vocal timber fail'd to Greece.

   But ftay, fond Youth, the danger is not paft: 755
You're not arriv'd in port, nor anchor caft.

From

From you my art may ſtill more bays deſerve,
If what by me you gain'd, by me you ſhall preſerve.
Nor than the conqueſt is the glory leſs
To fix the throne on that which you poſſeſs.   740
Now, Erato, divineſt, ſofteſt Muſe,
Whoſe name and office both do Love infuſe,
Aſſiſt my great deſign: If Venus' Son,
That vagabond, would from his Mother run,
And then, with ſoaring wings and body light,   745
Thro' the vaſt world's extent would take his flight;
By artful bonds let me ſecure his ſtay,
And make his univerſal Power obey.
　　　Whilſt I my art would thus improve,
　　And fondly thought to ſhackle Love,   750
　　Two neighbours that were ſtanding by,
　　Tormented both with jealouſy,
　　Told me it was in vain to try.
When one began his tale, as thus:
　　" Perhaps you've heard of Dædalus,   755
" When Minos would have made him ſtay,
" How through the clouds he found his way.
" He was a workman wiſe and good,
" Building was what he underſtood.
" Like to the houſe where we act Plays,   760
" He made a turning winding maze,
" Fitting to harbour acts of ſin,
" And put a Whore and Baſtard in.
　　" I've done your work; and now my truſt is,
" Good Sir, that you will do me juſtice.   765
" 'Tis true I hither fled for murther;
" Let my misfortunes go no further:
" Some end all puniſhments ſhould have.
" Birth to the wretch my country gave:
" Let it afford me now a grave.
" Diſmiſs my ſon; at leaſt, if rather
" You'd keep the boy, diſmiſs his Father.
" This he might ſay, and more, or ſo;
" But Minos would not let him go.
" At this he was enrag'd, and cried,   775
　" It is in danger wit is tried:

" Minos poffeffes Earth and Sea;
" The fky and fire are left for me.
" Pardon my fond attempt, great Jove,
" If I approach your feats above.
" It is neceffity that draws
" A new-invented rule for Nature's laws.

    " Thus he began: Full many a feather
" With twine of thread he ftitch'd together:
" (Abundance more than are enough
" To make your wife and mine a muff.)
" Thus he frames wings, and nothing lacks.
" To fix the whole, but melted wax:
" That was the work of the young boy
" Pleas'd at the fancy of the toy;
" Not gueffing, ere he was much older,
" He fhould have one upon each fhoulder.
" To whom his Father: Here's the Ship
" By which we muft from Minos flip.
" Child, follow me juft as I fly on,
" And keep your eye fix'd on Orion:
" I'll be your guide; and never fear,
" Conducted by a Father's care.
" The Virgin and Bootes fhun.
" Take heed left you approach the Sun;
" His flaming influence will be felt,
" And the diffufive wax will melt.
" The fea by rifing fogs difcover;
" O'er that, be fure, you never hover.
" It would be difficult to drag
" Your wetted pinions, fhould they flag.
" Between them both, the fky is fair,
" No winds or hurricanes are there,
" But you may fan the fleeting air.
    " Thus fpeaking, he with whipcord ftrings
" Faftens, and then extends, the wings:
" And, when the youth's completely dreft,
" Juft as the Eag'e from her neft
" By gentle flights her Eaglet tries
" To dare the fun, and mount the fkies;

" The Father fo his Boy prepares,
" Not without kifs and falling tears.
" In a large plain, a rifing height
" Gives fome affiftance to their flight,
" With a quick fpring and fluttering noife,   820
" They in the fky their bodies poife.
" Back on his Son the Father looks,
" Praifing his fwift and even ftrokes.
" Now dreadlefs, with bold art fupplied,
" He does on airy billows ride,
" And foar with an ambitious pride.
" Mortals, who by the limpid flood
" With patient angle long have ftood,
" On the fmooth water's fhining face
" See the amazing creatures pafs,   830
" Look up aftonifh'd, whilft the reed
" Drops from the hand whofe fenfe is dead;
" Roll'd by the wind's impetuous hafte
" They Samos now and Naxos paft,
" Paros, and Delos bleft abode   835
" And parent of the Clarian God.
" Lebinthus on their right hand lies,
" And fweet Calydne's Groves arife,
" And fam'd Aftypalæa's Fens
" Breeds fhoals of fifh in owzy dens ;   840
" When the unwary Boy, whofe growing years
" Ne'er knew the worth of cautious fears,
" Mounts an æthereal hill, whence he might fpy
" The lofty regions of a brighter fky.
" Far from his Father's call and aid   845
" His wings in glittering fire difplay'd,
" Whofe ambient heat their plume involves,
" And all their liquid bands diffolves.
" He fees his loofen'd pinions drop ;
" On naked arms lies all his hope.   850
" From the vaft concave precipice he finds
" A fwift deftruction finking with the winds.
" Beneath him lies a gaping deep,
" Whofe womb is equally as fteep.

L 2

" Then,

 " Then, " Father! Father!" he'd have cried:
 " Tempests the trembling sounds divide,
 " Whilst difmal fear contracts his breath,
 " And the rough wave completes his death.
" My Son! my Son!" long might the Father cry:
" There is no track to feek him in the Sky.
 " By floating wings his body found
 " Is cover'd with the neighbouring ground.
" His art, though not fuccefsful, has its fame,
" And the Icarian feas preferve his name."
     If men from Minos could efcape,
And into Birds transform their fhape,
And there was nothing that could hold them,
Provided feathers might be fokl them;
The thought from madnefs furely fprings
To fix a God that's born with wings.
     Quoth t'other man, " Sir, if you'll tarry,
" I'll tell you a tale of my Boy Harry,
" Would make a Man afraid to marry.
" This Boy does oft from paper white
" In miniature produce a Kite.
" With tender hands the wood he bends,
" On which the body he extends:
" Pafte made of flour with water mix'd
" Is the cement by which 'tis fix'd:
" Then fciffars from the maid he'll borrow,
" With promife of return to-morrow.
" With thofe he paper nicely cuts,
" Which on the fides for wings he puts.
" The tail, that's an effential part,
" He manages with equal art;
" With paper fhreds at diftance tied,
" As not too near, nor yet too wide,
" Which he to fitting length extends,
" Till with a tuft the fabrick ends.
" Next packthread of the eveneft twine,
" Or fometimes filk, he'll to it join,
" Which, by the guidance of his hand,
" Its rife or downfall may command;

" Or carry meſſengers, to ſee
" If all above in order be.   895
" Then wanton Zephyrs fan it till it riſe,
" And through æthereal rills ploughs up the azure ſkies.
      " Sometimes in ſilent ſhade of night
" He'll make it ſhine with wondrous light
" By lanthern with tranſparent folds,   900
" Which flaming wax in ſafety holds.
" This glittering with myſterious rays
" Does all the neighbourhood amaze.
" Then comes the Conjurer o'th' place,
" With legs aſquint and crooked face,   905
" Who with his ſpying-pole from far
" Pronounces it a Blazing-ſtar :
" That wheat ſhall fall, and oats be dear,
" And barley ſhall not ſpring that year:
" That murrain ſhall infect all kine,   910
" And meaſles will deſtroy the ſwine :
" That fair maids ſweethearts ſhall fall dead
" Before they loſe their maidenhead ;
" And widows ſhall be forc'd to tarry
" A month at leaſt before they marry.   915
" But, whilſt the fool his thought enjoys,
" The whole contrivance was my Boy's.
" Now, mark me, 'twas from ſuch like things
" The Poets fram'd out Cupid's wings.
" If a Child's nature thus can ſoar,
" And all this lies within his power,
" His Mother ſurely can do more:
" Pray tell me what is to be done,
" If ſhe'll with Cuckold-makers run.
" No watchful care of jealous eye
" Can hinder, if eſcape ſhe'll try ;
" The Kite will to her carrion fly."
Where native Modeſty the mind ſecures,
The Huſband has no need of locks and doors;
The ſpecious Comet fram'd by Jealouſy   930
Will prove deluſion all, and all a lie.

PART VII.

NOT all the Herbs by sage Medea found,
Not Marsan drugs, though mixt with magic sound,
Not philtres studied by Thessalian art,
Can fix the mind, and constancy impart.   935
Could these prevail, Jason had felt their charms;
Ulysses still had died in Circe's arms.
Continue lovely, if you'll be belov'd:
Virtue from Virtue's bands is ne'er remov'd.
Like Nireus beautiful, like Hylas gay;   940
By Time the blooming outside will decay.
See Hyacinth again of form bereft,
And only thorns upon the rose-tree left.
Then lay up stores of learning and of wit,
Whose fame shall scorn the Acherontic pit,   945
And, whilst those fleeting shadows vainly fly,
Adorn the better part which cannot die.

Ulysses had no magick in his face;
But then his eloquence had charming grace,
Such as could force itself to be believ'd,   950
And all the watery Goddesses deceiv'd:
To whom Calypso from her widow'd shore
Sends him these sighs, which furious tempests bore.
 " Your passage often I by art delay'd;
 " Oblig'd you more, the more to be betray'd.   955
 " Here you have often on this rolling sand
 " Describ'd your scene of war with slender wand.
 " Here's Troy, and this circumference its walls:
 " Here Simoïs gently in the ocean falls:
 " Here lies my camp: these are the spacious fields   960
 " Where to this sword the crafty Dolon yields.
 " This of Sithonian Rhesus is the tent——
 " On with the pleasing tale your language went,
 " When a tenth wave did with one flash destroy
 " The platform of imaginary Troy.   965
 " By fear like this I would enforce your stay,
 " To see what names the waters toss'd away.

" I took

" I took you caſt up helpleſs by the ſea:
" Thouſands of happy hours you paſs'd with me;
" No mention made of old Penelope.
" On adamant our wrongs we all engrave,
" But write our benefits upon the wave.
" Why then be gone, the ſeas uncertain truſt;
" As I found *you*, ſo may you find them juſt.
" Dying Calypſo muſt be left behind,   975
" And all your vows be wafted with the wind!"
    Fond are the hopes he ſhould be conſtant now,
Who to his tendereſt part had broke his vow.
By artful charms the Miſtreſs ſtrives in vain
The looſe inconſtant wanderer to gain.
Shame is her entrance, and her end is pain.

PART VIII.

INDULGENCE ſoon takes with a noble mind:
Who can be harſh that ſees another kind?
Moſt times the greateſt art is to comply
In granting that which juſtice might deny.   985
We form our tender plants by ſoft degrees,
And from a warping ſtem raiſe ſtately trees.
To cut th' oppoſing waves we ſtrive in vain;
But, if we riſe with them, and fall again,
The wiſh'd-for land with eaſe we may attain.
Such complaiſance will a rough humour bend,
And, yielding to one failure, ſave a friend.
Mildneſs and temper have a force divine,
To make ev'n paſſion with their nature join.
The Hawk we hate, as living ſtill in arms,   995
And Wolves aſſiduous in the Shepherd's harms.
The ſociable Swallow has no fears:
Upon our towers the Dove her neſt prepares,
And both of them live free from human ſnares.
Far from loud rage and echoing noiſe of fights   1000
The ſofteſt Love in gentle ſound delights.

L 4

Smooth

Smooth mirth, bright smiles, calm peace, and flowing joy,
Are the companions of the Paphian boy :
Such as when Hymen first his mantle spread
All o'er the sacred down which made the bridal bed.   1005
These blandishments keep Love upon the wing,
His presence fresh, and always in the spring :
This makes a prospect endless to the view,
With light that rises still, and still is new.
At your approach find every thing serene,   1010
Like Paphos honour'd by the Cyprian Queen,
Who brings along her daughter Harmony,
With Muses sprung from Jove and Graces Three.
Birds shot by you, Fish by your angle caught,
The Golden Apples from Hesperia brought,   1015
The blushing Peach, the fragrant Nectareens,
Laid in fresh beds of flowers and scented greens,
Fair Lilies strew'd with bloody Mulberries,
Or Grapes whose juice made Bacchus reach the skies,
May oftentimes a grateful present make,   1020
Not for the value, but the giver's sake.

    Perhaps she may at vacant hours peruse
The happy product of your easy Muse.
Far from intrigue and scandal be your verse ;
But praise of virgin modesty rehearse :   1025
Mausolus by his consort deified :
How for Admetus blest Alcestis died.
Since Overbury's " Wife [e]," no Poets seem
T' have chose a wiser or a nobler theme.

You'd

[e] This poem, supposed to have been written for the earl of Somerset,
is the character of a good woman; just the reverse of the lady that
his friend married. It is printed with his Characters, &c. and had gone
through sixteen editions in 1638 ; the last, a very accurate one,
was published by Mr. Capell, with other pieces of antient Poetry, in
8vo, 1770.—Sir Thomas Overbury, a gentleman of eminent parts and
learning, and of judgement and experience beyond his years, was
long the friend and confident of Robert Car, earl of Somerset. His
abilities were of singular service to that favourite, who did nothing without
his advice and direction ; and was accustomed to make use of his pen in
his addresses to the king and to his mistress. Overbury, who was naturally
haughty and overbearing, presumed to oppose the earl's marriage with the
countess

You'd help a neighbour, would a friend prefer,   1030
Pardon a fervant, let all come from her.
Thus what you grant if fhe muft recommend,
'Twill make a mutual gift and double friend.
So, when pale want is craving at the door,
We fend our favourite fon to help the poor;   1035
Pleas'd with their grateful prayers that he may live,
And find what heavenly pleafure 'tis to give.
Praife all her actions, think her drefs is fine ;
Embroideries with gold, pearl, diamonds, join :
Your wealth does beft, when plac'd on beauty, fhine.
If fhe in tabby waves encircled be,
Think Amphytrite rifes from the fea.
If by her the purpureal velvet's worn,
Think that fhe rifes like the blufh of morn ;

countefs of Effex, and expected the fame deference to be paid to his judgement on this as upon every other occafion. This oppofition drew upon
him the rage of the earl, and the fury of the countefs ; who determined on
his ruin, and fpeedily effected it. In the guife of friendfhip, Car reprefented to the king that it was neceffary to remove Overbury from the
court by fome honourable employment, and advifed his being fent ambaffador to Mufcovy. The king confented. But the perfidious minion
prevailed on his credulous friend to decline the appointment ; and then
requefted the monarch to punifh him for his refufal. He was committed
to The Tower ; where his death, which was feveral times in vain attempted, was at laft effected, by a poifoned clyfter, Sept. 15, 1613. A
tragedy founded on this fad event, is among the works of Mr. Savage.—
Mrs. Turner, who has been mentioned vol. I. p. 162, was an active accom-
plice in this murder. We are told by Mr. Oldmixon, in " The Life and
" Pofthumous Works of Arthur Maynwaring, efq." p. 3, that fhe was
a known miftrefs of that gentleman's grandfather, Sir Arthur ; who was a
courtier in the reign of James I, a favourite of Prince Henry, and a man
of gallantry. When the Countefs and Mrs. Turner intended to practice
their infernal experiments on the Earl of Effex by powders and philtres,
they were affifted with drugs by Dr. Foreman, of Lambeth, an eminent
Quack ; and Mrs. Turner, to try how effectually they would operate,
gave them firft to Sir Arthur Maynwaring, who was fo enflamed by
them, that he rode fifteen miles, through a ftorm of rain and thunder,
to Turner's houfe. Wilfon, in his Life of King James, fays, he fcarce
knew where he was, till he was there.

And

And when her filks afar from Indus come,
Wrought in Chinefe or in the Perfian loom,
Think that fhe then like Pallas is array'd,
By whofe myfterious art the wheel was made.
Each day admire her different graceful air,
In which fhe winds her bright and flowing hair.
With her when dancing let your genius fly :
When in her fong the note expires, then die.
    If in the Autumn, when the wafting year
Its plenty fhews, that foon muft difappear ;
When fwelling Grape and Peach with lovely hue,
And Pear and Apple, frefh with fragrant dew,
By tempting look and tafte perhaps invite
That which we feldom rule, our appetite ;
When noxious heat and fudden cold divides
The time o'er which bale influence prefides ;
Her feverifh blood fhould pulfe unufual find, ,
Or vaporous damps of fpleen fhould fink her mind ;
Then is the time to fhew a Lover's cares :
Sometimes enlarge her hopes, contract her fears.
Give the falubrious draughts with your own hand :
Perfuafion has the force of a command.
Watch and attend ; then your reward will prove,
When fhe recovers, full increafe of Love.
        Far from this Love is haughty pride,
        Which antient Fables beft deride :
        Women imperious, void of fhame,
        And carelefs of their Lovers' fame,
        Who of tyrannic follies boaft,
        Tormenting him that loves them moft.
        When Hercules, by labours done,
        Had prov'd himfelf to be Jove's fon ;
        By peace which he to Earth had given,
        Deferv'd to have his reft in Heaven ;
        Envy, that ftrives to be unjuft,
        Refolv'd to mortify him firft ;
        And that he fhould enamour'd be
        Of a proud jilt call'd Omphalé,
        Who fhould his Herofhip expofe
        By fpinning hemp in womens cloaths.

Her mind she did vouchsafe one day,   1085
Thus to her Lover to display :
 " Come quickly, Sir, off with this Skin :
" Think you I'll let a Tanner in ?
" If you of Lions talk, or Boars,
" You certainly turn out of doors.   1090
" Your club's abundantly too thick
" For one shall move a fiddle-stick.
" What should you do with all those arrows ?
" I will have nothing kill'd but Sparrows.
" Heccy, this day you may remember ;   1095
" For you shall see a Lady's chamber.
" Let me be rightly understood :
" What I intend is for your good.
" In boddice I design to lace ye,
" And so among my Maids I'll place ye.   1100
" When you're genteeler grown, and thinner,
" May be I'll call you up to dinner.
" With arms so brawny, fists so red,
" You'll scrub the rooms, or make the bed.
" You can't stick pins, or frieze my hair.   1105
" Bless me ! you've nothing of an air.
" You'll ne'er come up to working point :
" Your fingers all seem out of joint.
" Then besides, Heccy, I must tell ye
" An idle hand has empty belly :   1110
" Therefore this morning I'll begin,
" Try how your clumsiness will spin.
" You are my shadow, do you see :
" Your hope, your thought, your wish all be,
" Invented and control'd by me.
" Look up whene'er I laugh ; look down
" With trembling horror, if I frown.
" Say as I say : servants can't lie.
" Your truth is my propriety.
" Nay, you should be to torture brought,   1120
" Were I but jealous you transgrest in thought ;
" Or if from Jove your single wish should crave
" The fate of not continuing still my slave.

           " There

" There is no Lover that is wife
" Pretends to win at cards or dice.   1125
" 'Tis for his Miftrefs all is thrown:
" Th' ill-fortune his, the good her own.
" Melanion, whilom lovely youth,
" Fam'd for his valour and his truth,
" Whom every beauty did adorn   1130
" Fresh as Aurora's blufhing morn,
" Into the horrid woods is run,
" Where he ne'er fees the ray of fun,
" Nor to his palace dares return,
" Where he for Pfyche's love did burn,   1135
" And found correction at her hands
" For difobeying juft commands ;
" But muft his filent penance do
" For once not buckling of her fhoe :
" A good example, child, for you.
" Which fhews you, when we have our fool,
" We've policy enough to rule :
" I might have made you fuch a fellow,
" As fhould have carried my umbrella,
" Or bore a flambeau by my chair,   1145
" And had the mob not come too near;
" Or lay the cloth, or wait at table ;
" Nay been a helper in the ftable.
     " To my commands obedience pay
" At dead of night, or break of day.   1150
" Speed is your province ; if 'tis I
" That bid you run, you ought to fly.
" He that Love's nimble paffion feels
" Will foon outftrip my chariot wheels.
" Thro' Dog-ftar's heat he'll tripping go,
" Nor leaves he print upon the fnow.
" The wind itfelf to him is flow.
" He that in Cupid's wars would fight,
" Grief, winter, dirty roads, and night,
" A bed of earth midft fhowers of rain,   1160
" After no fupper, are his gain.
" Bright Phœbus took Admetus' pay,
" And in a little cottage lay :

" All

" All this he did for fear of Jove;
" And who would not do more for Love?   1165
" If entrance is by locks denied,
" Then through the roof or window flide,
" Leander each night fwam the feas,
" That he might thereby Hero pleafe.
" Perhaps I may be pleas'd to fee   1170
" Your life in danger, when for me.
" You'll find my fervants in a row;
" Remember then you make your bow;
" For they are your fuperiors now.
" No matter if you do engage   1175
" My Porter, Woman, favourite Page,
" My Dog, my Parrot, Monkey, Black, -
" Or any thing that does partake
" Of that admittance which you lack.
" But after all you mayn't prevail,   1180
" And your moft glittering hopes may fail:
" For Ceres does not always yield
" The crop entrufted to the field.
" Fair gales may bring you to a coaft
" Where you'll by hidden rocks be loft.   1185
" Love is tenacious of its joys,
" Gives fmall reward for great employs;
" But has as many griefs in ftore
" As Shells by Neptune caft on fhore.
" As Athos Hares, as Hybla Bees,   1190
" Olives on the Palladian trees.
" And, when his angry arrows fall,
" They're not found ting'd with common gall.
" You're told I'm not at home, 'tis true:
" I may be there, but not for you;
" And I may let you fee it too.
" Perhaps I bad you come at night:
" If the door's fhut, ftay till 'tis light.
" Perhaps my Maid fhall bid you go:
" A thing fhe knows you dare not do.   1200
" Your rival fhall admiffion gain,
" And laugh to fee his foe in pain.

" All

" All this and more you muſt endure,
" If you from me expect a cure.
" 'Tis fitting I ſhould ſearch the wound,　　1205
" Leſt all your danger be not found."
When eaſy fondneſs meets with woman's pride,
Nothing which *that* can aſk muſt be denied.
He that enjoy'd the names of great and brave
Is pleas'd to ſeem a female and a ſlave:　　1210
The Hero, number'd with the gods before,
Is ſo debas'd as to be man no more.

P A R T　IX.

NOT by the ſail with which you put to ſea
Can you where Thetis ſwells conducted be,
To the ſame port you'll different paſſage find　　1215
And fill your ſheets ev'n with contrarious wind.
You nurs'd the Fawn, now grown Stag wondrous big,
And ſleep beneath the ſhade you knew a twig.
The bubbling ſpring, increas'd by floods and rain,
Rolls with impetuous ſtream, and foams the main:　　1220
So Love augments in juſt degrees; at length
By nutrimental fires it gains its ſtrength.
Daily till midnight let kind looks or ſong,
Or tales of love, the pleaſing hours prolong.
No wearineſs upon their bliſs attends　　1225
Whom marriage vows have render'd more than friends.
So Philomels of equal mates poſſeſſ,
With a congenial heat, and downy reſt,
And care inceſſant, hover o'er their neſt:
Hence from their eggs (ſmall worlds whence all things ſpring)　1230
Produce a race by nature taught to ſing;
Who ne'er to this harmonious air had come,
Had their parental love ſtray'd far from home.
By a ſhort abſence mutual joys increaſe:
'Tis from the toils of war we value peace.　　1235
When Jove a while the fruitful ſhower reſtrains,
The field on his return a brighter verdure gains.

So let not grief too much difturb thofe hearts,
Which for a while the war or bufinefs parts.
'Twas hard to let Protefilaus go,   1240
Who did his death by oracles foreknow.
Ulyffes made indeed a tedious ftay,
His twenty winters abfence was delay;
But happinefs revives with his return,
And Hymen's altars with frefh incenfe burn :   1245
Tales of his fhip, her web, they both recount;
Pleas'd that their wedlock faith all dangers could furmount.
    Make thou fpeed back; hafte to her longing arms :
She may have real or impending harms.
There are no minutes in a Lover's fears :   1250
They meafure all their time by months and years.
        Poets are always Virtue's friends,
    'Tis what their Mufe ftill recommends: |
    But then the fatal track it fhows
    Where devious vice through trouble goes.   1255
    They tell us, how a hufband's care
Negle&ed leaves a wife too fair
In hands of a young fpark call'd Paris;
And how the beauteous truft mifcarries.
With kindnefs he receives the youth,   1260
Whofe modeft looks might promife truth :
Then gives him opportunity
To throw the fpecious vizard by.
The man had things to be adjufted,
With which the wife fhould not be trufted;   1265
And, whilft he gave himfelf the loofe,
Left her at home to keep the houfe.
    When Helen faw his back was turn'd,
The devil a bit the gipfy mourn'd.
Says fhe, " 'Tis his fault to be gone;   1270
" It fha'n't be mine to lie alone.
" A vacant pillow's fuch a jeft,
" That with it I could never reft.
" He ne'er confider'd his own danger,
" To leave me with a handfome ftranger.   1275
" Wolves would give good account of Sheep,
" Left to their vigilance to keep.

                                            " Pray

" Pray who, except 'twere Geese or Widgeons,
" Would hire a Hawk to guard their Fidgeons?
     " Suppofing then it might be faid   1280
     " That Menelaus now were dead:
     " A pretty figure I fhould make
     " To go in mourning for his fake.
     " She that in widow's garb appears,
     " Efpecially when at my years,
     " May feem to be at her laft prayers.
     " But I'll ftill have my heart divided
     " 'Twixt one to lofe, and one provided.
     " He that is gone, is gone: lefs fear
     " Of wanting him that I have here."   1290
     The fequel was the Fire of Troy
Brought to deftruction by this Boy.
     They tell us, How a Wife provok'd,
And to a brutifh Hufband yok'd,
Who, by diftracting paffion led,   1295
Scorns all her charms, and flies her bed,
When on her Rival fhe has feiz'd,
Seems with a fecret horror pleas'd.
They then defcribe her like fome Boar
Plunging his tufk in Maftiff's gore;   1300
Or Lionefs, whofe ravifh'd whelp
Roars for his Mother's furious help;
Or Bafilifk when rouz'd, whofe breath,
Teeth, fting, and eye-balls, all are death;
Like franticks ftruck by magic rod   1305
Of fome defpis'd avenging God:
Make her through blood for vengeance run,
Like Progne facrifice her fon,
And like Medea dart thofe fires
By which Creüfa's ghoft expires.   1310
Then let her with exalted rage
Her grief with the fame crimes affuage.
To heighten and improve the curfe,
Becaufe he's bad, they make her worfe.
So Tyndaris diffolves in tears,   1315
When firft fhe of Chryfeïs hears;

                                                     But

But when Lyrneffis captive's led,
And ravifh'd to defile her bed,
Her patience leffens by degrees;
But when at laft fhe Priameïs fees,
Revenge does to Ægyftus fly for eafe;
In his adulterous arms does plots difclofe,
Which fill Mycenæ with ftupendous woes,
And parricide and hell around her throws.

Ye Heavenly Powers, the female truth preferve,   1325
And let it not from native goodnefs fwerve;
And let no wanton toys become the caufe
Why men fhould break Hymen's eternal laws;
But let fuch fables and fuch crimes remain
Only as fictions of the Poet's brain: 1330
Yet marks fet up to fhun thofe dangerous fhelves
On which deprav'd mankind might wreck themfelves!

PART X.

AT firft, the ftars, the air, the earth, and deep,
Lay all confus'd in one unorder'd heap.
Till Love Eternal did each being ftrike   1335
With voice Divine to march, and feek its Like.
Then feeds of Heavens, then Air of vapourous found,
Then fertile Earth circled with Waters round,
On which the Bird, the Beaft, the Fifh, might move,
All center'd in that univerfal Love.   1340
Then Man was fram'd with foul of godlike ray,
And had a nobler fhare of Love than they:
To him was Woman crown'd with virtue given,
The moft immediate work and care of Heaven.

Whilft thus my darling thoughts in raptures fung,   1345
Apollo to my fight in vifion fprung.
His lyre with golden ftrings his touch commands,
And wreaths of laurel flourifh in his hands.
Says he, " You Bard that of Love's precepts treat,
" Your art at Delphi you will beft complete.   1350

" There's a fhort maxim, prais'd when underftood,
" Ufeful in practice, and divinely good,
" LET EACH MAN KNOW HIMSELF: ftrive to excel;
" The pleafure of the bleft is doing well.
   " 'Tis wifdom to difplay the ruling grace.   1355
" Some men are happy in a charming face:
" Know it, but be not vain. Some manly fhow
" By the exploded gun and nervous bow.
" There let them prove their fkill; perhaps fome heart
" May find that every fhot is Cupid's dart.   1360
" The prudent Lover, if his talent lies
" In eloquence, e'nt talkative, but wife;
" So mixes words delicious to the ear,
" That all muft be perfuaded who can hear.
" He that can fing, let him with pleafing found,   1365
" Though 'tis an air that is not mortal, wound.
" Let not a Poet my own art refufe:
" I'll come, and bring affiftance to his Mufe."
   But never by ill means your fortune pufh,
Nor raife your credit by another's blufh.   1370
The fecret rites of Ceres none profane,
Nor tell what Gods in Samo-thracia reign.
'Tis virtue by grave filence to conceal
What talk without difcretion would reveal.
For fault like this now Tantalus does lie   1375
In midft of fruits and water, ftarv'd and dry.
But Cytherea's modefty requires
Moft care to cover all her lambent fires.
   Love has a pleafing turn, makes that feem beft,
Of which our lawful wifhes are poffeft.   1380
Andromeda, of Libyc hue and blood,
Was chain'd a prey to monfters of the flood:
Wing'd Perfeus faw her beauty through that cloud.
Andromache had large majeftic charms;
Therefore was fitteft grace to godlike Hector's arms. 1385
Beauties in fmaller airs bear like commands,
And wondrous Magick acts by flendereft wands.
Like Cybele fome bear a mother's fway,
Whilft infant Gods and Heroines obey.

Some

Some rule like ftars by guidance of their eyes,　1390
And others pleafe when like Minerva wife.
Love will from 'Heaven, Art, Nature, Fancy raife
Something that may exalt its Confort's praife.
　　There will be little jealoufies,
　　By which Love's art its fubjects tries.　1393
　　They think it languifhes with reft;
　　But rifes, like the palm, oppreft.
　　And as too much profperity
　　Often makes way for luxury,
　　Till we, by turn of fortune taught,　1400
　Have wifdom by experience bought :
　　So when the hoary afhes grow
　　Around Love's coals, 'tis time to blow :
　　And then its craftinefs is fhown,
　　To raife your cares, to hide its own ;　1405
　And have you by a rival croft,
　　Only in hopes you mayn't be loft.
　　Sometimes they fay that you are faulty,
　　And that they know where you were naughty ;
　　And then perhaps your eyes they'd tear,
　Or elfe dilacerate your hair,
　　Not fo much for revenge as fear.
　　But fhe perhaps too far may run,
　　And do what fhe would have you fhun,
　　Of which there's a poetic ftory　1411
　That, if you pleafe, I'll lay before you.
　　Old Juno made her Jove comply
　　For fear, not afking when or why,
　　Unto a certain fort of matter,
　　Marrying her fon unto his daughter :　1420
　And fo to bed the couple went,
　　Not with their own, but friends confent.
　　This Vulcan was a Smith, they tell us,
　　That firft invented tongs and bellows ;
　　For breath and fingers did their works　1425
　(We'd fingers long before we'd forks) ;
　　Which made his hands both hard and brawny,
　　When wafh'd, of colour orange-tawny.

M 2

His

His whole complexion was a fallow,
Where black had not deſtroy'd the yellow.   1430
One foot was clump'd, which was the ſtronger,
T'other was ſpiny, though much longer ;
So both to the proportion come
Of the fore-finger and the thumb.
In ſhort, the whole of him was naſty,   1435
Ill-natur'd, vain, imperious, haſty :
Deformity alike took place
Both in his manners and his face.
Venus had perfect ſhape and ſize ;
But then ſhe was not over-wiſe :   1440
For ſometimes ſhe her knee is crimping
To imitate th' old man in limping.
Sometimes his dirty paws ſhe ſcorns,
Whilſt her fair fingers ſhew his horns.
But Mars, the Bully of the place, is   1445
The chiefeſt ſpark in her good graces.
At firſt they're ſhy, at laſt grow bolder,
And conjugal affection colder.
They car'd not what was ſaid or done,
Till impudence defied the Sun.   1450
   Vulcan was told of this; quoth he,
" Is there ſuch roguery ? I'll ſee !"
He then an iron net prepar'd,
Which he to the bed's teſter rear'd ;
Which, when a pully gave a ſnap,   1455
Would fall, and make a cuckold's trap.
All thoſe he plac'd in the beſt room,
Then feign'd that he muſt go from home ;
For he at Lemnos forges had,
And none but he to mind the trade.   1460
   Love was too eager to beware
Of falling into any ſnare.
They went to bed, and ſo were caught ;
And then they of repentance thought.
The ſhow being ready to begin,   1465
Vulcan would call his neighbours in.
Jove ſhould be there, that does make bold
With Juno, that notorious ſcold ;

Neptune

Neptune firſt Bargeman on the water ;
Thetis the Oyſter-woman's daughter ;   1470
Pluto that Chimney-ſweeping ſloven,
With Proſerpine hot from her oven ;
And Mercury, that's ſharp and cunning
In ſtealing cuſtoms and in running ;
And Dy the Midwife, though a Virgin ;   1475
And Æſculapius the Surgeon ;
Apollo, who might be Phyſician,
Or ſerve them elſe for a Muſician ;
The Piper Pan, to play her up ;
And Bacchus, with his chirping cup ;   1480
And Hercules ſhould bring his club in,
To give the Rogue a luſty drubbing ;
And all the Cupids ſhould be by,
To ſee their Mother's infamy.
    One Momus cried, " You're hugely pleas'd ;   1485
" I hope your mind will ſoon be eas'd :
" For, when ſo publicly you find it,
" People, you know, will little mind it.
" They love to tell what no one knows,
" And they themſelves only ſuppoſe.   1490
" Not every huſband can afford
" To be a Cuckold on record ;
" Nor ſhould he be a Cuckold ſtyl'd,
" That once or ſo has been beguil'd ;
" Unleſs he makes it demonſtration,
" Then puts it in ſome proclamation,
" With general voice of all the nation."
The company were come, when Vulcan hopping
And for his key in left-ſide pocket groping,
    Cries, " 'Tis but opening of that door   1500
" To prove myſelf a Cuckold, her a Whore."
    They all deſir'd his leave that they might go ;
They were not curious of ſo vile a ſhow :
Perſons concern'd might one another ſee,
And they'd believe ſince witneſſes were three.   1505
And they, thus prov'd to be ſuch fooliſh elves,
Might hear, try, judge, and e'en condemn themſelves.

M 3

Diſcretion

Difcretion covers that which it would blame,
Until fome fecret blufh and hidden fhame
Have cur'd the fault without the noife of fame.
　　The work is done : and now let Ovid have
Some gratitude attending on his grave ;
Th' afpiring palm, the verdant laurel ftrow,
And fweets of myrtle wreaths around it throw.
In Phyfick's Art as Podalirius fkill'd,   1515
Neftor in Court, Achilles in the Field ;
As Ajax had in fingle Combat force,
And as Automedon beft rul'd the Horfe ;
As Chalcas vers'd in Prophecies from Jove :
So Ovid has the Mafterfhip of Love.   1520
The Poet's honour will be much the lefs
Than that which by his means you may poffefs
In choice of Beauty's lafting happinefs.
But, when the Amazonian quits the field,
Let this be wrote on the triumphant fhield,
That fhe by Ovid's Art was brought to yield.
　　When Ovid's thoughts in Britifh ftyle you fee,
Which mayn't fo founding as the Roman be ;
Yet then admittance grant : 'tis fame to me.

P A R T XI.

I Who the art of war to Danaans gave,   1530
Will make Penthefilea's force as brave :
That both, becoming glorious to the fight,
With equal arms may hold a dubious fight.
What though 'twas Vulcan fram'd Achilles' fhield,
My Amazonian darts fhall make him yield.   1535
A myrtle crown with victory attends
Thofe who are Cupid's and Dione's friends.
When Beauty has fo many arms in ftore,
(Some men will fay) why fhould you give it more ?
Tell me who, when Penelope appears   1540
With conftancy maintain'd for twenty years ;

                                                   Who

Who can the fair Laodamia fee
In her Lord's arms expire as well as he;
Can view Alceftis, who with joy removes
From earth, inftead of him fhe fo much loves;   1545
Can hear of bright Evadne, who in fires
For her lov'd Capaneus prepar'd, expires,
When Virtue has itfelf a female name,
So Truth, fo Goodnefs, Piety, and Fame;
Would headftrong fight, and would not conquer'd be,   1550
Or ftoop to fo much generofity?
    'Tis not with fword, or fire, or ftrength of bow,
That Female warriors to their battle go:
They have no ftratagem, or fubtile wile;
Their native innocence can ne'er beguile: 1555
The Fox's various maze, Bear's cruel den,
They leave to fiercenefs and the craft of men.
'Twas Jafon that transferr'd his broken vows
From kind Medea to another fpoufe:
Thefeus left Gnoffis on the fands, to be   1560
Prey to the birds, or monfters of the fea:
Demophoon, nine times recall'd, forbore
Return, and let his Phillis name the fhore.
Æneas wrackt, and hofpitably us'd,
Fam'd for his piety, yet ftill refus'd   1565
To ftay where lov'd, but left the dangerous fword
By which fhe died to whom he broke his word.
Piteous examples! worthy better fate,
If my inftructions had not come too late:
For then their art and prudence had retain'd   1570
What firft victorious rays of beauty gain'd.
Whilft thus I thought, not without grief to find
Defencelefs Virtue meet with fate unkind,
Bright Cytherea's facred voice did reach
My tingling ears, and thus fhe bad me teach: 1575
    " What had the harmlefs maid deferv'd from thee?
" Thou haft given weapons to her enemy;
" Whilft in the field fhe muft defencelefs ftand,
" With want of fkill, and more unable hand.
" Stefichorus, who would no fubject find   1580
" But harm to maids, was by the Gods ftruck blind:

M 4

" But,

" But, when his song did with their glories rise,
" He had his own restor'd, to praise their eyes.
" Be rul'd by me, and arms defensive give;
" 'Tis by the Ladies favours you must live."   1585
    She then one mystic leaf with berries four
(Pluckt from her myrtle crown) bad me with speed devour.
I find the power infpir'd; through purer sky
My breath diffolves in verse, to make young Lovers die.
Here Modesty and Innocence shall learn   1590
How they may truth from flattering speech discern.
But come with speed: lose not the flying day.
See how the crowding waves roll down away,
And neither, though at Love's command, will stay.
These waves and time we never can recal;   1595
But, as the minutes pass, must lose them all.
Nor like what's past are days succeeding good,
But slide with warmth decay'd and thicker blood.
Flora, although a Goddess, yet does fear
The change that grows with the declining year;   1600
Whilst glistering snakes, by casting off their skin,
Fresh courage gain, and life renew'd begin.
The Eagles cast their bills, the Stag its horn;
But Beauty to that blessing is not born.

    Thus Nature prompts its use to forward Love,   1605
Grac'd by examples of the Powers above.
Endymion pierc'd the chaste Diana's heart,
And cool Aurora felt Love's fiery dart.

PART XII.

A Person of some quality
    Happen'd, they say, in Love to be   1610
With one who held him by delay,
Would neither say him No nor Ay,
Nor would she have him go his way.
    This Lady thought it best to send
For some experienc'd trusty friend,   1615

To whom she might her mind impart,
T' unchain her own, and bind his heart.
A Tire-woman by occupation,
A useful and a choice vocation.
She saw all, heard all, never idle;   1620
Her fingers or her tongue would fiddle;
Diverting with a kind of wit,
Aiming at all would sometimes hit;
Though in her sort of rambling way
She many a serious truth would say.   1625
Thus in much talk among the rest
The oracle itself exprest:
    " I've heard some cry, Well, I profess
" There's nothing to be gain'd by dress !
" They might as well say that a field,   1630
" Uncultivated, yet would yield
" As good a crop as that which skill
" With utmost diligence should till.
" Our vintage would be very fine,
" If nobody should prune their vine !   1635
" Good shape and air, it is confest,
" Is given to such as Heaven has blest ;
" But all folks have not the same graces ;
" There is distinction in our faces.
" There was a time I'd not repine   1640
" For any thing amiss in mine,
" Which, though I say it, still seems fair ;
" Thanks to my art as well as care !
" Our grandmothers, they tell us, wore
" Their Fardingale and their Bandore,   1645
" Their Pinners, Forehead-cloth, and Ruff,
" Content with their own cloth and stuff ;
" With Hats upon their pates like Hives,
" Things might become such Soldiers wives ;
" Thought their own faces still would last them   1650
" In the same mould which Nature cast them.
" Dark Paper Buildings then stood thick ;
" No Palaces of Stone or Brick :
" And then, alas ! were no Exchanges :
" But see how time and fashion changes !   1655
4   " I hate

" I hate old things and age. I fee,
" Thank Heaven, times good enough for me.
" Your Goldfmiths now are mighty neat :
" I love the air of Lombard-ftreet.
" Whate'er a Ship from India brings,   1660
" Pearls, Diamonds, Silks, are pretty things.
" The Cabinet, the Screen, the Fan,
" Pleafe me extremely, if Japan :
" And, what affects me ftill the more,
" They had none of them heretofore.   1665
" When you're unmarried, never load ye
" With Jewels; they may incommode ye.
" Lovers mayn't dare approach ; but moftly
" They'll fear when married you'll be coftly.
" Fine Rings and Lockets beft are tried   1670
" When given to you as a Bride.
" In the mean time you fhew your fenfe
" By going fine at fmall expence.
" Sometimes your Hair you upwards furl,
" Sometimes lay down in favourite curl.   1675
" All muft through twenty fiddlings pafs,
" Which none can teach you but your glafs.
" Sometimes they muft difhevel'd lie
" On neck of polifh'd ivory.
" Sometimes with ftrings of pearl they're fix'd,   1680
" And the united beauty mix'd;
" Or, when you won't their grace unfold,
" Secure them with a bar of gold.
" Humour and fafhions change each day ;
" Not birds in forefts, flowers in May,
" Would fooner number'd be than they.
" There is a fort of negligence,
" Which fome efteem as excellence,
" Your art with fo much art to hide,
" That nothing of it be defcried;   1690
" To make your carelefs treffes flow
" With fo much air, that none fhould know
" Whether they had been comb'd or no.
" But, in this fo neglected Hair,
" Many a heart has found its fnare.   1695

" Nature

" Nature indeed has kindly sent
" Us many things; more we invent:
" Little enough, as I may say,
" To keep our Beauty from decay.
" As leaves that with fierce winds engage,   1700
" Our curling tresses fall with age.
" But then by German herbs we find
" Colour, for locks to grey inclin'd.
" Sometimes we purchase hair; and why?
" Is not all *that* our own we buy?   1705
" You buy it publicly, say they:
" Why tell us that, when we don't pay.
" Of French *pomades* the town is full:
" Praise Heaven, no want of Spanish Wool!
" Let them look flusht, let them look dead,   1710
" That can't afford the White and Red.
" In Covent Garden you buy posies,
" There we our Lilies and our Roses.
" Who would a charming Eyebrow lack,
" Who can get any thing that's black?   1715
" Let not these boxes open lie:
" Some folks are too much given to pry.
" Art not dissembled would disgrace
" The purchas'd beauties of our face:
" This if such persons should discover,   1720
" 'Twould rather lose than gain a Lover.
" Who is there now but understands
" Searcloths to flea the face or hands?
" Though the idea's not so taking,
" And the skin seems but odd in making,   1725
" Yet, when 'twill with fresh lustre shine,
" Her spark will tell you 'tis divine.
" That Picture there your eye does strike;
" It is the work of great Van Dyck,
" Which by a Roman would be sainted: 1730
" What was't but canvas till 'twas painted?
" There's several things should not be known:
" O'er these there is a curtain drawn,
" 'Till 'tis their season to be shown.

" Your

" Your door on fit occasions keep   1735
" Fast shut: who knows but you're asleep?
" When our teeth, colour, hair, and eyes,
" And what else at the toilet lies,
" Are all put on, we're said to rise:
" There was a Lady whom I knew,   1740
" That must be nameless 'cause 'tis true,
" Who had the dismallest mischance
" I've heard of since I was in France?
" I do protest, the thoughts of it
" Have almost put me in a fit.   1745
" Old Lady Meanwell's chamber-door,
" Just on the stairs of the first floor,
" Stood open: and pray who should come,
" But Knowall flouncing in the room?
" No single hair upon her head: 1750
" I thought she would have fell down dead.
" At last she found a cap of hair,
" Which she put on with such an air,
" That every lock was out of place,
" And all hung dangling down her face.   1755
" I would not mortify one so,
" Except some twenty that I know.
" Her carelessness and her defect
" Were laid to Mistress Prue's neglect;
" And much ill-nature was betray'd   1760
" By noise and scolding with the maid.
" The young look on such things as stuff,
" Thinking their bloom has art enough.
" When smooth, we matter it not at all;
" 'Tis when the Thames is rough, we squawl.   1765
" But whate'er 'tis may be pretended,
" No face or shape but may be mended.
" All have our faults, and must abide them,
" We therefore should take care to hide them.
" You're short; sit still, you'll taller seem: 1770
" You're only shorter from the stem.
" By looser garb your leanness is conceal'd;
" By want of stays the grosser shape reveal'd.

                                        " The

" The more the blemishes upon the feet,
" The greater care the lace and shoes be neat.   1775
     " Some backs and sides are wav'd like billows:
     " These holes are best made up with pillows.
     " Thick fingers always should command
     " Without the stretching out the hand.
     " Who has bad teeth should never see   1780
     " A play, unless a Tragedy.
     " For we can teach you how to simper,
     " And when 'tis proper you should whimper.
     " Think that your grace and wit is now
" Not in your laughing at a thing, but how.   1785
     " Let room for something more than breath
     " Just shew the ends of milk-white teeth.
     " There is a *je n' scai quoy* is found
     " In a soft smooth affected sound :
     " But there's a shrieking crying tone,   1790
     " Which I ne'er lik'd, when all is done :
     " And there are some, who laugh like men,
     " As ne'er to shut their mouths again ;
     " So very loud and *mal-propos*,
     " They seem like hautboys to a show.   1795
     " But now for the reverse : 'tis skill
     " To let your tears flow when you will.
     " It is of use when people dye ;
     " Or else to have the spleen, and cry,   }
     " Because you have no Reason why.
     " Now for your talk—Come, let me see:
     " Here lose your *H*, here drop your *T* ;
     " Despise that *R* : your speech is better
     " Much for destroying of one letter.
     " Now lisp, and have a sort of pride   1805
     " To seem as if your tongue were tied.
     " This is such a becoming fault,
     " Rather than want, it should be taught,
        " And now that you have learnt to talk,
     " Pray let me see if you can walk.   1810
     " There's many dancing-masters treat
     " Of management of ladies feet.

                                    " There's

" There's fome their mincing gait have chofe,
" Treading without their heel or toes.
" She that reads Taffo f, or Malherbe g,   1815
" Chufes a ftep that is *fuperbe*.
" Some giddy creatures, as if fhunning
" Something diflik'd, are always running.
" Some prance like Frenchwomen, who ride
" As our Life-guard-men, all aftride.   1820
" But each of thefe have decoration
" According to their affectation,
" That dance is grateful, and will pleafe,
" Where all the motions glide with eafe.
" We to the fkilful theatre   1825
" This feeming want of art prefer.
 " 'Tis no fmall art to give direction
" How to fuit knots to each complexion,
" How to adorn the breaft and head,
" With blue, white, cherry, pink, or red.   1830
" As the morn rifes, fo that day
" Wear purple, fky-colour, or grey :
" Your black at Lent, your green in May,
" Your filamot with leaves decay.
" All colours in the fummer fhine :   1835
" The nymphs fhould be like gardens fine.

f Torquato Taffo, the celebrated epic poet of Italy, was born March 11, 1544, and died April 25, 1595. His works have been often printed feparately at various places; but the whole together, with his life, and feveral pieces for and againft his Gierufalemme Liberata, were printed at Florence, 1724, in fix vols. folio. The Englifh verfion of the " Jerufalem " Delivered," publifhed in 1763, by Mr. Hoole, in 2 vols. 8vo. will extend the fame of Taffo in this country.

g Francis de Malherbe, confidered by his countrymen as the father of the French poetry, was born about 1555, and died in 1628. His poetical works, though divided into fix books, make but a fmall volume. They confift of paraphrafes upon the Pfalms, odes, fonnets, and epigrams; and were publifhed in feveral forms to the year 1666, when a very compleat edition of them came out at Paris, with the notes of M. Menage. Malherbe alfo tranflated fome works of Seneca, and fome books of Livy.—By the manner in which Taffo and Malherbe are mentioned by Dr. King, they feem not to have been the moft fafhionable authors of that age. Our Author has tranflated what he calls " an admirable Ode of Malherbe," which will be inferted in this volume.

" It

" It is the fashion now-a-days,
" That almost every Lady plays.
" Basset and Piquet grow to be
" The subject of our Comedy :
" But whether we diversion seek
" In these, in Comet, or in Gleek,
" Or Ombre, where true judgement can
" Disclose the sentiments of man ;
" Let's have a care how we discover,
" Especially before a Lover,
" Some passions which we should conceal,
" But heats of play too oft reveal.
" For, be the matter small or great,
" There's like abhorrence for a cheat.
" There's nothing spoils a Woman's graces
" Like peevishness and making faces :
" Then angry words and rude discourse,
" You may be sure, become them worse.
" With hopes of gain, when we're beset,
" We do too commonly forget
" Such guards as screen us from those eyes
" Which may observe us, and despise.
" I'd burn the cards, rather than know
" Of any of my friends did so :
" I've heard of some such things ; but I,
" Thanks to my stars, was never by.
    " Thus we may pass our time : the men
" A thousand ways divert their spleen,
" Whilst we sit peevishly within ;
" Hunting, cocking, racing, joaking,
" Fuddling, swimming, fencing, smoaking :
" And little thinking how poor we
" Must vent our scandal o'er our tea.
" I see no reason but we may
" Be brisk, and equally as gay.
" Whene'er our Gentlemen would range,
" We'll take our chariot for the Change :
" If they're disposing for the Play,
" We'll hasten to the Opera :

" Or

1840
1845
1850
1855
1860
1870
1875

" Or when they'll luftily caroufe,
" We'll furely to the Indian Houfe :
" And at fuch coft whilft thus we roam,
" For cheapnefs fake they'll ftay at home.
" Few wife mens thoughts e'er yet purfued   1880
" That which their eyes had never view'd :
" And fo our never being feen
" Is the fame thing as not t'have been.
" Grandeur itfelf and Poverty
" Were equal if no witnefs by :   1885
" And they who always fing alone
" Can ne'er be prais'd by more than one.
" Had Danaë been fhut up ftill,
" She'd been a Maid againft her will,
" And might have grown prodigious old,   1890
" And never had her ftory told.
" 'Tis fit fair maids fhou'd run a-gadding
" To fet the amourous Beaux a-madding.
" To many a Sheep the Wolf has gone
" Ere it can neatly feize on one,   1895
" And many a Partridge fcapes away
" Before the Hawk can pounce its prey :
" And fo, if pretty Damfels rove,
" They'll find out one perhaps may love ;
" If they no diligence will fpare,   1900
" And in their dreffing ftill take care.
" The Fifher baits his hook all night,
" In hopes by chance fome Eel may bite.
" Each with their different grace appears,
" Virgins with blufh, Widows with tears,   1905
" Which gain new Hufbands tender-hearted,
" To think how fuch a couple parted.
" But then there are fome foppifh Beaux
" Like us in all things but their cloaths.
" That we may feem the more robuft,   1910
" And fitteft to accoft them firft,
" With powder, paint, falfe locks, and hair,
" They give themfelves a female air ;
" Who, having all their tale by rote,
" And harping ftill on the fame note,   1915

" Will

" Will tell us that, and nothing more
" Than what a thoufand heard before.
" Though they all marks of Love pretend,
" There's nothing which they lefs intend :
" And, 'midft a thoufand hideous oaths,   1920
" With jewels falfe and borrow'd cloaths,
" Our eafinefs may give belief
" To one that is an errant thief."
   The fpark was coming ; fhe undreft
Scuttles away as if poffeft.   1925
The Governefs cries, " Where d'ye run ?"
" Why, Madam, I've but juft begun."
She bawls ; the other nothing hears,
But leaves her prattling to the chairs.
   Virtue, without thefe little arts,   1930
At firft fubdues, then keeps, our hearts :
And though more gracefully it fhows
When it from lovely perfons flows ;
Yet often Goodnefs moft prevails
When Beauty in perfection fails.   1935
Though every feature mayn't be well,
Yet all together may excel.
There's nothing but will eafy prove,
When all the reft's made up by Love.

P A R T   XIII.

VIRGINS fhould not unfkill'd in Mufic be ;   1940
   For what's more like themfelves than Harmony ?
Let not Vice ufe it only to betray,
And Syrens by their Songs entice their prey.
Let it with fenfe, with voice, and beauty join,
Grateful to eyes and ear, and to the Mind Divine :   1945
For there's a double grace when pleafing ftrings
Are touch'd by her that more delightful fings.
Thus Orpheus did the rage of deferts quell,
And charm'd the monftrous inftruments of Hell,

New walls to Thebes Amphion thus began,　　　1950
Whilst to the work officious marble ran.
Thus with his harp and voice Arion rode
On the mute Fish safe through the rolling flood.
Nor are the essays of the Female wit
Less charming in the verses they have writ.　　　1955
From antient ages, Love has found the way
Its bashful thoughts by Letters to convey;
Which sometimes run in such engaging strain,
That pity makes the Fair write back again.
What's thus intended, some small time delay:　　　1960.
His passion strengthens rather by our stay.
Then with a cautious wit your pen with-hold,
Lest a too free expression make him bold.
Create a mixture 'twixt his hope and fear,
And in reproof let tenderness appear.　　　1965
As he deserves it, give him hopes of life:
A cruel Mistress makes a froward Wife.
Affect not foreign words: Love will impart
A gentle style more excellent than art.
Astrea's h lines flow on with so much ease,　　　1970
That she who writes like them must surely please.
Orinda's i works, with courtly graces stor'd,
True sense in nice expressions will afford:

Whilst

h Astrea was a name assumed by Mrs. Aphra Behn, a lady well known in the gay and poetical world, in the licentious reign of King Charles II. She was Authoress of seventeen Plays, besides two volumes of Novels, several Translations, and many Poems. She died April 16, 1689. Mr. Pope, speaking of her dramatic pieces, says,

"The stage how loosely does Astrea tread,
"Who fairly puts all characters to bed!"

i Orinda, the poetical name of Mrs. Catharine Philips. She was the daughter of John Fowler, merchant, and born in London 1631; was married to James Philips, of the Priory of Cardigan, esq. about the year 1647; and died in Fleet-street, in the month of June, 1664. Her poems have been several times printed. She was also the writer of a volume of Letters, published many years after her death, to Sir Charles Cotterel, intituled, "Letters from Orinda to Poliarchus;" which have been admired —Mrs. Philips was as much famed for her friendship, as for her poetry; and had the good fortune to be equally esteemed by the

best

Whilſt Chudleigh's [k] words ſeraphic thoughts expreſs
In lofty grandeur, but without exceſs.   1975
Oh, had not Beauty parts enough to wound,
But it muſt pierce us with Poetic ſound!
Whilſt Phœbus ſuffers-female powers to tear
Wreaths from his Daphne, which they juſtly wear!
    If greater things to leſſer we compare,   1980
The ſkill of Love is like the art of War.
The General ſays, " Let him the Horſe command :
" You by that Enſign, you that Cannon ſtand :
-" Where danger calls, let t'other bring ſupplies."
With Pleaſure all obey, in hopes to riſe.   1985
So, if you have a ſervant ſkill'd in Laws,
Send him with moving ſpeech to plead your cauſe.
He that has native unaffected voice,
In ſinging what you bid him, will rejoice.
And wealth, as beauty orders it, beſtow'd,   1990
Would make ev'n Miſers in expences proud.
But they, o'er whom Apollo rules, have hearts
The moſt ſuſceptible of Lovers ſmarts,
And like their God ſo they feel Cupid's darts.
The Gods and Kings are by their labours prai,'d,   1995
And they again by them to honour rais'd.
For none to Heaven or Majeſty expreſt
Their duty well, but in return were bleſt.
Nor did the mighty Scipio think it ſcorn
That Ennius, in Calabrian Mountains born,   2000
His wars, retirements, councils, ſhould attend,
In all diſtinguiſh'd by the name of Friend.
He that, for want of worlds to conquer, wept,
Without conſulting Homer never ſlept.

beſt poet and the beſt divine of her age.   Dr. Jeremy Taylor addreſſed his
diſcourſe " on the nature and effects of friendſhip" to this lady ; and Mr.
Cowley has celebrated her memory, in an Ode preſerved amongſt his
" Select Works."

    [k] This lady was daughter to Richard Lee, of Winſlade, in the county
of Devon, eſq.   She was born in the year 1656 ; became the wife of S:r
George Chudleigh, of Aſhton, in the ſame county, bart. ; and died Dec.
15, 1710.   Her Poems were twice printed in her life-time in one volume,
8vo ; the ſecond edition in 1709.

The Poets' cares all terminate in fame ;   2005
As they obtain, they give, a lasting name.
Thus from the dead Lucrece and Cynthia rise,
And Berenice's hair adorns the skies.
The sacred Bard no treacherous craft displays,
But virtuous actions crowns with his own bays.   2010
Far from Ambition and Wealth's sordid care
In him good-nature and content appear :
And far from Courts, from studious parties free,
He sighs forth Laura's charms beneath some tree ;
Despairing of the valued prize he loves,   2015
Commits his thoughts to winds and echoing groves.
    Poets have quick desire and passion strong ;
Where once it lights, there it continues long.
They know that Truth is the perpetual band,
By which the world and heaven of Love must stand.   2020
The Poet's art softens their tempers so,
That manners easy as their verses flow.
Oh could they but just retribution find,
And as themselves what they adore be kind !
In vain they boast of their celestial fire,   2025
Whilst there remains a Heaven to which they can't aspire !
Apelles first brought Venus to our view,
With blooming charms and graces ever new,
Who else unknown to mortals might remain
Hid in the caverns of her native main :   2030
And with the Painter now the Poets join
To make the Mother and her Boy divine.
Therefore attend, and from their musick learn
That which their minds inspir'd could best discern.
    First see how Sidney [l], then how Cowley [m] mov'd,   2035
And with what art it was that Waller [n] lov'd.

Forget

[l] See an account of Sir Philip Sidney, vol. II. p. 89.

[m] Mr. Abraham Cowley was born in 1618 ; and died July 28, 1667. His " Poetical Blossoms," which are an abundant proof of his talent for poetry, were generally regarded as an earnest of that fame to which he afterwards rose, and which, in the opinion of some of his contemporaries, eclipsed that of every other English poet.—Cowley, who helped to corrupt the taste of the age in which he lived, and had himself been corrupted by

it,

Forget not Dorfet *, in whofe generous mind
Love, fenfe, wit, honour, every grace combin'd :

And

it, was a remarkable inftance of true genius, feduced and perverted by falfe
wit. But this wit, falfe as it was, raifed his reputation to a much higher
pitch than that of Milton. There is a want of elegance in his words,
and of harmony in his verfification ; but this was more than atoned for
by, his greateft fault, the redundancy of his fancy. His Latin poems,
which are efteemed the beft of his works, are written in the various mea-
fures of the ancients, and have much of their unaffected beauty. He was
more fuccefsful in imitating the eafe and gaiety of Anacreon, than the
bold and lofty flights of Pindar. His metaphors, which are not only
beyond, but contrary to nature, were generally admired in the reign of
Charles II. To the merit of a good poet, may be added that of his being
an admirable profe writer ; and his " Cutter of Coleman Street," a comedy
which might even have claimed a place in the late judicious feléction of
his writings, where it is commended and the Preface to it preferred, is
a ftriking inftance of dramatic merit. See Granger.

a Edmund Waller, efq. born March 3, 1605 ; died Oct. 1, 1687. He is
commonly ftyled the Englifh Tibullus, and was the firft who fhewed us cur
tongue had beauty and numbers in it. The beft edition of his works is
in 4to, 1730, with elegant and ufeful notes by Mr. Fenton.—Mr. Waller
excelled all his predeceffors in harmonious verfification. His love verfes
have all the tendernefs and politenefs of the Roman poet he fo much re-
fembled ; and his panegyrick on Cromwell has been ever efteemed a
mafter-piece in its kind. His vein is never redundant, like that of
Cowley : we frequently wifh he had faid more, but never that he had faid
lefs. His perfonal qualities were as amiable as his poetical ; and he was
equally formed to pleafe the witty and the fair. He not only retained all
his faculties, but much of his ufual vivacity, at eighty years of his age.

o Charles lord Buckhurft, who was created earl of Middlefex in the life-
time of his father, April 4, 1674, fucceeded to the earldom of Dorfet in
Auguft, 1677.—This noble lord was the juft admiration of the age he lived
in. The fprightlinefs of his wit recommended him to the efteem and
intimacy of King Charles II. He was a bountiful patron to poets and to
men of parts ; and had a particular character for univerfal generofity. In
the reign of James II, he atoned for the follies of his youth, by a firm ad-
herence to the Proteftant religion ; for which he fhewed his concern, by
conveying the princefs Anne into Derbyfhire, from the tumult of thofe
times ; and, having been further inftrumental in the happy Revolution,
was made lord chamberlain of the houfehold to king William, and knight

of

And if for me you one kind wish would spare,
Answer a Poet to his friendly prayer.   2940
Take Stepney's P verse, with candour ever blest;
For Love will there still with his ashes rest.
There let warm spice and fragrant odours burn,
And everlasting sweets perfume his urn.
⌐ Not that the living Muse is to be scorn'd ;   2045
Britain with equal worth is still adorn'd.
See Halifax q, where sense and honour mixt
Upon the merits just reward have fixt :
And read their works, who, writing in his praise,
To their own verse immortal laurels raise.   2050
                                                               Learn

of the Garter. He had the honour of being appointed one of the lords
justices four years successively; and died Jan. 29, 1705-6. His works,
consisting chiefly of sprightly songs, are printed with the Minor Poets.

   P George Stepney, esq. a man more famous as a Statesman than a Poet.
He was born 1663, became acquainted at Cambridge with the celebrated
Charles Montague, afterwards earl of Halifax; and through his interest
was employed in several foreign negotiations, which he conducted with
great reputation and success. He died in the year 1707, and was buried in
Westminster Abbey. His works are amongst those of the Minor Poets.

   q Mr. Charles Montague was constituted one of the lords commissioners
of the treasury, March 2, 1691-2 ; chancellor of the exchequer, in May,
1694. The coin being exceedingly debased and diminished, he formed the
design of calling in the money, and re-coining it, in 1695 ; and effected it
in two years : to supply the immediate want of cash, he projected the
issuing of exchequer bills. For this service, he had the thanks of the house
of commons in 1697. He was next year appointed first lord commissioner
of the treasury ; and, resigning that post in June 1700, obtained a grant of
the office of auditor of the receipt of the exchequer ; and the same year,
Dec. 13, was created baron Halifax. On the accession of king George I,
he was a member of the regency ; was appointed first lord commissioner of
the treasury, Oct. 5, 1714 ; created viscount Sunbury and earl of Halifax,
Oct. 15 ; and died May 15, 1715. He was a magnificent patron of learning ; and was himself an elegant writer, as may be seen by his works in
the Minor Poets.

   r Matthew Prior has been reputed a native of London ; but was born
at Winburn in Dorsetshire, July 21, 1664. (Hutchins's Hist. vol. II.
p. 75.) His father dying while he was very young, his uncle (a vintner
near Charing Cross) had the charge of him, sent him to Westminster
School, and afterward took him into his own business. In this situation,
                                                               he

Learn Prior's [r] lines; for they can teach you more
Than facred Ben [s], or Spenfer [t], did before:

And he was accidentally diftinguifhed by Charles earl of Dorfet; who, deter-
mining to place him in a fituation more fuited to his fine parts, fent him
to St. John's College, Cambridge, in 1682; where he proceeded bachelor
of arts in 1686, and was fhortly after chofen fellow. At the univerfity,
he contracted an intimate acquaintance with Mr. Charles Montague, afterward earl of Halifax. On the Revolution, he was brought to court by
his great patron the earl of Dorfet. In 1690, he was fecretary to the pleni-
potentiaries at The Hague; and king William was fo fatisfied with his
fervices, that, in the refolution to keep him near his perfon, he appointed
him a gentleman of the bed-chamber. He was again employed as fecretary,
at Ryfwick, in 1697; having been the fame year nominated principal
fecretary of ftate in Ireland. In 1697, he went fecretary to the earl of
Portland, in his embaffy to France. In 1699, he was made under-fecretary
in the office of the earl of Jerfey; and in a few days was ordered back to
Paris, to affift the ambaffador in the Partition-treaty; which he difpatched
to the fatisfaction of both Sovereigns. In 1700, he was appointed one of
the lords commiffioners for trade and plantations, and was elected member
for Eaft Grinfted. In 1704 and 1706, he exerted his poetical talent in
honour of his country, on the fuccefs of her Majefty's arms. In July,
1711, he was employed in a fecret negotiation at Paris. In Auguft 1712,
being fent again to France, to accommodate fuch matters as then remained
unfettled in the congrefs at Utrecht, he had the honour of being prefented
with the French king's picture fet with diamonds. From the end of that
month, he had the appointment and authority of an ambaffador, till the
death of the Queen; and remained at Paris in a public character fome
months after the acceffion of king George I. On his arrival in England,
March 25, 1715, he was taken into cuftody. In 1717, he was excepted
out of the act of grace; and, at the clofe of that year, being difcharged
from his confinement, retired from bufinefs, to Down Hall, in Effex;
where he died, of a lingering fever, Sept. 11, 1721.—'One Prior (fays
"Bp. Burnet), who had been Jerfey's fecretary, upon his death, was em-
"ployed to profecute that which the other did not live to finifh. Prior
"had been a boy taken out of a tavern by the earl of Dorfet, who acci-
"dentally found him reading Horace."—This *ill-natured* reflection produced the following epigram by Mr. Dodfley, "Trifles," p. 241.

> "*One Prior !* and is this, this all the fame,
> "The Poet from th' Hiftorian can claim?
> "No; Prior's verfe pofterity fhall quote,
> "When 'tis forgot *one Burnet* ever wrote!"

s See fome account of Jonfon, vol. II. p. 89.

                    s Edmund

And mark him ^u well that uncouth Phyſick's art
Can in the ſofteſt tune of Wit impart.
See Paſtorella o'er Florello's grave ^w,
See Tamerlane ^x make Bajazet his ſlave ;
And Phædra ^y with her antient vigour rave.

Through

^t Edmund Spenſer, the celebrated author of the " Fairy Queen," father of the Engliſh heroic poem, and of true paſtoral poetry in England, was born in London, and educated at Pembroke Hall, Cambridge; B. A. 1573; M. A. 1576. His " Shepherd's Calendar," introducing him to that great judge of merit Sir Philip Sidney, raiſed him from a ſort of obſcurity to the office of poet laureat to Elizabeth ; but for ſome time he only wore the barren laurel, without receiving any penſion. Burghley, it is ſaid, prevented his receiving an hundred pounds which the queen intended for him. We find him, however, in conſiderable eſteem with many eminent men in his time. He was ſent abroad by Leiceſter ; and was ſecretary to Lord Grey of Wilton when deputy of Ireland. The queen alſo at laſt rewarded his ſervices with a conſiderable grant of lands in Ireland. In the Iriſh rebellion under Deſmond, he was plundered, and deprived of his eſtate, and ſpent the latter part of his life with much grief of heart under the diſappointment of a broken fortune : he died in 1598-9.— Spenſer ſtands diſtinguiſhed from almoſt all other poets in that faculty by which a poet is diſtinguiſhed from other writers, namely, invention ; and excelled all his contemporaries in harmonious verſification.

^u Dr. Samuel Garth, the celebrated author of " The Diſpenſary."—The firſt edition of this admirable poem came out in 1694 ; and it went through three impreſſions in a few months. This extraordinary encouragement put him upon making ſeveral improvements in it ; and in 1706, he publiſhed the fourth edition, with ſeveral additions. It was dedicated to Anthony Henley, eſq. and had commendatory verſes before it by Charles Boyle afterward earl of Orrery, Col. Chriſt. Codrington, Thomas Cheeke, eſq. and Col. Henry Blount.—Major Pack (Miſcell. p. 102.) obſerves, that " The Diſpenſary had loſt and gained in every edition ; almoſt every " thing that Sir Samuel left out being a robbery from the publick, whilſt " every thing that he added was an embelliſhment to his poem."—On the acceſſion of king George I, he had the honour of being knighted with the duke of Marlborough's ſword. He died Jan. 18, 1718-19. His other pieces are printed in the collection of the Minor Poets.

^w Characters which the Editor acknowledges he does not recollect.

^x See Rowe's Play of Tamerlane.—Mr. Nicholas Rowe was born in 1673, was bred to the law, but ſeduced by the Muſes. Beſides " Tamer-" lane," he wrote ſix other tragedies, a comedy, and ſeveral poems pub-
liſhed

Through Rapin's [z] nurferies and gardens walk,
And find how Nymphs transform'd by amorous colours talk.
Pomona [a] fee with Milton's grandeur rife,   2060
The moft delicious fruit of Paradife,
With Apples might the firft-born man deceive,
And more perfuafive voice than tempting Eve,
Not to confine you here; for many more
Britain's luxuriant wealth has ftill in ftore,   2065

liſhed in one volume under the title of "Mifcellaneous Works."—He was appointed poet laureat on the acceffion of king George I; and died Dec. 6, 1718.—His tranflation of Lucan was not publiſhed till ten years after his death; but a fmall fpecimen of it, which was printed by Mr. Collins in 1713, underwent a fevere cenfure from Dr. Bentley, in his "Remarks on a Difcourfe on Freethinking."

y Phædra and Hippolitus, a Tragedy, by Edmund Smith, firft acted in 1707. Its excellence confifts in the beauty and harmony of the verfification. It was honoured with a prologue by Mr. Addifon, to railly the tafte of the publick for Italian operas.—This ingenious poet was the fon of Mr. Neale; but, affumed the name of Smith in compliment to an uncle who was his guardian. He was born in 1686, and died in 1710. He was a good-natured man, a finiſhed fcholar, a great poet, and a difcerning critic. From an affected carelefsnefs in drefs, he was diſtinguiſhed by his friends by the name of "Captain Ragg;" and was ftyled by the fair fex "the "handfome Sloven." His Works, confifting of the abovementioned Tragedy, three or four odes, and a Latin oration, were publiſhed by Mr. Oldifworth in 1719.

z Renatus Rapin, a French Jefuit, born in 1621, died Oct. 27, 1687. He publiſhed "Hortorum Libri Quatuor," a work which has been much admired. An Engliſh tranflation of it was publiſhed by Mr. Evelyn in 1673; and another, in 1706, by James Gardener, M. A. of Jefus College, Cambridge.

a John Philips, born Dec. 30, 1676, was educated at Chrift Church, Oxford. The firft poem which diftinguiſhed him was his "Splendid "Shilling," which the author of the Tatler ftyles "the fineft burlefque "poem in the Britiſh language." His next was "Blenheim." The third, "Upon Cyder," founded upon the model of the Georgics, is a very excellent piece in its kind, and has been tranflated into Italian by a Florentine nobleman. A Latin Ode to Mr. St. John, which is alfo a mafter-piece, completes his works. He died at Hereford, Feb. 15, 1708. He was one of thofe few poets whofe Mufe and manners were excellent and amiable; and both were fo in a very eminent degree.

Whofe

Whom would I number up, I muſt outrun
The longeſt courſe of the laborious ſun.

XXXXX

PART XIV.

OUR manners like our countenance ſhould be;
   They always candid, and the other free:
But, when our mind by anger is poſſeſt, 2070
Our noble manhood is transform'd to beaſt.
No feature then its wonted grace retains,
When the blood blackens in the ſwelling veins:
The eye-balls ſhoot out fiery darts would kill
Th' oppoſer, if the Gorgon had its will. 2075
When Pallas in a river ſaw the flute
Deform'd her cheeks, ſhe let the reed be mute.
Anger no more will mortify the face,
Which in that paſſion once conſults her glaſs.
Let Beauty ne'er be with this torment ſeiz'd, 2080
But ever reſt ſerene, and ever pleas'd.
A dark and ſullen brow ſeems to reprove
The firſt advances that are made to Love,
To which there's nothing more averſe than pride.
Men without ſpeaking often are denied: 2085
And a diſdainful look too oft reveals
Thoſe ſeeds of hatred which the tongue conceals.
When eyes meet eyes, and ſmiles to ſmiles return,
'Tis then both hearts with equal ardour burn,
And by their mutual paſſion ſoon will know 2090
That all are darts, and ſhot from Cupid's bow.
But, when ſome lovely form does ſtrike your eyes,
Be cautious ſtill how you admit ſurprize.
What you would love, with quick diſcretion view:
The object may deceive by being new. 2095
You may ſubmit to a too haſty fate,
And would ſhake off the yoke when 'tis too late.
We often into our deſtruction ſink
By not allowing time enough to think.

Reſiſt

Refift at firft : for help in vain we pray,   2100
When ills have gain'd full ftrength by long delay.
Be fpeedy; left perhaps the growing hour
Put what is now within, beyond our power.
Love, as a fire in cities finds encreafe,
Proceeds, and till the whole's deftroy'd won't ceafe.] 2105
It with allurements does, like rivers, rife
From little fprings, enlarg'd by vaft fupplies.
Had Myrrha kept this guard, fhe had not ftood
A monumental crime in weeping wood.
Becaufe that Love is pleafing in its pain,   2110
We not without reluctance health obtain.
Phyfick may tarry till to-morrow's fun,
Whilft the curs'd poifons through the vitals run.
The tree not to be fhook has pierc'd the ground,
And death muft follow the neglected wound.   2115
   O'er different ages Love bears different fway,
Takes various turns to make all forts obey.
The Colt unback'd we footh with gentle trace:
We feed the Runner deftin'd for the race;
And 'tis with time and mafters we prepare   2120
The manag'd Courfers rufhing to the war.
Ambitious Youth will have fome fparks of pride,
And not without impatience be denied.
If to his Love a Rival you afford,
You then prefent a trial for his fword: 2125
His eager warmth difdains to be perplext,
And rambles to the beauty that is next.
Maturer years proceed with care and fenfe,
And, as they feldom give, fo feldom take offence:
For he that knows refiftance is in vain,   2130
Knows likewife ftruggling will increafe his pain.
Like wood that's lately cut in Paphian Grove,
Time makes him a fit facrifice for Love.
By flow degrees he fans the gentle fire,
Till perfeverance makes the flame afpire.   2135
This Love's more fure, the other is more gay;
But then he roves, whilft this is forc'd to ftay.
There are fome tempers which you muft oblige,
Not by a quick furrender, but a fiege;

3   That

That moſt are pleas'd, when driven to deſpair   2140
By what they're pleas'd to call a cruel fair.
They think, unleſs their uſage has been hard,
Their conqueſt loſes part of its reward.
Thus ſome raiſe ſpleen from their abounding wealth,
And, clog'd with ſweets, from acids ſeek their health.   2145
And many a boat does its deſtruction find
By having ſcanty ſails, too full of wind.
    Is it not treachery to declare
The feeble parts we have in war?
Is it not folly to afford   2150
Our enemy a naked ſword?
Yet 'tis my weakneſs to confeſs
What puts men often in diſtreſs:
But then it is ſuch Beaux [b] as be

Poſſeſt with ſo much vanity,   2155
To think that wherefoe'er they turn,
Whoever looks on them muſt burn.
What they deſire they think is true,
With ſmall encouragement from you.
They will a ſingle look improve,   2160
And take civilities for love.
    " We all expected you at play:
" Was't not a Miſtreſs made you ſtay?"
The Beau is fir'd, cries, " Now I find
" I out of pity muſt be kind: 2165
" She ſigh'd, impatient till I came."
Thus, ſoaring to the lively flame,
We ſee the vain ambitious Fly
Scorch its gay wings, then unregarded die.

[b] It is obvious that this word conveys at preſent a very different idea from its original ſignification ; which was plainly that of *an accompliſhed gentleman.*—How different are the manly Beaux of Farquhar from the preſent Macaronies! and how many intermediate gradations have ariſen between them ! The genuine Beau appears to have been corrupted by a ſervile imitation of that ludicrous character the *petit-maitre* of our neighbour nation ; a title affected by ſuch of that vain people as had no other, in humble emulation of their *grand-maitre,* Louis the Fourteenth. From theſe came the Lord Foppingtons and Sir Harry Wildairs ; and from them degenerated by degrees the Fribble and the Macarony !

Both fexes have their jealoufy,   2170
And ways to gain their ends thereby,
But oftentimes too quick belief
Has given a fudden vent to grief,
Occafion'd by fome perfons lying,
To fet an eafy wife a-crying :   2175
And Procrjs long ago, alas !
Experienc'd this unhappy cafe.
    There is a Mount, Hymettus ftyl'd,
Where Pinks and Rofemary are wild,
Where Strawberries and Myrtles grow,   2180
And Violets make a purple fhow ;
Where the fweet Bays and Laurel fhine,
All fhaded by the lofty Pine ;
Where Zephyrs, with their wanton motion,
Have all the leaves at their devotion.   2185
Here Cephalus, who Hunting lov'd,
When dogs and men were both remov'd,
And all his dufty labour done,
In the meridian of the fun,
Into fome fecret hedge would creep,   2190
And fing, and hum himfelf afleep.
But commonly being hot and dry,
He thus would for fome cooler cry :
    " O now, if fome
    " Cooler would come !   2195
        " Deareft, rareft,
        " Lovelieft, faireft,
    " Cooler, come !
        " Oh, AIR,
    " Frefh and rare ;   2200
    " Deareft, rareft,
    " Lovelieft, faireft,
    " Cooler, come ; Cooler, come ; Cooler, come !"
    A Woman, that had heard him fing,
Soon had her malice on the wing :   2205
For Females ufually don't want
A Fellow Goffip that will cant ;
Who ftill is pleas'd with others ails,
And therefore carries fpiteful tales.

                                        She

She thought that she might raise some strife 2210
By telling something to his Wife:
That once upon a time she stood
In such a place, in such a wood,
On such a day, and such a year,
There did, at least there did appear 2215
('Cause for the world she would not lie,
As she must tell her by the bye)
Her Husband; first more loudly bauling,
And afterwards more softly calling
A person not of the best fame, 2220
And Mistress Cooler was her name.
" Now, Gossip, why should she come thither?
" But that they might be naught together?"
When Cris heard all, her colour turn'd,
And though her heart within her burn'd, 2225
And eyeballs sent forth sudden flashes;
Her cheeks and lips were pale as ashes.
Then, " Woe the day that she was born!"
The nightrail innocent was torn:
Many a thump was given the breast, 2230
" And she, oh, she should never rest:
" She strait would heigh her to the wood,
" And he'd repent it—that he should."
With eager haste away she moves,
Never regarding scarf or gloves: 2235
Into the grotto soon she creeps,
And into every thicket peeps,
And to her eyes there did appear
Two prints of bodies—that was clear:
" And now (she cries) I plainly see 2240
" How time and place, and all agree:
" But here's a covert where I'll lie,
" And I shall have them by and by."
　　'Twas noon; and Cephalus, as last time,
Heated and ruffled with his pastime, 2245
Came to the very self-same place
Where he was us'd to wash his face;
And then he sung, and then he hum'd,
And on his knee with fingers thrum'd.

When

When Criffy found all matters fair, 2250
And that he only wanted Air ;
Saw what device was took to fool her,
And no fuch one as Miftrefs Cooler.
Miftrufting then no future harms,
She would have rufh'd into his arms. 2255
But, as the leaves began to ruftle,
He thought fome beaft had made the buftle.
He fhot, then cried, " I've kill'd my Deer."—
" Ay, fo you have," (fays Cris) " I fear."—
" Why, Criffy, pray what made you here ?"
" By Goffip Trot, I underftood
" You kept a fmall Girl in this wood."
Quoth Ceph, " 'Tis pity thou fhould'ft die
" For this thy foolifh jealoufy :
" For 'tis a paffion that does move 2265
" Too often from excefs of love."
But, when they fought for wound full fore,
The petticoat was only tore,
And fhe had got a lufty thump,
Which in fome meafure bruis'd her rump. 2270
Then home moft lovingly they went:
Neither had reafon to repent.
Their following years pafs'd in content;
And Criffy made him the beft wife
For the remainder of his life. 2275
  The Mufe has done, nor will more laws obtrude,
Left fhe, by being tedious, fhould be rude.
Unbrace Love's fwans, let them unharnefs'd ftray,
And eat Ambrofia through the milky way.
Give liberty to every Paphian Dove, 2280
And let them freely with the Cupids rove.
But, when the Amazonian trophies rife
With monuments of their paft victories;
With what difcretion and what art they fought :
Let them record, " They were by OVID taught." 2285

P O E M S

BY

DR. K I N G:

THE FURMETARY,

MULLY OF MOUNTOWN,

ORPHEUS AND EURYDICE,

RUFINUS, OR THE FAVOURITE,

BRITAIN'S PALLADIUM,

AND

MISCELLANY POEMS.

VOL. III.

POEMS

by

DR. KING:

CONTAINING

THE FURMETARY,

MULLY OF MOUNTOWN,

ORPHEUS AND EURYDICE,

RUFINUS, OR THE FAVOURITE,

BRITAIN'S PALLADIUM,

AND

MISCELLANY POEMS.

THE FURMETARY;

A very Innocent and Harmlefs P O E M [a],

IN THREE CANTO'S.

Firft printed in 1699.

P R E F A C E.

THE Author of the following Poem may be thought to write for fame, and the applaufe of the town: but he wholly difowns it; for he writes only for the public good, the benefit of his country, and the manufacture of England. It is well known, that *grave Senators* have often, at the Palace-yard, refrefhed themfelves with Barley-broth in a morning, which has had a very folid influence on their counfels; it is therefore hoped that other perfons may ufe it with the like fuccefs. No man can be ignorant, how of late years Coffee and Tea in a morning has prevailed; nay, Cold Waters have obtained their commendation, and Wells are fprung up from Acton to Iflington, and crofs the water to Lambeth. Thefe liquors have feveral eminent champions of all profeffions. But there have not been wanting perfons, in all ages, that have fhewn a true love for their country, and the proper diet of it, as Water-gruel, Milk-porridge, Rice-milk, and efpecially Furmetry both with Plums and without. To this end, feveral worthy perfons have encouraged the eating fuch wholefome diet in a morning; and, that the poor may be provided, they have defired feveral Matrons to ftand at Smithfield-

---

[a] " The Furmetary" was written to pleafe a Gentleman, who thought nothing fmooth or lofty could be written upon a mean fubject; but had no intent of making any reflection upon " The Difpenfary," which has defervedly gained a lafting reputation. Dr. King's Preface to his Mifcellanies.—See an account of Sir Samuel Garth above, p. 184.

bars,

bars, Leaden-Hall-market, Stocks-market, and divers other noted places in the City, efpecially at Fleet-ditch; there to *difpenfe* Furmetry to labouring people, and the poor, at reafonable rates, at three-half-pence and two-pence a difh, which is not dear, the Plums being confidered.

The places are generally ftiled Furmetaries, becaufe that food has got the general efteem; but that at Fleet-ditch I take to be one of the moft remarkable, and therefore I have ftyled it " The " Furmetary:" and could eafily have had a certificate of the ufe-fulnefs of this Furmetary, figned by feveral eminent Carmen, Gardeners, Journeymen Taylors, and Bafket-women, who have promifed to contribute to the maintenance of the fame, in cafe the Coffee-houfes fhould proceed to oppofe it.

I have thought this a very proper fubject for an Heroic Poem; and endeavoured to be as fmooth in my verfe, and as inoffenfive in my characters, as was poffible. It is my cafe with Lucretius, that I write upon a fubject not treated of by the Ancients. But, " the greater labour, the greater glory."

Virgil had a Homer to imitate; but I ftand upon my own legs, without any fupport from abroad. I therefore fhall have more occafion for the Reader's favour, who, from the kind acceptance of this, may expect the defcription of other Furmetaries about this City, from his moft humble fervant,

AND PER SE AND,

C A N T O I.

NO fooner did the grey-ey'd Morning peep,
    And yawning mortals ftretch themfelves from fleep;
Finders of gold were now but newly paft,
And Bafket-women did to Market hafte;
The Watchmen were but juft returning home,   5
To give the Thieves more liberty to roam;
When from a hill, by growing beams of light,
A ftately pile was offer'd to the fight;
Three fpacious doors let paffengers go through,
And diftant ftones did terminate their view: 10

Juft

Juſt here, as ancient Poets ſing, there ſtood,
The noble palace of the valiant Lud;
His image now appears in Portland ſtone,
Each ſide ſupported by a god-like ſon [b].
But, underneath, all the three heroes ſhine,
In living colours, drawn upon a ſign,
Which ſhews the way to Ale, but not to Wine.

   Near is a place entlos'd with iron-bars,
Where many mortals curſe their cruel ſtars,
When brought by Uſurers into diſtreſs,   10
For having little, ſtill muſt live on leſs:
Stern Avarice there keeps the relentleſs door,
And bids each wretch eternally be poor.
Hence Hunger riſes, diſmally he ſtalks,
And takes each ſingle priſoner in his walks;   15
This duty done, the meager monſter ſtares,
Holds up his bones, and thus begins his prayers:
  " Thou, Goddeſs Famine, that canſt ſend us blights,
" With parching heat by day, and ſtorm by nights,
" Aſſiſt me now: ſo may all lands be thine,   20
" And ſhoals of orphans at thy altars pine:
" Long may thy reign continue on each ſhore,
" Where-ever Peace and Plenty reign'd before!
" I muſt confeſs, that to thy gracious hand,
" I widows owe, that are at my command;   35

  [b] As Dr. King's deſcription of Ludgate, though familiar to the preſent
age, will be leſs intelligible to the riſing generation, it may not be improper to obſerve, that its name, which Geoffry of Monmouth has aſcribed
to King Lud, was with greater propriety derived from its ſituation near
the rivulet Flud, or Fleet, which ran near it.—So early as 1373, Ludgate
was conſtituted a priſon for poor debtors who were free of the city; and
was greatly enlarged in 1454, by Sir Stephen Forſter, who, from having
been himſelf confined there, became lord mayor of London, and eſtabliſhed
ſeveral benevolent regulations for its government.—The old gate becoming
ruinous, an elegant building, as above deſcribed by Dr. King, was erected
in 1586, with the ſtatue of Queen Elizabeth on the Weſt front, and thoſe
of the pretended King Lud and his two ſons on the Eaſt. This was pulled
down in 1760, and the ſtatue of Elizabeth placed againſt the church of St.
Dunſtan in the Weſt. Since that time, the city debtors have been confined in a part of the London workhouſe in Biſhopſgate ſtreet.

O 3

" I joy

" I joy to hear their numerous childrens cries ;
" And blefs thy power, to find they've no fupplies.
" I thank thee for thofe Martyrs, who would flee
" From fuperftitious rites and tyranny,
" And find their fullnefs of reward in me.
" But 'tis with much humility I own,
" That generous favour you have lately fhown,
" When men, that bravely have their country ferv'd,
" Receiv'd the juft reward that they deferv'd,
" And are preferr'd to me, and fhall be ftarv'd.
" I can, but with regret, I can defpife,
" Innumerable of the London cries :
" When Peafe, and Mackarel, with their harfher found,
" The tender organs of my ears confound ;
" But that which makes my projects all mifcarry,   50
" Is this inhuman, fatal FURMETARY.
    " Not far from hence, juft by the Bridge of Fleet.
" With Spoons and Porringers, and Napkin neat,
" A faithlefs Syren does entice the fenfe,
" By fumes of viands, which fhe does difpenfe,
" To mortal ftomachs, for rewarding pence.
" Whilft each man's earlieft thoughts would banifh me,
" Who have no other oracle but thee."

CANTO II.

WHILST fuch-like prayers keen Hunger would advance,
    Fainting and weaknefs threw him in a trance :   60
Famine took pity on her careful flave,
And kindly to him this affiftance gave.
She took the figure of a thin parch'd Maid,
Who many years had for a Hufband ftaid ;
And, coming near to Hunger, thus fhe faid :
    " My darling fon, whilft Peace and Plenty fmile,
" And Happinefs would over-run this ifle,
" I joy to fee, by this thy prefent care,
" I've ftill fome friends remaining fince the war :

                                          " In

" In fpite of us, A does on Venifon feed,   70
" And Bread and Butter is for B decreed;
" C D combines with E F's generous foul,
" To pafs their minutes with the fparkling bowl,
" H, I's good-nature, from his endlefs ftore,
" Is ftill conferring bleffings on the poor,
" For none, except 'tis K, regards them more.
" L, M, N, O, P, Q, is vainly great,
" And fquanders half his fubftance in a treat:
" Nice eating by R, S, is underftood,
" T's fupper, though but little, yet is good;   80
" U's converfation's equal to his wine,
" You fup with W, whene'er you dine:
" X, Y, and Z, hating to be confin'd,
" Ramble to the next Eating-houfe they find.
" Pleafant, good-humour'd, beautiful, and gay,
" Sometimes with mufick, and fometimes with play,
" Prolong their pleafures till th'approaching day.
" AND PER SE AND alone, as Poets ufe,
" The ftarving dictates of my rules purfues;
" No fwinging coachman does afore him fhine,
" Nor has he any conftant place to dine,
" But all his notions of a meal are mine.
" Hafte, hafte, to him, a bleffing give from me,
" And bid him write fharp things on FURMETRY:
" But I would have thee to Coffedro go,   95
" And let Tobacco too thy bufinefs know;
" With famous Teedrums in this cafe advife,
" Rely on Sagoe, who is always wife:
" Amidft fuch counfel, banifh all defpair;
" Truft me, you fhall fucceed in this affair: 100
" That project which they FURMETARY call,
" Before next Breakfaft-time fhall furely fall!"
   This faid, fhe quickly vanifh'd in a wind
Had long within her body been confin'd:
Thus Hercules, when he his miftrefs found,   105
Soon knew her by her feent, and by her found.

O 4   CANTO

CANTO III.

HUNGER rejoic'd to hear the bleſt command,
 That FURMETARY ſhould no longer ſtand;
With ſpeed he to Coffedro's manſion flies,
And bids the pale-fac'd mortal quickly riſe.
 " Ariſe, my friend; for upon thee do wait
" Diſmal events and prodigies of Fate !
" 'Tis break of day, thy footy broth prepare,
" And all thy other liquors for a war :
" Rouſe up Tobacco, whoſe delicious ſight,
" Illuminated round with beams of light,
" To my impatient mind will cauſe delight.
" How will he conquer noſtrils that preſume
" To ſtand th' attack of his impetuous fume !
" Let handſome Teedrums too be call'd to arms,
" For he has courage in the midſt of charms :
" Sagoe with counſel fills his wakeful brains,
" But then his wiſdom countervails his pains ;
" 'Tis he ſhall be your guide, he ſhall effect
" That glorious conqueſt which we all expect :
" The brave Hectorvus ſhall command this force ;
" He'll meet Tubcarrio's Foot, or, which is worſe,
" Oppoſe the fury of Carmanniel's Horſe.
" For his reward, this he ſhall have each day,
" *Drink Coffee, then ſtrut out, and never pay.*"
 It was not long e'er the Grandees were met,
And round *news-papers* in full order ſet;
Then Sagoe, riſing, ſaid, " I hope you hear
" Hunger's advice with an obedient ear;
" Our great deſign admits of no delay,
" Famine commands, and we muſt all obey :
" That Syren which does FURMETARY keep
" Long ſince is riſen from the bands of ſleep;
" Her Spoons and Porringers with art diſplay'd,
" Many of Hunger's ſubjects have betray'd."
 " To arms," Hectorvus cried : " Coffedro ſtout,
" Iſſue forth liquor from thy ſcalding ſpout !"

Great One-and-all-i gives the firſt alarms ;
Then each man ſnatches up offenſive arms.
To Ditch of Fleet courageouſly they run,   145
Quicker than thought ; the battle is begun :
Hectorvus firſt Tubcarrio does attack,
And by ſurprize ſoon lays him on his back ;
Thirſto and Drowtho then, approaching near,
Soon overthrow two magazines of Beer.   150
  The innocent Syrena little thought
That all theſe arms againſt herſelf were brought ;
Nor that in her defence the drink was ſpilt :
How could ſhe fear, that never yet knew guilt ?
Her fragrant Juice, and her delicious Plums,   155
She does *diſpenſe* (with gold upon her thumbs) :
Virgins and Youths around her ſtood ; ſhe ſate,
Environ'd with a Wooden-chair of ſtate.
  In the mean time, Tobacco ſtrives to vex
A numerous ſquadron of the tender ſex ;   160
What with ſtrong ſmoak, and with his ſtronger breath,
He funks Baſketia and her ſon to death.
  Coffedro then, with Teedrums and the band
Who carried ſcalding liquors in their hand,
Throw watery ammunition in their eyes ;   165
On which Syrena's party frighten'd flies :
Carmannio ſtraight drives up a bulwark ſtrong,
And horſe oppoſes to Coffedro's throng.
Coledrivio ſtands for bright Syrena's guard,
And all her rallied Forces are prepar'd ;   170
Carmannio then to Teedrum's ſquadron makes,
And the lean mortal by the buttons takes ;
Not Teedrum's arts Carmannio could beſeech,
But his rough valour throws him in the ditch.
Syrena, though ſurpriz'd, reſolv'd to be   175
The great Bonduca of her FURMETRY :
Before her throne courageouſly ſhe ſtands,
Managing ladles-full with both her hands.
The numerous Plums like hail-ſhot flew about,
And Plenty ſoon diſpers'd the *meagre* rout.   180
  So have I ſeen, at Fair that's nam'd from Horn,
Many a Ladle's blow by Prentice borne ;

In

In vain he strives their passions to assuage,
With threats would frighten; with soft words engage;
Until, through Milky gauntlet soundly beat, 185
His prudent heels secure a quick retreat.

Jamque opus exegi, quod nec Jovis ira nec ignis,
Nec poterit ferrum, nec edax abolere vetustas!

MULLY

MULLY OF MOUNTOWN [c].

First printed by the Author in 1704.

I.

MOUNTOWN [d]! thou sweet retreat from Dublin cares,
    Be famous for thy Apples and thy Pears;
For Turnips, Carrots, Lettuce, Beans, and Pease;
For Peggy's Butter, and for Peggy's Cheese.   5
May clouds of Pigeons round about thee fly;
But condescend sometimes to make a Pye.
May fat Geese gaggle with melodious voice,
And ne'er want Gooseberries or Apple-sauce: 10
Ducks in thy Ponds, and Chicken in thy Pens,
And be thy Turkeys numerous as thy Hens:
May thy black Pigs lie warm in little stye,
And have no thought to grieve them till they die.
Mountown! the Muses' most delicious theme;   15
Oh! may thy Codlins ever swim in Cream!
Thy Rasp- and Straw-berries in Bourdeaux drown,
To add a redder tincture to their own!
Thy White-wine, Sugar, Milk, together club,
To make that gentle viand Syllabub [e].   20

[c] It was taken for a State Poem, and to have many mysteries in it; though it was only made, as well as "Orpheus and Eurydice," for country diversion. Dr. King's Preface to his Miscellanies.

[d] A pleasant villa to the South of Dublin, near the sea.

[e] "Peace to thy gentle shade, sweet-smiling Henniver!"—would have been our Author's ejaculation, if he had lived in 1775; when the admirers of this "gentle viand" lamented the irreparable loss of the foundress of the Lactarium.

    Lac mihi non æstate novum, non frigore desit;

    " My milk in summer's drought, nor winter fails;

was the Matron's invitation to the publick; whilst her happy cottage presented the liveliest reflection of its benignant owner:

    Quam dives pecoris nivei, quam lactis abundans!

    " What luscious milk, what rural stores are mine!"

Thy

Thy Tarts to Tarts, Cheefe-cakes to Cheefe-cakes join,
To fpoil the relifh of the flowing Wine.
But to the fading palate bring relief,
By thy Weftphalian Ham, or Belgic Beef;
And, to complete thy bleffings in a word,
May ftill thy foil be generous as its Lord [f] !

II.

Oh ! Peggy, Peggy, when thou goeft to brew,
Confider well what you're about to do ;
Be very wife, very fedately think.
That what you're going now to make is *drink* :
Confider who muft drink that drink, and then,
What 'tis to have the praife of *boneft* men :
For furely, Peggy, while that drink does laft,
'Tis Peggy will be *toafted* or *difgrac'd*.
Then, if thy Ale in *glafs* thou would'ft confine,
To make its fparkling rays in beauty fhine,
Let thy clean Bottle be entirely dry,
Left a white fubftance to the furface fly,
And, floating there, difturb the curious eye.
But this great maxim muft be underftood,
" Be fure, nay very fure, thy *cork* be good !"
Then future ages fhall of Peggy tell,
That Nymph that *brew'd* and *bottled* Ale fo well.

III.

How fleet is air ! how many things have breath
Which in a moment they refign to death ;
Depriv'd of light, and all their happieft ftate,
Not by their fault, but fome o'er-ruling Fate !
Although fair flowers, that juftly might invite,
Are cropt, nay torn away for man's delight ;
Yet ftill thofe flowers, alas ! can make no moan,
Nor has Narciffus now a power to groan !
But all thofe things which breathe in different frame,
By tie of common breath, man's pity claim.
A gentle Lamb has rhetorick to plead,
And, when fhe fees the Butcher's knife decreed,
Her voice intreats him not to make her bleed :

[f] Judge Upton.

But cruel gain, and luxury of taste,
With pride, still lays man's *fellow-mortals* waste :
What earth and waters breed, or air inspires,
Man for his palate fits by torturing fires.   60
   MULLY, a Cow sprung from a beauteous race,
With spreading front, did Mountown's pastures grace.
Gentle she was, and, with a gentle stream,
Each morn and night gave Milk that equal'd Cream,
Offending none, of none she stood in dread,   65
Much less of persons which she daily *fed :*
" But Innocence cannot itself defend,
" 'Gainst treacherous arts, veil'd with the name of Friend."
   ROBIN of Derby-shire, whose temper shocks
The constitution of his native rocks ;   70
Born in a place g, which, if it once be nam'd,
Would make a blushing modesty asham'd :
He with indulgence kindly did *appear*
To make poor Mully his peculiar care,
But inwardly this sullen churlish thief   75
Had all his mind plac'd upon Mully's Beef;
His fancy fed on her, and thus he'd cry,
" Mully, as sure as I'm alive, you die !
" 'Tis a brave Cow.   O, Sirs, when Christmas comes,
" These Shins shall make the Porridge grac'd with Plums,   80
" Then, midst our cups, whilst we profusely *dine,*
" This blade shall enter deep in Mully's Chine,
" What Ribs, what Rumps, what bak'd, boil'd, stew'd, and roast !
" There shan't one single Tripe of her be lost !"
   When Peggy, Nymph of Mountown, heard these sounds,   85
She griev'd to hear of Mully's future wounds.
" What crime," said she, " has gentle Mully done ?
" Witness the rising and the setting Sun,
" That knows what Milk she constantly would give !
" Let that quench Robin's rage, and Mully live."   90
   Daniel, a sprightly Swain, that us'd to slash
The vigorous Steeds that drew his Lord's calash,

g The Devil's Arse of Peak ; described by Hobbes in a poem " De
" Mirabilibus Pecci," the best of his poetical performances. See an account of Hobbes, vol. II. p. 142.

To

To Peggy's fide inclin'd, for 'twas well known
How well he lov'd thofe Cattle of his own.
    Then Terence fpoke, oraculous and fly,
He'd neither grant the queftion nor deny;
Pleading for Milk, his thoughts were on Mince-pye :
But all his arguments fo dubious were,
That Mully thence had neither hopes nor fear.
    " You've fpoke," fays Robin ; " but now, let me tell ye,   100
" 'Tis not fair fpoken *words* that fill the *belly* ;
" Pudding and Beef I love ; and cannot floop
" To recommend your bonny-clapper Soup ;
" You fay fhe's innocent : but what of that ?
" 'Tis more than crime fufficient that fhe's *fat !*   105
" And that which is prevailing in this cafe
" Is, there's another Cow to fill her place.
" And, granting Mully to have Milk in ftore,
" Yet ftill this other Cow will give us more.
" She dies."—Stop here, my Mufe : forbear the reft :   110
And veil that grief which cannot be expreft !

ORPHEUS

ORPHEUS AND EURYDICE.

Firſt printed by the Author in 1704.

A S Poets ſay, one Orpheus went
  To Hell upon an odd intent,
Firſt tell the ſtory, then let's know,
If any one will do ſo now.
  This Orpheus was a jolly boy,   5
Born long before the Siege of Troy ;
His parents found the lad was ſharp,
And taught him on the Iriſh Harp ;
And, when grown fit for marriage life,
Gave him Eurydice for wife,   10
And they, as ſoon as match was made,
Set up the Ballad-ſinging trade.
  The cunning varlet could deviſe,
For country folks, ten thouſand lies ;
Affirming all thoſe monſtrous things   15
Were done by force of *harp* and *ſtrings* ;
Could make a Tiger in a trice
Tame as a Cat, and catch your Mice ;
Could make a Lion's courage flag,
And ſtraight could animate a Stag,   20
And, by the help of pleaſing ditties,
Make Mill-ſtones run, and build up Cities ;
Each had the uſe of fluent tongue,
If Dicé ſcolded, Orpheus ſung.
And ſo, by diſcord without ſtrife,   25
Compos'd one harmony of life ;
And thus, as all their matters ſtood,
They got an honeſt livelihood :
  Happy were mortals, could they be
From any ſudden danger free !   30
Happy were Poets, could their ſong
The feeble thread of life prolong !
  But, as theſe two went ſtroling on,
Poor Dicé's ſcene of life was done ;

4   Away

Away her fleeting breath muſt fly,
Yet no one knows wherefore, or why.
   This eaus'd the general lamentation,
To all that knew her in her ſtation;
How briſk ſhe was ſtill to advance,
The Harper's gain, and lead the dance,
In every tune obſerve her thrill,
Sing on, yet change the money ſtill.
   Orpheus beſt knew what loſs he had,
And, thinking on't, fell almoſt mad,
And ¡in deſpair to Linus ran,
Who was eſteem'd a Cunning-man;
Cried, " He again muſt Dicé have,
" Or elſe be buried in her grave."
   Quoth Linus, " Soft, refrain your ſorrow:
" What fails to-day, may ſpeed to-morrow.
" Thank you the Gods for whate'er happens,
" But don't fall out with your fat capons.
" 'Tis many an honeſt man's petition,
" That he may be in your condition.
" If ſuch a bleſſing might be had,
" To change a living wife for dead,
" I'd be your chapman; nay, I'd do't,
" Though I gave forty pounds to boot.
" Confider firſt, you ſave her diet;
" Confider next, you keep her·quiet:
" For, pray, what was ſhe all along,
" Except the burthen of your ſong?
" What, though your Dicé's under ground,
" Yet many a woman may be found,
" Who, in your gains if ſhe may part take,
" Truſt me, will quickly make your heart ake:
" Then reſt content, as widowers ſhould—
" The Gods beſt know what's for our good!"
   Orpheus no longer could endure
Such wounds where he expeᵭed cure.
   " Is't poſſible?" cried he; " and can
" That noble creature, married man,
" In ſuch a cauſe be ſo profane?

5

" I'll fly thee far as I would death,
" Who from my Dicé took her breath."   75
    Which faid, he foon outftript the wind,
Whilft puffing Boreas lagg'd behind,
And to Urganda's cave he came,
A lady of prodigious fame ;
Whofe hollow eyes and hopper breech   80
Made common people call her Witch ;
Down at her feet he proftrate lies,
With trembling heart and blubber'd eyes.
    " Tell me," faid he, " for fure you know
" The Powers above, and thofe below,   85
" Where does Eurydice remain ?
" How fhall I fetch her back again ?"
    She fmilingly replied, " I'll tell
" This eafily without a fpell :
" The wife you look for's gone to Hell—
" Nay, never ftart, man, for 'tis fo ;
" Except one ill-bred wife or two,
" The fafhion is, for all to go.
" Not that fhe will be damn'd ; ne'er fear
" But fhe may get preferment there.   95
" Indeed, fhe might be fried in pitch,
" If fhe had been a bitter bitch ;
" If fhe had leapt athwart a fword,
" And afterwards had broke her word.
" But your Eurydice, poor foul !   100
" Was a good-natur'd harmlefs fool ;
" Except a little cattervawling,
" Was always painful in her calling ;
" And, I dare truft old Pluto for't,
" She will find favour in his Court :   105
" But then to fetch her back, that ftill
" Remains, and may be paft my fkill ;
" For, 'tis too fad a thing to jeft on,
" You're the firft man e'er afk'd the queftion ;
" For hufbands are fuch felfifh elves,   110
" They care for little but themfelves.
" And then one rogue cries to another,
" Since this wife's gone, e'en get another :

" Though moſt men let ſuch thoughts alone,
" And ſwear they've had enough of *one.*
" But, ſince you are ſo kind to Dicé,
" Follow the courſe which I adviſe ye ;
" E'en go to Hell yourſelf, and try
" Th' effect of Muſick's harmony ;
" For you will hardly find a friend,
" Whom you in ſuch a caſe might ſend ;
" Beſides, their Proſerpine has been
" The briſkeſt dancer on the green,
" Before old Pluto raviſh'd her,
" Took her to Hell—and you may ſwear
" She had but little Muſick there ;
" For, ſince ſhe laſt beheld the ſun,
" Her merry dancing-days are done ;
" She has a colt's tooth ſtill, I warrant,
" And will not diſapprove your errand.
" Then your requeſt does reaſon ſeem,
" For what's one ſingle ghoſt to them ?
" Though thouſand *phantoms* ſhould invade ye,
" Paſs on—Faint Heart ne'er won fair Lady !
" The bold a way will find, or make,
" Remember, 'tis for Dicé's ſake."
    Nothing pleas'd Orpheus half ſo well,
As news that he muſt go to Hell.
Th' impatient wight long'd to be going,
As moſt folk ſeek their own undoing ;
Ne'er thought of what he left behind,
Never conſider'd he ſhould find
Scarce any paſſenger beſide
Himſelf, nor could he hire a guide.
    " Will Muſick do't ?" cried he. " Ne'er heed,
" My harp ſhall make the marble bleed ;
" My harp all dangers ſhall remove,
" And dare all flames, but thoſe of Love."
    Then kneeling begs, in terms moſt civil,
Urganda's paſsport to the Devil ;
Her paſs ſhe kindly to him gave,
Then bad him 'noint himſelf with ſalve ?

Such as thofe hardy people ufe,
Who walk on fire without their fhoes;
Who, on occafion, in a dark hole,   155
Can gormondize on lighted Charcoal;
And drink eight quarts of flaming Fuel,
As men in flux do Water-gruel.
She bad him then go to thofe-caves,
Where Conjurers keep Fairy flaves,   160
Such fort of creatures as will bafte ye
A Kitchen-wench for being nafty:
But, if fhe neatly fcour her pewter,
Give her the money that is due t'her.
    Orpheus went down a narrow hole,   165
That was as dark as any coal;
He did at length fome glimmering fpy,
By which, at leaft, he might defcry
Ten thoufand little Fairy elves,
Who there were folacing themfelves.   170
    All ran about him, cried, " Oh, dear!
" Who thought to have feen Orpheus here?
" Tis that Queen's birth-day which you fee,
" And you are come as luckily:
" You had no Ballad but we bought it,   175
" Paid Dicé when fhe little thought it;
" When you beneath the yew-tree fat,
" We've come, and all danc'd round your Hat;
" But whereabouts did Dicé leave ye?
" She had been welcome, Sir, believe me."   180
    " Thefe little chits would make one fwear,"
Quoth Orpheus, 'twixt difdain and fear.
" And dare thefe Urchins jeer my croffes,
" And laugh at mine and Dicé's loffes.
" Hands off—the monkeys hold the fafter;   185
" Sirrahs, I am going to your Mafter!"
    " Good words," quoth Oberon: " don't flinch;
" For, every time you ftir, I'll pinch;
" But, if you decently fit down,
" I'll firft equip you with a crown;   190
" Then for each dance, and for each fong,
" Our pence apiece the whole night long."

P 2

Orpheus,

Orpheus, who found no remedy,
Made virtue of neceſſity,
Though all was out of tune, their dance   195
Would only hinder his advance.
Each note that from his fingers fell
Seemed to be Dicé's paſſing-bell,
At laſt, night let him eaſe his crupper,
Get on his legs, to go to ſupper.   200
    Quoth Nab, " We here have ſtrangers ſeldom,
" But, Sir, to what we have you're welcome."
    " Madam, they ſeem of light digeſtion.
" Is it not rude to aſk a queſtion?
" What they may be, fiſh, fleſh, or fruit?   205
" For I ne'er ſaw things ſo minute."

    " S I R,

    " A roaſted ant, that's nicely done,
" By one ſmall atom of the ſun.
" Theſe are flies eggs, in moon-ſhine poach'd,
" This a flea's thigh in collops ſcotch'd,   210
" 'Twas hunted yeſterday i' th' Park,
" And like t' have ſcap'd us in the dark.
" This is a diſh entirely new,
" Butterflies brains diſſolv'd in dew;
" Theſe lovers vows, theſe courtiers hopes,
" Things to be eat by microſcopes: 215
" Theſe ſucking mites, a glow-worm's heart,
" This a delicious rainbow-tart !"
    " Madam, I find, they're very nice,
" And will digeſt within a trice;
" I ſee there's nothing you eſteem,   220
" That's half ſo groſs as our whipt-cream.
" And I infer, from all theſe meats,
" That ſuch light ſuppers keep clean ſheets."
    " But, Sir," ſaid ſhe, " perhaps you're dry !"
Then, ſpeaking to a Fairy by,   225
" You've taken care, my dear Endia,
" All's ready for my Ratifia."

                                    " S I R,

"SIR,

"A drop of water, newly torn
"Fresh from the rosy-finger'd Morn;
"A pearl of milk, that's gently preſt   230
"From blooming Hebe's early breaſt;
"With half a one of Cupid's tears;
"When he in embryo firſt appears;
"And honey from an infant bee
"Makes liquor for the Gods and Me!"   235
"Madam," ſays he, "an't pleaſe your Grace,
"I'm going to a droughty place;
"And, if I an't too bold, pray charge her,
"The draught I have be ſomewhat larger."
"Fetch me," ſaid ſhe, "a mighty bowl,   240
"Like Oberon's capacious ſoul,
"And then fill up the burniſh'd gold
"With juice that makes the Britons bold.
"This from ſeven barley-corns I drew, ⎫
"Its years are ſeven, and to the view ⎬
"'Tis clear, and ſparkles fit for you. ⎭
"But ſtay —
"When I by Fate was laſt time hurl'd,
"To act my pranks in t'other world,
"I ſaw ſome ſparks as they were drinking,   250
"With mighty mirth and little thinking,
"Their jeſts were *ſupernaculum*,
"I ſnatch'd the rubies from each thumb,
"And in this cryſtal have them here,
"Perhaps you'll like it more than Beer."   255
Wine and late hours diſſolv'd the feaſt,
And Men and Fairies went to reſt.
The bed where Orpheus was to lie
Was all ſtuff'd full of Harmony,
Purling ſtreams and amorous rills,   260
Dying ſound that never kills:
Zephyrus breathing, Love delighting,
Joy to ſlumber ſoft inviting:
Trembling ſounds that make no noiſe,
And ſongs to pleaſe without a voice,   265

P 3

Were

Were mixt with down that fell from Jove,
When he became a Swan for love.

'Twas night, and Nature's felf lay dead,
Nodding upon a feather-bed;
The mountains feem'd to bend their tops,
And fhutters clos'd the milleners fhops,
Excluding both the punks and fops,
No ruffled ftreams to mill do come,
The filent fifh were ftill more dumb;
Look in the chimney, not a fpark there,
And darknefs did itfelf grow darker.

But Orpheus could not fleep a wink,
He had too many things to think:
But, in the dark, his harp he ftrung,
And to the liftening Fairies fung.

Prince Prim, who pitied fo much youth
Join'd with fuch conftancy and truth,
Soon gave him thus to underftand;

" Sir, I laft night receiv'd command
" To fee you out of Fairy Land,
" Into the Realm of Nofnotbocai;
" But let not fear or fulphur choak ye;
" For he's a Fiend of fenfe and wit,
" And has got many rooms to lett."

As quick as thought, by glow-worm glimpfe,
Out walk the Fidler and the Prince.
They foon arrive; find Bocai brewing
Of Claret for a Vintner's ftewing.

" I come from Oberon," quoth Prince Prim.

" 'Tis well," quoth Bocai: " what from him?"

" Why, fomething ftrange; this honeft man
" Had his wife died; now, if he can,
" He fays, he'd have her back again."

Then Bocai, fmiling, cried, " You fee,
" Orpheus, you'd better ftay with me.
" For, let me tell you, Sir, this place,
" Although it has an ugly face,
" If to its value it were fold,
" Is worth ten thoufand ton of gold;

" And very famous in all ftory,   305
" Call'd by the name of Purgatory.
" For, when fome ages fhall have run,
" And Truth by Falfehood be undone,
" Shall rife the Whore of Babylon ;
" And this fame Whore fhall be a Man,   310
" Who, by his lies and cheating, can
" Be fuch a trader in all evil,
" As to outdo our friend the Devil :
" He and his pimps fhall fay, that when
" A man is dying, thither then   315
" The Devil comes to take the foul,
" And carry him down to this hole ;
" But, if a man have ftore of wealth,
" To get fome prayers for his foul's health,
" The Devil has then no more to do,   320
" But muft be forc'd to let him go ;
" But we are no more fools than they,
" Thus to be bubbled of our prey.
" By thefe fame pious Frauds and Lies,
" Shall many Monafteries rife :   325
" Friars fhall get good meat and beer,
" To pray folks out that ne'er came here ;
" Pans, pots, and kettles, fhall be given,
" To fetch a man from hence to Heaven.
" Suppofe a man has taken purfes,   330
" Or ftolen fheep, or cows, or horfes,
" And chances to be hang'd ; you'd cry,
" Let him be hang'd, and fo good by.
" Hold, fays the Friar ; let me alone,
" He's but to Purgatory gone ;   335
" And if you'll let our Convent keep
" Thofe purfes, cows, horfes, and fheep ;
" The fellow fhall find no more pain,
" Than if he were alive again."
    Here Orpheus figh'd, began to take on,
Cried, " Could I find the Whore you fpake on,
" I'd give him my beft flitch of bacon :
" I'd give him cake and fugar'd fack,
" If he would bring my Dice back :

P 4

" Rather j

" Rather than she should longer stay,   345
" I'd find some lusty man to *pray*.
" And then poor Dicé, let him try her,
" I dare say, would requite the Friar."
    Great Nosnotbocai smil'd to see
Such goodness and simplicity.   350
Then kindly led them to a cell,
An outward granary of Hell;
A filthy place, that's seldom swept,
Where feeds of villainy are kept.
    " Orpheus," said he, " I'd have you take   355
" Some of these feeds here, for my fake;
" Which, if they are discreetly hurl'd
" Throughout the parts of t'other world,
" They may oblige the Fiend you sue to,
" And fill the palace of old Pluto.   360
    " Sow *pride-feed* uppermost ; then above
" *Envy* and *scandal* plant *self-love*.
" Here take *revenge*, and *malice without cause*,
" And here *contempt of honesty and laws* ;
" This hot feed's *anger*, and this hotter *lust*,   365
" Best sown with *breach of friendship*, and *of trust* :
    " These *storm, hail, plague,* and *tempest* feeds,
" And this a quintessence of weeds,
" This the worst fort of artichoke,
" A plant that Pluto has himself bespoke ;   370
" Nourish it well, 'tis useful *treachery*.
" This is a choice though little feed, a *lye* :
" Here take some new from these prodigious loads,
    " Of tender things that look like Toads.
" In future times, these, finely dreft,   375
" Shall each invade a Prince's breast ;
" 'Tis *flattery* feed, though thinly sown,
" It is a mighty plant when grown,
" When rooted deep, and fully blown ;
" Now see these things like bubbles fly,   380
" These are the feeds of *vanity*.
" Take *tyrant acorns*, which will best advance,
" If sown in Eastern climates, or in France ;

" But

" But thefe are things of moft prodigious hopes,
" They're *Jefuit bulbs* tied up with ropes,
" And thefe the Devil's grafts for future popes,
" Which with Fanaticifm are join'd fo clean,
" You'd fcarce believe a knife had pafs'd between :
" *Falfe-witnefs* feed had almoft been forgot,
" 'Twill be your making, fhould there be a plot :
" And now, dear Orpheus, fcatter thefe but well ;   390
" And you'll deferve the gratitude of Hell."
          Quoth Orpheus, " You fhall be obey'd
" In every thing that you have faid,
" For mifchief is the Poet's trade :
" And whatfoever they fhall bring,
" You may affure yourfelf, I'll fing.
" But pray what Poets fhall we have,
" At my returning from the grave ?"
          " Sad dogs !" quoth Bocai — " let me fee —   395
" But, fince what I fay cannot fhame them,
" I'll e'en refolve to never name them."
          " But now," fays Bocai, " Sir, you may
" Long to be going on your way,
" Unlefs you'll drink fome Arfenick Claret :   400
" 'Tis burnt, you fee; but Sam can fpare it.
          Orpheus replied, " Kind Sir, 'tis neither
" Brandy nor whets that brought me hither ;
" But Love, and I an inftance can be,
" Love is as hot as pepper'd brandy ;   405
" Yet, gentle Sir, you may command
" A tune from a departing hand ;
" The ftyle and paffion both are good,
" 'Tis *The Three Children in the Wood.*"
          He fang ; and pains themfelves found eafe ;   410
For griefs, when well exprefs'd, can pleafe.
When he defcrib'd the childrens lofs,
And how the Robins cover'd them with mofs ;
          To hear the pity of thofe birds,
E'en Bocai's tears fell down with Orpheus' words.   415
          &c.

RUFINUS;

R U F I N U S;

O R,

THE FAVOURITE*.

Imitated from CLAUDIAN.

OFT, as I wondering stand, a secret doubt
Puzzles my reason, and disturbs my thought,
Whether this lower world by Chance does move,
Or guided by the guardian hand of Jove.
When I survey the world's harmonious frame, 5
How Nature lives immutably the same;
How stated bounds and ambient shores restrain
The rowling surges of the briny main;
How constant Time revolves the circling year;
How Day and Night alternately appear; 10
Then am I well convinc'd some secret soul,
Some First Informing Power directs the whole;
Some great Intelligence, who turns the Spheres,
Who rules the steady motion of the Stars,
Who decks with *borrow'd light* the waning Moon, 15
And fills with *native light* th' unchanging Sun,
Who hangs the Earth amidst surrounding skies,
And bids her various Fruits in various Seasons rise.
But, soon as I reflect on human state,
How blind, how unproportion'd, is our fate; 20
How *ill men*, crown'd with blessings, smoothly pass
A golden circle of delightful days;
How *good men* bear the rugged paths of life,
Condemn'd to endless cares, to endless strife:
Then am I lost again; Religion fails, 25
Then Epicurus' bolder *scheme* prevails;

* This was written in 1711, and seems to be a harsh satire on the duke
of Marlborough; but was perhaps dictated rather by party rage than truth.

Which through the void makes wandering *atoms* dance,
And calls the medley world the work of Chance;
Which God's eternal Providence denies,
And feigns him nodding in the diftant fkies.   30

  At length RUFINUS' fate my doubt removes,
And God's *exiftence* and his *juftice* proves.
Nor do I longer undeceiv'd complain,
The Wicked flourifh, and triumphant reign;
Since they to Fortune's heights are rais'd alone,   35
To rufh with greater ruin headlong down [b].

But

[b] The Reader (if fuch an one by chance there be) who has received no
entertainment from the preceding lines may fpare himfelf the trouble of
perufing a mafterly imitation of the fame original; which we are tempted
to annex, as a rich repaft for the Literati. To the very learned and now
right reverend author of them our beft excufe is fuggefted by his own
motto—*Licebit interdum* NOTISSIMA *eligere*.

    " Oft have thefe thoughts my anxious foul opprefs'd,
" With fluctuating fury tore my breaft,
" Whether Omnifcient Powers, all good, beftow
" Their care and blefling on mankind below;
" Or doth fole arbitrefs, blind Chance, prefide.
" And things at random drive the giddy guide.
    " When this harmonious whole I wondering found
" By laws directed, ftricteft union bound;
" How circling feafons in their turns appear,
" To pour their products, and complete the year;
" How Night and Day in grateful change move round;
" How ftraggling deeps, unwilling, own a bound;
" The tumult ceas'd.—Yet, though reprefs'd my fears,
" My mind ftill labours with the leflening cares.
" As when retiring ftorms forfake the deep,
" Pant to the fhore, and o'er the billows creep;
" While Ocean yet not all his peace regains,
" Nor baffled Boreas quits the heaving plains,
" Thick fluttering blafts die in a diftant roar,
    " And fainter murmurs fall along the fhore.
    " But now a confcious guidance I defcry,
" Now fee a Mind Almighty, thron'd on high:
" Who points the planets their unvaried way;
" Fills the fair womb of Earth with offspring gay;
" Gives changing Phœbe fplendours not her own,
" And ftores with unlent light the conftant Sun;
" On central axes hangs the fteady ball,
" Secure in air, and gives it laws to roll.

" When

But here inſtruct thy Bard, Pierian Dame,
Whence, and of whom, the dire contagion came.
    Alecto's breaſt with rage and envy glows,
To ſee the world poſſeſs'd of ſweet repoſe.   40
Down to the dreary realms below ſhe bends,
There ſummons a *cabal* of Siſter Fiends.
Thither unnumber'd Plagues direct their flight,
The curſed progeny of Hell and Night.
Firſt, Diſcord rears her head, the nurſe of War;   45
Next, Famine fiercely ſtalks with haughty air;
Then Age ſcarce drags her limbs, ſcarce draws her breath,
But, tottering on, approaches neighbouring Death;
Here grows Diſeaſe, with inbred tortures worn;
There Envy ſnarls, and others good does mourn;
There Sorrow ſighs, her robe to tatters torn;
Fear ſkulks behind, and trembling hides her face,
But Raſhneſs headlong thruſts her front of braſs;
Then Luxury, wealth's bane, profuſely ſhines,
Whilſt Want, attending in a *cloud*, repines.   55

───────────

" When lo! again ——
" My views no more a certain proſpect boaſt,
" And all the promiſe of a God is loſt.
" Black gathering clouds my ruffled mind o'er-ſpread,
" Bewilder'd in the maze of life I tread,
" See the ſucceſsful Villain ride the ſtate;
" The Patriot ſinking in the ſtorms of Fate.
" Sudden Religion's ſtrong ſupports decay,
" And all the towering fabrick falls away;
" With mournful eyes the fleeting form I view,
" And forc'd, unwilling, other guides purſue;
" That through the void teach ſtooping atoms rain'd,
" By Chance aſſociate, and by Chance detain'd.
" While lucky jumbles of a thoughtleſs rout
" A world produce, and at an heat ſtrike out.
" Exiſts the whole, ungovern'd, ſelf-combin'd,
" Nor wants the ſtay of an immortal Mind.
    " But all my doubts RUFINUS' fall remov'd;
" Abſolv'd the Gods, and Providence approv'd.
" Of tardy Vengeance now no more I rave,
" When proſtituted Purple courts the Slave;
" Hoiſted aloft, juſt ſhewn, then headlong flung,
" To deck the dunghill whence the inſect ſprung."
        Miſcellaneous Tranſlations in Proſe and Verſe, 1724.

A train

A train of fleeplefs felf-tormenting cares,
Daughters of meagre Avarice, appears [e];
Who, as around her wither'd *neck* they cling,
Confefs the parent *bag* from whence they fpring.
Here ills of each malignant kind refort,   60
A thoufand monfters guard the dreadful court.
Amidft th' *infernal crowd*, Alecto ftands,
And a deep filence awfully commands;
Then, in tumultuous terms like thefe, exprefs'd
A paffion long had fwell'd within her breaft :   65
" Shall we fupine permit thefe *peaceful days*,
" So fmooth, fo gay, fo undifturb'd, to pafs?
" Shall Pity melt, fhall Clemency controul,
" A Fury's fierce and unrelenting *foul?*
" What do our iron whips, our brands, avail;   70
" What all the horrid implements of Hell;
" Since mighty Jove debars us of his *fkies*,
" Since Theodofius too his *earth* denies ?
" Such were the days, and fo their tenor ran,
" When the firft happy Golden Age began :   75
" Virtue and Concord, with their heavenly train,
" With Piety and Faith, fecurely reign;
" Nay, Juftice, in imperial pomp array'd,
" Boldly explores this everlafting fhade;
" Me fhe, infulting, menaces and awes;   80
" Reforms the world, and vindicates her laws.
" And fhall we then, neglected and forlorn,
" From every region banifh'd, idly mourn ?
" Affert yourfelves; know what, and whence, you are:
" Attempt fome glorious mifchief worth your care;
" Involve the Univerfe in endlefs war.
" Oh ! that I could in Stygian vapours rife,
" Darken the *fun*, pollute the balmy *fkies*;
" Let loofe the *rivers*, deluge every plain,
" Break down the *barriers* of the roaring main,
" And fhatter Nature into Chaos once again !"
    So rag'd the Fiend, and tofs'd her *vipers* round,
Which hiffing pour'd their poifon on the ground.

    [e] This is an inftance in which Dr. King, in common with greater
Poets, has facrificed Grammar to (even a very indifferent) Rhyme.

A murmur

A murmur through the jarring audience rung,
Different resolves from different reasons sprung.   95
So when the fury of the storm is past,
When the rough winds in softer murmurs waste;
So sounds, so fluctuates, the troubled sea,
As the expiring *tempest* plows its way.

 Megæra, rising then, addrefs'd the throng,   100
To whom Sedition, Tumult, Rage, belong;
Whofe food is entrails of the guiltlefs dead,
Whofe drink is childrens blood by parents shed.
She scorch'd Alcides with a frantic flame,   105
She broke the bow, the favage world did tame;
She nerv'd the arm, she flung the deadly dart,
When Athamas transfix'd Learchus' heart:
She prompted Agamemnon's monftrous Wife
To take her injur'd Lord's devoted life: 110
She breath'd revenge and rage into the Son,
So did the Mother's blood the Sire's atone:
She blinded Oedipus with kindred charms,
Forc'd him inceftuous to a Mother's arms;
She ftung Thyeftes, and his fury fed;   115
She taught him to pollute a Daughter's bed.
Such was her dreadful fpeech:

  " Your *fchemes* not practical nor lawful are,
 " With Heaven and Jove to wage unequal war:
 " But, if the peace of Man you would invade,   120
 " If o'er the ravag'd Earth *deftruction* fpread.
 " Then shall RUFINUS, fram'd for every *ill*,
 " With your own vengeance execute your will;
 " A prodigy from favage parents fprung,
 " Impetuous as a Tigrefs new with young;   125
 " Fierce as the Hydra, fickle as the Flood,
 " And keen as meagre Harpies for their food.
 " Soon as the infant drew the vital air,
 " I firft receiv'd him to my nurfing care;
 " And often he, when tender yet and young,   130
 " Cried for the teat, and on my bofom hung:
 " Whilft my *horn'd ferpents* round his *vifage* play'd;
 " His features form'd, and there their *venom* shed,

" Whilft

"Whilft I, infuling, breath'd into his heart
"*Deceit* and *craft*, and every hurtful art;
"Taught him t'involve his foul in fecret clouds,
"With falfe diffembling fmiles to veil his frauds.
"Not dying patriots' tortures can affuage
"His inborn cruelty, his native rage:
"Not Tagus' yellow torrent can fuffice
"His boundlefs and unfated *avarice*;
"Nor all the metal of Pactolus' ftreams,
"Nor Hermus glittering as the folar beams.
"If you the ftratagem propos'd approve,
"Let us to Court this *bane* of *crowns* remove.
"There fhall he foon, with his intriguing art,
"Guide uncontroul'd the willing Prince's *heart*.
"Not Numa's wifdom fhall that *heart* defend,
"When the falfe *Favourite* acts the faithful *Friend*."
Soon as fhe ended, the furrounding crowd
With peals of joy the black defign applaud.
Now with an *adamant* her hair fhe bound,
With a blue *ferpent* girt her veft around;
Then haftes to Phlegethon's impetuous ftream,
Whofe pitchy waves are flakes of rolling flame;
There lights a torch, and ftraight, with wings difplay'd,
Shoots fwiftly through the *dun* Tartarian glade.
A place on Gallia's utmoft verge there lies,
Extended to the fea and Southern fkies;
Where once Ulyffes, as old Fables tell,
Invok'd and rais'd th'inhabitants of Hell;
Where oft, with ftaring eyes, the trembling *hind*
Sees airy *phantoms* fkim before the wind:
Hence fprings the Fury into upper fkies,
Infecting all the region as fhe flies:
She roars, and fhakes the atmofphere around,
And Earth and Sea rebellow to the found.
Then ftraight transform'd her fnakes to filver hairs,
And like an old decrepid *fage* appears;
Slowly fhe creeps along with trembling gait,
Scarce can her languid limbs fuftain her weight.
At length, arriving at RUFINUS' cell,
Which, from his monftrous birth, fhe knew fo well,

She

She mildly thus Hell's *darling hope* addref's'd,
Sooth'd his ambition, and inflam'd his breaft :   175
 " Can Sloth diffolve RUFINUS ? canft thou pafs
" Thy fprightly youth in foft inglorious eafe ?
" Know, that thy better Fate, thy kinder Star,
" Does more exalted paths for thee prepare.
" If thou an *old* man's counfel canft obey,   180
" The fubject world fhall own thy fovereign fway :
" For my enlighten'd foul, my confcious breaft,
" Of Magic's *fecret fcience* is poffefs'd.
" Oft have I forc'd, with *myftic midnight* fpells,
" Pale *fpectres* from their fubterranean cells : 185
" Old Hecaté attends my powerful fong,
" Powerful to haften fate, or to prolong ;
" Powerful the rooted ftubborn oak to move,
" To ftop the thunder burfting from above,
" To make the rapid flood's defcending ftream 190
" Flow backward to the fountain whence it came.
" Nor doubt my truth — behold, with juft furprize,
" An effort of my art—a *palace rife*."
 She faid ; and, lo ! a *palace* towering feems,
With Parian pillars and metallic beams.   195
RUFINUS, ravifh'd with the vaft delight,
Gorges his *avarice,* and gluts his fight.
Such was his tranfport, fuch his fudden pride,
When Midas firft his *golden wifh* enjoy'd :
But, as his ftiffening food to metal turn'd, 200
He found his rafhnefs, and his ruin mourn'd.
 " Be thou or Man or God," Rufinus faid,
" I follow wherefoe'er thy dictates lead."
 Then from his *hut* he flies, affumes the ftate
Propounded by the Fiend, prepar'd by Fate. 205
Ambition foon began to lift her head,
Soaring, fhe mounts with reftlefs pinions fpread ;
But Juftice, confcious, fhuns the poifon'd air,
Where only *proftituted tools* repair ;
Where STILICO and Virtue not avail ;   210
Where *royal favours* ftand expos'd to fale ;

           Where

Where now Rufinus [d], scandalously great,
Loads labouring nations with oppreffive weight;

Keeps

[d] To the elegant writer whom we have already quoted in p. 219, the Curious are also indebted for the following valuable Fragment:

— Slow daftard Dulnefs is his native vice,
But Mifchief quickens, and informs the mafs,
From realm to realm as the Deftroyer flies,
A following tract of bloody ruin lies :
Beneath the Line with fiercer fires he glows,
And adds new winter to Rhiphean fnows.
An horrid refpite chains and racks afford,
The cruel mercies of th' impending fword :
Worfe than th' impending fword protracted breath,
A life prolong'd to wail the woes of death.
   If any, bolder than the reft, deny
When call'd the Tyrant's coffers to fupply ;
Stung with the dire difgrace, he foams with ire,
And his red eye-balls dart deftructive fire.
So the ftruck Savage roves Getulia's plain,
Tries the barb'd javelin, and provokes the pain;
Robb'd of her young, fo the mad tigrefs roars,
Hangs on the parth, and thunders to the fhores ;
So hiffes fierce, fo meditates her foe,
The trodden fnake, while her big columns glow :
But ftill he thirfts, ftill pines amidft his ftore,
A wretch, that's always craving, always poor.
   See great Fabricius, great in indigence,
Slight the deluding tribute of a prince ;
His fmall paternal plot Serranus plows,
While fweat bedews the toiling conful's brows.
Thofe lowly cots, the Curian names adorn,
On cloud-hid Palatine look down with fcorn.
O facred ftate ! where wealth or want ne'er come ;
To ferve no motive, to enflave no Rome !
Let luxury thy o'er-charg'd nature load,
And with fantaftic dainties heap thy board.
To her full breafts, me Mother Earth receives ;
Cheaply I'll riot on the wealth fhe gives.
There, figur'd walls betray the Tyrian loom,
Th' imperial *murix* * proudly paints thy dome.
Here, blooming meads their fragrant fweets difpenfe ;
Here, living pleafures court the ravifh'd fenfe ;
Embroider'd carpets every field adorn,
Blows in the grove, and opens in the lawn ;

* A fhell fifh ; of the liquor whereof a purple colour is made.

Keeps the obfequious world depending ftill
On the proud dictates of his lawlefs will;   215
Advances thofe, whofe fierce and factious zeal
Prompts ever to *refift*, and to *rebel* :
But thofe *impeaches*, who their Prince commend,
Who, dauntlefs, dare his *facred rights* defend.
Expounds fmall *riots* into *higheft crimes*,   220
Brands *loyalty* as *treafon* to the *times*.
An *haughty Minion*, mad with *empire* grown,
Enflaves the *fubjects*, and infults the *Throne*.

A thoufand difemboguing *rivers* pay
Their everlafting homage to the *fea* ;   225
The Nile, the Rhine, the Danube, and the Thames,
Pour conftant down their tributary ftreams :
But yet the *fea* confefles no increafe,
For all is fwallow'd in the deep abyfs.

In craving, ftill RUFINUS' foul remains,   230
Though fed with fhowers of gold, and floods of gains ;
For he defpoils and ravages the land,
No ftate is free from his rapacious hand ;
Treafures immenfe he hoards.; erects a tower,
To lodge the plunder'd world's collected ftore :
Unmeafur'd is his wealth, unbounded is his power.

* * * * *

The flowery couch and gently-murmuring ftreams
Lull to foft flumbers and unbroken dreams.
There, clamorous clients croud long rooms of ftate,
And fawning levees call the Wretched, Great !
Here, on fmooth whifpers, balmy Zephyr blows,
And every Mufick wakes from calm repofe.
A virtuous Poverty's a good confefs'd,
When Nature made us men, fhe made us blefs'd.
So live the Wife, who hear her heavenly voice,
Who know to make, and know to ufe, their choice *.

* " Adeo tritum thema eft, atque ab omnibus jactatam, otium & fe-
" ceffum præponere vitæ forenfi, & occupatæ, propter fecuritatem, liber-
" tatem, dulcedinem, dignitatem, aut faltem ab indignitatibus immuni-
" tatem, *ut nemo tractet hunc locum quin bene tractet* ; ita humanis concep-
" tibus in experiendo, & confenfibus in approbando confonat." Bacon,
de Augm. Scient.

Oh !

Oh! whither would'ft thou rove, *miftaken man?*
Vain are thy hopes, thy acquifitions vain:
For now, fuppofe thy *avarice* poffefs'd   240
Of all the fplendour of the glittering Eaft,
Of CROESUS' mafs of wealth, of CYRUS' crown,
Suppofe the ocean's treafure all thy own;
Still would thy foul repine, ftill afk for more,
Unbleft with plenty, with abundance poor.   245
FABRICIUS, in himfelf, in virtue great,
Difdain'd a monarch's bribe, defpis'd his ftate.
SERRANUS, as he grac'd the Conful's chair,
So could he guide the plough's laborious fhare.
The fam'd, the warlike, CURII deign'd to dwell   250
In a poor lonely cot and humble cell.
Such a retreat to me's more glorious far,
Than all thy pomp, than all thy triumphs are:
Give me my folitary native home,
Take thou thy rifing tower, thy lofty *dome*;   255
Though there, thy furniture of radiant die
Abftracts and ravifhes the curious eye;
Though each apartment, every fpacious room,
Shines with the glories of the Tyrian *loom*;
Yet here I view a more delightful fcene,   260
Where Nature's frefheft bloom and beauties *reign*;
Where the warm Zephyr's genial balmy wing,
Playing, diffufes an eternal fpring:
Though there thy lewd lafcivious limbs are laid,
On a rich downy couch, or *golden bed*;   265
Yet here, extended on the flowery grafs,
More free from care, my guiltlefs hours I pafs:
Though there, thy *fycophants*, a fervile race,
Cringe at thy levees, and refound thy praife;
Yet here a murmuring ftream, or warbling bird,   270
To me does fweeter harmony afford.
NATURE on all the power of blifs beftows,
Which from her bounteous fource perpetual flows.
But he alone with happinefs is bleft,
Who knows to ufe it rightly when poffeft: 275
A doctrine, if well poiz'd in Reafon's fcale,
Nor Luxury nor Want would thus prevail.

Q 2

Nor

Nor would our fleets fo frequent plow the main,
Nor our embattled *armies* ftrew the plain.
　　But, oh! RUFINUS is to reafon blind!　　　　　280
A ftrange hydropic thirft inflames his mind.
No *bribes* his growing appetite can fate;
For new poffeffions new defires create.
No fenfe of fhame, no modefty, reftrains,
Where Avarice or where Ambition reigns.　　　　285
When with ftrict *oaths* his profer'd faith he binds,
Falfe are his vows, and treacherous his defigns.
　　Now, fhould a Patriot rife, his power oppofe,
Should he affert a finking *nation's* caufe,
He ftirs a vengeance nothing can controul,　　　290
Such is the rancour of his haughty foul;
Fell as a lionefs in Libya's plain,
When tortur'd with the javelin's pointed gain:
Or a fpurn'd ferpent, as fhe fhoots along,
With lightening in her eyes, and poifon in her tongue.　295
Nor will thofe families eraz'd fuffice;
But provinces and cities he deftroys:
Urg'd on with blind revenge and fettled hate,
He labours the confufion of the *ftate*;
Subverts the nation's old-eftablifh'd frame,　　　300
Explodes her laws, and tramples on her fame.
　　If e'er in *mercy* he pretends to fave
A man purfued by *faction* from the *grave*;
Then he invents new punifhments, *new pains*,
Condemns to *filence*, and from *truth* reftrains ᵉ:　　305
Then *racks* and *pillories*, and *bonds* and *bars*,
Then *ruin* and *impeachments* he prepares.
O dreadful mercy! more than death fevere!
That doubly tortures whom it feems to fpare!
　　All feem enflav'd, all bow to him alone;　　　310
Nor dare their hate their juft refentments own:
But inward grieve, their fighs and pangs confin'd,
Which with *convulfive forrow* tear the *mind*.

　　ᵉ Alluding to the fentence then recently paffed on Dr. Sacheverell, for whom our Author was a profeffed Advocate. See vol. II. p. 180.

Envy

Envy is mute—'tis treafon to difclofe
The baneful fource of their eternal woes.   315
   But STILICO's fuperior foul. appears
Unfhock'd, unmov'd, by bafe ignoble fears.
He is the Polar Star, directs the *ftate*,
When *parties* rage, and *public tempefts* beat;
He is the fafe *retreat*, the fweet repofe,   320
Can footh and calm afflicted Virtue's *woes*.
He is the folid, firm, unfhaken force,
That only knows to ftem th' invader's courfe.
   So when a river, fwell'd with Winter's rains,
The limits of its wonted fhore difdains;   325
Bridges, and ftones, and trees, in vain oppofe;
With unrefifted rage the torrent flows :
But as it, rolling, meets a mighty rock,
Whofe fix'd foundations can repel the fhock,
Elided *furges* roar in *eddies* round,   330
The rock, *unmov'd*, reverberates the found,

BRITAIN'S PALLADIUM;

OR,

Lord BOLINGBROKE'S Welcome from FRANCE f.

" Et thure, et fidibus juvat
  " Placare, et vituli sanguine debito
" Custodes Numidæ Deos."
                    HOR. lib. I. Od. xxxvi. ad Pomponium
                        Numidam, ob cujus ex Hispaniâ red-
                        ditum gaudio exultat.

WHAT noise is this, that interrupts my sleep ?
    What echoing shouts rise from the briny deep ?
Neptune a solemn festival prepares,
And Peace through all his flowing orb declares:
That dreadful trident, which he us'd to shake,   5
Make Earth's foundations and Jove's palace quake,
Now, by his side, on ouzy couch reclin'd,
Gives a smooth surface and a gentle wind :
Innumerable Tritons lead the way,
And crouds of Nereids round his chariot play.   10
The ancient Sea-gods with attention wait,
To learn what's now the last result of Fate ;
What earthly Monarch Neptune now decrees
Alone his great vicegerent of the seas.   –

    By an auspicious gale, Britannia's fleet   15
On Gallia's coast this shining triumph meet ;
These pomps divine their mortal sense surprize,
Loud to the ear, and dazzling to the eyes :
Whilst scaly Tritons, with their shells, proclaim
The names that must survive to future fame ;   20
And Nymphs their diadems of pearl prepare
For monarchs who, to purchase peace, make war :

f Lord Bolingbroke set out for France, accompanied by Mr. Hare
one of his under-secretaries, Mr. Prior, and the Abbé Gualtier, Aug. 2 ;
and arrived again in London, Aug. 21, 1712. See the note, p. 234.

Then

Then Neptune his majeſtic ſilence broke,
And to the trembling ſailors mildly ſpoke :
" Throughout the world Britannia's flag diſplay ;   25
" 'Tis my command, that all the globe obey :
" Let Britiſh ſtreamers wave their heads on high,
" And dread no foe beneath Jove's azure ſky ;
" The reſt let Nereus tell" —
     " If I have truth," ſays Nereus, " and foreſee   30
" The intricate deſigns of Deſtiny ;
" I, that have view'd whatever fleets have rode
" With ſharpen'd keels to cut the yielding flood ;
" I, that could weigh the fates of Greece and Rome,
" Phœnician wealth, and Carthaginian doom ;
" Muſt ſurely know what, in the womb of time,   35
" Was fore-ordain'd for Britain's happy clime ;
" How wars upon the watery realms ſhall ceaſe,
" And Anna give the world a glorious peace :
" Reſtore the ſpicy traffick of the Eaſt,
" And ſtretch her empire to the diſtant Weſt :   40
" Her fleets deſcry Aurora's purple bed,
" And Phœbus' ſteeds after their labours fed.
" The Southern coaſts, to Britain ſcarcely known,
" Shall grow as hoſpitable as their own :
" No monſters ſhall be feign'd, to guard their ſtore,   45
" When Britiſh trade ſecures their golden ore :
" The fleecy product of the Cotſwold field
" Shall equal what Peruvian mountains yield :
" Iron ſhall there intrinſic value ſhow,
" And by Vulcanian art more precious grow.   50
     " Britannia's royal fiſhery ſhall be
" Improv'd by a kind guardian deity ;
" That mighty taſk to Glaucus we aſſign,
" Of more importance than the richeſt mine ;
" He ſhall direct them how to ſtrike the Whale,   55
" How to avoid the danger, when prevail ;
" What treaſure lies upon the frozen coaſt
" Not yet explor'd, nor negligently loſt.
     " In vaſt Acadia's plains, new theme for fame,
" Towns ſhall be built, ſacred to Anna's ſ name ;   60

ſ Annapolis, the capital of Nova Scotia.

Q 4

" The

" The filver fir and lofty pines fhall rife
" From Britain's own united Colonies ;
" Which to the maft fhall canvas wings afford,
" And pitch, to ftrengthen the unfaithful board ;
" Norway may then her naval ftores with-hold,   65
" And proudly ftarve for want of Britifh gold.
  " O happy Ifle ! to fuch advantage plac'd,
" That all the world is by thy counfels grac'd ;
" Thy nation's genius, with induftrious arts,
" Renders thee lovely to remoteft parts.   70
" Eliza firft the fable fcene withdrew,
" And to the ancient world difplay'd the new ;
" When Burleigh h at the helm of ftate was feen,
" The trueft fubject to the greateft Queen :
" The Indians, from the Spanifh yoke made free,   75
" Blefs'd the effects of Englifh liberty ;
" Drake i round the world his Sovereign's honour fpread,
" Through ftraights and gulphs immenfe her fame convey'd ;
" Nor refts enquiry here ; his curious eye
" Defcries new conftellations in the fky,   80
" In which vaft fpace, ambitious mariners
" Might place their names on high, and chufe their ftars,
" Raleigh k, with hopes of new difcoveries fir'd,
" And all the depths of human wit infpir'd,
" Rov'd o'er the Weftern world, in fearch of fame,   85
" Adding frefh glory to Eliza's name ;
" Subdued new empires, that will records be
" Immortal of a Queen's virginity l.
  " But think not, Albion, that thy fons decay,
" Or that thy princes have lefs power to fway ;   90

h Sir William Cecil was made prefident of the court of wards Jan. 10, 1561, at which time he was alfo fecretary of ftate ; and was created lord Burleigh, Feb. 25, 1570-1. He died Aug. 4, 1598, in his 78th year, after having had a principal fhare in the adminiftration 40 years. He has been defervedly placed at the head of our Englifh ftatefmen ; not only for his great abilities and indefatigable application, but alfo for his inviolable attachment to the intereft of his fovereign. See more in Granger.

  i See above, p. 92.

  k See vol. II. p. 93.

  l Alluding to the firft fettlement of Virginia.

                           " Whatever

" Whatever in Eliza's reign was feen,
" With a re-doubled vigour fprings again :
" Imperial Anna fhall the feas controul,
" And fpread her naval laws from Pole to Pole :
" Nor think her conduct or her counfels lefs,   95.
" In arts of war, or treaties for a peace ;
" In thrifty management of Britain's wealth,
" Embezzled lately, or purloin'd by ftealth.
" No nation can fear want, or dread furprize,
" Where Oxford's ᵐ prudence Burleigh's lofs fupplies ;   100.
" On him the publick moft fecurely leans,
" To eafe the burthen of the beft of Queens :
" On him the merchants fix their longing eyes,
" When war fhall ceafe, and Britifh commerce rife.
    " Alcides' ftrength and Atlas' firmer mind   105.
" To narrow ftreights of Europe were confin'd.
" The Britifh Sailors, from their Royal Change,
" May find a nobler liberty to range.
" Oxford fhall be their Pole-ftar to the South,
" And there reward the efforts of their youth :   110

ᵐ Robert Harley, efq. was born Dec. 5, 1661. On the acceffion of king William, he was elected member for Tregony; and afterward for Radnor, which he reprefented till called to the upper houfe. Feb. 11, 1701-2, he was chofen fpeaker; as he was again, 31 Dec. following; and a third time, in the firft parliament of queen Anne. April 17, 1704, he was fworn of the privy council; and, May 18 following, appointed fecretary of ftate, being ftill fpeaker of the houfe of commons. His office of fecretary he refigned Feb. 12, 1707-8. Aug. 10, 1710, he was made a commiffioner of the treafury and chancellor of the exchequer; and three days after fworn again of the privy council; where, on the 8th of March following, his life was attacked by Guifcard. The addrefs of both houfes of parliament fhews their great anxiety on that alarming occafion. Her majefty, in reward for his many fervices, advanced him to the peerage, by the title of baron Harley, earl of Oxford and earl Mortimer. On the 29th of May, he was appointed lord treafurer; Aug. 15, chofen governor of the South Sea company, of which he had been the founder; and, Oct. 26, 1712, was honoured with the Garter. July 27, 1714, he refigned the treafurer's ftaff. June 10, 1715. his lordfhip was impeached by the houfe of commons; and was committed to The Tower July 9, where he was confined till July 2, 1717, when the impeachment was difmiffed. He died May 21, 1724.

                                        " Whence,

" Whence, through his conduct, traffick shall encrease,
" Ev'n to those Seas which take their *name* from *peace*[a].
   " Peace is the found muft glad the Britons' ears
" But fee ! the noble Bolingbroke[b] appears ;
" Gefture compos'd and looks ferene declare   115
" The approaching iffue of a doubtful war.
" Now my coerulean race fafe in the deep,
" Shall hear no cannons' roar difturb their fleep ;
" But fmootheft tides and the moft halcyon gales
" Shall to their port direct Britannia's fails.
   " Ye Tritons, fons of Gods ! 'tis my command,   120
" That you fee Bolingbroke in fafety land ;
" Your concave fhells for fofteft notes prepare,
" Whilft Echo fhall repeat the gentleft air ;
" The River-gods fhall there your triumphs meet,
" And, in old Ocean mix'd, your hero greet ;
" Thames fhall ftand wondering, Ifis fhall rejoice,   125
" And both in tuneful numbers raife their voice.

  [a] The Pacific Ocean.
  [b] Henry St. John, efq. was fecretary at war from April 20, 1704;
to Feb. 22, 1707-8. He fucceeded Mr. Boyle as fecretary of ftate, Sept.
21, 1710 ; and July 7, 1712, was created baron St. John and vifcount
Bolingbroke : an honour he received reluctantly, having been difappointed
of an earldom and of the Garter. On the acceffion of king George I, he
was made lord lieutenant and cuftos rotulorum of the county of Effex.
The feals were taken from him Oct. 13, 1715, and all the papers in his
office fecured. Soon after the meeting of the new parliament, perceiving
himfelf in danger, he withdrew into France. In 1723, his majefty having
granted him a full and free pardon, he returned to his native country ;
and in about two years obtained an act of parliament, to reftore him to
his family inheritance. He remained, however, ftill a mere titular lord,
not being admitted to take his feat in parliament. Inflamed with this
taint, he again entered upon the public ftage, and embarked ftrongly in
oppofition againft Sir Robert Walpole ; which he carried on with inimit-
able fpirit, till, in 1735, on a difagreement with his principal coadjutors,
he retired to France, with a full refolution never more to engage in public
bufinefs. On the death of his father, who lived to be extremely old, he
fettled at Batterfea, the ancient feat of the family, where he paffed the
remainder of his days in the higheft dignity ; and died, Nov. 15, 1751,
on the verge of fourfcore. During the latter part of his life, he was much in
the confidence of Frederick prince of Wales, and is fuppofed to have been
the advifer of the moft important fteps in that prince's political conduct.

                                                   " The

" The rapid Medway, and the fertile Trent,
" In fwifteft ftreams, confefs their true content.
" Avon and Severn fhall in raptures join,
" And Fame convey them to the Northern Tine :   130
" Tweed then no more the Britons fhall divide,
" But Peace and Plenty flow on either fide ;
" Triumphs proclaim, and mirth and jovial feafts,
" And all the world invite for welcome guefts."
Faction, that through the land fo fatal fpread,   135
No more fhall dare to raife her Hydra's head ;
But all her votaries in filence mourn
The happinefs of Bolingbroke's return ;
Far from the common pitch, he fhall arife,
With great defigns, to dazzle Envy's eyes ;   140
Search deep, to know of Whiggifh plots the fource,
Their ever-turning fchemes, and reftlefs courfe.
   Who fhall hereafter Britifh annals read,
But will reflect with wonder on this deed ?
How artfully his conduct overcame   145
A ftubborn race, and quench'd a raging flame ;
Retriev'd the Britons from unruly fate,
And overthrew the Phaëtons of ftate !
Thefe wife exploits through Gallia's nation ran,
And fir'd their fouls, to fee the wondrous man :   150
The aged counfellors, without furprize,
Found wit and prudence fparkling in his eyes ;
Wifdom that was not gain'd in courfe of years,
Or reverence owing to his hoary hairs,
But ftruck by force of genius ; fuch as drove   155
The Goddefs Pallas from the brain of Jove.
The youth of France, with pleafure, look'd to fee
His graceful mien and beauteous fymmetry :
The virgins ran, as to unufual fhow,
When he to Paris came, and Fontainbleau ;   160
Viewing the blooming minifter defir'd,
And ftill, the more they gaz'd, the more admir'd.
Nor did the Court, that beft true grandeur knows,
Their fentiments by leffer facts difclofe,
By common pomp, or ceremonious train,   165
Seen heretofore, or to be feen again ;

But

But they devis'd new honours, yet unknown,
Or paid to any subject of a crown.
  The Gallic King, in age and counsels wise,   170
Sated with war, and weary of disguise,
With open arms salutes the British Peer,
And gladly owns his prince and character.
As Hermes from the throne of Jove descends,
With grateful errand, to Heaven's choicest friends;
As Iris from the bed of Juno flies,   175
To bear her Queen's commands through yielding skies,
Whilst o'er her wings fresh beams of glory flow,
And blended colours paint her wondrous bow;
So Bolingbroke appears in Louis' sight,
With message heavenly; and, with equal light,   180
Dispels all clouds of doubt, and fear of wars,
And in his Mistress' name for Peace declares:
Accents divine! which the great King receives
With the same grace that mighty Anna gives.
  Let others boast of blood, the spoil of foes,   185
Rapine and murder, and of endless woes,
Detested pomp! and trophies gain'd from far,
With spangled ensigns, streaming in the air:
Count how they made Bavarian subjects feel
The rage of fire, and edge of harden'd steel: 190
Fatal effects of foul insatiate pride,
That deal their wounds alike on either side:
No limit's set to their ambitious ends,
For who bounds them, no longer can be friends.
By different methods Bolingbroke shall raise   195
His growing honours and immortal praise.
  He, fir'd with glory and the public good,
Betwixt the people and their danger stood:
Arm'd with convincing truths, he did appear;
And all he said was sparkling, bright, and clear. 200
The listening Senate with attention heard,
And some admir'd, while others trembling fear'd;
Not from the tropes of formal eloquence,
But Demosthenic strength, and weight of sense:
Such as fond Oxford to her Son supplied,   205
Design'd her own, as well as Britain's pride.

Who,

Who, lefs beholden to the ancient ftrains,
Might fhew a nobler blood in Englifh veins;
Out-do whatever Homer fweetly fung
Of Neftor's counfels, or Ulyffes' tongue.   210
   Oh! all ye Nymphs, whilft time and youth allow,
Prepare the Rofe and Lily for his brow.
Much he has done, but ftill has more in view;
To Anna's intereft and his country true.
More I could prophefy; but muft refrain: 215
Such truths would make another mortal vain!

TO THE DUKE OF BEAUFORT [r].

T H E time will come (if Fate fhall pleafe to give
   This feeble thread of mine more fpace to live)
When I fhall you and all your acts rehearfe,
In a much loftier and more fluent verfe;
To Ganges' banks, and China farther Eaft,
To Carolina, and the diftant Weft,
Your name fhall fly, and every where be bleft;
Through Spain and tracts of Libyan fands fhall go
To Ruffian limits, and to Zembla's fnow.
Then fhall my eager Mufe expand her wing,
Your love of juftice and your goodnefs fing;
Your greatnefs, equal to the ftate you hold;
In counfel wife, in execution bold:
How there appears, in all that you difpenfe,
Beauty, good-nature, and the ftrength of fenfe.
Thefe let the world admire.—From you a fmile
Is more than a reward of all my toil.

P A paraphrafe on Naudæus's Addrefs to Cardinal de Bagni. Dr. King
dedicated his Englifh verfion of that work to the duke of Beaufort.

MISCELLANY POEMS.

✳✳✳✳

S O N G.

YOU fay you love; repeat again,
　　Repeat th' amazing found,
Repeat the eafe of all my pain,
　　The cure of every wound.

What you to thoufands have denied,
　　To me you freely give;
Whilft I in humble filence died
　　Your mercy bids me live.

So upon Latmos' top each night
　　Endymion fighing lay,
Gaz'd on the Moon's tranfcendent light;
　　Defpair'd, and durft not pray.

But divine Cynthia faw his grief,
　　Th' effect of conquering charms:
Unafk'd the Goddefs brings relief,
　　And falls into his arms.

SONG, TO CÆLIA.

THE cruel Cælia loves, and burns
　　In flames fhe cannot hide;
Make her, dear Thyrfis, cold returns,
　　Treat her with fcorn and pride.

You know the captives fhe has made,
　　The torment of her chain:
Let her, let her be once betray'd,
　　Or rack her with difdain!

See

See tears flow from her piercing eyes,
    She bends her knee divine;
Her tears for Damon's fake defpife;
    Let her kneel ftill for mine.

Purfue thy conqueft, charming youth,
    Her haughty beauty vex,
Till trembling virgins learn this truth—
    Men can revenge their fex.

An incomparable ODE of MALHERBE's q, written by
him when the Marriage was on foot between this
King of FRANCE r and ANNE of AUSTRIA.

Tranflated by a great Admirer of the Eafinefs of French Poetry.

Cette Anne fi belle,	This Anna fo fair,
Qu'on vante fi fort,	So talk'd of by fame,
Pourquoy ne vient elle ?	Why don't fhe appear ?
Vrayment, elle a tort !	Indeed, fhe's to blame !
Son Loüis foûpire	Lewis fighs for the fake
Apres fes appas :	Of her charms, as they fay;
Que veut elle dire,	What excufe can fhe make
Que elle ne vient pas ?	For not coming away ?
Si il ne la poffède,	If he does not poffefs,
Il s'en va mourir ;	He dies with defpair ;
Donnons y reméde,	Let's give him redrefs,
Allons la querir.	And go find out the Fair.

q The Tranflator propofed to turn this Ode with all imaginable exact-
nefs ; and he hopes he has been pretty juft to Malherbe : only in the fixth
line he has made a fmall addition of thefe three words, " as they fay;"
which he thinks is excufable, if we confider the French Poet there talks a
little too familiarly of the king's paffion, as if the king himfelf had
owned it to him. The Tranflator thinks it more mannerly and refpect-
ful in Malherbe to pretend to have the account of it only by hearfay.
                                                                KING.

r Lewis the Fourteenth.

                                                        T H E

THE LAST BILLET.

SEPTEMBER and November now were paſt,
When men in bonfires did their firing waſte;
Yet ſtill my monumental log did laſt:
To begging boys it was not made a prey
On the King's birth or coronation day.
Why with thoſe oaks, under whoſe ſacred ſhade
Charles was preſerv'd, ſhould any fire be made?
At laſt a froſt, a diſmal froſt, there came,
Like that which made a market upon Thame:
Unruly company would then have made
Fire with this log, whilſt thus its owner pray'd:
" Thou that art worſhip'd in Dodona's grove,
" From all thy ſacred trees fierce flames remove:
" Preſerve this groaning branch, O hear my prayer,
" Spare me this one, this one poor Billet ſpare;
" That, having many fires and flames withſtood.
" Its antient teſtimonial may laſt good
" In future times to prove, I once had Wood!"

✶✶✶✶✶

TO LAURA,

In Imitation of PETRARCH.

AT ſight of murder'd Pompey' head
Cæſar forgets his ſex and ſtate,
And, whilſt his generous tears are ſhed,
Wiſhes he had at leaſt a milder fate.

At Abſalom's untimely fall,
David with grief his conqueſt views;
Nay weeps for unrelenting Saul,
And in ſoft verſe the mournful theme purſues.

The

The mightier Laura, from Love's darts secure,
Beholds the thousand deaths that I endure,
Each death made horrid with most cruel pain;
    Yet no frail pity in her looks appears,
    Her eyes betray no careless tears,
But persecute me still with anger and disdain.

⁂⁂⁂⁂

To the Right Honourable the late Earl of ——— *, upon his disputing publicly at Christ Church, Oxford.

MUSE, to thy master's lodgings quickly fly;
    Entrance to thee his goodness won't deny:
With due submission, tell him you are mine,
And that you trouble him with this design,
Exactly to inform his noble youth
Of what you heard just now from vanquish'd Truth:
" Conquer'd, undone! 'Tis strange that there should be
" In this confession pleasure ev'n to me.
" With well-wrought terms my hold I strongly barr'd,
" And rough distinctions were my surly guard.
" Whilst I, sure of my cause, this strength possess,
" A noble youth advancing with address,
" Led glittering falsehood on with so much art,
" That I soon felt sad omens in my heart.
" Words with that grace," said I, " must needs persuade;
" I find myself insensibly betray'd.
" Whilst he pursues his conquest, I retreat,
" And by that name would palliate my defeat.
    " But here methinks I do the prospect see
" Of all those triumphs he prepares for me,
" When Virtue or when Innocence opprest
" Fly for sure refuge to his generous breast;
" When with a noble mien his youth appears,
" And gentle voice persuades the listening peers.
" Judges shall wonder when he clears the laws,
" Dispelling mists, which long have hid their cause:

* Probably James the third of Anglesea. See the Memoirs of Dr. King, in our First Volume.

" Then, by his aid, aid that can never fail,
" Ev'n I, though conquer'd now, ſhall ſure prevail :
" Thouſands of wreaths to me he ſhall repay
" For that one laurel Error wears to-day."

A GENTLEMAN TO HIS WIFE.

WHEN your kind wiſhes firſt I ſought,
   'Twas in the dawn of youth :
I toaſted you, for you I fought,
   But never thought of truth.

You ſaw how ſtill my fire encreas'd ;
   I griev'd to be denied :
You ſaid, " till I to wander ceas'd
   " You'd guard your heart with pride."

I, that once feign'd too many lies,
   In height of paſſion ſwore
By you and other deities,
   That I would range no more.

I've ſworn, and therefore now am fix'd,
   No longer falſe and vain :
My paſſion is with honour mix'd,
   And both ſhall ever reign.

THE MAD LOVER.

I'LL from my breaſt tear fond deſire,
   Since Laura is not mine :
I'll ſtrive to cure the amorous fire,
   And quench the flame with wine.

Perhaps in groves and cooling ſhade
   Soft ſlumbers I may find :
There all the vows to Laura made
   Shall vaniſh with the wind.

The fpeaking ftrings and charming fong
  My paffion may remove:
Oh, Mufick will the pain prolong,
  And is the food of love.

I'll fearch heaven, earth, hell, feas, and air,
  And 'that fhall fet me free :
Oh, Laura's image will be there
  Where Laura will not be.

My foul muft ftill endure the pain,
  And with frefh torment rave :
For none can ever break the chain
  That once was Laura's flave.

THE SOLDIER'S WEDDING.

A Soliloquy by NAN THRASHERWELL, being Part
of a Play called " The New Troop."

O MY dear Thrafherwell, you're gone to fea,
  And happinefs muft ever banifh'd be
From our flock-bed, our garret, and from me !
Perhaps he is on land at Portfmouth now
In the embraces of fome Hampfhire Sow,
Who, with a wanton pat, cries, " Now, my Dear,
" You're wifhing for fome Wapping doxy here."—
" Pox on them all ! but moft on bouncing Nan,
" With whom the torments of my life began :
" She is a bitter one !"—You lye, you Rogue ;
You are a treacherous, falfe, ungrateful dog.
Did not I take you up without a fhirt ?
Woe worth the hand that fcrubb'd off all your dirt !
Did not my intereft lift you in the Guard ?
And had not you ten fhillings, my reward ?
Did I not then, before the Serjeant's face,
Treat Jack, Tom, Will, and Martin, with difgrace ?

R 2

And

And Thrasherwell before all others chuse,
When I had the whole Regiment to louse.
Curs'd be the day when you produc'd your sword,
The just revenger of your injur'd word:
The martial Youth round in a circle stood,
With envious looks of love, and itching blood.
You, with some oaths that signified consent,
Cried " Tom is Nan's !" and o'er the sword you went.
Then I with some more modesty would step :
The Ensign thump'd my bum, and made me leap.
I leap'd indeed ; and you prevailing men
Leave us no power of leaping back again.

✹✹✹✹

THE OLD CHEESE.

YOUNG Slouch the Farmer had a jolly Wife,
 That knew all the conveniencies of life,
Whose diligence and cleanliness supplied
The wit which Nature had to him denied :
But then she had a tongue that would be heard,
And make a better man than Slouch afeard.
This made censorious persons of the town
Say, Slouch could hardly call his soul his own :
For, if he went abroad too much, she'd use
To give him slippers, and lock up his shoes.
Talking he lov'd, and ne'er was more afflicted
Than when he was disturb'd or contradicted :
Yet still into his story she would break
With, " 'Tis not so—pray give me leave to speak."
His friends thought this was a tyrannic rule,
Not differing much from calling of him fool ;
Told him, he must exert himself, and be
In fact the master of his family.

 He said, " That the next Tuesday noon would shew
" Whether he were the lord at home, or no ;

" When

" When their good company he would entreat
" To well-brew'd ale, and clean, if homely, meat."
With aking heart home to his wife he goes,
And on his knees does his rash act disclose,
And prays dear Sukey, that one day, at least,
He might appear as master of the feast.
" I'll grant your wish," cries she, " that you may see
" 'Twere wisdom to be govern'd still by me."
The guests upon the day appointed came,
Each bowsy Farmer with his simpering dame.
" Ho ! Sue !" cries Slouch, " why dost not thou appear ?
" Are these thy manners when Aunt Snap is here ?"
" I pardon ask," says Sue; " I'd not offend
" Any my dear invites, much less his friend."
    Slouch by his kinsman Gruffy had been taught
To entertain his friends with finding fault,
And make the main ingredient of his treat
His saying, " There was nothing fit to eat :
" The boil'd Pork stinks, the roast Beef's not enough,
" The Bacon's rusty, and the Hens are tough ;
" The Veal's all rags, the Butter's turn'd to Oil ;
" And thus I buy good meat for sluts to spoil.
" 'Tis we are the first Slouches ever sate
" Down to a Pudding without Plums or Fat.
" What Teeth or Stomach's strong enough to feed
" Upon a Goose my Grannum kept to breed ?
" Why must old Pidgeons, and they stale, be drest,
" When there's so many squab ones in the nest ?
" This Beer is sour, this musty, thick, and stale,
" And worse than any thing, except the Ale."
    Sue all this while many excuses made,
Some things she own'd, at other times she laid
The fault on chance, but oftener on the maid.
Then Cheese was brought.   Says Slouch, " This e'en shall roll :
" I'm sure 'tis hard enough to make a Bowl :
" This is Skim-milk, and therefore it shall go ;
" And this, because 'tis Suffolk, follow too."
But now Sue's patience did begin to waste.
Nor longer could dissimulation last.

R 3

Pray

" Pray let me rife," fays Sue, " my dear : I'll find
" A Cheefe perhaps may be to Lovy's mind."
Then in an entry, ftanding clofe, where he
Alone, and none of all his friends might fee ;
And brandifhing a cudgel he had felt,
And far enough on this occafion fmelt ;
" I'll try, my joy," fhe cried, " if I can pleafe
" My Deareft with a tafte of his Old Cheefe."
  Slouch turn'd his head, faw his wife's vigorous hand
Wielding her oaken fapling of command,
Knew well the twang : " Is't the Old Cheefe, my Dear !
" No need, no need of Cheefe," cries Slouch : " I'll fwear,
" I think I've din'd as well as my Lord Mayor !"

THE SKILLET.

TWO neighbours, Clod and Jolt, would married be ;
  But did not in their choice of Wives agree.
Clod thought a Cuckold was a monftrous beaft
With two huge glaring eyes and fpreading creft :
Therefore, refolving never to be fuch,
Married a Wife none but himfelf could touch,
Jolt, thinking marriage was decreed by Fate,
Which fhews us whom to love, and whom to hate,
To a young handfome jolly lafs made court,
And gave his friends convincing reafon for't,
That, fince in life fuch mifchief muft be had,
Beauty had fomething ftill that was not bad.
Within two months, Fortune was pleas'd to fend
A Tinker to Clod's houfe, with " Brafs to mend."
The good old wife furvey'd the brawny fpark,
And found his chine was large, though countenance dark.
Firft fhe appears in all her airs, then tries
The fquinting efforts of her amorous eyes.
Much time was fpent, and much defire expreft :
At laft the Tinker cried, " Few words are beft ;

" Give

" Give me that Skillet then ; and, if I'm true,
" I dearly earn it for the work I do."
They 'greed ; they parted. On the Tinker goes,
With the fame ftroke of pan and twang of nofe,
Till he at Jolt's beheld a fprightly dame
That fet his native vigour all on flame.
He looks, fighs, faints, at laft begins to cry,
" And can you then let a young Tinker die ?"
Says fhe, " Give me your Skillet then, and try."
" My Skillet ! Both my heart and Skillet take ;
" I wifh it were a Copper for your fake."
    After all this, not many days did pafs
Clod, fitting at Jolt's houfe, furvey'd the Brafs
And glittering Pewter ftanding on the fhelf.
Then, after fome gruff muttering with himfelf,
Cried, " Pr'ythee, Jolt, how came that Skillet thine ?"
" You know as well as I," quoth Jolt ; " 't'en't mine ;
" But I'll afk Nan."   'Twas done ; Nan told the matter
In truth as 'twas ; then cried, " You've got the better :
" For tell me, Deareft, whether would you chufe
" To be a gainer by me, or to lofe.
" As for our Neighbour Clod, this I dare fay,
" We've Beauty and a Skillet more than they."

THE FISHERMAN.

TOM Banks by native induftry was taught
    The various arts how Fifhes might be caught.
Sometimes with trembling reed and fingle hair,
And bait conceal'd, he'd for their death prepare,
With melancholy thoughts and downcaft eyes,
Expecting till deceit had gain'd its prize.
Sometimes in rivulet quick and water clear
They'd meet a fate more generous from his fpear.
To bafket oft he'd pliant oziers turn,
Where they might entrance find, but no return.

His

His net well pois'd with lead he'd fometimes throw,
Encircling thus his captives all below.
But, when he would a quick deftruction make,
And from afar much larger booty take,
He'd through the ftream, where moft defcending, fet
From fide to fide his ftrong capacious net ;
And then his ruftic crew with mighty poles
Would drive his prey out from their owzy holes,
And fo purfue them down the rolling flood,
Gafping for breath, and almoft choak'd with mud,
Till they, of farther paffage quite bereft,
Were in the mafh with gills entangled left.

   Trot, who liv'd down the ftream, ne'er thought his beer
Was good, unlefs he had his water clear.
He goes to Banks, and thus begins his tale :
" Lord ! if you knew but how the people rail !
" They cannot boil, nor wafh, nor rinfe, they fay,
" With water fometimes ink, and fometimes whey,
" According as you meet with mud or clay.
" Befides, my wife thefe fix months could not brew,
" And now the blame of this all's laid on you ;
" For it will be a difmal thing to think
" How we old Trots muft live and have no drink :
" Therefore, I pray, fome other method take
" Of fifhing, were it only for our fake."
  Says Banks, " I'm forry it fhould be my lot
" Ever to difoblige my goffip Trot :
" Yet 't'en't my fault ; but fo 'tis Fortune tries one
" To make his meat become his neighbour's poifon ;
" And fo we pray for winds upon this coaft,
" By which on t'other navies may be loft.
" Therefore in patience reft, though I proceed :
" There's no ill-nature in the cafe, but need.
" Though for your ufe this water will not ferve,
" I'd rather you fhould choak, than I fhould ftarve."

A C A S E

A CASE OF CONSCIENCE.

OLD Paddy Scot, with none of the beſt faces,
   Had a moſt knotty pate at ſolving caſes ;
In any point could tell you to a hair
When was a grain of honeſty to ſpare.
It happen'd, after prayers, one certain night,
At home he had occaſion for a light
To turn Socinus [t], Leſſius, Eſcobar,
Fam'd Covarruvias, and the great Navarre :
And therefore, as he from the chapel came,
Extinguiſhing a yellow taper's flame,
By which juſt now he had devoutly pray'd,
The uſeful remnant to his ſleeve convey'd.
There happen'd a Phyſician to be by,
Who thither came but only as a ſpy,
To find out others faults, but let alone
Repentance for the crimes that were his own.
  This Doctor follow'd Paddy ; ſaid, " He lack'd
" To know what made a ſacrilegious fact."
  Paddy with ſtudious gravity replies,
" That's as the place or as the matter lies :
" If from a place unſacred you ſhould take
" A ſacred thing, this ſacrilege would make ;
" Or an unſacred thing from ſacred place,
" There would be nothing different in the caſe ;
" But, if both thing and place ſhould ſacred be,
" 'Twere height of ſacrilege, as Doctors all agree."
  " Then," ſays the Doctor, " for more light in this,
" To put a ſpecial caſe, were not amiſs.
" Suppoſe a man ſhould take a Common Prayer
" Out of a Chapel where there's ſome to ſpare."
  " A Common Prayer !" ſays Paddy, " that would be
" A ſacrilege of an intenſe degree."

  t Marianus Socinus, an eminent civilian, born in Tuſcany in 1482, died in Auguſt, 1556. He is introduced here, as are the following perſonages, for his great ſkill in caſuiſtry. He was grandfather to Fauſtus Socinus, the founder of the ſect which bears their name.

" Suppoſe

" Suppofe that one fhould in thefe holidays
" Take thence a bunch of Rofemary or Bays."
  " I'd not be too cenforious in that cafe,
" But 'twould be facrilege ftill from the place."
  " What if a man fhould from the chapel take
" A taper's end : fhould he a fcruple make,
" If homeward to his chambers he fhould go,
" Whether 'twere theft, or facrilege, or no ?"
  The fly infinuation was perceiv'd,
Says Paddy, " Doctor, you may be deceiv'd,
" Unlefs in cafes you diftinguifh right ;
" But this may be refolv'd at the firft fight.
" As to the taper, it could be no theft,
" For it had done its duty, and was left :
" And facrilege in having it is none,
" Becaufe that in my fleeve I now have one."

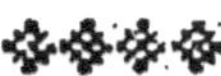

THE CONSTABLE.

ONE night a fellow wandering without fear,
    As void of money as he was of care,
Confidering both were wafh'd away with beer,
With Strap the Conftable by Fortune meets,
Whofe lantherns glare in the moft filent ftreets.
Refty, impatient any one fhould be
So bold as to be drunk that night but he :
" Stand ; who goes there," cries Strap, " at hours fo late ?
" Anfwer.   Your name ; or elfe have at your pate."—
  " I wo'nt ftand, 'caufe I can't.   Why muft you know
" From whence it is I come, or where I go ?"
  " See here my ftaff," cries Strap ; " trembling behold
" Its radiant paint, and ornamental gold :
" Wooden authority when thus I wield,
" Perfons of all degrees obedience yield.
" Then, be you the beft man in all the city,
" Mark me ! I to the Counter will commit ye,"

" You !

" You ! kifs, and fo forth.   For that never fpare :
" If that be all, commit me if you dare ;
" No perfon yet, either through fear or fhame,
" Durft commit me, that once had heard my name."—
" Pray then, what is't ?"—" My name's ADULTERY ;
" And, faith, your future life would pleafant be
" Did your wife know you once committed *me*."

XXXXX

LITTLE MOUTHS.

FROM London, Paul the Carrier coming down
     To Wantage, meets a beauty of the town,
They both accoft with falutation pretty,
As, " How do'ft, Paul ?"—" Thank you : and how do'ft, Betty !"
" Didft fee our Jack, nor Sifter ? No, you've feen,
" I warrant, none but thofe who faw the Queen."
    " Many words fpoke in jeft," fays Paul, " are true,
" I came from Windfor *; and, if fome folks knew
" As much as I, it might be well for you,"
" Lord, Paul ! what is't ?"—" Why give me fomething for't,
" This kifs ; and this.   The matter's then in fhort :
" The Parliament have made a proclamation,
" Which will this week be fent all round the nation ;
" That Maids with little mouths do all prepare
" On Sunday next to come before the Mayor,
" And that all Batchelors be likewife there :
" For Maids with little mouths fhall, if they pleafe,
     " From thefe young men choofe two apiece."
    Betty, with bridled chin, extends her face,
And then contracts her lips with fimpering grace,
Cries, " Hem ! pray what muft all the huge ones do
" For hufbands, when we little mouths have two ?"
    " Hold, not fo faft," cries he ; " pray pardon me :
" Maids with huge gaping wide mouths muft have three."

　　　 u Where Queen Anne and her Court frequently refided.

Betty

Betty diftorts her face with hideous fquawl,
And mouth of a foot wide begins to bawl,
" Oh! ho! is't fo? The cafe is alter'd, Paul.
" Is that the point ? I wifh the three were ten ;
" I warrant I'd find mouth, if they'll find men."

XXXX

HOLD FAST BELOW.

THERE was a lad, th' unluckieft of his crew,
   Was ftill contriving fomething bad, but new.
His comrades all obedience to him paid,
In executing what defigns he laid :
'Twas they fhould rob the orchard, he'd retire,
His foot was fafe whilft theirs was in the fire.
He kept them in the dark to that degree,
None fhould prefume to be fo wife as he,
But, being at the top of all affairs,
The profit was his own, the mifchief theirs ;
'There fell fome words made him begin to doubt,
The rogues would grow fo wife to find him out ;
He was not pleas'd with this, and fo next day
He cries to them, as going juft to play,
" What a rare Jack-daw's neft is there ! look up,
" You fee 'tis almoft at the fteeple's top."
" Ah," fays another, " we can have no hope
" Of getting thither to't without a rope."
Says then the fleering fpark, with courteous grin,
By which he drew his infant cullies in ;
" Nothing more eafy; did you never fee
" How, in a fwarm, bees, hanging bee by bee,
" Make a long fort of rope below the tree.
" Why mayn't we do the fame, good Mr. John ?
" For that contrivance pray let me alone.
" Tom fhall hold Will, you Will, and I'll hold you,
" And then I warrant you the thing will do.

" But,

" But, if there's any does not care to try,
" Let us have no Jack-daws, and what care I ?"
    That touch'd the quick, and so they soon complied,
No argument like that was e'er denied,
And therefore inftantly the thing was tried.
 They hanging down on ftrength above depend :
Then to himfelf mutters their trufty friend,
" The dogs are almoft ufelefs grown to me,
" I ne'er fhall have fuch opportunity
" To part with them ; and fo e'en let them go."
Then cries aloud, " So ho ! my lads ! fo ho !
" You're gone, unlefs ye all hold faft below.
" They've ferv'd my turn, fo 'tis fit time to drop them ;
" The Devil, if he wants them, let him ftop them."

✳✳✳✳

THE BEGGAR WOMAN.

A GENTLEMAN in hunting rode aftray,
    More out of choice, than that he loft his way,
He let his company the Hare purfue,
For he himfelf had other game in view.
A Beggar by her trade ; yet not fo mean,
But that her cheeks were frefh, and linen clean.
" Miftrefs," quoth he, " and what if we two fhou'd
" Retire a little way into the wood ?"
    She needed not much courtfhip to be kind,
He ambles on before, fhe trots behind ;
For little Bobby, to her fhoulders bound,
Hinders the gentle dame from ridding ground.
He often afk'd her to expofe ; but fhe
Still fear'd the coming of his Company.
Says fhe, " I know an unfrequented place,
" To the left hand, where we our time may pafs,
" And the mean while your horfe may find fome grafs."
Thither they come, and both the horfe fecure ;
Then thinks the Squire, I have the matter fure.

She

She's afk'd to fit : but then excufe is made,
" Sitting," fays fhe, " 's not ufual in my trade
" Should you be rude, and then fhould throw me down,
" I might perhaps break more backs than my own."
He fmiling cries, " Come, I'll the knot untie,
" And, if you mean the Child's, we'll lay it by."
Says fhe, " That can't be done, for then 'twill cry.
" I'd not have us, but chiefly for your fake,
" Difcover'd by the hideous noife 'twould make.
" Ufe is another nature, and 'twould lack
" More than the breaft, its cuftom to the back."
" Then," fays the Gentleman, " I fhould be loth
" To come fo far and difoblige you both :
" Were the child tied to me, d'ye think 'twould do?"
" Mighty well, Sir! Oh, Lord! if tied to you !"
    With fpeed incredible to work fhe goes,
And from her fhoulders foon the burthen throws ;
Then mounts the infant with a gentle tofs
Upon her generous friend, and, like a crofs,
The fheet fhe with a dextrous motion winds,
Till a firm knot the wandering fabrick binds.
    The Gentleman had fcarce got time to know
What fhe was doing; fhe about to go,
Cries, " Sir, good b'ye; ben't angry that we part,
" I truft the child to you with all my heart :
" But, ere you get another, 'ten't amifs
" To try a year or two how you'll keep this."

THE VESTRY.

WITHIN the Shire of Nottingham there lies
    A parifh fam'd, becaufe the men were wife :
Of their own ftrain they had a teacher fought,
Who all his life was better fed than taught.
It was about a quarter of a year
Since he had fnoar'd, and eat, and fatten'd there,

When

When he the houfe-keepers, their wives, and all,
Did to a fort of Parifh-meeting call;
Promifing fomething, which, well underftood,
In little time would turn to all their good :
  When met, he thus harangues : " Neighbours, I find,
" That in your principles you're well inclin'd :
" But then you're all folicitous for Sunday,
" None feem to have a due regard for Monday,
" Moft people then their dinners have to feek,
" As if 'twere not the firft day of the week ;
" But, when you have hafh'd meat and nothing more,
" You only curfe the day that went before.
" On Tuefday all folks dine by one confent :
" And Wednefdays only faft by Parliament,
" But Fafting fure by Nature ne'er was meant.
" The Market will for Thurfday find a difh,
" And Friday is a proper day for fifh,
" After Fifh, Saturday requires fome Meat,
" On Sunday you're oblig'd by law to treat ;
" And the fame law ordains a Pudding then,
" To children grateful, nor unfit for men.
" Take Hens, Geefe, Turkies, then, or fomething light,
" Becaufe their legs, if broil'd, will ferve at night,
" And, fince I find that roaft Beef makes you fleep,
" Corn it a little more, and fo 'twill keep.
" Roaft it on Monday, pity it fhould be fpoil'd,
" On Tuefday Mutton either roaft or boil'd.
" On Wednefday fhould be fome variety,
" A Loin or Breaft of Veal, and Pigeon Pye.
" On Thurfday each man of his difh make choice,
" 'Tis fit on Market-days we all rejoice.
" And then on Friday, as I faid before,
" We'll have a difh of Fifh, and one difh more.
" On Saturday ftew'd Beef, with fomething nice,
" Provided quick, and tofs'd up in a trice,
" Becaufe that in the afternoon, you know,
" By cuftom, we muft to the Ale-houfe go ;
" For elfe how fhould our houfes e'er be clean,
" Except we gave fome time to do it then?

" From whence, unlefs we value not our lives,
" None part without remembering firft our Wives,
" But thefe are ftanding rules for every day,
" And very good ones, as I fo may fay :
" After each meal, let's take a hearty cup ;
" And where we dine, 'tis fitting that we fup.
  " Now for the application, and the ufe,
" I found your care for Sunday an abufe :
" All would be afking, Pray, Sir, where d'you dine ?
" I have roaft Beef, choice Venifon, Turkey, Chine :
" Every one's hawling me. Then fay poor I,
" It is a bitter bufinefs to deny ;
" But, who is't cares for fourteen meals a day,
" As for my own part, I had rather ftay,
" And take them now and then — and here and there, —
" According to my prefent bill of fare.
" You know I'm fingle : if you all agree
" To treat by turns, each will be fure of me."
  The Veftry all applauded with a hum,
And the feven wifeft of them bad him come.

❋❋❋❋

THE MONARCH.

WHEN the young people ride the Skimmington,
    There is a general trembling in a town.
Not only he for whom the perfon rides
Suffers, but they fweep other doors befides ;
And by that hieroglyphic does appear
That the good woman is the mafter there.
At Jenny's door the barbarous Heathens fwept,
And his poor wife fcolded until fhe wept,
The mob fwept on, whilft fhe fent forth in vain,
Her vocal thunder and her briney rain.
Some few days after two young fparks came there,
And whilft fhe does her Coffee frefh prepare,
One for difcourfe of news the mafter calls,
T'other on this ungrateful fubject falls.

" Pray,

" Pray, Mrs. Jenny, whence came this report,
" For I believe there's no great reason for't,
" As if the folks t'other day swept your door,
" And half a dozen of your neighbours more ?"
" There's nothing in't," says Jenny ; " that is done
" Where the wife rules, but here I rule alone,
" And, gentlemen, you'd much mistaken be,
" If any one should not think that of me.
" Within these walls, my suppliant vassals know
" What due obedience to their prince they owe,
" And kiss the shadow of my papal toe.
" My word's a law ; when I my power advance,
" There's not a greater Monarch ev'n in France.
" Not the Mogul or Czar of Muscovy,
" Not Prester John, or Cham of Tartary,
" Are in their houses Monarch more than I.
" My House my Castle is, and here I'm King,
" I'm Pope, I'm Emperor, Monarch, every thing.
" What though my wife be partner of my bed,
" The Monarch's Crown fits only on this head."
   His wife had plaguy ears, as well as tongue,
And, hearing all, thought his discourse too long :
Her conscience said, he should not tell such lies,
And to her knowledge such ; she therefore cries,
" D'ye hear — you — Sirrah — Monarch — there ?— Come down
" And grind the Coffee — or I'll crack your Crown."

THE INCURIOUS.

A VIRTUOSO had a mind to see
   One that would never discontented be,
But in a careless way to all agree.
He had a Servant, much of Æsop's kind,
Of personage uncouth, but sprightly mind,
" Humpus," says he, I order that you find
" Out such a man, with such a character,
" As in this paper now I give you here,

" Or I will lug your ears, or crack your pate,
" Or rather you fhall meet with a worfe fate,
" For 1 will break your back, and fet you ftrait.
" Bring him to dinner."   Humpus foon withdrew,
Was fafe, as having fuch a one in view
At Covent Garden dial, whom he found
Sitting with thoughtlefs air and look profound,
Who, folitary gaping without care,
Seem'd to fay, " Who is't? wilt go any where?"

    Says Humpus, " Sir, my Mafter bad me pray
" Your company to dine with him to-day."
He fnuffs; then follows; up the ftairs he goes,
Never pulls his off his hat, nor cleans his fhoes,
But, looking round him, faw a handfome room,
And did not much repent him he was come ;
Clofe to the fire he draws an elbow chair,
And, lolling eafy, doth for fleep prepare.
In comes the family, but he fits ftill,
Thinks, " Let them take the other chairs that will !"

    The Mafter thus accofts him, " Sir, you're wet,
" Pray have a cufhion underneath your feet."
Thinks he, " If I do fpoil it, need I care ?
" I fee he has eleven more to fpare."

    Dinner's brought up ; the Wife is bid retreat,
And at the upper end muft be his feat.
" This is not very ufual," thinks the Clown r
" But is not all the family his own ?
" And why fhould I, for contradiction's fake
" Lofe a good dinner, which he bids me take ?
" If from his table fhe difcarded be,
" What need I care ? there is the more for me."

    After a while, the Daughter's bid to ftand,
And bring him whatfoever he'll command.
Thinks he, " The better from the fairer hand."

    Young Mafter next muft rife, to fill him wine,
And ftarve himfelf, to fee the booby dine :
He does.   The Father afks, " What have you there ?
" How dare you give a ftranger Vinegar ?"
" Sir, 'twas Champagne I gave him."—" Sir, indeed !
" Take him and fcourge him till the rafcal bleed,

" Don't fpare him for his tears nor age, I'll try
" If Cat of nine tails can excufe a lye."
   Thinks the Clown, " That 'twas wine, I do believe;
" But fuch young rogues are apteft to deceive :
" He's none of mine, but his own flefh and blood,
" And how know I but 'tmay be for his good ?"
   When the defert came on, and jellies brought,
Then was the difmal fcene of finding fault,
They were fuch hideous, filthy, poifonous ftuff,
Could not be rail'd at nor reveng'd enough.
Humpus was afk'd who made them.   Trembling he
Said, " Sir, it was my Lady gave them me."—
" I'll take care fhe fhall no more Poifon give,
" I'll burn the witch; 't'ent fitting fhe fhould live,
" Set faggots in the court, I'll make her fry,
" And pray, good Sir, may't pleafe you to be by ?"
   Then, fmilling, fays the Clown, " Upon my life,
" A pretty fancy this, to burn one's Wife !
" And, fince that actually is your defign,
" Pray let me juft ftep home, and fetch you mine."

✻✻✻✻

A P P L E - P Y E.

OF all the Delicates which Britons try,
   To pleafe the palate, or delight the eye;
Of all the feveral kinds of fumptuous fare;
There's none that can with APPLE-PYE compare,
For coftly flavour, or fubftantial pafte,
For outward beauty, or for inward tafte.
   When firft this infant-difh in fafhion came,
Th' ingredients were but coarfe, and rude the frame;
As yet unpolifh'd in the modern arts,
Our Fathers eat Brown Bread inftead of Tarts:
Pyes were but indigefted lumps of Dough,
Till time and juft expence improv'd them fo,

S 2

King Cole (as ancient Britifh Annals w tell)
Renown'd for fiddling and for eating well,
Pippins in homely Cakes with Honey ftew'd,   15
" Juft as he bak'd," the Proverb fays, " he brew'd !"
Their greater art fucceeding Princes fhow'd,
And model'd Pafte into a neater mode ;
Invention now grew lively, palate nice,
And Sugar pointed out the way to Spice.   20
   But here for ages unimprov'd we ftood,
And Apple-pye was ftill but homely food ;
When god-like Edgar, of the Saxon Line,
Polite of tafte, and ftudious to refine,
In the Defert perfuming Quinces caft,   25
And perfected with Cream the rich repaft.
Hence we proceed the outward parts to trim,
With Crinkumcranks adorn the polifh'd brim ;
And each frefh Pye the pleas'd fpectator greets
With virgin-fancies, and with new conceits.   30
   Dear Nelly, learn with care the Paftry art,
And mind the eafy precepts I impart :
Draw out your Dough elaborately thin,
And ceafe not to fatigue your Rolling-pin :
Of Eggs and Butter fee you mix enough :   35
For then the Pafte will fwell into a Puff,
Which will, in crumpling founds, your praife report,
And eat, as Houfewives fpeak, " exceeding fhort."
Rang'd in thick order let your Quinces lie ;
They give a charming relifh to the Pye.   40
If you are wife, you'll not Brown Sugar flight,
The browner (if I form my judgement right)
A deep Vermillion tincture will difpenfe,
And make your Pippin redder than the Quince.
   When this is done, there will be wanting ftill,   45
The juft referve of Cloves and Candied Peel ;
Nor can I blame you, if a drop you take
Of Orange-water, for perfuming-fake.
But here the nicety of art is fuch,
There muft not be too little, nor too much :   50

w See the old Ballad of " King Cole," in the original Anglo-Saxon
language, in the fecond volume of this collection, p. 87.

If with difcretion you thefe cofts employ,
They quicken appetite; if not, they cloy.
   Next, in your mind this maxim firmly root,
" Never o'ercharge your PYE with coftly fruit :"
Oft let your Bodkin through the lid be fent,   55
To give the kind imprifon'd treafure vent ;
Left the fermenting liquor, clofely preft,
Infenfibly, by conftant fretting, wafte,
And o'er-inform your tenement of Pafte.
   To chufe your Baker, think, and think again   60
(You'll fcarce one honeft Baker find in ten) :
Aduft and bruis'd, I've often feen a PYE,
In rich difguife and coftly ruin lie,
While penfive Cruft beheld its form o'erthrown,
Exhaufted Apples griev'd, their moifture flown,
And Syrup from the fides ran trickling down.
   O be not, be not tempted, lovely NELL,
While the hot-piping odours ftrongly fmell,
While the delicious fume creates a guft,
To lick th' o'erflowing juice, or bite the cruft.   70
You'll rather ftay (if my advice may rule)
Until the hot's corrected by the cool ;
Till you've infus'd the lufcious ftore of Cream,
And chang'd the purple for a filver ftream ;
Till that fmooth viand its mild force produce,   75
And give a foftnefs to the tarter juice.
   Then fhalt thou, pleas'd, the noble fabrick view,
And have a flice into the bargain too ;
Honour and fame alike we will partake,
So well I'll eat, what you fo richly make.   80

The ART of making PUDDINGS.

"   —PUDDING is own'd to be
" Th' effect of NATIVE INGENUITY."
ART of COOKERY, ver. 358.

I. HASTY PUDDING.

I SING of FOOD, by British Nurse defign'd,
  To make the Stripling brave, and Maiden kind,
Delay not, Muse, in numbers to rehearse
The pleasures of our life, and sinews of our verse.
Let PUDDING's dish, most wholesome, be thy theme,   5
And dip thy swelling plumes in fragrant Cream.
  Sing then that Dish so fitting to improve
A tender modefty and trembling love;
Swimming in Butter of a golden hue,
Garnish'd with drops of Rose's spicy dew.   10
  Sometimes the frugal Matron seems in hafte,
Nor cares to beat her Pudding into Pafte:
Yet Milk in proper Skillet she will place,
And gently spice it with a blade of Mace;
Then set some careful Damsel to look to't,   15
And still to stir away the Bishop's-foot;
For, if burnt Milk should to the bottom stick,
Like over-heated zeal, 'twould make folks fick.
Into the Milk her Flour she gently throws,
As Valets now would powder tender Beaux: 20
The liquid forms in HASTY MASS unite,
Forms equally delicious as they're white.
In shining dish the HASTY MASS is thrown,
And seems to want no graces but its own.
Yet still the Housewife brings in fresh supplies,   25
To gratify the tafte, and please the eyes.
She on the surface lumps of Butter lays,
Which, melting with the heat, its beams difplays;
From whence it caufes, wondrous to behold,
A Silver foil bedeck'd with streams of Gold!   30

II. A

II. A Hedge-Hog after a Quaking Pudding.

AS Neptune, when the three-tongued fork he takes,
With ftrength divine the globe terreftrial fhakes.
The higheft Hills, Nature's ftupendous Piles,
Break with the force, and quiver into Ifles;
Yet on the ruins grow the lofty Pines,   35
And Snow unmelted in the vallies fhines:
  Thus when the Dame her HEDGE-HOG-PUDDING breaks,
Her Fork indents irreparable ftreaks,
The trembling lump, with Butter all around,
Seems to perceive its fall, and then be drown'd;   40
And yet the tops appear, whilft Almonds thick
With bright Loaf-fugar on the furface ftick.

III. Puddings of various Colours in a Difh.

YOU, Painter-like, now variegate the fhade,
And thus from PUDDINGS there's a Landfcape made.
And WISE and LONDON [x], when they would difpofe   45
Their Ever-greens into well-order'd rows,
So mix their colours, that each different plant
Gives light and fhadow as the others want.

[x] The two Royal Gardeners. KING.—Mr. Addifon was of opinion,
that "there are as many kinds of gardening as of poetry. Your makers
"of paftures and flower-gardens are epigrammatifts and fonneteers in
"this art: contrivers of bowers and grottoes, treillages and cafcades, are
"romance-writers. WISE and LONDON are our heroic poets; and if,
"as a critic, I may fingle out any paffage of their works to commend, I
"fhall take notice of that part in the upper garden at Kenfington, which
"was firft nothing but a gravel-pit. It muft have been a fine genius for
"gardening, that could have thought of forming fuch an unfightly hol-
"low into fo beautiful an area, and to have hit the eye with fo un-
"common and agreeable a fcene as that which it is now wrought into.—
"I never yet met with any one, who has walked in this garden, who was
"not ftruck with that part of it." Spectator, No 477; and fee above,
p. 126.—A good poem, by Mr. Tickell, intituled, "Kenfington Garden,"
is printed in the firft volume of Dodfley's Collection.

S 4

IV. Making

IV. Making of a GOOD PUDDING gets a GOOD HUSBAND.

YE Virgins, as thefe lines you kindly take,
So may you ftill fuch glorious Pudding make,　　　　50,
'That crouds of Youth may ever be at ftrife,
To gain the fweet compofer for his Wife!

V. SACK and SUGAR to QUAKING-PUDDING.

"Oh, Delicious!"

BUT where muft our Confeffion firft begin,
If Sack and Sugar once be thought a Sin?

VI. BROILED PUDDING.

HID in the dark, we mortals feldom know　　　　55
From whence the fource of happinefs may flow:
Who to Broil'd Pudding would their thoughts have bent
From bright PEWTERIA's love-fick difcontent?
Yet fo it was, PEWTERIA felt Love's heat
In fiercer flames than thofe which roaft her meat.　　60
No Pudding's loft, but may with frefh delight,
Be either *fried* next day, or *broil'd* at night.

VII. MUTTON PUDDING.

BUT Mutton, thou moft nourifhing of meat,
Whofe fingle joint *y* may conftitute a treat;
When made a Pudding, you excel the reft　　　　65
As much as That of other Food is beft!

y A Loin. KING.

To

To Mr. CARTER, Steward to the Lord CARTERET.

ACCEPT of health from one who, writing this,
Wifhes you in the fame that now he is;
Though to your perfon he may be unknown,
His wifhes are as hearty as your own.
For CARTER's drink, when in his Mafter's hand,
Has pleafure and good-nature at command.
What though his Lordfhip's lands are in your truft,
'Tis greater to his BREWING to be juft.
As to that matter, no one can find fault,
If you fupply him ftill with WELL-DRIED MALT.
Still be a fervant conftant to afford
A liquor fitting for your generous Lord;
Liquor, like him, from feeds of worth in light,
With fparkling atoms ftill afcending bright.
May your accompts fo with your Lord ftand clear,
And have your reputation like your Beer;
The main perfection of your life purfue,
In March, October, every month, ftill brew,
And get the character of " Who but You?"

NERO. A SATIRE.

WE know how ruin once did reign,
When Rome was fir'd, and Senate flain;
The Prince, with Brother's gore imbrued,
His tender Mother's life purfued;
How he the carcafe, as it lay,
Did without tear or blufh furvey,
And cenfure each majeftic grace
That ftill adorn'd that breathlefs face:
Yet he with fword could domineer
Where dawning-light does firft appear
From rays of Phœbus; and command
Through his whole courfe, even to that ftrand
Where he, abhorring fuch a fight,
Sinks in the watery gloom of night:

Yet

Yet he could death and terror throw,
Where Thulé ſtarves in Northern ſnow ;
Where Southern heats do fiercely paſs
O'er burning ſands that melt to glaſs.
    Fond hopes ! Could height of Power aſſuage
The mad exceſs of NERO's rage ?
Hard is the fate, when ſubjeĉts find
The Sword unjuſt to Poiſon join'd !

Ad A M I C U M.

P RIMUS ab Angliacis, Carolinæ Tyntus [z] in oras,
    Palladias artes ſecum, cytharamque ſonantem
Attulit ; aſt illi comites Parnaſſido una
Adveniunt, autorque viæ conſultus Apollo :
Ille idem ſparſos longè latéque colonos
Legibus in cœtus æquis, atque oppida cogit ;
Hinc hominum molliri animos, hinc mercibus optis
Creſcere divitias et ſurgere teĉta Deorum.
Talibus auſpiciis doĉtæ conduntur Athenæ,
Sic byrſa ingentem Didonis crevit in urbem
Carthago regum domitrix ; ſic aurea Roma
Orbe triumphato nitidum caput intulit aſtris.

Attempted in ENGLISH,

    TYNTE was the man who firſt, from Britiſh ſhore,
Palladian arts to Carolina bore ;
His tuneful harp attending Muſes ſtrung,
And Phœbus' ſkill inſpir'd the lays he ſung.
Strong towers and palaces their riſe began,
And liſtening ſtones to ſacred fabricks ran.
Juſt laws were taught, and curious arts of peace,
And trade's briſk current flow'd with wealth's increaſe.
On ſuch foundations learned Athens roſe ;
So Dido's thong did Carthage firſt incloſe :
So Rome was taught OLD Empires to ſubdue,
As Tynte creates and governs, now, the NEW.
        [z] Major Tynte, Governor of Carolina.
                                    ULYSSES

ULYSSES and TIRESIAS.

ULY. TELL me, old Prophet, tell me how,
      Eftate when funk, and pocket low,
    What fubtle arts, what fecret ways,
    May the defponding fortune raife?
    You laugh: thus Mifery is fcorn'd!
TIR.   Sure 'tis enough you are return'd
    Home by your Wit, and view again
    Your Farm of Ithac, and Wife Pen.
ULY.   Sage friend, whofe word's a law to me,
    My want and nakednefs you fee:
    The fparks, who made my wife fuch offers,
    Have left me nothing in my coffers;
    They've kill'd my oxen, fheep, and geefe,
    Eat up my bacon and my cheefe.
    Lineage and virtue, at this pufh,
    Without the *gelt*, 's not worth a rufh.
TIR.   Why, not to mince the matter more,
    You are averfe to being poor;
    Therefore find out fome rich old cuff,
    That never thinks he has enough:
    Have you a Swan, a Turkey-pye,
    With Woodcocks, thither let them fly.
    The Firft-fruits of your early Spring,
    Not to the Gods, but to Him bring.
    Though he a foundling Baftard be,
    Convict of frequent perjury;
    His hands with brother's blood imbrued,
    By juftice for that crime purfued.
    Never the wall, when afk'd, refufe,
    Nor lofe your friend, to fave your fhoes.
ULY.   'Twixt Damas and the kennel go!
    Which is the filthieft of the two?
    Before Troy-town it was not fo.
    There with the beft I us'd to ftrive.
TIR.   Why, by that means you'll never thrive.
ULY.   It will be very hard, that's true:
    Yet I'll my generous mind fubdue.

Tranflation

Tranſlation from TASSO, Canto iii. St. 3.

SO when bold Mariners, whom hopes of ore
Have urg'd to ſeek ſome unfrequented ſhore:
The ſea grown high, and pole unknown, do find :
How falſe is every wave, and treacherous every wind !
If wiſh'd-for land ſome happier ſight deſcries,
Diſtant huzzas, ſaluting clamours, riſe :
Each ſtrives to ſhew his mate th' approaching bay,
Forgets paſt danger, and the tedious way.

From HESIOD.

WHEN Saturn reign'd in Heaven, his ſubjects here
Array'd with godly virtues did appear ;
Care, Pain, Old Age, and Grief, were baniſh'd far,
With all the dread of Laws and doubtful War :
But chearful Friendſhip, mix'd with Innocence,
Feaſted their underſtanding and their ſenſe ;
Nature abounded with unenvied ſtore,
Till their diſcreeteſt wits could aſk no more ;
And when, by fate, they came to breathe their laſt,
Diſſolv'd in ſleep their flitting vitals paſs'd.
Then to much happier manſions they remov'd,
There prais'd their God, and were by him belov'd [a].

VERSES left in the King of FRANCE's Bed-chamber, after the Death of the Duke DE MONT-MORENCY.

ON ne ſe jouvient que du Mal ;
Ingratitude regne au monde :
L'Injure ſe grave au metal,
Et le Bien-fait s'ecrit ſur l'onde.

[a] That is, they were as happy as the day is long. KING.

THAME

THAME and ISIS.

SO the God Thame, as through some pond he glides,
  Into the arms of wandering Isis slides :
His strength, her softness, in one bed combine,
And both with bands inextricable join ;
Now no cærulean Nymph, or Sea god, knows
Where Isis, or where Thame, distinctly flows ;
But with a lasting charm they blend their stream,
Producing one imperial River—THAME.

❊❊❊❊

Of DREAMS.

"For a Dream cometh through the multitude of Business."
                                  Ecclef. v. 4.

    "Somnia, quæ ludunt mente volitantibus umbris,
    "Non delubra deûm nec ab æthere numina mittunt
    "Sed sibi quisque facit," etc.   PETRONIUS.

THE flitting Dreams, that play before the wind,
  Are not by Heaven for Prophesies design'd ;
Nor by æthereal Beings sent us down,
But each man is creator of his *own* :
For, when their weary limbs are sunk in ease,
The souls essay to wander where they please ;
The scatter'd images have space to play,
And Night repeats the labours of the Day.

❊❊❊❊

I waked, speaking these out of a Dream in the
Morning.

NATURE a thousand ways complains,
  A thousand words express her pains :
But for her Laughter has but three,
And very small ones, HA, HA, HE !

One of Lord Blessington's Similes in his Play, called, "The Lost Princess, a Tragedy."

BUT, as a Huntsman going out to *hawk*,
And finds *two* Filberds growing on *one* stalk;
The *one* he cracks, and, finding it not *found*,
Fancies the other *so*, that's on the ground.

A Passage from the same PLAY.

——" Stand here alive !
" Nay, he shall die," quoth he, " so may I thrive.
" That is to say, One, Two, and likewise Three."
To the *first* Knight thus instantly spake he,
" I did condemn thee, therefore thou shalt dye,
" And for your death there's a necessity;
" For you have been the cause of *that* [b] Knight's death."
Then, turning to the *third* Knight, thus he saith,
" Thou hast not done what I commanded thee."
And thus he caus'd them to be slain *all Three!*

Another, from the same.

Upon a day, betwixt them *two* said thus,
A Lord is lost if he be vicious.
And drunkenness will be a foul record
Of any man, and chiefly of a Lord :
For there are many an eye, and many an ear,
Still waiting on a Lord, he knows not where.
For God's love, therefore, drink more temperately;
Wine makes a man to lose most wretchedly,
His mind, his sense, and his limbs every one.
Thou shalt see the reverse, quoth he, anon,
And prove it by your own experience,
That wine's not guilty of so great offence.
There is no wine bereaves me of my sense.

[b] i. e. The *second* Knight. KING.

A LETTER TO A FRIEND.

DEAR DICK!

I HEARD yesterday, that on Friday last your hopes of marrying the fair lady Melinda were all vanished, and that she is in the embraces of your rival. I protest, it made strong impressions on me, so that I fled to Boëthius for Consolation. But, his notions being too philosophical for me (yet to comfort you I was resolved), I set myself to search my constant guide in affairs of this life, to see if I might find any thing that in such distress might be an assistance to my Friend. The guide I mention is my little Grammar, which, for the many Receipts, both in the Syntax and *Qui mihi*, may vie with any Philosopher who pretends to Morality or Politicks. I considered, Why may not he, that treats so much of Words and Speech, have something concerning Women, who have so vast a talent in them both? and at least, if any thing concerning Matrimony may be found, it will be in his description of the Three Concords. I went therefore to my fate, and, as a lucky omen, the first line I met with was,

Omnia vincit amor ; et nos cedamus amori :

" Love all things conquers ; e'en we yield to Love."

And here, thought I, appears the cause how so ingenious, sedate, and thoughtful a man as my Friend could let himself be ruffled with the passion of Love : but it is like our Destiny ; sooner or later we must all come to it, and therefore, resistance being in vain, we ought to comply with its first motions, that so our doom may be quickly known, without the torment of expectation : and this agrees excellently with the verses of an old Friend of mine ;

" Might o'ercomes Right ; and powerful Love can conquer
" The grey-hair'd Senator and sparkish Yonker.
" Then, since this Love will conquer one by one,
" Let's all agree to yield ; the work is done."

I had scarce given myself time to look on the Book, but I again cast my eye on a passage, which I thought might justify my Friend in his endeavours to " alter his condition," as the married people term it, which was this ;

                                          Tempora

Tempora mutantur et nos mutamur in illis.

" The Times are chang'd; and with them, chang'd are we."

But then I again confidered, that this change is not always for the better, and that it might happen to my Friend as it did to Jack Crofly,

" Times change; we change: but, Jack, it is thy curfe,

" Ever to change, and ever for the worfe."

So that there may happen that, in my Friend's cafe, a danger may have been avoided, inftead of a blefling being loft. For we find in the Accidence, that happinefs in Marriage feems to be confined only to Kings and Queens. There is no fuch expreffion as *Ricardus et Melinda funt beati,* " Richard and Melinda are " happy;" but only, *Rex et Regina funt beati,* " The King and " the Queen are happy;" which made me fall into this pathetic expreffion;

" If Kings and Queens are only to be bleft

" When join'd together, e'en God help the reft !"

fo that the Comforts of Matrimony feem to be the flowers and prerogatives of the Crown, never to be alienated.

Indeed, let my Friend remember the troubles he underwent in his Courtfhip, the tempefts, the hopes, the jealoufies, the contempt, and the defpair; and I think I ought to congratulate my Friend's deliverance. To fee the hard-heartednefs of thefe Women;

Pectora percuffit, pectus quoque robora fiunt.

Upon which, an Acquaintance of mine made this Paraphrafe:

" At Cynthia's feet, the victim of her eyes,

" The wretched, fad, defpairing, Damon lies,

" And does fuch piteous tales of love rehearfe

" As might an adamantine fortrefs pierce:

" He ftrikes his breaft, but with a wondrous ftroke

" 'Tis Cynthia's breaft that hardens into *oak.*

" Each fainting figh and each heart-rending groan

" Increafe her inclinations to be *ftone.*

" But, O ! that ftone her charming beauty keeps;

" Cynthia's the marble, but 'tis Damon weeps.

I know my dear Friend, as he can have no defire of torments, fo for the continuance of fuch, he has in him an infeparable appetite after liberty, and being the mafter of his time as well as inclinations. How fweet is the found of *Diluculo furgere faluberrimum eft*, when it can be pronounced without any one to contradict it !

 " O, may your hours of life be unconfin'd,
 " And wear an equal freedom with your mind !
 " And may no Screech-owl's voice from curtains prate,
 " How your diverting friends have kept you late !
 " And, when Aurora rouzes you to wealth,
 " And with her fragrant dawn would give you health,
 " Obey her voice : and let it not be faid,
 " You were commanded then to lie in bed."

I will detain you but with one contemplation more, which fhall be upon thefe words, in the fame place,

 Amantium iræ amoris redintegratio eft ;

which plainly feems to me to defcribe this opinion of fome old Philofophers, that envy and ftrife were the firft principles of all things ; and that, when people had fought and fquabbled till they were weary, they became very loving, and fell to the pro- duction of creatures. I have fent you this Tranflation out of a Fragment which may belong to Lucretius or fome other Author :

 " Men fay, the goddefs Strife prefides above,
 " And caufes things, and mixes e'en with Love.
 · " He that adores her muft expect her fcorn,
 " Whilft crowds of bleeding flaves her ftate adorn.
 " She wars, makes peace, is crofs, gay, four, and kind,
 " And flies the compafs of the various wind.
 " But, when fhe feems the conquerefs in the field,
 " She'll in that unexpected minute yield.
  " Then let Hymen's rites begin ;
  " Io, triumph ; enter in.
 " But you that have th' inconftant torment got,
 " Confider not the fortune of your lot ;
 " That Goddefs, who now bears the name of Wife,
 " Was *yours* for hours before ; now *his* for life."

For my part, I fhould not envy his bargain ; and I am fure I wifh you as well as myfelf ; and I am, with all fincerity,

 Your obliged Friend (though perhaps out of your memory)
    BALTHASAR ICHENKEVELT.

P. S. If you fhew this to any perfon breathing, you fhall furely be pinched by the Fairies.

A PINDARIC ODE

TO THE MEMORY OF

DR. WILLIAM KING[c].

I.

A WIDOW'D Friend invites a widow'd Mufe
  To tell the melancholy news,
  And cloath herfelf with fable weeds,
Such as will fhew her heart with forrow bleeds ;
  With grief fhe can't exprefs,   5
  But in foft moving verfe,
Which melts to tears, like that dark night
In which thou vanifhed'ft from fight,
To mount the regions of eternal light.
For Heaven, it feems, denied a longer date.   10
  Thy happy courfe was run,
  Thy bufinefs here was done,
And thou art fet, like the all-glorious fun.
  Yet, juft before thy death,
  Thou rais'dft thy tuneful breath.   15
Like dying fwans at their approaching fate.

II.

Come hither, friendly Mufe, and tell
  How this good Prophet fell,
  That liv'd fo well :
What faucy meffenger durft ftrike the blow   20
  Of fatal Death,
  And feize his breath,
Who always was in readinefs to go ?

c Written by Mr. Oldifworth, who continued the Examiners when Dr. Swift had given them up, and whom our Author is fuppofed occafionally to have affifted in thofe papers.—Whatever may be thought of Mr. Oldifworth's poetry, the warmth of friendfhip which breathes through this Pindarick demands our commendation.

           Could

Could not thy wit command
The Fugitive to ftand,   25
Which others could forbid to die,
And blefs their names with immortality ?
Hadft thou but us'd thy art,
Death would have dropt his dart,
And wondering ftopt the preffure of his leaden hand.   30

III.

Alas, he's cold ! Oh, for a grave
To bury the fad tale ;
For tears will not prevail
Where Humour, Wit, or Virtue, could not fave !
Learning we boaft in vain :   35
A tomb is all we gain
For a life fpent in ftudy and in pain.
Wretched Mortality !
Couldft thou thyfelf but fee,
Thou wouldft hate life as we love thee.   40
Why then fo fond to live are vain mankind ?
Why all thofe joys purfue,
That feem to make life new ?
Becaufe they can no greater pleafures find.
But thou, my Friend, didft higher go,   45
Refolv'd fublimer things to know,
Wing'd Heaven, and left us here below.

IV.

How fhouldft thou live in fuch an age of vice ?
The Phœnix only dwells in Paradife.
Earth was too narow for thy mind,   50
And thou, to all its flatteries blind,
Now in the bowers of blifs
Strikeft thy harmonious Lyre,
Where endlefs Pleafures reign,
And Peace and Piety remain   55
Amidft the blifsful choir ;
Thou doft in all perfections fhine,
And add'ft frefh luftre to the courts divine ;

T 2   Whilft

Whilſt we lament thy too, too early fate :
But greateſt bleſſings have the ſhorteſt date.
   In mournful Poetry
   Our laſt efforts we'll try,
Who beſt can write upon a theme ſo great.

V.

Like warriours well appointed for the fight,
   Poſſeſs'd with generous rage,
   Each Poet ſhould engage ;
   Each ſtrive who beſt could prove
    His duty or his love ;
Each freely pay his tributary mite.
Well may we grieve, well may we mourn thy loſs,
   From whom ſo many drew
   Such Heliconian dew,
From whoſe celeſtial ſpring ſuch influence flows.
   Thy wit did kindly give
   Food by which others live :
For, at thy call, mirth ſat on every face ;
   The ſavage throng
   Follow'd thy ſong :
   Thus raviſh'd and amaz'd,
They danc'd around in one harmonious pace ;
   And ſtill with aweful ſilence gaz'd.

VI.

   But why do I expoſtulate,
   Since ſorrow comes too late
To hinder thine or ſave another's fate ?
When Heaven doth a deſiring ſoul receive,
He ſeems to envy, that pretends to grieve.
   Of what ſtrange atoms are we made,
   That we of Death ſhould be afraid,
   That's but a ſtill, refreſhing dream !
Why ſhould we dread to mix with Earth,
Our parent-clay that gave us birth :
Or meet the Tyrant who hath loſt his ſting.
The King of Terrors ; then no more a King,
But we triumphant o'er the Grave and Him ?

VII.

The world, ungrateful, feldom doth produce   95
A fruitful harveft for a virtuous Mufe;
  If Piety appear
  To crown the happy year,
'Tis always with indifference heard,
  And with fuch cool regard,   100
The grudging foil juft nourifhment denies,
And fo the hopeful plant too early dies;
  Such marks of goodnefs feldom laft,
  But where they're rooted faft.
Religion here and Duty eafy grew,   105
Thy Loyalty no new-taught doctrines knew,
But principles from education drew.
  Envy herfelf muft ftop ev'n here,
  And clofe the falfe malicious ear.

VIII.

Thy Virtue's fled beyond her poifonous blaft,   110
  Which can no longer laft;
Since Heaven, from her peculiar care,
  Did for thy fame prepare,
For fear the vicious world fhould fpoil the growth,
Have chang'd thy virtue, or debas'd thy worth!   115
  But pity 'twas that thou fhouldft die,
  Firft-born of modeft Poetry;
  Pity, thy gaiety and wit,
Should only now for worms be fit,
And, mix'd with Nature's rubbifh, huddled lie!   120

                    CRAPU-

C R A P U L I A;

O R,

The Region of the Cropsicks[d]:

A Fragment, in the Manner of Rabelais[e].

CHAP. I.

The Situation of the Country.

CRAPULIA is a very fair and large territory, which on the North is bounded with the Æthiopic Ocean, on the East with Laconia and Viraginia, on the South by Moronia Felix, and Weftward with the Tryphonian Fens. It lies in that part of the Univerfe where is bred the monftrous bird called Ruc, that for its prey will bear off an Elephant in its talons; and is defcribed by the modern Geographers.

The foil is too fruitful, and the heavens too ferene; fo that I have looked upon them with a filent envy, not without pity, when I confidered they were bleffings fo little deferved by the inhabitants. It lies in feventy-four degrees of longitude, and fixty degrees of latitude, and eleven degrees diftant from the Cape of Good Hope; and lies, as it were, oppofite to the whole coaft of Africa. It is commonly divided into two provinces, Pamphagonia and Ivronia, the former of which is of the fame length and breadth as Great Britain (which I hope will not be taken as any reflection), the other is equal to the High and Low Dutch Lands. Both obey the fame prince, are governed by the fame laws, and differ very little in their habit or their manners.

d "A fatire on the Dutch," fays the Editor of Dr. King's "Remains."—His conjecture may poffibly be right; or, having Dr. King's papers in his poffeffion; it may even have appeared from them that fuch was the intention if it had been completed. But, in its prefent unfinifhed ftate, it muft be owned, there is no ftriking refemblance.

e Of whom, fee above, p. 96.

CHAP. II.

PAMPHAGONIA: or, *Glutton's Paradise.*

PAMPHAGONIA is of a triangular figure, like that of antient Ægypt, or the Greek letter *Delta*, Δ. It is mountainous, inclofed with very high hills : its foil is of the richeft, fo that birds which come thither to feed, if they tarry but three months, grow fo very fat and weighty, that they cannot fly back again over the mountains, but fuffer themfelves to be taken up in the hand, and are as delicious as the Ortolan or the Beccaficos of the Italians. And it is no wonder to them who know that Geefe in Scotland are generated from leaves fallen into the water, and believe the teftimony of one of our Embaffadors· that in the North-Eaft parts of the world Lambs grow upon ftalks like Cabbages and eat up the grafs all round about them, to find the fame fort of provifions in this country. Befides, the Fifh upon that coaft are in fuch plenty, and fo voracious (whether they conform themfelves to the genius of the place and people, or prefage to themfelves the honour of fo magnificent a fepulchre as was given to Nero's Turbot), that, as foon as the hook is caft in, they prefs to it as the Ghofts in Lucian did to Charon's boat, and cling to the iron as Miners do to a rope that is let down when the light of their candle forebodes fome malignant exhalation.

The fea-ports, with which this country abounds more than any other, are of no other ufe than to receive and take in fuch things as are edible, which they have for their fuperfluous wool and hides : nor may the inhabitants export any thing that has the leaft relation to the palate. You fee nothing there but Fruit-trees. They hate Plains, Limes, and Willows, as being idle and barren, and yielding nothing ufeful but their fhade. There are Hops, Pears, Plumbs, and Apples, in the hedge-rows, as there is in all Ivronia ; from whence the Lombards, and fome counties in the Weft of England, have learned their improvements. In antient times, Frugonia, or the Land of Frugality, took in this country as one of its provinces; and Hiftories tell us, that, in Saturn's time, the Frugonian Princes gave laws to all this part of the world, and had their palace there ; and that their country was called Fagonia, from the fimplicity of their diet, which confifted

T 4   only

only in Beech-maft. But that yoke has been long ago fhaken off; their manners are wholly changed, and, from the univerfality of their food, they have obtained, in their own country language, the title of Pamphagones.

CHAP. III.

The Firft Province of PAMPHAGONIA.

FRIVIANDY, or Tight-bittia (that we may take the pro-vinces in their order), were it not for a temperament peculiar to the place, is rather of the hotteft to produce thofe who are pro-perly called good Trencher-men. Its utmoft point, which other Geographers call the Promontory of the Terra Auftralis, is of the fame latitude as the moft Southerly parts of Caftile, and is about forty-two degrees diftant from the Æquator. The inha-bitants have curled hair and dufky complexions, and regard more the delicacy than the largenefs and number of their difhes. In this very promontory, which we fhall call the Black one from its colour (for it is a very fmoaky region, partly from the fre-quent vapours of the place, partly from its vicinity to the Terra del Fogo, which, by the common confent of Geographers, lies on the right-hand of it, but rather nearer than they have placed it) is the city Lucina, whofe buildings are lofty, but apt to be fmoaky and offenfive to the fmell; from whence a colony went, perhaps, as far as the Indies, where it remains to this day by the name of Cochin-China.

Here is the famous temple of the great Deity Omafius Gorgut, or Gorbelly. It is a vaft pile, and contains a thoufand hearths, and as many altars, which are conftantly employed in the Rucal Feftivals. In the midft is a high pyramid, as lofty as the hand of man can erect it, little inferior to thofe of Memphis. It is called the Chemilnean Tower. This, rifing high, gives the fignal of war to the adjoining countries : for, as we by Beacons lighted upon a high hill difcover the danger of an approaching enemy, fo thefe, on the contrary, do the fame by letting their fmoke ceafe and their fires go out : for, when the perpetual va-pour ceafes to roll forth in thick and dark clouds of fmoke, it is

a token

a token that the Hambrians are drawing nearer, than whom there
can be no enemy more terrible to this nation. There are several
smaller towns, that lie under the dominion of this supreme city.
Charbona is the largest village, and, what is seldom seen elfewhere, lies all under ground. Upon its barren foil arises another, though of lefs note, called Favillia. After thefe lies
Tenaille, a narrow town, and Batillû, a broad one, both confiderable. On the left are fome fubfervient petty hamlets, as
Affadora, Marmitta, Culliera, as ufeful for the reception of
ftrangers, amongft which, that of Marmitta is watered by the
river Livenza; which, as is faid of a fountain in the Peak of
Derby, boils over twice in four-and-twenty hours.

CHAP. IV.

The Second Province of PAMPHAGONIA.

NEXT to this is the Golofinian diftrict, the moft pleafant
part of Pamphagonia, covered with Dates, Almonds, Figs,
Olives, Pomegranates, Oranges, Citrons, and Piftaches; through
which run the fmootheft of ftreams, called the Oglium. Here is
the beautiful city of Marzapane, with noble turrets glittering
with gold, but lying too open to the enemy. Over it hang the
Zucker hills, out of whofe bowels they draw fomething that is
hard, white, and fparkling, but fweet as that moifture which the
Ancients gathered out of the reeds which grew in Arabia and
the Indies. You fhall find few people here, who are grown up,
but what have loft their teeth, and have ftinking breaths. Near
to this is the little city Seplafium, which admits of no tradefmen
but Perfumers. It is a town of great commerce with the people
of Viraginia, efpecially the Locanians, who ufe to change their
Looking-glafs with them for Oils and Paftils. The agreeable-
nefs of the place, and the bounty of the Heavens, is favourable to
their art; for the whole track of land, at certain feafons, is covered with aromatic comfits, that fall like hail-ftones: which
Anathumiafis I take to be effentially the fame as that aërial
Honey which we often find upon our oaks, efpecially in the
fpring, and that it differs only In thicknefs: for whereas that

Honey

Honey is fprinkled in drops, the little globules are hardened by
the intenfe cold of the middle region, and rebound in falling.

✳✳✳✳

C H A P. V.

Of the Third Province of PAMPHAGONIA.

IN the fifty-fifth degree, we come into the plains of Lecania,
and fo into the very heart of Pamphagonia, where the chief
city we meet with is Cibinium, which is wafhed with the acid
ftreams of the river Affagion. In the Forum, or market-place,
is the tomb (as I conjecture by the footfteps of fome letters now
remaining) of Apicius, that famous Roman, not very beautiful,
but antique. It is engraved upon the fhell of a Sea-crab; and it
might happen, notwithftanding what Seneca fays, that this famous Epicure, after having fought for larger Shell-fifh than the
coafts of Gallia could fupply him with, and then going in vain
to Africa to make a farther enquiry, might hear fome rumour
concerning this coaft, fteer his courfe thither, and there dye of a
furfeit. But this I leave to the Criticks. Here I fhall only
mention the moft fertile fields of Lardana and Offulia. The
delicious fituation of Mortadella, the pleafanteft of places, had
wonderfully delighted me, had it not been for the Salt-works
which often approach too near it. There is an offenfive ftinking
town called Formagium, alias Butterboxia, and Mantica a boggy
place near the confines of Ivronia.

I haften to the metropolis of the whole region, which, whether
you refpect the uniformity of the building, the manners of the
people, or their way of living, their rules for behaviour, their
law and juftice, will fhew as much as if I were to defcend to
particulars.

〰〰〰

C. H A P. VI.

Of the Metropolis of PAMPHAGONIA, and the Cuftoms of the Inhabitants.

THERE are but very few villages in this country, as well
as in fome others; from whence a Traveller may conjecture, that the country-towns are devoured by the cities, which

are not fo many in number as they are large and populous; of
which the mother and governefs is called Artocreopolis. The
report goes, that in ancient times there were two famous cities,
Artopolis and Creatium, which had many and long contefts about
the fuperiority: for fo it happens to places, as well as men, that
increafe in power; infomuch as the two moft flourifhing Uni-
verfities in the world (to both of which I bear the relation of a
Son, though I am more peculiarly obliged to one of them for my
education), notwithftanding they are fifters, could not abftain
from fo ungrateful a contention.

Artopolis boafted of its antiquity, and that it had flourifhed in
the Saturnian age, when it had as yet no rival. Creatium fet
forth its own fplendour, pleafantnefs, and power. At laft, a
council being called, Creatium got the preference by the univerfal votes of the affembly : for fuch is the iniquity of the
times, that though the head be covered with grey hairs, yet nothing is allowed to the reverence of Antiquity, when encountered
by a proud and upftart Novelty. The other city is now fo far
neglected, that the ruins or footfteps of its magnificence are
fcarce remaining, any more than of Verulam, as is moft elegantly fet forth by our noble Poet Spenfer in his verfes on that
fubject; the latter ufurping the name of the other, as well as
the other has now the double title of Artocreopolis. The city
is more extenfive than beautiful : it is fortified with a large and
deep ditch of running water, which wafhes almoft all the ftreets,
wherein are a thoufand feveral ponds for Fifh ; upon which fwim
Ducks, Geefe, Swans, and all forts of Water-fowl, which has
been wifely imitated by the people of Augfburg. This ditch is
called Gruefla. There are two walls, whofe materials were furnifhed by the Flefh-market; for they are made of Bones, the
larger ferving for the foundations, the leffer for the fuperftruc-
ture, whilft the fmalleft fill up what is wanting in the middle;
being all cemented with the Whites of Eggs, by a wonderful
artifice. The houfes are not very beautiful, nor built high after
the manner of other cities ; fo that there is no need of an Auguftus to reftrain the buildings to the height of feventy feet, as
was done at Rome ; nor is there room for a Seneca or Juvenal
to complain of the multitude of their ftairs and number of
their ftories.

They

They have no regard for Stair-cafes; for indeed none of the
citizens care for them, partly from the trouble of getting up
them (efpecially when, as they often do, they have drunk heartily) as much as for the danger of getting down again. Their
houfes are all covered with large bladebones, very neatly joined
together. There are no free citizens admitted, but fuch whofe
employment has more immediately fome relation to the Table.
Hufbandmen, Smiths, Millers, and Butchers, live in their colonies, who, when they have a Belly of an unwieldy bulk, are promoted to be Burgeffes; to which degree none were anciently admitted but Cooks, Bakers, Victualers, and the graveft Senators,
who are chofen here, as in other places, not for their prudence,
riches, or length of beard; but for their meafure, which they
muft come up to yearly if they will pretend to bear any office in
the public. As any one grows in dimenfions, he rifes in honour; fo that I have feen fome who, from the meaneft and moft
contemptible village, have, for their merits, been promoted to a
more famous town, and at laft obtained the fenatorial dignity in
this moft celebrated city: and yet, when by fome difeafe (as it
often happens), or by age, they have grown leaner than they are
allowed to be by the Statutes, have loft their honour, together
with the bulk of their carcafe. Their ftreets were paved with
polifhed Marble; which feemed ftrange amongft a people fo incurious, both becaufe the workmanfhip was troublefome, and
there might be danger in its being flippery. But the true reafon
of it was, that they might not be forced to lift their feet higher
than ordinary by the inequality of the pavement, and likewife
that the chairs of the fenators might the more eafily be pufhed
forward: for they never go on foot, or on horfe-back, nor even in
a coach, to the Exchange, or their public feafts, becaufe of their
weight; but they are moved about in great eafy Elbow-chairs,
with four wheels to them; and continue fitting fo fixed, in the
fame pofture, fnoring and flabbering till they are wheeled home
again.

At the four gates of this city, whofe form is circular, there
fit in their turns as many fenators, who are called Bufcadores.
Thefe carefully examine all who come in and go out: thofe that
go out, left they fhould prefume by chance to do it fafting, which
they can eafily judge of by the extent of their bellies; and, the
matter being proved, they are fined in a double fupper: thofe

that come in, to fee what they bring with them upon their return; for they muft neither depart with empty ftomachs, nor
come back with empty hands. Every month, according to the
laws, which they unwillingly tranfgrefs, there are ftated Feafts,
at which all the fenators are obliged to be prefent, that after
dinner (for no perfon can give his vote before he has dined)
they may deliberate concerning the public affairs. The name of
their Common-hall is Pythanos-come [f]. Every one knows his
own feat, and his conveniences of a clofe-ftool, and a couch to
repofe upon when the heat of their wine and feafoned dainties
incline them to it. Their greateft delicacies are ferved up at the
firft courfe; for they think it foolifh not to eat the beft things
with the greateft appetite: nor do they cut their Boars, Sheep,
Goats, and Lambs, into joints, or quarters, as commonly we do,
but convey them whole to table, by the help of machines, as I
remember to have read in Petronius Arbiter. They are fineable
who rife before they have fet fix hours; for, when the edge of
their ftomach is blunted, they do, what they call, " fit and pid-
" dle." They eat and drink fo leifurely, for the fame reafon as
the famous Epicure of old wifhed that his neck were as long as
a Crane's. They meafure the feafonable time for their departure
after this method: they have a door to their Town-houfe, which
is wide enough for the largeft man to enter when he is fafting;
through this the guefts pafs; and when any one would depart,
if he ftops in this paffage, he is trufted to go out at another door;
but if it be as eafy as if he were fafting, the Mafter of the Ceremonies makes him tarry till he comes to be of a ftatutable mag-
nitude: after which example, Willfrid's needle in Belvoir Caftle [g]
was a pleafant trial of Roman Catholic fanctity. They have
Gardens of many acres extent, but not like thofe of Adonis or
Alcinoüs; for nothing delightful is to be expected in them, neither order, nor regularity of walk, nor grafs-plots, nor variety of
flowers in the borders; but you will find all planted with Cabbages, Turnips, Garlick, and Mufk-melons, which were carried
hence to Italy, and are in quantity fufficient to feaft an hundred
Pythagoreans.

There is a public College, or Hofpital, whither they are fent
who have got the Dropfy, Gout, or Afthma, by their eating and

[f] The Devil take the hindmoft. — King.
[g] The beautiful refidence of the duke of Rutland.

drinking;

drinking; and there they are nourished at the public expence.
As for such as have lost their teeth by their luxury, or broken
them by eating too greedily or incautiously, they are provided
for in the Island of Sorbonia. All the richer sort have several
servants, in the nature of vassals, to cultivate their gardens, and
be employed in inferior offices, who have their liberty when
they can arrive at such a bulkiness. If any of the Grandees
of the country die of a surfeit, he is given, as being all made
up of the most exquisite dainties, to be eaten up by his servants; and this they do that nothing should be lost that is so delicate. The men are thick and fat to a miracle; nor will any
one salute another, whose chin does not come to the midst
of his breast, and his paunch fall to his knees. The women
are not unlike them, and in shape resemble the Italians, and
have breasts like the Hottentots. They go almost naked, having
no regard to their garments. The magistrates and persons of
better figure have gowns made of the skins of such beasts as
they have eaten at one meal. All wear a knife, with a large
spoon, hanging upon their right-arm. Before their breasts they
wear a smooth skin, instead of a napkin, to receive what falls out
of their mouths, and to wipe them upon occasion; which whether it be more black or greasy, is hard to determine.

 They are of a very slow apprehension, and no way fit for any
science; but yet understand such arts as they have occasion for.
Their Schools are Public-houses, where they are educated in the
sciences of Eating, Drinking, and Carving; over which, one
Archisilenius, an exquisite Epicure, was then Provost, who, instead of Grammar, read some Fragments of Apicius. Instead of
a Library, there is a public repository of Drinking-vessels, in
which Cups of all orders and sizes are disposed into certain
classes. Cups and Dishes are instead of Books. The younger
Scholars have less, the elder have greater; one has a Quart, the
other a Pottle, the other a Gallon: this has a Hen, that a Goose,
a third a Lamb or a Porker: nor have they any liberty, or
recess, till the whole is finished; and if, by a seven years stuf-
fing, they are no proficients in Fatness, are presently banished
into the Fancetic Islands; nor are they suffered long to stay there
idle and without improvement. Hither likewise are sent all
Phyficians who prescribe a course of diet to any person. When

any

any one is fick, without recourfe to Æfculapius, they make him
eat Radifh, and drink warm Water; which, according to Celfus,
will purge and vomit him. Venifon is that which they moft
delight in; but they never take it in Hunting, but by Nets and
Gins. They look upon the Swine as the moft profitable and
beft of all animals; whether it is for the likenefs of its manners,
as being good for nothing but the table, or elfe from its growing
fat on the fudden with the worft of nutriment. It may not
feem credible; yet parfimony appears in the midft of their pro-
fufenefs: but then it is very ill placed, for it is in Crumbs,
Bones, and Crufts. They do not fo much as keep any Dogs,
Cats, Hawks, or any thing that eats flefh. If any Perfon fuffer
meat to ftink, he is impaled; but Venifon and Rabbits are to
have the *baut-gout:* and then their Cheefe is kept till it is over-
run with little Animals, which they devour with Muftard and
Sugar. This is an odd fort of cuftom, derived from the Dutch.

　　The country abounds with Rivers, which ebb and flow according to their digeftion, and generally overflow at the beginning of January, and towards the end of February, and do mifchief to the neighbouring country.

※※※※

C H A P. VII.

Of *the Wars of the* PAMPHAGONIANS.

THE Pamphagones have perpetual wars with the Hambrians, or the Fancetic Iflands, and the Frugonians. * *
*　*　*　*　*　*　*　*　*　*　*　*　*

Cætera defunt.

FOUR DEDICATIONS.

I.

To my Honoured Friend Sir EDMUND WARCUPP, of Oxfordshire, Knight [h].

S I R,

I SHALL make you but a bad return for lending me these Memoirs, by sending them back in *my* English. However, I did not think I could be too intent upon them, when, the longer I read and considered this Book, the characters of two *such Brothers* as the Duke of Bouillon and Marefchal Turenne raised in me a true and more lively idea of your Sons, the Colonel and the Captain. It is true, that the *former*, being born Princes, became great Generals; but then they lived long in the world to obtain it: whereas the other *two Brothers*, though cut off in their bloom, had done more than any of such an age could do, towards equalling *their* great examples.

The Battle of Sedan, in which the duke of Bouillon got his greatest glory, has nothing more considerable in it than the action by which he gained the enemy's cannon: and, upon reading this, who could not but have an image of colonel Warcupp's bravery in the battle of Steynkirk [i], where he drove the French from their cannon, and laid his own half-pike upon them. In the same battle, when the count de Soiffons should have received the advantage of the victory, it is with surprize that we find him dead. This naturally brings captain Warcupp to our remembrance, who, when *he* should have received the new commands which for his valour the King designed him, was (in-

h Prefixed by Dr. King to " New Memoirs and Characters of the " Two Great Brothers, the Duke of Bouillon and Marefchal Turenne." Tranflated by him, from the French, in 1693.

i In this battle, which was fought Aug. 3, 1692, the Confederates were commanded by king William in person, and the French by the duke of Luxemburg. The English were forced to retreat, with the loss of several thousand brave officers and soldiers.

stead

ſtead of enjoying the reward) found mortally wounded in his Majeſty's ſervice.

This, to a common Reader, may ſeem a melancholy and an improper addreſs to a Father; but then they muſt be ignorant of the greatneſs of Sir Edmund Warcupp's mind, and his true notions of honour. Lacedæmon heretofore gloried in ſo great a man as Thraſibulus, who, receiving his ſon Pitanas dead upon a ſhield in his country's ſervice, interred him with theſe ex-preſſions: " Let other Fathers ſhed tears; I will not. This " Youth died like mine, like a Spartan."

England has reaſon to boaſt of a double honour in Sir Edmund Warcupp, who, with ſuch an evenneſs of temper and heroic patience, could bear the loſs of *two Sons*, ſo young, ſo brave, ſo very much his own, and ſo true Engliſhmen.

As for my own part, were I to be a Father, I ſhould wiſh for ſuch Sons; and, muſt they die! I would loſe them after the ſame manner. And I am ſure that, in bearing of my misfortune, I could have no better pattern than yourſelf.

But, in the circumſtances I am in at preſent, there is nothing I am more ambitious of, than to be admitted amongſt the number of,

S I R,

Your moſt faithful friends,

and humble ſervants,

W. KING.

II [k].

To the Right Honourable LORDS and GENTLEMEN, Members of the Immortal BEEF-STEAK CLUB [l].

LORDS, and GENTLEMEN,

IT is generally prefumed, that a Mifcellany fhould confift of what the world moft delights in, that is, Variety. There the Serious may find Contemplation; the Witty, Mirth; the Po-liticians, State Maxims; the Humourfome, frefh Airs; the Amo-rous, new Sonnets; true Worth may gain Preferment, and Vice meet with its due Correction: in fhort, it fhould contain fuch things as may fatisfy the mind when its thoughts incline either to Inftruction or Pleafure. It feems, therefore, moft proper that fuch a Mifcellany fhould be dedicated to fome Club, or col-lection of perfons; that, if any part fhould not pleafe all, yet it may have its lucky chance, and at one time or another find a Patron amongft fome of them. To whom then fhould the Au-thor addrefs fooner than to the noble BEEF-STEAK-CLUB, where every valuable quality reigns differently, but are all ce-mented by the ties of good-nature and good-humour? When Dido laid the foundations of Carthage, fhe enclofed her fubjects, the wife and valiant Phœnicians, within the compafs of a thong, which fhe cut out of an Ox's hide; and from thence arofe a for-midable Empire: So this Club, under the denomination of ano-ther part of the Ox, comprehends perfons of fuch valour, worth, and conduct, as may render their Country happy, and their Miftrefs great and glorious.

But now to the Meat—Beef has been that which has al-ways relifhed with the world, either whole or in pieces, in ima-gination or reality. Jupiter made his court to Europa in the fhape of a Bull, and brought her over to this continent, which ftill retains her name: it was the fame Jupiter who turned the fair Io to a beautiful Cow, and fo preferved his Miftrefs from the fury of his Wife, and for a reward caufed her to be wor-

[k] Prefixed to a Collection of our Author's Mifcellanies, publifhed by himfelf, in one volume 8vo, in or about the year 1709.

[l] See an account of Eftcourt, their Proveditor, above, p. 86; and fome further particulars of him, in the Obfervations annexed to this Volume.

fhiped.

shiped throughout all Ægypt. Pasiphaë fell in love with a natural Bull, and so got a whimsical heir to the Cretan kingdom. But now, since the Britons have brought the French Mushrooms, Trufles, and Kickshaws, into contempt, people begin to relinquish Fables, and come to solid Beef and fat Lincolnshire Oxen. Patroclus and Achilles of old delighted most in Chines, Barons, Ribs, and Surloins roasted; and that not without reason, for they are excellent. Guy of Warwick regaled himself with boiled Rumps, Buttocks, Flanks, and Briskets, not less admirable. There is no reason but to believe that Beef-steaks, when nicely broiled with the Gravy in them, may produce as good blood and vigorous spirits as either of the former; seeing they, approaching nearest to the fire, the place of greatest danger, have consequently gained to themselves the post of honour. Such bravery cannot fail of success; and I doubt not but in a little while the Members of this Club will be able to broil their Steaks upon the magnificent and stupendous Gridiron of the Escurial. In the mean time, I desire them to accept of the hearty wishes for their prosperity, of

Their most obedient humble servant,

WILLIAM KING.

III^m.

To the Reverend Dr. KNIPE, Master of Westminster School[n].

S I R,

THOUGH I have lost my *natural* Parents, who were most indulgent to me, and the great Dr. Busby[o], whose memory

[m] Prefixed to " An Historical Account of the Heathen Gods and " Heroes," printed in the beginning of the year 1711.

[n] Thomas Knipe, D. D. was also a prebendary of Westminster. He did not long survive the date of this Dedication; dying 8 Id. Aug. 1711, aged 73. His epitaph is printed in Dart's History of that Abbey.

[o] Richard Busby, D. D. was born Sept. 22, 1606; and, having passed

U 2

through

mory to me shall be for ever sacred; yet, I thank God, I have a Master still remaining, to whom I may pay my duty and acknowledgment for the benefits I have received by my education. It is in some measure to express this duty, that I lay the following papers before you, expecting pardon for the faults that may be in them, from your innate goodness, which I have so often experienced.

The subject of the Poetical History has exercised the pens of Clemens Alexandrinus, Lactantius, Minutius Felix, Arnobius, St. Austin, and the learned Bishops Fulgentius and Eustathius; and is useful, not only for the better knowledge of the Classicks and all other polite Literature, but even of the Holy Scriptures themselves. It must be acknowledged, that the utmost end of your instruction tends to the understanding of the Text of the Holy Bible in all the learned Languages; and the Fundamentals of our Religion, as taught in the Catechism, Nine and Thirty Articles, and Homilies, of the Church of England: so that whosoever has had the happiness of an education under you at Westminster must attribute it to his own neglect, if he be not a good Christian, and consequently a loyal Subject. That, by your wholesome instructions to the young Gentlemen of this nation, you may long contribute to the good of the Church and State, and the honour of her Majesty's Royal Foundation in which you are so eminently placed, is the hearty wish of, Sir,

Your most dutiful and obedient servant,

WILLIAM KING.

through the classes of Westminster School as a king's scholar, was elected student of Christ Church in 1624; made prebendary of Wells and rector of Cudworth, July 1, 1639; master of Westminster School, Dec. 13, 1640; and by his skill and diligence in the discharge of this most laborious and important office for the space of fifty-five years, bred up the greatest number of eminent men, in church and state, that ever adorned at one time any age or nation. He was installed prebendary of Westminster, July 5, 1660; died April 6, 1695, aged 89; and was buried in Westminster Abbey, where a fine monument is erected to his memory.

IV. To

IV P.

To the moſt Noble Prince HENRY SOMERSET Duke of BEAUFORT, Marquis and Earl of WOR- CESTER, Earl of GLAMORGAN, Baron HERBERT, and Lord of CHEPSTOW, RAGLAND, and GOWER, Lord-Lieutenant of the County of SOUTHAMPTON, Lord Warden of the New Foreſt, and One of Her MAJESTY's moſt Honourable Privy Council, &c. q

May it pleaſe your GRACE,

THE ſubjeƈt of the following papers makes it ſeem proper that they ſhould be preſented to your Grace : for, ſince you have been admitted to her Majeſty's Council, it is convenient you ſhould ſee all the meaſures that have been taken by perſons advanced to the like ſtation. Mr. Gabriel Naude r, who was the Author of the French from which this is a Tranſlation, is accounted one of the moſt celebrated geniuſes of the latter age, for his knowledge of men and books, the variety and extenſive- neſs of his converſation, and his good fortune in being admitted to the ſervice of the moſt illuſtrious perſons then in Europe. His wiſdom, prudence, good humour, and temperance, recom- mended him ſo far, that, having ſtudied Phyſick in Padua, with the famous Mr. Patin, under Mr. Moreau, and being returned from his travels, he was, in the year 1630, being then about

P Prefixed to " Political Conſiderations on Refined Politicks, &c." tranſlated from the French of Gabriel Naudæus in 1711.

q See a poem, addreſſed to this noble peer, above, p. 237. He ſuc- ceeded to his grandfather's titles in 1699, and died in 1714. His grace was twice married, and had the misfortune to loſe both ladies in child- bed ; the firſt of them (lady Mary Sackvile, only daughter to Charles earl of Dorſet) in 1705, without Iſſue ; the ſecond (lady Rachel Noel, ſecond daughter to Wriotheſley Baptiſt earl of Gainſborough) in September 1709. By the ſecond ducheſs, he had three ſons, two of which ſucceſſively in- herited the titles.

r He was born at Paris, Feb. 12, 1600.

thirty, fent by Cardinal Richlieu [s] upon an efpecial occafion to Rome, where he remained above twelve years as Library-keeper [t] to the Cardinal de Bagni, a perfon that had improved himfelf fo far in all good Authors relating to Politicks, and efpecially in Ariftotle's Rhetorick, which was his favourite, that Cardinal Pamphilio, who afterwards fucceeded by the name of Innocent the Tenth [u], faid, he feared no other rival befides him for the popedom; but death prevented it. Mr. Naude was after-wards Library-keeper to Antonio Barbarini, nephew to Pope Urban VIII [w]. Upon his coming back from Rome, he was ad-mitted into the fervice of the Cardinal Mazarine [x], of whofe penetration into mankind the whole world is fenfible. To thefe patrons he owed his preferments of canon of Verdun and

[s] John Armand du Pleffis de Richlieu, the illuftrious ftatefman of France, was born Sept. 5, 1685; obtained a difpenfation for being made bifhop of Lucon at the early age of 22; was dignified with the title of cardinal in 1622; was prime minifter in 1624, and died in 1642. The hiftory of his life would be the hiftory of France. We fhall therefore only add, that, amidft other qualifications, his various political treatifes demonftrate him to have been an able writer; he was alfo a poet, and, in the true fpirit of that *genus irritabile*, is faid to have envied Corneille the glory of his " Cid," and to have obliged the French academy to publifh a cri-ticifm in 1637 to its difadvantage.

[t] He had been before employed in a like capacity by Henry de Mefmes, prefident à mortier.

[u] He filled the pontifical chair from 1644 to 1655.

[w] Better known by the name of Cardinal Maffeo Barbarini. He was advanced to the pontifical chair in 1623, and died July 29, 1644. He was equally famous for the variety of his learning and the elegance of his genius. His Latin poems were re-publifhed, by Jof. Browne, A. M. in 1726.

[x] This celebrated fucceffor of Richlieu had the happinefs of com-pleating many of the great plans his predeceffor had fchemed, but left unfinifhed.—Naudæus founded for this minifter a library of 40,000 volumes, at that period an immenfe collection; but had the mortification, on the cardinal's difgrace, of feeing the whole, which he had collected with fo much labour, difperfed. Naudæus himfelf purchafed all the books in phyfic, for 3500 livres. His abilities in the felecting of books may be difcovered in his " Avis pour dreffer un Bibliotheque," which was tranf-lated into Englifh, under the title of " Inftructions for creating a " Library, written by Gabriel Naude, publifhed in Englifh, with fome " Improvements, by John Evelyn, Efq. Lond. 1661."

prior

prior of Artige in the Limoiſin. Queen Chriſtina, who re‑
ſolved to make Sweden famous by her encouragement of learn‑
ing, invited him to Stockholm, where ſhe ſhewed him particular
marks of her eſteem. Upon his journey thence, he died at
Abbeville, July 29, 1653, and ſo hindered us from ſeveral things
he had deſigned to perfect *y*. Pardon this ſhort account of the
Author; for it is in ſome meaſure an apology for the preſumption
of the Dedication; for I would have nothing approach your
Grace, but what had formerly been ſo far received in the world
as that it might juſtify its appearance once again in publick.

The Author, in his Work, has made a ſufficient apology for
his ſearching ſo far into " the Secrets of State;" and ſhewn that
a great ſpirit can have no prejudice, but rather reap advantage,
from the diſcovery of them. Now if Youth, under all the
temptations of the world, can produce commendable actions fit‑
ting the dignity of a perſon's birth and grandeur; if the ſtricteſt
rules of œconomy are preſerved, and temperance mixed with the
ſweeteſt affability be always the product of his converſation,
either in friendſhip or conjugal affection, the niceſt trials of huma‑
nity; what may be expected from the finiſhed years of ſuch a
one, when he knows the rocks and quick-ſands he is to avoid,
and has no other port in view but where his anceſtors ſafely
harboured? It cannot be doubted, therefore, but the virtues
and honour inherent in your Grace's family and perſon will al‑
ways conduct you through the difficulties of ſtate affairs, and
guard you againſt the crafts of policy, preſerving you in the love
of your countrymen and the favour of your Prince.

That your Grace will accept of this firſt eſſay of my gratitude,
is the utmoſt ambition of your Grace's

Moſt obliged, moſt dutiful, humble ſervant,

WILLIAM KING.

y Naudæus was very prudent and regular in his conduct, very ſober,
never drinking any thing but water. Study being his principal occupation,
he wrote a great number of books; from which Mr. Bayle embelliſhed
his Dictionary with many extracts.

ADDITIONAL OBSERVATIONS.

Vol. I. p. 1. It fhould have been mentioned, that another young ftudent of Chrift-Church, Mr. Edward Hannes, had a hand in the " Reflections on Varillas." This gentleman was, in 1690, elected profeffor of chemiftry; and was the author of feveral ingenious Latin poems, fome of which are printed in the " Mufæ Anglicanæ" and in other Mifcellanies. Mr. Addifon has addreffed a Poem, " Ad D. D. Hannes, infigniffimum Medi- " cum et Poetam."

P. 2. M. Varillas intituled his book, " Hiftoire des Revolutions " arrivées en Europe en matiere de Religion." Paris, 6 vols. 4to, 1686, &c.; and again in 1687, 12mo. It was alfo printed in both fizes at Paris in 1690; and had before been publifhed at Amfter- dam. It begins with the year 1374, and ends in 1650. At the head of the firft volume, Varillas had put the following adver- tifement: " In compofing this work, I have taken my materials " indifferently from Catholic and Proteftant writers; citing thefe " laft in their own words as often as I found them ingenuous " enough not to fupprefs or difguife the moft important truths; " and it is through their own fault that I have been obliged to " have recourfe to the Catholicks."

P. 5. l. 18. This extract of M. Hozier's letter is cited in the Preface to M. Larroque's " Nouvelles Accufations contre M. " Varillas, ou Remarques Critiques contre une partie de fon " premier livre de l'Hiftoire de l'Herefie. Amftelod. 1687."

Ibid. l. 27. It fhould be obferved, in juftice to Varillas, that he denied this matter of the penfion. It is true, Le Long tells us (Biblotheque Hiftorique de la France, art. Varillas), " that " he was offered fuch by feveral French noblemen, as well as by " foreigners; which he always refufed: and particularly the " States of Holland offered him one, in 1669, to write their " hiftory; but he alfo refufed this, by the advice of M. Pom- " pone. He accepted that only of the clergy of France, which " M. de Harlai, Archbifhop of Paris, had procured for him." But Varillas contradicts this; and, in his anfwer to Burnet, fays, " that he never accepted the penfion which M. Harlai had ob- " tained for him from the clergy of France in 1670; nor yet that " which he procured of the King for him, charged upon the ab- " bey of La Victoire, in 1672; and that all that he received by " the Archbifhop's means was, a prefent from the affembly of the " Clergy in 1670, and a grant from the King of two thoufand " livres in 1685." See Niceron's Memoires, tom. V. p. 64. Paris, 1728, 8vo.

P. 93. July 24, 1775, the Emprefs beftowed on the marfhal Romanzow an eftate of 5000 Peafants, 100,000 roubles in money; a fervice of plate; a hat with a wreath of laurel, enriched with

precious

precious ftones to the value of 30,000 roubles, a diamond ftar and fhoulder-knot, &c. &c.

P. 135. Dr. Richard Bentley [z] was born at Wakefield in Yorkfhire, Jan. 27, 1661-2, and received there the firft part of his education; whence being removed to St. John's college, Cambridge, he followed his ftudies with indefatigable induftry. In 1689, being then mafter of arts, he was incorporated in the fame degree at Wadham college, Oxford. Oct. 2, 1692, he was inftalled in a prebend at Worcefter, by Bp. Stillingfleet, to whom he was domeftic chaplain; and whofe recommendations, with thofe of Bp. Lloyd, obtained for him the honour of opening Mr. Boyle's famous lectures. In April 1694, he obtained the patent of keeper of the royal library; in 1700, was prefented to the mafterfhip of Trinity college; was collated archdeacon of Ely, June 12, 1707; had a good benefice in that ifland; and was chaplain to queen Anne, as he had been to king William. In 1709, a complaint was laid againft him by feveral of the fellows, before the bifhop of Ely as vifitor, which, after above twenty years continuance, was terminated in his favour. In 1717, he had another difpute with his college, on the fees of creation for a doctorate; on which occafion he was fufpended and degraded; but reftored by a mandamus from the king's bench. He died July 14, 1742.

Ibid. Dr. Aldrich died Dec. 14, 1710. He was a learned and pious Divine; a warm zealot for the church intereft; a ftout champion for the prerogatives of the crown; and made himfelf famous, by contriving the hieroglyphical figures of the Oxford Almanacks; in fome of which, many people fancied ftrange allufions, particularly in favour of the Pretender.

Ibid. Mr. Charles Boyle, born in Auguft 1676, was entered, when only 15, of Chrift Church, Oxford. He fucceeded to the title of earl of Orrery, Aug. 23, 1703, on the death of his elder brother Lionel, and had a regiment given him; was elected a knight of the thiftle, Oct. 13, 1705; raifed to the rank of major general in 1709, and fworn of the privy council. At the time the peace of Utrecht was fettling, he was appointed envoy extraordinary to the ftates of Flanders and Brabant, Jan. 11, 1710-11; and, for his fervices, was created baron Boyle of Marfton, Somerfetfhire, Sept. 10, 1711. He refided at Bruffels, as envoy, till June 1713; and, on the acceffion of king George I, was continued in his command in the army, made a lord of the bed-chamber; and lord lieutenant of the county of Somerfet, Dec. 3, 1714. He refigned his poft in the bed-chamber in 1716, his regiment having before been taken from him. He was committed to The Tower,

---

[z] He was " the fon a tradefman," fays the writer of his article in the " Biographia Britannica;" which Mr. Cumberland, in his " Letter to " the Bp. of Oxford, 1767," p. 23, ftyles " a mifreprefentation," and a " debafing of his condition from that of a gentleman to a mean tradefman."

Sept.

Sept. 28, 1721, on suspicion of being concerned in Layer's plot;
whence he was at length discharged, after suffering severely in his
health. He died Aug. 28, 1731, aged 57. His taste as a fine
writer is well established; and the noble instrument which bears
his name is a proof of his mechanical genius; he had also a peculiar turn to medicine; and bought and read whatever was published on that subject.

P. 139. l. 3. *Add, as a Note,* An English translation of Phalaris was published in 1634; but the Translator confessed he had
no skill in Greek, and that he did it from " the most approved ver-
" sions in three several languages."—Another translation was published by Mr. Whately of Magdalen College [probably that said
to be by J. S. 1699.]—Mr. Budgell translated a few particular
Letters, which he annexed to his Memoirs of the Boyles.—And,
lastly, Dr. Franklin hath given a translation of the whole, in
1749. From the last-mentioned writer, we have extracted the
following remarks:—" The controversy was on both sides carried
" on with great learning and spirit; and convinced the world
" that no subject was so inconsiderable, but, if in the hands of
" able men, might produce something worthy of their attention.
" I never heard my lord Orrery's abilities as a scholar called in
" question; and Dr. Bentley was always looked on as a man of
" wit and parts; and yet I have been assured that, whilst the dif-
" pute was in its height, the partizans of each side behaved with
" a partiality usual in such cases. The friends of Phalaris and
" Mr. Boyle would not allow their adversary any wit; whilst the
" Doctor's advocates, on the other hand, made it their business to
" represent Mr. Boyle as void of learning,; and attributed all
" the merit of his book to the assistance of some men of distin-
" guished merit in the college and university of which he was a
" member; and so far did this malicious affectation prevail, that
" Dr. Swift alludes to it as a fact in his " Battle of the Books,"
" where he says, " that Boyle had a suit of armour given him by
" all the gods." Many indeed, who gave into this foolish opinion,
" did at the same time allow, in justice to the late lord Orrery,
" that, if the weapons were put into his hand, he had at least the
" skill to manage them to the best advantage. To recompense
" any uneasiness, which might arise from reports of this kind,
" Mr. Boyle had the secret satisfaction of seeing his enemies, whilst
" they endeavoured to lessen his reputation, pay him the highest
" compliment, by attributing his work to the Literati of Christ
" Church; who, if they had really been concerned in it any far-
" ther than casual hints of conversation on the subject, would, I
" believe, long before this time have cleared their titles to a share
" in the reputation acquired by it; which as they have never yet
" done, I see no reason why Mr. Boyle should not be looked
" upon as the sole author of that piece; or why, as the labour
" and merit of it was his own, his claim to the deserved ap-
" plause

"plaufe it has met with fhould ever for the future be called in
"queftion."

Ibid. *After* l. 25, *add,* This occafioned the three following
treatifes :

"An Effay concerning Critical and Curious Learning; in
"which are contained fome fhort Reflections on the Controverfy,
"&c. by T. R. efq. 1698." [Q. Thomas Rymer, efq.]

"View of Differtation, &c. [by John Milner, D. D. late vicar
"of Leeds, in Yorkfhire], 1698."

"A Chronological Account of the Life of Pythagoras, and
"other famous Men his Contemporaries; with an Epiftle to the
"Rev. Dr. Bentley, concerning Porphyry's and Jamblichus's Lives
"of Pythagoras. By the Right Reverend Father in God William
"[Lloyd] Lord Bifhop of Coventry and Lichfield, 1699." The
Letter is dated Dec. 30, 1698.

Ibid. Mr. Boyle, in his *second* edition, corrected fome miftakes; and annexed to it "A fhort Account of Dr. Bentley, by
"way of Index."—To the *third* edition, he added a fmall Appendix, of four pages, occafioned by "A View of the Controverfy
"between Dr. Bentley and Mr. Boyle, upon the Epiftles of Pha-
"laris, &c. in order to the manifefting the Incertitude of Heathen
"Chronology." [This feems to be Dr. Milner's book.]

P. 140. *After* l. 15, *add,* "An Anfwer to the "Short Ac-
"count, &c." in relation to fome Mf. Notes on Callimachus and
"Mr. Bennet's Appendix," was publifhed, in 1699, by Mr.
Whately.

Ibid. Dr. Bentley gave a very full and particular anfwer to
the accufation relative to Sir Edward Sherburn, in the Preface to his Differtation, p. xliii. et feqq.; which was as pofitively
contradicted by Sir Edward, in the "Short Account, &c." p. 134.
—Sir Edward was born Sept. 18, 1618; was clerk of the
ordnance to King Charles I, but ejected in 1641 for adhering to
the royal caufe. Retiring with the King to Oxford, he was there
made mafter of arts. On the furrender of that city to the parliament, he fettled in the Middle Temple, and publifhed feveral
learned works. He recovered his office under King Charles II,
but was again turned out by James II; and betook himfelf ever
after to a retired and ftudious courfe of life. He died Nov. 4,
1702, in his 85th year.

P. 141. *Add to Note,* Dr. Bentley's memory failed him here: it
was not Rupilius, but his adverfary, who *permagna negotia dives
habebat Clazomenis.* Or perhaps he miftook wittingly, in order to
compare the *permagna negotia* with the *pus atque venenum.*

P. 142. This Letter from Dr. King was not immediately addreffed to Mr. Boyle, but "to a Friend of that Gentleman." See
"Boyle againft Bentley," p. 6.

P. 143. The following P. S. was annexed to Dr. King's Letter, in the "Short Account, &c." p. 138. "I hope, Sir, this

X 4

"anfwer

" anfwer of Dr. Bentley will divert you as much as his former
" *Differtation*, his *own few Notes on Callimachus*, or his extra-
" ordinary *Collection of Pills to purge Melancholy* (London, 8vo,
" 1698, printed for *Playford*); which He may have more ufe of,
" than when it was firft publifhed."

P. 150. *Add to Note*, Mr. Prefton has given a good defcription
of a fimilar amphitheatre, at Hockley in the Hole, under the title
of " Æfop at the Bear-garden, a Vifion, 1715." It was dedicated
originally, he fays, to Bull-baiting, Bear-baiting, Prize-fighting,
and all other forts of *rough game*; and was not only attended by
Butchers, Drovers, and great crowds of all forts of mob, but
likewife by Dukes, Lords, Knights, Squires, &c. There were
feats particularly fet apart for the quality, ornamented with old
tapeftry hangings, into which none were admitted under half a
crown at the leaft. Its neighhourhood was famous for fheltering
Thieves, Pickpockets, and infamous Women; and for breeding
Bull-dogs.

P. 152. *Add to Note*, St. Nicholas ftill holds his rank and
veneration in the Ruffian Calendar, and has almoft as many altars
as the Virgin himfelf. Wraxall's Tour, 1774, p. 233.

P. 165. l. 5. *Add to Note*, Wotton's attainments in the lan-
guages were fo remarkable, as to be fet forth by his father, in a
Pamphlet dedicated to King Charles II, intituled, " An Effay on
" the Education of Children in the firft Rudiments of Learning;
" together with a Narrative of what Knowledge William Wot-
" ton, a Child of Six Years of Age, hath attained unto, upon the
" Improvement of thofe Rudiments in the Latin, Greek, and
" Hebrew Tongues. By Henry Wotton, of Corpus Chrifti
" College, Cambridge, and Minifter of Wrentham in Suffolk."
Re-printed in 8vo. 1752.

Ibid. l. 16. Dr. King was very right in this affertion; the
fhape of Neftor's cup hath been miftaken by all who have written
about it, from the days of Martial to thofe of our Englifh Homer;
as is very fatisfactorily fhewn by Mr. Clarke, in " The Con-
" nection of Roman, Saxon, and Englifh Coins," p. 218.

P. 170. l. 12. *read* How far.

P. 174. Richard Flecknoe, who lived in the reigns of Charles
the Firft and Second, was better acquainted with the Nobility
than with the Mufes. If his own works are not fufficient to
tranfmit his name to pofterity, Mr. Dryden has effectually performed that office in his celebrated fatire called " Mac Flecknoe."
Langbaine enumerates five of his dramatic productions. His
other works confift of Epigrams and Ænigmatical Characters,
and of a Diary, in burlefque verfe, 12mo, 1655. Dryden, in his
Dedication to Limberham, has feverely raillied an Epiftle Dedi-
catory of Flecknoe's to a Nobleman; but to what book it was
prefixed is now unknown.—Langbaine tells us, he never could
get one of his plays acted: but this is a miftake. His " Love's

" King-

" Kingdom, a Paſtoral Tragi-comedy," appears, by the Dedication to William Marquis of Newcaſtle, to have been acted and
damned. Q. If this is not the Dedication Dryden alludes to ? His
" Love's Dominion, a Dramatique Piece full of excellent Mora-
" litie, written as a Pattern for the reformed Stage, 1654," 12ᵐᵒ,
is dedicated to Lady Eliz. Claypole, Cromwell's daughter.

Ibid. Thomas Decker was contemporary with Ben Jonſon,
and contended with that celebrated Laureat for the bays. Though
his writings are in ſmall eſtimation, he had in that age many
friends amongſt the Poets, particularly the ingenious Richard
Brome. He wrote eight plays; clubbed with Webſter in writing three more; and with Rowley and Ford in another. That
which was in moſt eſteem was " The Untruſſing the humourous
" Poet," publiſhed in 1602, in his own defence, againſt " The
" Poe aſter" of Jonſon, in which he was laſhed under the title of
Criſpinus. Though far inferior to his antagoniſt, Decker gained
ſome applauſe, and retaliated on the Laureat under the name of
Horace Junior.

P. 175. l. ult. r Critick.—Ibid Note, l. 1, " The Generous
" Enemies, or the Ridiculous Lovers," a comedy, 1672, was written by John Carey; or rather, according to Langbaine, ſtolen
by him from four eminent poets.

Ibid. l. 2. " Secret Love, or the Maiden Queen," 1679, was
a tragedy of Dryden's; the plot of it is founded on the hiſtory of
Cleobuline queen of Corinth.

P. 179. l. 34. One of the firſt efforts of the Engliſh Stage;
it was printed in the year 1575, under the following title, " A right
" pithy pleaſaunt and merie Comedie, intytuled Gammer Gur-
" tons Nedle played on Stage not longe ago in Chriſtes Col-
" ledge, in Cambridge, made by Mr. S. Maiter of Arts." It is
alſo printed in Dodſley's Collection of Old Plays, vol. I. and in
Hawkins's " Origin of the Engliſh Drama," vol. I.

Ibid. l. 37. Printed in Dodſley's Collection, vol. V. under
the title of " Grim the Collier of Croydon, or the Devil and his
" Dam; with the Devil and S. Dunſtan, by J. T." It was firſt
printed in 1662, 8vo. The plot is taken from Machiavel's " Mar-
" riage of Belphegor."

P. 185. Add, See vol. II. p. 130.

P. 200. John Swammerdam, born at Amſterdam in 1637,
applied himſelf early in life to anatomical and medical ſtudies,
purſuing at the ſame time his favourite amuſement of diſcover-
ing, catching, and examining, flying inſects. In 1651, he went
to Leyden; and was admitted a candidate of phyſic in 1663.
From this time he applied diligently to anatomy; and in 1667
firſt injected the uterine veſſels of a human ſubject with ceraceous
matter, which uſeful attempt he afterward improved and perfected. In 1668, he declined a ſplendid offer of an eſtabliſhment
under the grand duke of Tuſcany; and publiſhed the next year
his

his general hiſtory of Inſects ; whoſe nature and properties were then his chief ſtudy. In 1673, he publiſhed his treatiſe on Bees ; but, after that fatiguing performance, never recovered his former health and vigour, and took a total diſtaſte to worldly affairs. He died Feb. 17, 1680.

P. 201. Lewis Maimbourg, born at Nancy in 1610, was admitted into the ſociety of Jeſuits in 1626; but being obliged in 1682 to quit it, for aſſerting too boldly the authority of the Gallican church, againſt the court of Rome, was rewarded, by Louis XIV, with a very honourable penſion, with which he retired to the abbey of St. Victor, where he died Aug. 13, 1686. He had great reputation as a preacher, and publiſhed two volumes of Sermons. He was a voluminous hiſtorian ; having written the Hiſtory of Arianiſm, of the Iconoclaſtes, of the Croiſades, of the Schiſm of the Weſt, of the Schiſm of the Greeks, of the Decay of the Empire, of the League, of Lutheraniſm, of Calviniſm, of the Pontificate of St. Leo ; and was compoſing the Hiſtory of the Schiſm of England when he died. Mr. Bayle ſays, " Father Maimbourg's hiſtories are very agree-" ably written, contain many lively ſtrokes, and a great variety of " occaſional inſtructions."

P. 202. Dr. Caſe (on Mr. Granger's authority) is ſaid to have been ſent for, to attend John Dennis in his phrenzy, though in fact it was to Partridge the Almanack-maker. We may the rather be excuſed in following this able Biographer in ſo ſmall a miſtake, as we have ſo frequently profited by his correct remarks. The fact, however, for which that circumſtance was mentioned, is equally true—that he was living in 1708. When Tutchin publiſhed his Obſervators, John Caſe uſed frequently to advertize himſelf at the end of that paper, beginning in this formal manner, " Your old Phyſician Dr. Caſe deſires you not to forget " him," &c. &c.

P. 205. l. 31. r. with chicken, white beets, &c.

P. 207. l. 4. r. remarkable.

Ibid. l. 7. *Add this Note*, In the Temple. This Pump has been perpetuated by Dr. Garth, in The Diſpenſary, canto ii.

" So glow-worms may compare with Titan's beams,
" And Hare Court pump with Aganippe's ſtreams."

Ibid. l. 18. This circumſtance is noted by The Tatler, vol. V. No 47.

P. 213. l. 12. Tom Britton, the famous muſical ſmall-coal-man, was born at or near Higham Ferrers in Northamptonſhire. He came to London ; and, having ſerved ſeven years to a ſmall-coal-man in St. John's Street, received a ſum of money from his maſter, not to ſet up in buſineſs. After having ſpent the money in Northamptonſhire, he returned to London, and ſet up the ſmall-coal trade in a houſe adjoining to the little gate of

St. John of Jerufalem next Clerkenwell Green, where he became a great proficient in chemiftry; and was as famous for his knowledge in the theory of mufic, in the practical part of which fcience he was alfo very confiderable. He left behind him a valuable collection of mufic, moftly pricked by himfelf, which was fold for near an hundred pounds; and an excellent collection of printed books of chemiftry and mufic. Befides thefe, he had in his life-time fold to lord Somers a curious collection of pamphlets, for about five hundred pounds; and had fold by auction a noble library, principally of Rofacrufian writings, which excited general admiration. He had alfo a confiderable collection of mufical inftruments, which were fold for fourfcore pounds after his death; which happened in September 1714, being upwards of threefcore years of age. The mufical club, alluded to by Dr. King, was kept up by Britton for many years, at his own charges, at his own little cell. He was univerfally efteemed for probity, fagacity, diligence, and humility; and continued in his original profeffion, though he might have lived very reputably without it, till the time of his death.

Ibid. l. 26. r. Grim.—Ibid. *Second Note*, r. Gervafe Markham, author of a play called "Herod and Antipater," 1622.

P. 214. l. 7. Dr. King here miftakes the perfon who wrote this piece. It was not the Author of "Oceana;" but Sir John Harrington, the Tranflator of Ariofto. It was called "A New "Difcourfe of a ftale Subject, called "The Metamorphofis of "A-Jax." Written by Mifacmos to his Friend and Cofin Phi- "loftilpnos," 8vo, 1596, printed by Field.

P. 240. l. 21. r. Codrington.   P. 244. l. 37. r. Florence.

P. 263. A cork tree is now (1776) growing at Wimbledon.

VOL. II.

P. 9. M. De Boodt publifhed, in 1637, "Hiftoria Gemmarum "& Lapidum, *Lugd. Bat.*" 8vo.

P. 20. Spencer Cowper, efq. was tried July 16, 1699. The ftory of Sarah Stout's death, which furnifhed the materials for feveral pamphlets at that time (re-printed with the State Trials) is recorded by Mrs. Manley, in the firft volume of her Atalantis. It alfo occafioned, in 1729, two indelicate poems, under the titles of "Sarah the Quaker to Lothario in the Shades," and "Lothario's Anfwer."

P. 60. There is a print of the queen of France and duke of Suffolk, engraved on a large fheet, from an original belonging to the late earl of Granville, now Mr. Walpole's. On the right hand of the duke is his lance, appendent to which is a label, infcribed,

"Cloth of gold, do not defpife,
"Though thou be match'd with cloth of frize:
                                        "Cloth

    " Cloth of frize, be not too bold,
    " Though thou be match'd with cloth of gold."

Mary queen of France, youngeft fifter to Henry VIII, was one
of the moft beautiful women of her age. It is pretty clear that
Charles Brandon gained her affections before fhe was married to
Lewis XII.; as, foon after the death of that monarch, which was
in about three months after his marriage, fhe plainly told him,
" that if he did not free her from all her fcruples within a certain
" time, fhe would never marry him." His cafuiftry fucceeded
within the time limited; and fhe became his wife. This was
probably with the king's connivance. It is however certain, that
no other fubject durft have ventured upon a queen of France, and
a fifter of the implacable Henry VIII.—Charles Brandon was remarkable for the dignity and gracefulnefs of his perfon, and his
robuft and athletic conftitution. He diftinguifhed himfelf in tilts
and tournaments (the favourite exercifes of Henry), and made a
confpicuous figure at the famous interview of the English and
French monarchs in the *camp de drap d'or*, between Guines and
Ardres. He was brought up with that prince, ftudied his difpofition, and exactly conformed to it. That conformity gradually
brought on a ftricter intimacy; and the king, to bring him nearer
to himfelf, raifed him from a private perfon to a duke. Granger.

    P. 145. Sir William Temple having in fome meafure been the
original caufe of the controverfy between Mr. Boyle and Dr.
Bentley; it may be entertaining to annex an extract of a letter
of his, from Moor Park, March 30, 1698. " I think there can
" be no exception to any thing in it [Mr. Boyle's Book], befides
" his partiality to me; which perhaps will be lefs forgiven him
" by the Doctor, than any other fault. For the reft, the com-
" pafs and application of fo much learning, the ftrength and per-
" tinence of arguments, the candour of his relations, in return to
" fuch foul-mouthed railing, the pleafant turns of wit, and the
" eafinefs of ftyle, are, in my opinion, as extraordinary, as the
" contrary of all thefe all appear to be in what the Doctor and
" his Friend have written. So that I have as much reafon to be
" pleafed with finding myfelf in Mr. Boyle's good opinion, as I
" fhould be forry to be in theirs." See the " Short Account of
" Dr. Bentley's Humanity, &c." p. 140.

    P. 165. l. 4. r. phyfician.—P. 169. Lotteries were firft drawn,
in St. Paul's Church, about 1569; and the drawing continued
night and day till all was finifhed.

    P. 170. " Plays, gaming-booths, and mufical-booths, at May-
Fair, were prohibited, by proclamation, April 21, 1709.

    P. 180. Dr. Sacheverell was the fon of Jofhua Sacheverell, of
Marlborough, clerk (whom Biffet, p. 255, calls a Dean). Henry
became demy of Magdalen College in 1687, at the age of 15.
A tranflation of his, from Virgil's Firft Georgick, dedicated to
Mr. Dryden, is in the third volume of " Mifcellany Poems," 1693.

P. 191. The benevolent chancellor of Winchester, whom we mentioned as the last surviving male of the Hoadly family, died March 11, 1776. He was master of the hospital of St. Cross, and had several other good preferments.

P. 198. Lieutenant-general Meredith, major-general Maccartney, and brigadier Honeywood, were cashiered, in December 1710, for drinking " Damnation to the present Ministry !"

P. 200. On the 11th of November, 1717, Dr. Welton, with his congregation, consisting of about 250 Nonjurors, was surprized by the justices and constables ; and most of them, refusing the oaths, were ordered to be prosecuted.

P. 233. Lancelot Addison, the son of Lancelot a clergyman, was born in 1632, educated at Appleby, and sent thence to Queen's College, Oxford ; admitted to the degree of B. A. Jan. 25, 1654 ; M. A. July 4, 1657. Being chosen a *terræ filius* for the act in 1658, his oration was so satirical, on the pride, ignorance, hypocrify, and avarice, of those then in power, that he was compelled to make a recantation, and ask pardon on his knees. He accepted the chaplainship of Dunkirk, where he continued till it was delivered to the French in 1662 ; and next year went chaplain to Tangier. In 1670, he was appointed king's chaplain ; soon after, prebendary of Sarum ; dean of Lichfield, July 3, 1683 ; and archdeacon of Coventry, Dec. 8, 1684. He died April 20, 1703, after having published many learned and useful treatises, which are enumerated in the Biographical Dictionary. The celebrated Joseph Addison was his son.

P. 245. Dr. Swift tells us, vol. XIV. p. 228, " Sir James of the " Peak said to Bouchier the gamester, Sirrah, I shall look better " than you, when I have been a month in my grave."

P. 268. Nicholas Lechmere, esq. representative in parliament for Cockermouth, and one of the Managers against Sacheverell, was an eminent Lawyer, a staunch Whig, and an Opposer of all the measures of the last four years of Queen Anne, having been removed from his office of queen's counsel in June 1711. He was appointed solicitor-general in October 1714; chancellor of the dutchy court of Lancaster; attorney-general in March, 1717-18 ; and was created a Peer. Dying June 18, 1727 ; the title became extinct. The Reader will find a very humorous Ballda, called " Duke upon Duke," on a quarrel between this Nobleman and Sir John Guise, in Swift's Works, vol. VI. p. 114.

P. 305. Dr. John Freind was born, in 1675, at Croton in Northamptonshire, where his father was rector. He was sent to Westminster-school, with his brother Robert, who was afterwards master of it. He was elected to Christ Church in 1690 ; and, under the auspices of Dean Aldrich, undertook, with another student, to publish two orations, one of Æschines, the other of Demosthenes, which were well received ; and was also prevailed upon to revise an edition of Ovid's Metamorphosis,

2
which

which Dr. Bentley feverely reprehends. He was director of the ftudies to Mr. Boyle; and, fays the great Critic, " was of the " fame fize for learning with the late Editor of the Æfopean " Fables [Mr. Alfop]. If they can but make a tolerable copy " of verfes, with two or three fmall faults in it, they muft pre- " fently fet up to be Authors." But, whatever may be thought of thofe ju enile performances, in his profeffional capacity he was a mafterly writer. After having publifhed feveral curious medical treatifes, he was chofen profeffor of chemiftry at Oxford in 1704; and the next year attended lord Peterborow on his Spanifh expedition; of which Dr. Freind publifhed an account in 1707. He was created M. D. that year; in 1712, was elected a Member of the Royal Society; and attended the duke of Ormond that year into Flanders. After his return, he refided chiefly at London, and gave himfelf up wholly to the cares of his profeffion. He was elected a burgefs for Launcefton in 1722; and, being fufpected of having a hand in Layer's plot, was committed to The Tower, March 15, 1722-3, where he continued a prifoner till the 21ft of June following. Soon after he obtained his liberty, he was made phyfician to the prince of Wales; and, upon that prince's acceffion to the crown, became phyfician to queen Caroline, who honoured him with a vaft fhare of her confidence and efteem. He did not enjoy this office long; dying July 26, 1728, in his 52d year. Their majefties, in confideration of his great merit, fettled a penfion upon his widow. His celebrated " Hiftory of Phyfic," the firft part of which was printed in 1725, was tranflated into Latin by Dr. Wigan, and publifhed, with the Latin works of Dr. Freind, at London, in folio, 1733. They were re-printed at Paris, in 4to, 1735.

V O L. III.

P. 8. Hedington, Hinkfey, Cowley, and Marfton, are all in the neighbourhood of Oxford.

P. 9. *Note*, l. 13. *r.* apophthegms. P. 17. l. 1. *r.* Franklin.

P. 56. l. 22. 'This claim ftill remains in force; at leaft, it was certainly exercifed, in 1727, by the lord of the manor of Bardolf, in Addington, Surrey. See " Verfes on the Coronation of their " late Majefties King George II, and Queen Caroline, 1761," 8vo, p. 64. The claim is mentioned in Speed's Hiftory, under Richard II.

P. 73. Sir Charles Sedley outlived all his contemporary Wits, except the duke of Devonfhire, the earl of Godolphin, and the duke of Buckingham, who married his granddaughter Catharine; fee above, p. 138.

P. 79. Jeffery Hudfon was born at Okeham in Rutland. He hath been celebrated by Davenant, in his " Jeffreidos," a poem in three cantos.

P. 84.

P. 84. Vinegar was the keeper of the Ring in Moor-fields, and was fo called from the fournefs of his looks, and the aufterity of his government. The rabble paid him a profound veneration, and allowed his determination in all difputes and controverfies, either at cudgels or wreftling, to be final and concluſive. Thus Mr. Prefton tells us, Æfop at the Bear Garden, p. 26,

"—great VINEGAR appear'd,
" By the whole rabble either lov'd or fear'd ;
" Father of noife ! Methought I heard him fay,
" Clear, clear the Ring ; the Bear fhall have fair play."

Ibid. Brawn was mafter of The Rummer Tavern in Great Queen-ftreet. See a character of his kitchen, vol. II. p. 304.

P. 86. Dick Eftcourt was Mr. Bickerftaff's apothecary; fee Tatler, Nº 2. His talents and extraordinary qualifications are celebrated in the Spectator, Nº 264. 358. 370. and 468. He was author of a play, called " The Fair Example," 1706.

P. 113. The Kit-cat Club, a Society of the firft rank, is faid to have been fo called from their meetings being originally at the houfe of one Chriftopher Catt.—Charles earl of Dorfet was one of the firft founders of this Club, which confifted of no more than thirty-nine members, all men of the firft rank for quality or learning, moft of whom had been employed in the greateft offices of ftate and in the army, and none were admitted but thofe of the greateft diftinction in fome way or other. All their pictures were drawn by that great mafter Sir Godfrey Kneller ; and were kept, in commemoration of the auguft affembly, by their ingenious Secretary Mr. Jacob Tonfon ; and are ftill in the poffeffion of his family. Sir Richard Blackmore publifhed, in 1708, a poem, called " The Rife and Progrefs of the Kit-cat " Club." A ludicrous account of it is alfo in Ned Ward's Hiftory " of Clubs," which reprefents Mr. Tonfon as the firft inftitutor.

P. 138. Richard Duke, M. A. was prefented by the bifhop of Winchefter to the rich living of Witney in Oxfordfhire, which was afterward enjoyed fucceffively by Dr. Freind, mafter of Weftminfter School, and his fon the dean of Canterbury. Fifteen of Mr. Duke's " Sermons on feveral Occafions" were printed in 1715, 8vo, and a third time in 1730. By the title-page, he appears to have been prebendary of Gloucefter, rector of Whitney, and chaplain in ordinary to queen Anne. His poems were collected by Mr. Tonfon, and publifhed with thofe of Rofcommon in 1717.

P. 175. l. 6. *Gleek* is ufed by Shakefpeare, as a noun, in the fenfe of mufick, or a mufician ; as a verb, in that of fneering, gibing, or drolling upon. In Scotland, it is ftill retained, and fignifies to fool or fpend time idly, with fomething of mimickry or drollery. See Johnfon's Dictionary.

P. 179. Lady Chudleigh alfo publifhed, in 1710, a volume of " Effays upon feveral Subjects, in Profe and Verfe ;" and com-

plains,

plains, in the Preface, of Mr. Lintott's having added, without her confent, to the fecond Edition of her Poems, " a Dialogue," (firft printed without a name in 1700) occafioned by a Wedding Sermon of Mr. John Sprint, a Nonconformift Divine, at Milton Port, Somerfetfhire, called " The Bride-woman's Counfellor, " 1699."

P. 185. Rowe's Lucan was firft publifhed, in folio, in 1718.

P. 259. The poem on " Apple Pye" hath been claimed as Mr. Welfted's, in " The Weekly Oracle," Auguft 16, 1735 ; with a remark, that " Dr. King, the Civilian, a gentleman of no mean re-" putation in the world of letters, let it pafs fome years, without " contradiction, as his own."

P. 263. A fourth edition of De la Quintinye's " Complete Gardener," 8vo. tranflated by George London and Henry Wife, was publifhed in 1704. They alfo wrote " The Retired Gardener."

⁎ In the progrefs of thefe Volumes through the prefs, the Editor could not but frequently remark a ftriking fimilarity between Dr. King and the Author of the " Epiftles to Lorenzo ;" an obfervation, however, which he had no thought of mentioning, till he obferved, in a monthly publication [a], the latter of thofe writers had been compared with Mr. Sterne.—Without the moft diftant intention either of " offering a fop to Cerberus [a]," or of degrading the abilities of Dr. Kenrick ; it is fubmitted to the attentive Reader, whether our parallel be not the more faithful refemblance. Dr. King's moft ftriking characterifticks were, an inexhauftible fund of real wit, and an irony moft feverely poignant; talents which Dr. Kenrick poffeffes in perfection. The former was properly a *bon vivant*, and had a heart fo exquifitely convivial, that he was the delight of all with whom he affociated : in this point of view, the comparifon will fcarcely be difputed. And even their poetry (admitting the remark of the Reviewer, " that it is eafier for a middling Poet in thefe " days to make good rhymes, than it was formerly for a good " one [a]") is not unlike. Our Author, in his " Art of Love," like the Writer of the " Epiftles," wifhed rather, perhaps, to attach his readers by the power of his philofophy, than by the fweetnefs of his poetry. Yet that many inftances might be produced, where the *fenfe* of *both* muft be allowed to be happily adorned with the moft judicious choice of *rhyme*, the flighteft infpection of the " Orpheus and Eurydice" of the one, or the " Moral Epiftles" of the other, will plainly teftify. In their *lighter* Effays, their manner is ftill more congenial : the fame concifenefs, the fame epigrammatic turn, is evidently confpicuous. And, to heighten the fimilarity, if Dr. King ventured boldly to enter the lifts with Dr. Bentley, Dr. Kenrick hath, not lefs daringly, waged literary war with a modern Ariftarchus, the juftly celebrated Author of The Rambler.

[a] Monthly Review, for December, 1775.

INDEX

INDEX of PERSONS, PLACES, BOOKS, &c. incidentally mentioned, and occasionally illuftrated, in the NOTES.

ADAMS, Dr. John, ii. 211.
Addifon, Dr. Lancelot, ii. 235. iii. 305.
Æfop, iii. 58. 120.
Aldrich, Dean, i. 135. iii. 297.
Alleyn, Edward, iii. 3.
Almanack-makers, ii. 115.
Alfop, Mr. i. 236. iii. 305.
Amboyna, i. 67.
Arthur, king, ii. 147.
Aftrop, i. 67.

Baker, Dr. William, ii. 217.
Baliol, John, ii. 64.
Bantam, i. 67.
Barbarini, cardinal, iii. 294.
Bardana, ii. 160.
Bartholinus, Thomas, i. 125.
Bartholomew Fair, ii. 169.
Bathurft, Dr. Ralph, i. 239.
Battle Royal, i. 221.
Bawd, iii. 14.
Baxter, Richard, ii. 185.
Bear-garden, iii. 306.
Beau, iii. 188.
Beaufort, duke of, iii. 293.
Bedell, bp. i. 227.
Behn, Mrs. Afra, iii. 178.
Bentley, Dr. Richard, i. 141. iii. 33. 35. 297.
Barnard, Dr. i. 226.
Betterton, Thomas, ii. 60.
Biffet, William, ii. 181. 261.
Borrichius, i. 125.
Boffu, Le Rene, iii. 188.
———, Charles, iii. 297.
Boyle, Robert, ii. 94.
Bradford, Dr. Samuel, ii. 217.
Bralesford, Humphry, ii. 255.
Brady, Dr. i. 235.
Brahe, Tycho, i. 124.

Brandon, Charles, iii. 303.
Brawn, of the Rummer, iii. 306.
Britton, Tom, iii. 302.
Buckingham, Sheffield duke of, iii. 138.
——————— Villiers, duke of, ii. 150.
Bunyan, John, ii. 184.
Burgefs, Daniel, ii. 191.
Burleigh, lord, iii. 232.
Burnet, bp. ii. 204.
Bufby, Dr. Richard, iii. 291.
Bufh, William, ii. 272.

Callimachus, i. 140.
Cantor, at Rome, iii. 5.
Carlifle, countefs of, i. 234.
Cartwright, William, i. 234.
Cafe, Dr. John, i. 202. iii. 302.
Charles, archduke, ii. 130.
Chudleigh, lady, 179. 307.
Cibber, Caius Gabriel, i. 127.
Ciofani, Hercules, iii. 120.
Cithern, ii. 79.
City Hunt, ii. 169.
Clarendon, earl, ii. 269.
Clarke, Pofture-mafter, ii. 18.
Coaches, i. 193.
Colman, George, iii. 4.
Compton, bp. ii. 253.
Cooper, Thomas, ii. 78.
Coward, Dr. William, i. 237.
Cowley, Abraham, iii. 180. His remark on Ovid, 117.
Cowper, lord, ii. 214.
——————— Spencer, ii. 20. iii. 303.
Creech, Thomas, iii. 9.
Crew, bp. i. 226.

Damaree, a Waterman, ii. 192.
Dampier, captain William, iii. 52.

VOL. III.   Y   Darien.

Darien, ii. 133.
De Boodt, iii. 333.
Decker, Thomas, iii. 301.
De Foe, Daniel, ii. 183.
Delegates, Court of, i. xiv.
Demoivois, i. 152.
Denham, Sir John, iii. 122.
Denmark, Reformation there, i. 119.
Derham, Dr. William, ii. 115.
Dervorgilla, queen, ii. 64.
Dialogues of the Dead, i. 144.
Domesday Book, i. 12.
Dorset, earl of, iii. 181.
Drake, Sir Francis, iii. 92.
Dryden, John, iii. 62. 139.
Duke, Richard, iii. 138. 307.
D'Urfey, ii. 118.
Dutch-woman, the tall, i. 204.

Eachard, Dr. John, i. 214.
Edwin, Sir Humphry, ii. 225.
Ely; see Ridel.
English Rogue, ii. 182.
Essex, Robert earl of, i. 228.
Estcourt, Dick, iii. 86. 306.

Farnaby, Thomas, i. 236.
Feast of the Oaks, iii. 58.
Fell, bp. i. 238.
Fernelius, Dr. iii. 70.
Fisher, Payne, i. 237.
Flamsteed, John, ii. 263.
Flecknoe, Richard, iii. 300.
Fleetwood, bp. ii. 246. 262.
Ford, Charles, i. xxiv.
Formosa, History of, ii. 133.
France, Mary queen of, iii. 303.
Franklin, Dr. Thomas, iii. 298.
Freind, Dr. John, iii. 305.
Fuller, William, ii. 253.

Gammer Gurton's Needle, iii. 301.
Garth, Sir Samuel, iii. 184.
Gaudy, iii. 30.
Gibson, bp. i. 236.

Gibson, James, ii. 249.
Gleek, iii. 307.
Gloucester, duke of, i. 44.
Goddard's Drops, ii. 126.
Goddard, Thomas, ii. 270.
Gouldman, Francis, iii. 102.
Granger, James, i. xv.
Greatrix, Valentine, ii. 45.
Grim the Collier of Croydon, iii. 301.
Grimston, lord, iii. 65.
Grout, iii. 306.

Halifax, earl of, iii. 182.
Hall, Jacob, i. 204.
Hannes, Dr. Edward, iii. 296.
Hare Court Pump, iii. 301.
Harley, Robert, iii. 233.
Harrington, Sir John, i. 224. iii. 303.
Harris, Dr. John, ii. 217.
Harvey, Dr. William, iii. 70.
Haversham, lord, i. xv.
Head, Richard, ii. 182.
Hearne, Thomas, iii. 75.
Henniver, Mrs. iii. 203.
Heylyn, Dr. Peter, i. 225.
Highgate, ii. 154.
Hoadly, bp. ii. 190.
———— chancellor, iii. 304.
Hobbes, Thomas, ii. 139. iii. 39.
Hobson the Carrier, iii. 51.
Holbein Hans, i. 261.
Holinshead, Raphael, iii. 74.
Horse-races, i. 152.
Hudson, Jeffery, iii. 79. 306.

James, Sir; see Peak.
———— Richard, i. 231.
Jenkins, Old, ii. 89.
Jews, many in Jamaica, i. 257.
Johnson, Samuel, ii. 215.
Jonson, Ben, ii. 89.

Kennet, bp. iii. 37.
Kenrick, Dr. William, iii. 308.
Kensington-

Kenfington-gardens, iii. 126. 263.
Kirkman, Francis, i. 180.
Kit-Cat Club, iii. 306.
Kneller, Sir Godfr. iii. 71. 307.
Knipe, Dr. Thomas, iii. 221.
Koningfmark, count, iii. 49.
Kynafton, Sir Francis, i. 235.

Lactarium, iii. 203.
Lady's Travels into Spain, ii. 151.
Le Brun Anthony, i. 278.
Lechmere, Nicholas, iii. 305.
Leeuwenhoeck, A. V. ii. 103.
Lilly, William, i. 161.
Linacre, Thomas, i. 240.
Lincoln's Inn Fields, i. 145.
Lintott's Mifcellanies, iii. 37.
Lifter, Dr. Martin, i. 161.
Littleton, Adam, ii. 83.
Lloyd, bp. ii. 233. 264.
Locman, iii. 58.
London, George, iii. 263. 307.
Lotteries, ii. 169. iii. 304.
Ludgate, iii. 197.
Ludolf, Job, ii. 91.

Malherbe, Francis, iii. 174.
Mandevile, Sir John, ii. 62.
Manethon, iii. 48.
Manley, Mrs. Delarivier, ii. 184.
Markham, Gerv. i. 213. iii. 303.
Marfham, Sir John, iii. 48.
May Fair, ii. 169. iii. 304;
Mazarin, cardinal, iii. 294.
Meeting-houfes, ii. 191. iii. 313.
Mentz; fee *Printing*.
Milner, Dr. John, iii. 299. 313.
Modena, duchefs of, ii. 128.
Moleworth, lord, i. 37.
Monfmouth, duke of, i. 217.
Moor Fields, ii. 145.
Moore, Francis, ii. 115.
More, Sir Thomas, i. 259.
Morland, lady, ii. 90. iii. 513.

Mofs, Dr. Robert, ii. 217.
Mufgrave, Dr. William, ii. 49.

Naudæus, Gabriel, ii. 9. iii. 294.
Neftor's Cup, iii. 300.
Nicholas, St. i. 152. iii. 300.
Nicolfon, bp. i. 256.

Ogilby, John, iii. 90.
Oldenburg, Henry, ii. 6.
Oldham, John, iii. 54.
Oldifworth, Mr. iii. 274.
Oliver's Porter, i. 217.
Orinda, iii. 178.
Ortelius, Abraham, iii 113.
Ofborn, Francis, ii. 84.
Otaheite, i. 162. ii. 81.
Overbury, Sir Thomas, iii. 152.
Ovid, a Canon Lawyer, iii. 117.
Oyfters, *green* Colchefter, iii. 100.

Park, St. James's, iii. 73.
Parliaments, i. 14.
Parr, Thomas, iii. 31.
Partridge, John, ii. 110. 263.
Peak, Sir James of the, ii. 245. iii. 305.
Pearfon, bp. ii. 221.
Pembroke, earl of, iii. 105.
Petit Maitre, iii. 188.
Phalaris, iii. 298.
Philip king of Spain, ii. 130.
Philips, Mrs. Catharine, iii. 178.
——— John, iii. 185.
Pie-powder Court, i. 176.
Planudes, iii. 120.
Plaxton, George, ii. 67.
Plot, Dr. Robert, ii. 7.
Poland, i. 70.
Politianus, Angelus, iii. 114.
Poor Robin, ii. 115.
Printing, when firft ufed at Mentz and at Spire, i. 259; at Oxford, 262.

Prior,

Prior, Matthew, iii. 182.
Pfalmanazar, George, ii. 133.

Rabelais, iii. 96.
Ralegh, Sir Walter, ii. 93. iii. 128.
Ramfey, John, ii. 218.
Randolph, Robert, ii. 118.
——————— Thomas, ibid.
Rapin, Renatus, iii. 185.
Ray, John, ii. 12.
Reformation of Manners, ii. 184.
Richlieu, cardinal, iii. 294.
Richmond, duchefs of, ii. 64.
Ridel, Geoffry, bp. of Ely, i. 256.
Ridpath, George, ii. 183.
Robinfon, Dr. Tancred, ii. 31.
——————— Thomas, i. 257.
Rochefter, earl of, ii. 253.
Rome, Stage-riots there, iii. 5.
Roper, Abel, ii. 183.
Rowe, Nicholas, iii. 184. 308.
Runic Poetry, ii. 176.
Ruffel, lady, ii. 66.
Ruffia, i. 95. 152. iii. 296. 300.

Sacheverell, Dr. Henry, ii. 180. 242. iii. 304.
Saffold, Dr. i. 202.
Saint John, Henry, iii. 234.
Salmon, Dr. William, ii. 4.
Sandys, George, iii. 121.
Savage, Dr. William, ii. 218.
Savile, Sir Harry, i. 262.
Scrope, Sir Car, iii. 138.
Sedley, Sir Charles, iii. 73.
Seyley the Chimney-fweeper, i, 213.
Sherburn, Sir Edward, iii. 299.
Sherlock, Dr. William, i. 210.
Sidney, Sir Philip, ii. 89.
Slavery, i. 93.
Sloane, Sir Hans, ii. 5.
Small-coal-man, the Mufical, iii. 302.

Smallridge, bp. ii. 217.
Smith, Edmund, iii. 185.
Snape, Dr. Andrew, ii. 218.
Socinus, Marianus, iii. 249.
Sorbiere, Samuel, i. 23.
South, Dr. Robert, i. 210.
Spain, ii. 151.
Spanheim, iii. 122.
Spenfer, Edmund, iii. 184.
Spira, Francis, ii. 160.
Stanihurft, Richard, i. 218.
Stat. 1 Geo. I, ii. 226.
Stepney, George, iii. 182.
Stillingfleet, bp. ii. 231.
Stow, John, iii. 184.
Stradling, Sir Edward, i. 230.
Strafford, earl of, ii. 192.
Sutton, Gibbon, ii. 218.
Swammerdam, John, iii. 301.
Sweden, i. 70.
Swift, Thomas, i. 218.
Sydenham, Dr. Thomas, i. 32.

Taliefin, iii. 56.
Taffo, Torquatus, iii. 174.
Temple, Sir William, ii. 146. iii. 304.
Thynne, Thomas, iii. 49.
Tillotfon, bp. ii. 230.
Timorodee, ii. 81.
Tonfon, Jacob, iii. 307.
Topography, i. 257.
Torpedo, iii. 100.
Tracey, Richard, i. 232.
Tuke, Sir William, iii. 8.
Turner, Dr. John, ii. 217.
——————— Mrs. i. 162. iii. 153.
Tutchin, capt. John, ii. 183. 279.
Tyrrel, Sir Thomas, i. 228.

Van Dyck, Sir Anthony, i. 261.
Varillas, Antoine, i. 2. iii. 296.
Vernon of Chrift Church, i. 236.
——————— George, i. 225.
Upton, judge, i. xviii.
Ufher, archbp. i. 227.

Wadham, lady, ii. 64.
Waller, Edmund, iii. 181.
Wallis, Dr. John, ii. 167.
Walter, Sir John, ii. 244.
Wanley, Humphry, ii. 61.
Ward, bp. ii. 208. iii. 38.
Welton, Dr. Richard, ii. 200.
   iii. 304.
Whaley, Nathanael, ii. 217.
Wheate, Sir Thomas, ii. 245.
Wickham, William of, i. 262.

Wickliff, John, i. 3.
Wilkins, bp. ii. 168.
Wife, Henry, iii. 263. 307.
Wolfey, cardinal, ii. 286.
Wotton, William, i. 167. iii.
   300.

York, Roger archbp. of, i. 253.

Zouch, Richard, i. 234.

Vol. II. p. 90. *Firſt Note, after* 1679-80, *add,* " ætatis 19°." She was his ſecond lady. There are three inſcriptions on her tomb, in Hebrew, Æthiopic, and Engliſh.

Reform the ſecond Note thus, On an adjoining tablet, are three inſcriptions, to the memory of Sir William's firſt lady, in Hebrew, Greek, and Engliſh, the latter of them in theſe words : " Carola " daughter of Roger Harſnett, eſq. and of Carola his wife, " the truly loving (and as truly beloved) wife of Samuel Mor- " land, knight and baronet, bare a ſecond ſon Oct. 4, died Oct. 10, " Anno Domini 1674, ætatis 23°."

P. 191. *Note.* The ſame mob deſtroyed the meeting-houſes of Mr. Earl in Long Acre, Mr. Bradbury in New-ſtreet, Mr. Taylor in Leather Lane, Mr. Wright in Black Fryars, and Mr. Hamilton in Clerkenwell ; and burnt the pulpit, pews, and ſome of the Bibles. They threatened to demoliſh Mr. Hoadly's church and houſe ; and, when the guards came up, were detaching parties to deſtroy Mr. Shower's meeting-houſe, and to pull down the Bank, which ſtood near it. " Hiſtorical Account of Sacheverell."

Vol. III. p. 299. The title of the tract mentioned in the fourth and ſixth paragraphs is, " A View of the Diſſertations upon the " Epiſtles of Phalaris, Themiſtocles, &c. lately publiſhed by the " Rev. Dr. Bentley ; alſo of the Examination of the Diſſertation " by the Hon. Mr. Boyle. In order to the manifeſting the Incer- " titude of Heathen Chronology."

CONTENTS OF VOL. III.

USEFUL Miscellanies, Part the Firſt.

1. Preface of the Publiſher of Joan of Hedington, a Tragi-comedy, Pag. 3
2. The Tragi-comedy, 17
3. Some Account of Horace's Behaviour during his Stay at Trinity College in Cambridge. With an Ode to entreat his Departure thence. Together with a Copy of his Medal, taken out of Trinity College Buttery, by a Well-wiſher to that Society, 24
4. An Anſwer to Clemens Alexandrinus's Sermon, upon *Quis Dives ſalvetur ?* "What Rich Man can be "ſaved ?" proving it eaſy for a Camel to go through the Eye of a Needle, 37

The Art of Cookery; in Imitation of Horace's Art of Poetry. With ſome Letters to Dr. Liſter and Others, occaſioned principally by the Title of a Book publiſhed by the Doctor, being the Works of Apicius Cœlius, "concerning the Soups "and Sauces of the Ancients :" With an Extract of the greateſt Curioſities contained in that Book, 41

The Art of Love : In Imitation of Ovid *De Arte Amandi.* With a Preface, containing the Life of Ovid, 103

The Furmetary, 195

Mully of Mountown, 203

Orpheus and Eurydice, 207

Rufinus, or The Favourite, 218

Britain's Palladium ; or, Lord Bolingbroke's Welcome from France, 230

Verſes to the Duke of Beaufort, 237

MISCELLANY POEMS.

Song, 238
An incomparable Ode of Malherbe's, written by him when the Marriage was on foot between Louis XIV and Anne of Auſtria, tranſlated by an Admirer of the Eaſineſs of French Poetry, 239
The laſt Billet, 240
To Laura, in Imitation of Petrarch, ibid.
To the Right Hon. the Earl of ——, upon his diſputing publicly at Chriſt Church, Oxford, 241
A Gentleman to his Wife, 242

The

The Mad Lover,   pag. 242
The Soldier's Wedding, a Soliloquy, by Nan Thrasher-
    well, being Part of a Play, called "The New Troop," 243
The Old Cheese,   244
The Skillet,   245
The Fisherman,   247
A Case of Conscience,   276
The Constable,   250
Little Mouths,   251
Hold fast below,   .   252
The Beggar Woman,   253
The Vestry,   254
The Monarch,   256
The Incurious,   257
Apple-Pye,   259
The Art of making Puddings,   262
A Panegyric on Beer, to Mr. Carter, Steward to the
    Lord Carteret,   265
Nero, a Satire,   ibid.
Verses to Major Tynte,   266
Ulysses and Tiresias, a Dialogue on Riches,   257
Translation from Tasso,   268
———— from Hesiod,   ibid.
Verses left in the King of France's Bed-chamber, after
    the Death of the Duke De Montmorency,   ibid.
Thame and Isis,   269
Of Dreams,   ibid.
Verses on waking out of a Dream,   ibid.
Extracts from " The Lost Princess," a Play of Lord
    Blessinton,   270
A merry Letter to a Friend, on Love, Marriage, and a Single
    Life, occasioned by his Mistress's marrying his Rival, 271
A Pindaric Ode to the Memory of Dr. King,   274
Crapulia, or the Region of the Cropsicks ; a Fragment, in the
    Manner of Rabelais,   278
Four DEDICATIONS, by Dr. KING :
    1. To Sir Edmund Warcupp,   288
    2. To the Beef-Steak Club,   290
    3. To Dr. Knipe,   292
    4. To the Duke of Beaufort,   293
Additional Observations,   296
Index to the Notes,   309
Addenda,   313

F I N I S.

www.ingramcontent.com/pod-product-compliance
Lightning Source LLC
Chambersburg PA
CBHW031029120726
47905CB00007B/2103